To Andrew, for all of your inspiration, love, and support

STEPHANIE FAZIO

HEX KITCHEN

Syafant Press

New York, New York

Cover designed by Keith Tarrier

This book is a work of fiction. Names, characters, places, and incidents either are the product of the author's imagination or are used fictionally, and any resemblance to actual persons, living or dead, business establishments, events, or locales is entirely coincidental.

Stephanie Fazio

Visit www.StephanieFazio.com

Printed in the United States of America
First Printing: May 2021

Library of Congress Control Number: 2021904018

ISBN 978-1-951572-22-8

CHAPTER 1

KENZIE

N*eed. Coffee. Now.*

Kenzie stumbled around her tiny apartment like a zombie. She didn't even bother turning on the lights—a decision she regretted when she whacked her knee against the edge of the tiny coffee table. Mumbling half-hearted curses, she wedged herself into her apartment's postage stamp-sized kitchen.

She managed to grind up the coffee beans and boil water without further maiming herself. Four agonizing minutes later, the silky, slightly bitter scent of coffee curled around her nostrils. Her beloved French Press was the sole relic of her life from *before*. Her dad always liked to say there was no greater crime than weak coffee and—

And why the hell was she thinking about her father? She really needed to get some caffeine into her system pronto.

Kenzie moaned in relief as the dark roast hit her tongue. The precious liquid transformed her from a scary approximation of a human being into herself. She flipped on lights and went to check on Kiwi.

Kiwi, her pet chameleon, was perched on a branch in his habitat. His bulging eyes rotated as he regarded her. In his resting state, Kiwi was romaine lettuce-green, with yellow stripes and orange dots all over his scaly body. As Kenzie reached into the enclosure to take out his food dish, Kiwi's coloring changed to match the red sleeve of her hoodie.

"Morning, bud," Kenzie told the little creature.

Kiwi responded with a yawn.

"Hungry, little dude?"

Kiwi cocked his head at her in the universal signal for *Duh*.

Kenzie hummed to herself as she pulled out a box of live crickets from the cabinet that was dedicated to Kiwi. She also got out a bag of wriggling waxworms.

"Sorry," Kenzie apologized to the insects. She fished them out and arranged them in a container.

Kenzie sprinkled vitamin supplements over the insects in a swirling motion, making the meal look like it was covered in a light dusting of powdered sugar. She retrieved a bunch of collard greens from her otherwise-empty fridge. Grabbing a knife from the block on her counter, she began to chiffonade the greens.

Kiwi didn't care about the presentation of his meal, but Kenzie had a long-standing habit of plating food so the colors and textures added to the eating experience. Not that a meal of crickets, waxworms, and greens could really be appealing no matter how it was arranged.

Preparing Kiwi's meals was as close as Kenzie came to gourmet cooking these days. Unless one counted boiling water for ramen or nuking Easy Mac….

Kenzie raked her dark hair into a high ponytail as she watched Kiwi's long tongue flick out to devour his meal. She finished her coffee as she put on the horrible pink monstrosity otherwise known as her uniform. The color washed out Kenzie's already-pale skin, making her appear ghostly. The uniform always smelled like grease no matter how many times she washed it. The pink fabric was also splotched from various food stains because Loretta was too cheap to ever replace her employees' uniforms.

Kenzie didn't bother with makeup, except to apply a double coat of mascara to her lashes. Her gunmetal-gray eyes were her most attractive feature, and since she had neither the sufficient assets nor the inclination to display cleavage, her eyes were her best shot at earning extra tips.

Kenzie scowled as a thunderous banging on the downstairs apartment's ceiling made her floorboards shudder.

"It's six o'clock in the morning!" Kenzie's grouchy downstairs neighbor and landlord shouted, his voice reverberating through the floor. He devolved into raspy smoker's coughs. He banged what must have been a broomstick handle on his ceiling again. "Hush your racket!"

Kenzie rolled her eyes and held back a sarcastic retort. She couldn't stop herself from shutting a cabinet door with more force than strictly necessary. Her neighbor really should know better than to test Kenzie's goodwill before she'd had her second cup of coffee.

"And your rent's two days past due!" he called. A corresponding bang on his ceiling accompanied the unwelcome reminder. "Get me my money, or you can find somewhere else to call home."

Home. Kenzie looked around at the bare walls and ratty furniture she'd inherited from the previous tenant. Despite the fact that she'd been living in this apartment for four years, ever since Nana had died and Kenzie decided it was high time to leave New York, this place wasn't home.

And that was precisely the point.

Kenzie had moved from Manhattan to this rusty Tennessee town because she wanted to leave home and everything that came with that loaded word behind. She'd had a little money from selling Nana's house in Queens, but it hadn't amounted to much after all her grandmother's debts were settled. Rent in this tired old building was stupid cheap…part of the reason she'd picked the place…but so was her boss.

"I'm getting paid on Friday," Kenzie called, infusing her voice with as much saccharine as she could stomach. She could almost taste that artificial, over-sweetened powder the old ladies in town swirled into their already-sweet tea.

"Goshdarn lazy kids and their crummy work ethic," her landlord muttered.

Because of the non-existent insulation, Kenzie heard every word. She could have informed him that, at the age of twenty-two, she wasn't a kid. And that putting in fourteen-hour shifts at the diner six days a week didn't match Kenzie's definition of lazy. But she kept her mouth shut. Kenzie knew from experience that goading her landlord only resulted in one outcome: late fees.

She could move, she supposed, but it wasn't like there was a plethora of apartment options in this town. Kenzie wasn't nomadic by nature, and the thought of needing to find a new apartment and new job was too exhausting to contemplate.

Kenzie sighed. Unless she could convince her cheapskate boss to give her a raise, she'd need to get a roommate. And aside from Kiwi, who didn't give a flying fig about Kenzie's past, a roommate would ask questions she didn't want to answer. Besides, Kenzie was better on her own.

After blowing a kiss to Kiwi, Kenzie wrestled her bike out of the narrow hallway, down the steps of her second-story unit, and onto the cracked cement walkway outside. Her breath immediately fogged the air.

Spring in East Tennessee meant it was chilly in the morning but would get up into the sixties later in the day. Not that Kenzie would be able to enjoy the milder weather. She got to work in the dark of morning and left in the dark of night. And Loretta was firmly opposed to giving her employees breaks that lasted longer than the time it took to pee.

Kenzie nestled deeper into her hoodie as the cold wind slapped at her cheeks. She pedaled harder to warm herself up.

It had been a shock to her system to come from Manhattan, where she'd grown up taking the subway and bus system for granted, to a town without any public transportation. But everything Kenzie had been through taught her how to adapt. Hence the bike. And some killer calf muscles, if she did say so herself.

It was four miles to *Good Ol' Apple Pie*, the diner where she worked. The darkness of pre-dawn was giving way to a murky gray. The light made the run-down houses on either side of the potholed road look haunted. It was eerily quiet, which only emphasized the spooky feel.

Kenzie pedaled into the *Good Ol' Apple Pie's* gravel lot and carried her bike onto the sagging porch. She parked it against the wall, where a layer of chipped, pink paint covered the ground like snow.

She glanced across the street and past the cornfield, where the sound of engines cut through the otherwise-silent morning. A tiny jet was racing down the short runway.

Kenzie watched as the jet took to the sky and headed off to deliver the important people within to important places. A minute later, a tiny, single-engine plane landed on the same airstrip to refuel before taking off again.

If it wasn't for this private airstrip, *Good Old Apple Pie* would have died along with so many of this town's businesses years ago. Since it was the only eatery within miles of the airfield, the diner got a steady flow of customers from the airfield's staff and families wanting to grab a bite while their private jets refueled. None of the planes stayed longer than it took to fuel up and the passengers to stretch their legs.

It was always a little jarring to see people wearing Armani and three-carat diamonds walk into this crap-hole diner. It was even stranger to see people who probably regularly dined in the world's finest restaurants sitting in plastic booths and eating soggy corned beef on rye.

"You're late," Loretta informed Kenzie the moment she stepped inside the restaurant.

Kenzie checked the rooster clock on the wall above the cash register. She met her boss's beady eyes and forced an approximation of a pleasant smile. "It's six fifty-five, Loretta. My shift starts at seven."

"And by the time you get the coffee going, you'll be late! We already have a customer."

Kenzie glanced at the man sitting at the counter. Billy-Joe—yep, that was seriously his name—swiveled on his stool to face her. He smiled, displaying his missing front tooth.

"My, Miss Kenzie," he drawled. "Aren't you a sight for sore eyes this mornin'."

Kenzie could never tell if Billy-Joe was creepily flirting or if he was simply exercising that southern friendliness she still hadn't gotten used to.

You could take the girl out of New York, but you couldn't take New York out of the girl, apparently.

"Hi, Billy-Joe," Kenzie replied with a curt nod. "The usual?"

"Yes ma'am. And if I may be so bold, you are lookin' mighty fine in that there dress."

"Ham-and-egg on Texas toast coming right up," Kenzie said.

There were two kinds of people who came to the diner. The first were out-of-towners who walked across the street from the airfield for a quick bite. The rest of the diner's patrons were townies. The old men especially liked to linger for hours because coffee refills were free and because they liked to leer at Kenzie.

"Six fifty-nine," Loretta announced.

In her head, Kenzie tore off her frilly uniform right in the middle of the dining room, threw it at her boss, and walked out the door. Out loud, she said, "Alrighty, then."

Maybe she'd wait until tomorrow to ask for that raise....

"Mornin' Kenzie." Max, the busboy, tipped his baseball cap to her. He ducked his head and began furiously scrubbing at a table's plastic covering.

"Morning, Max," Kenzie replied.

Max's face turned pink. The teen's cheeks were cut up from his daily battle with his razor. Judging from the little smears of blood and dots of tissue still stuck to his skin, the razor had triumphed this morning.

"Howdy, Miss Kenzie." Roger, the diner's cook, popped his head out of the service window. The six-foot-six man had to crouch to get his head at the level of the window. "Ready for another day in the salt mines?"

"I don't pay you to socialize!" Loretta called. She snapped her newspaper and settled herself on the stool behind the cash register.

Roger rolled his eyes and grumbled something under his breath. Kenzie winked at Max, who blushed even harder.

The bells above the diner door clanged, and a woman stepped inside. Kenzie could tell from the woman's crisp business suit, diamond stud earrings, and Chanel perfume that she'd come from the airfield rather than town. The woman's nose wrinkled slightly as she took in the smells of old grease, watered-down bleach, and stale coffee.

"Are you serving breakfast?" the woman asked, her voice as cool as her matching navy blazer and pumps.

"Certainly," Loretta chirped, almost falling off her stool as she heaved herself to her feet. "Sit anywhere you like."

The woman nodded and perched on one of the plastic booths.

"Give her an extra slice of lemon in her water," Loretta hissed at Kenzie. "And cover up you tattoos, for Pete's sake!"

Kenzie bit her tongue hard enough to make her eyes water. She rolled down her sleeves, hiding the tattoos that covered her from wrists to shoulders. The cut of her uniform didn't completely hide the dragon tail that snaked across her collarbone.

Sorry, not sorry.

"Loretta, a word?" Roger called.

Kenzie sent the cook a silent thanks as Loretta bustled past Kenzie and through the swinging doors that led to the kitchen.

Kenzie grabbed one of the plastic menus from the bin by the cash register and brought it, along with the water (and two lemon slices) to their patron.

The woman waved away the menu when Kenzie held it out to her.

"Just bring me whatever's fresh," the woman said before taking out her phone and tapping away.

Whatever's fresh…. Hah. Fresh out of the freezer was the only kind of fresh that came from this kitchen.

Kenzie headed to the back to relay the woman's order, which would no doubt send Roger into near-hysterics. Max, who was peeking into the kitchen through the gap between the swinging doors, widened his eyes at Kenzie in warning. Kenzie could hear Loretta and Roger's raised voices coming from inside.

Bracing herself for the impending storm within, Kenzie stepped into the kitchen.

Loretta and Roger were facing off on opposite sides of the island. A mountain of limp vegetables covered the countertop, along with other leftover ingredients from the previous night. A pile of tomato guts was oozing into a heap of already-wilted lettuce.

Yummy.

Roger's bushy eyebrows were pulled together and his bulky arms were crossed over his chest. Kenzie had seen Roger's temper flare on occasion and could tell he was gearing up for a fight.

Loretta's special talent was bringing out the worst in all of them.

"You cheap old bitch," Roger growled. "I'm here busting my ass every day, and for what? A measly thirteen bucks an hour?"

"Be grateful you get anything at all," Loretta snapped back. "Your food isn't fit for a pigsty. I should fire you right now, you ungrateful little rat!"

Alrighty, then.

"Fuck you, Loretta Jones!" Roger shouted. "I'm done."

A small pulse of regret zinged through Kenzie. She didn't know Roger well, but he was nice enough and always served as a good buffer between the staff and Loretta.

"If you walk outta here, you ain't comin' back, you hear?" Loretta yelled.

Roger yanked off his apron and tossed it on top of the tomato guts.

"Roger, wait." Kenzie put a hand on his arm. "Maybe…think about this for a hot sec?"

He shook his head. "Sorry to leave you in the lurch, Miss Kenzie." He lifted his chin at Max, who was standing just inside the swinging doors. "Same to you, kid. You've both been swell coworkers."

Roger turned to glower at Loretta. He gave her the finger before stalking out the back.

Loretta's double chin was wobbling from rage, and her breath huffed out in wheezing gasps. Kenzie didn't have time to react before Loretta whirled on her and Max. Max, the little coward, stepped behind Kenzie so she became a living shield between him and their enraged boss.

"One of you will have to cook today," Loretta announced. "And get moving. We have a customer, for Pete's sake!" She clutched at her heart, and for a second, Kenzie thought the woman might be having a heart attack.

Wishful thinking. Their boss waddled over to the two of them. Her heavy scent of diner grease and drugstore perfume filled the air.

"Well?" Loretta barked.

"I—I can't cook," Max stammered, looking at the wilted vegetables like they might grow fangs and bite him.

Loretta turned her vulture eyes on Kenzie.

Kenzie shook her head. When she left New York City, she'd sworn to herself she would never go near the restaurant industry again. She'd had to amend that promise when she wound up in Ellingreer, Tennessee, and her options for a job were either gas station attendant or waitress. But it wasn't like waitressing for *Good Ol' Apple Pie* resembled her old life in one of Manhattan's premier gourmet hotspots. Aside from delivering plates from the kitchen to the customers, she didn't have to go near the food.

"You hired me to be a waitress," Kenzie reminded her boss.

"My husband divorced me because of my cooking," Loretta said, a note of panic entering her voice.

Surrre. That's *why he divorced you.*

"Sorry, not interested," Kenzie said, even though she wasn't feeling especially sorry. Loretta had made her own bed, and now she could lie in it.

"I'll—I'll pay you extra," Loretta said, desperate now.

Kenzie hesitated. Her landlord's threats from this morning warred with the nausea that filled her at the thought of being back inside a kitchen.

For the first seventeen years of her life, food had been Kenzie's world. It had meant passion and comfort and creativity. Until it transformed into her own personal hell.

Kenzie had run halfway across the country to escape her old life. She'd spent the last five years trying to forget her past…and doing a damn good job of it.

But she really needed the money.

"Time-and-a-half," Kenzie told her boss. "Plus a dollar-an-hour raise from here on out."

Loretta gaped at her.

"Take it or leave it." Kenzie slowly and deliberately rolled up her sleeves, displaying her tattoos.

Sweat beaded on Loretta's brow and darkened her thinning gray hair.

"Fine," Loretta mumbled. She snapped at Max. "Get our new customer coffee and OJ, on the house. You're her waiter now." To Kenzie, she said, "If I'm going to empty my bank account over you, this better be the best meal you've ever made."

Kenzie almost laughed at that. Instead of demanding to know what kind of miracle she was supposed to work from a handful of sad ingredients, she just gave her boss a salute and tucked her loose hairs back into her ponytail.

Left alone in the kitchen, Kenzie surveyed her domain.

The stained countertops, warped old griddle, and dull knives were a far cry from the one-star Michelin restaurant she'd grown up in. If her dad could see her now—

Kenzie stopped that thought in its tracks before her sanity derailed. Thinking about her dad always inspired a simultaneous urge to break down sobbing and punch through the nearest wall. Since neither would keep her from getting fired, she pushed all thoughts of him and her former life out of her mind.

Kenzie focused on the task at hand. She began to cook.

Her hands remembered what to do, even if it had been five years since she'd made a real meal for anyone besides Kiwi. She opened the industrial fridge and began pulling out every ingredient that looked to be in reasonable shape. She ignored the freezer.

Everything else faded away as she began to chop her veggies. Without slowing, she added olive oil to a pan before tossing in finely-diced shallot, red chiles, and jalapeno.

Kenzie didn't see the whole dish in her mind, but every step presented itself to her as though she were following a recipe. Her mind went blissfully empty of everything except for the rhythmic *tap tap tap* of her blade on the board. Soon, the sizzle of cubed potatoes joined the harmony in her pan.

Kenzie added the mostly-cooked potatoes and veggies to a cast iron skillet before topping it with two raw eggs. She put her sunrise-in-a-pan in the hot oven. Then, she concentrated on her avocado crema. A fresh citrus scent filled the kitchen as she zested a lime. A sprinkle of coarse sea salt, and…*perfect.*

The timer in Kenzie's head told her the eggs were almost done. She found a small packet of surprisingly-unexpired pine nuts on a back shelf. She poured them into a dry pan, tossing the seeds until their earthy scent suffused the air.

Kenzie moved around the kitchen, as light on her feet as a ballerina. Music played in her head. She was dragged back to all the times the sous chefs at Ashner's blasted music in the wee morning hours after the customers were long gone.

Kenzie hummed along with the phantom music as she pulled her bubbling pan out of the oven. The golden yolk embedded in the chile-studded potatoes looked exactly like a sunrise.

She would have liked some fresh cilantro to finish off the dish, but since there was none to be had, she sprinkled some finely-chopped parsley over the eggs for another burst of freshness.

"Now, that's what I call a breakfast," Kenzie said to herself as she marveled at her creation.

"Er, Kenzie?" Max poked his head into the kitchen. "Loretta says, um, hurry up—" His jaw clicked shut and his eyes bugged at the sight of Kenzie's creation. "That smells…. Wow." He shook his head in disbelief.

"I've got this," she told him, wrapping a towel around the pan's hot handle and carrying it out to the dining area.

Maybe it was juvenile, but she wanted to see the customer's face when the woman took her first bite.

Kenzie couldn't ignore the soft warmth that was lighting up her insides. She'd had more fun cooking this meal than she'd had in…way too long.

Damn. She really needed to get out more….

"That smells just wonderful." The woman put down her phone and tipped her chin up, sniffing as steam wafted from the pan toward her. "Reminds me of Barcelona."

Kenzie couldn't help but smile at that. She'd never been to Spain herself, but one of the chefs at Ashner's was from Madrid. He'd cooked comfort food from his childhood for her any time she was nervous or scared about something. She'd earned her love of Spanish cuisine from him.

"Enjoy," Kenzie said, feeling as sunny as the glossy yolks she set before the woman. She stepped back, conscious that most people didn't like their wait staff hovering over them like weirdos while they ate.

The woman was so intent on her food that she didn't seem to notice Loretta and Max, who were also creeping forward to judge the woman's reaction.

Instead of digging right in, the woman closed her eyes and lowered her head, inhaling.

"Very nice," she murmured. "I wouldn't have thought of pine nuts, but I imagine their butteriness will complement the jalapenos nicely." She turned the pan's handle so she could examine the dish from another angle.

This woman knew food, Kenzie realized. She'd seen restaurant critics in Ashner's do the same thing with their dishes before they even took a bite.

After the customer finished her examination of the dish, she unwrapped the sticky paper from her napkin to free the cutlery rolled inside. With the tip of her blunt knife, she pierced one of the egg yolks.

The golden cream oozed over the potatoes…just like a sunrise spilling over the horizon. Kenzie released the breath she hadn't known she'd been holding.

Kenzie turned back toward the kitchen, satisfied that the dish's taste would live up to every expectation. A gasp had her spinning back around.

Kenzie froze.

The woman had stopped mid-chew with her fork raised above her eggs. That was the only part of the scene that made any sense. The restaurant had…transformed.

The plastic booths were gone. So were the beige walls and chipped red-and-white tile floor. Kenzie was staring at a scene out of a magazine.

They were on a cobbled patio surrounded by pink and purple flowers. A palm tree swayed lazily in the breeze that smelled like sea salt and sun. The stone balustrade overlooked a cerulean ocean. Kenzie could hear the waves gently breaking on the white sand.

What the——?

Kenzie reached out her hand to brush the palm tree in front of her. Her fingers went right through the tree, finding nothing of substance except for the plastic tablecloth that she could only feel rather than see.

"How on earth did you do this?" the woman asked, her voice full of wonder.

Um…good question.

Kenzie was an excellent cook. She'd been trained by a James Beard Award winner. But even her father couldn't give someone a transcendent experience through his food.

Don't be stupid, she told herself. *This isn't the food. It can't be.*

There had to be some other…some *reasonable*…explanation.

"It feels so real," the woman breathed. She reached out to touch one of the flowering bushes, but her fingers couldn't grab hold of anything. As real as the scene looked, they were still in the diner. They hadn't actually been transported to…wherever this was.

Obviously.

Although it certainly felt real. Too real.

"I've never eaten something so good it actually made me feel as if I was elsewhere," the woman continued. She put another bite of food into her mouth and chewed slowly.

Kenzie glanced at Max and Loretta. From the awed expressions on their faces, it was obvious they were seeing the same thing she was.

This wasn't just a customer with a fantastic imagination and an appreciation for food. They were all seeing the same illusion.

Loretta was the first to recover.

"Well, we do like to *wow* our customers," she said. She wiped her sleeve across her sweaty forehead and gave Kenzie a look that was part disbelief, part admiration, and part fear.

"Yeah." Kenzie managed a small chuckle. "Here at the *Good Ol' Apple Pie*, we want everyone to feel like they're somewhere—" She grasped for the right word. "Magical."

Kenzie offered the customer a wobbly smile, trying to reassure both of them. She had no idea what on earth was happening, but one truth was clear. She had to play this whole thing off like this tropical oasis was in their heads…a shared delusion. Because that was the only reasonable explanation for what she'd done.

The only other explanation was preposterous. Impossible.

CHAPTER 2

BRAXTON

Braxton was fucked. Well and truly fucked.

Here he was, sitting in rush hour traffic in the middle of Sydney. Meanwhile, three kilometers away, one of his family's restaurants was collapsing into rubble.

"Are you there yet?" a frantic female voice demanded through his car's speaker system.

"No, Sofia," he growled at his sister. "And you asking me every two seconds isn't going to get me there any faster."

The light turned green.

Braxton floored the accelerator. And then immediately had to brake hard when some idiot cut him off. Braxton groaned.

"Don't get pulled over," his sister said in an imperious tone. "That's all we need."

Sofia might be two years younger than Braxton, but she sometimes acted more like an extraneous and unwelcome third parent than a twenty-one-year-old.

"If you're going to keep me on the phone," Braxton grated out, "why don't you be useful. Like figure out whether it would be faster for me to ditch the car and just run the rest of the way."

"Car," Sofia said immediately, making it clear she'd done the calculation before he even asked.

The next light turned yellow.

"Come on!" Braxton shouted at the car in front of him.

It came to a slow stop with seconds to spare before the light turned red.

"Fuck!" He slammed his hand down on the steering wheel.

"Okay, just relax," Sofia said. "You can't be panicked when you get there. You're going to have to talk to police and reporters, and whatever you say is going to reflect on our entire operation. Just stay cool."

Stay cool. *Right*. Because a three-story building collapsing on top of a restaurant full of people wasn't worthy of panic.

"I'm working on some damage control issues," Sofia said. The sound of her fingers tapping away at her keyboard came through the speaker. "Hopefully we'll be able to keep the general population from wondering why only half the building got destroyed."

Braxton winced. He didn't even want to think about what would happen if the Gourmands, the culinary magic authorities, thought his family was flouting their cardinal law: no one in the general populace could find out what they did. Ever.

The law was harsh and unyielding, but it wasn't without merit. Braxton could only imagine the pandemonium that would erupt if the whole world discovered that a small number of people had the ability to infuse actual magic into food. Everyone would want a piece of them. They'd be under constant threat of enslavement and dissection by those who wanted their power for themselves.

A notification popped up on Braxton's screen, alerting him to another incoming call. The number was blocked.

"Let me call you back," he told Sofia.

He didn't wait for her permission before switching to the unknown caller.

"Braxton McKaid," he said. He uttered a silent prayer of thanks when the light turned green again.

"Braxton, darling," said a warm, grandmotherly voice that was familiar even though Braxton had never actually met the woman. "This is Polly Berrywhite."

Braxton's stomach flipped. There was only one reason why the most famous person in the culinary magic community was calling him personally.

His palms, already sweaty, slid off the steering wheel.

"Do you have good news for me?" Braxton managed. His mouth had gone dry.

"I certainly do, dearest. The official invitation is in the mail, but I love to deliver the invitation personally whenever possible." She let out a hearty chuckle. "Of course, with you being in Australia, it's more than a hop, skip, and a jump from the US. I hope you understand."

"Of course," Braxton managed. His heart was racing.

He wanted to ask for clarification. Was he really, truly invited? This was too important to be working off veiled assurances.

"Let me just spell it out," Polly said, like she was reading his mind. "I'd like to invite you to be one of the eight competitors for this decade's tournament."

Thank God. Thank God.

Years of preparation and training and sleepless nights…all for this. All so he could compete in the tournament. So he could win.

Then, he'd finally be able to yank his family back from the pit of despair they'd been teetering on for the last five years.

"…will be so much fun," Polly was chattering. "I'm sure you have mixed feelings about returning to New York, however—"

She kept talking, but Braxton wasn't listening anymore.

New York.

A shudder rolled through him. He'd known he would have to go to Manhattan if he was chosen to compete in the tournament, but Braxton had been trying not to think about it. Images flashed through his mind of his last trip to the Big Apple, back when his family had been whole.

"So, what do you say, dearest?" Polly asked. "Can I tell the Gourmands that you've officially accepted our invitation?"

"Yes, of course," Braxton said without a moment's hesitation. "I'll be there. Thank you."

"Oh, excellent," Polly gushed. "All of the details will be enclosed in the official invitation. And, Braxton?" She took a dramatic breath. "Welcome to Hex Kitchen!"

Most culinary magicians would feel elation at being invited to the most prestigious competition in the world. Braxton was just relieved.

The tournament was a means to an end for him.

Whatever positive emotions he was feeling evaporated as the road curved and his restaurant finally came into view. He slammed on the brake and got out, barely remembering to shut off his car.

He began to cough from the sooty air. Chalky dust was billowing up from the building, which looked like it had been torn right down the center. Half of the building was still standing and appeared utterly unscathed. The other half—the magic half—looked like it had been struck by a wrecking ball…or several.

Braxton ran forward.

"Hey, you can't go near there!" someone yelled.

Braxton ignored them. He sprinted toward the building, choking on the dust clouds and shielding his face against the gritty particles that swirled in the air.

A heavy grip came down on his forearm. Braxton turned to see a fireman holding him back.

"You can't go any closer," the man said. "It isn't safe."

"Is anyone still inside?" Braxton's voice was barely audible over all the yelling and sirens and the sound of his brother's legacy collapsing into ruin.

"Everything's going to be fine, Sir. Please just wait over there."

The fireman had barely finished speaking when a hoarse scream came from the fallen building.

"Help!" a woman cried.

Braxton's heart leapt into his throat. The fireman, clearly sensing Braxton's panic, tightened his grip.

More screams were cut off as another section of the building toppled down. More filthy dust clogged the air.

Forcing himself to calm down, Braxton gave the fireman a tight nod and extricated himself from the other man's grip. He walked a few steps away and took the foil packet out of his pocket. He unwrapped the packet that enclosed a small salmon patty.

Braxton shoved it in his mouth, not even tasting the mixture of salmon, spinach, and breadcrumbs. It wasn't the flavor or sustenance he was after. It was the magic it contained.

The patty was one of his brother's recipes. But, like everything Aidan had made, Braxton's recreation wasn't nearly as potent. Still, it was better than nothing. He hoped.

"Come on, Aid," he whispered to his dead twin. "I need this recipe to work, okay?"

Braxton stopped himself before he glanced to the side, where his twin should have been standing. Even after five years without his brother, he still looked for him. Still talked to him.

Aidan never talked back.

Seconds after he'd swallowed the salmon patty, Braxton felt a subtle change throughout his body. Energy coursed through him, but it wasn't the manic fear he'd felt on his drive here. This was more contained…more purposeful. His biceps and calf muscles twitched. Then, his muscles began to expand. The seams of his T-shirt strained as his body swelled. His breathing came easier.

He felt *strong*.

With the distraction of a collapsing building, no one noticed the change that had come over him. He just hoped his altered body would be enough for what he was about to do.

Braxton waited until no one seemed to be looking in his direction. Then, he sprinted toward the building. He heard shouting behind him, but he didn't stop.

Braxton leapt over crumbled stone, twisted piping, and shattered glass. He was practically blind from the haze of dust, but he forged on.

"Is anyone in here?" he called out, coughing as he inhaled a lungful of polluted air.

Cement beams were crossed over a sagging doorway, blocking his way forward. Braxton knelt down and grasped one of the beams. It must have weighed over a hundred kilos, but thanks to the magic he'd just ingested, Braxton lifted it without so much as breaking a sweat.

The inside of the dilapidated building was even worse than it had seemed from the other side. Crumpled tables, smashed produce, and tens of thousands of dollars' worth of kitchen equipment were strewn all over the place. An arrangement of red orchids hung precariously off the remains of a chandelier.

Braxton was staring at what had become of his brother's wish. The transformation of their father's dream.

Dust and rubble.

It was enough to break his goddamn heart.

The timing made sense. They were coming up on exactly a decade since Aidan made his wish that resulted in their family's restaurants. Now, without the wisher to keep the wish alive, it had turned into…this.

The uneven ground beneath Braxton's feet shuddered, reminding him of why he was here.

"Can you hear me?" Braxton called out.

He thought he heard coughing from somewhere nearby. Braxton followed the sound, using his enhanced strength to plow through the destruction.

He thrust aside the mangled remains of a fridge and part of a collapsed wall.

There.

A couple was huddling amid the rubble and clinging to each other.

"Hey, come on." Braxton swallowed a cough.

The man said something that Braxton didn't catch. He pointed to the woman, who Braxton assumed was his wife.

The woman made a whimpering sound and grabbed at her leg. When Braxton glanced down and saw bone protruding from her calf, he went lightheaded.

Her injury wasn't even the worst of it. The woman's leg was caught beneath a metal beam. From the looks of it, it had fallen from the ceiling. It was enormous.

Braxton heaved against the beam. His muscles screamed in protest and spots flashed across his vision as fought the metal's dead weight. Finally, there was enough space for the woman to crawl away.

"Go!" he ordered, his muscles quivering from the strain.

He waited until the couple had dragged themselves out of the beam's path. Then, he let it fall through the marble floor with a terrific crash.

Braxton leapt over the fallen beam and lifted the injured woman into his arms.

"Look out!" she wheezed.

Braxton hunched over her as more of the ceiling collapsed. He clenched his teeth as a falling chunk of cement and plaster struck his back.

"I'm gonna get you out of here," Braxton rasped. "Just hang on."

"Anthony!" the woman shrieked. Her limbs flailed as she tried to get free of Braxton's grip.

Braxton looked around for the man. He wasn't behind them like he had been a few seconds ago.

Braxton spun in a slow circle. He froze.

Acid surged into his throat. The woman was sobbing uncontrollably as she weakly fought against Braxton's hold.

The man's lower legs were the only part of his body that was visible. The rest of him had disappeared beneath the giant chunk of concrete that had crushed him. A trickle of blood was sliding across the marble floor's crumbled remains.

"Anthony! Anthony!" The woman pounded her fists against Braxton's chest. "*Anthony!*"

"There's nothing we can do." The words scraped out of Braxton's throat. "We have to go."

There was a dull crash as another chunk of concrete hit the ground nearby. The pieces exploded into small shards. Braxton's bare arms were bleeding, and his eyes burned.

He searched for any other sign of life as he carried the woman out of the restaurant. He found none.

Had it not been for his enhanced strength, he and the woman would have been among the body count.

Braxton kicked through a brick wall—something that wouldn't have been possible without the magic coursing through his system—and stumbled outside.

After the airless interior, it was pure bliss out here. Braxton focused on breathing as he tried not to listen to the woman as she sobbed for her husband.

I'm sorry, Braxton wanted to say. His throat was burning, though—from the dust, he told himself—and he didn't think he could get the words out. Not that they would help, anyway.

Braxton knew better than anyone that *sorry* wasn't enough to change what had happened. So, he kept his useless apologies to himself and helped get the survivor over to the paramedics.

As an oxygen mask was shoved onto his own face, Braxton turned to look at the ruins of his restaurant. The non-magic part of the building was still standing tall and naked without its other half.

There was only one way to prevent anyone else from getting hurt. He had to shut down the rest of his family's restaurants. At least for the next two weeks, until the tournament was over.

Braxton pulled out his cell phone, which was still somehow in one piece, and started texting Sofia.

As he did, he couldn't stop himself from thinking about what two weeks of lost revenue would do to their bottom line. It would shift their family's precarious financial position firmly into the red. They'd be bankrupt by the end of the first week, and by the second, there'd be nothing left of their restaurants at all.

It would be the final nail in the coffin of his father's dream.

There was only one path to salvation for his family. He had to win Hex Kitchen. They all just needed to hang on long enough for him to do it.

CHAPTER 3

BRAXTON

Braxton parked his car in the underground garage beneath his family's flagship restaurant and penthouse apartment. He desperately needed a shower…preferably before his mum caught sight of him and had a heart attack. One glance in his rearview mirror told him he looked like death warmed up.

With a heavy sigh, Braxton got out of his car. The magic from the salmon patty had worn off. Now, his muscles felt like gelatin. Exhaustion and grief weighed on his every step. He couldn't stop thinking about that man's crushed body.

If he'd closed the restaurant sooner….

Shower and sleep, he told himself sternly, before his regrets could spiral out of control.

Once he was in a better head space, he would meet with his mum and sister. Together, they'd figure out how to pay their employees without any source of income for two more weeks.

Braxton was so focused on his to-do list that he didn't pay any attention to the heavy footsteps behind him.

Braxton let out an affronted *oof* as a heavy weight at his back sent him sprawling. He hit the unforgiving cement floor with a hard *smack*.

Braxton turned his head to the side so he wasn't eating the ground. "What the—"

A fist came at his face.

This time, his vision went black for several seconds.

Braxton struggled, but the man straddling him was as heavy as a beached whale.

The man hit Braxton again. It wasn't hard enough to break any bones, but it hurt like hell. Braxton let out a garbled curse as blood spilled down his chin.

"That's enough," a crisp, male voice commanded.

Braxton sucked in a breath as the weight on his back disappeared.

Ignoring the stars that danced across his vision, Braxton scrambled to his feet.

Five men were standing in a semi-circle, blocking Braxton's path to the building. The metallic gleam of guns poked out of more than one waistband.

Braxton's gaze immediately landed on the man in the center of the group. He was in his late sixties, but he didn't look his age. His skin was wrinkle-free and the kind of tan that couldn't be bought. His black hair was thick and combed so that not even a strand was out of place. He was dressed in a meticulous three-piece suit that made Braxton feel like a downright caveman.

"Mr. Santiori," Braxton said. "Nice of you to drop by." His words were a little thick since he couldn't feel half his face, but he was impressed that he sounded much more in control than he felt.

Veneziano Santiori was the head of one of the oldest and most prestigious culinary magic families in the world. He was also a notorious mobster.

"I thought it might be nice to have a little in-person conversation," Veneziano said in that cool-as-ice voice.

"Nice of you to make the trip all the way from Chicago," Braxton said with more confidence than he was feeling. "I'm flattered."

"You shouldn't be," said a different voice.

That surly response came from the anemic-looking bloke standing on Veneziano's right. Rick Santiori, Veneziano's son, was wearing a matching three-piece suit that seemed to swallow him whole. On him, it looked ridiculous.

After Braxton, Rick was probably the most talented culinary magician in the world. He was also the meanest son-of-a-bitch Braxton had ever met.

"Congratulations on your acceptance into Hex Kitchen," Veneziano told Braxton. "My son has also been invited to compete."

Well, that didn't come as much of a shock.

"Oh? How much did it cost you to get an invitation?" Braxton asked.

He was feeling bolder now. If Rick was in the tournament, that meant he was under the same scrutiny by the Gourmands as Braxton. And that meant Braxton was safe until Hex Kitchen began.

Most likely. Probably. Maybe.

Rick scowled. His father laughed, seemingly unconcerned by the insult.

"There is nothing wrong with using money and influence to get ahead," Rick said in his annoying American accent. He gave Braxton a sour look. "Not that you'd know about that."

"You're right," Braxton agreed. "What my family has, we've earned. I wouldn't expect you to understand."

Rick started forward, but he hadn't made it a step before his father's hand came down on his bony shoulder.

"That'll do, Son," his father said in a patronizing tone.

Rick's pale cheeks turned red.

"Well, this has been nice and all," Braxton said, inching forward.

The three burly thugs reached for their guns. Braxton froze.

"You've been having some problems with your restaurant empire," Veneziano said softly. "Specifically, the magic part of your restaurants."

Rick snickered but quieted at a look from his father. Braxton didn't say anything.

"Your family's in debt," Veneziano continued. "Pouring all your savings into a sinking ship. Sad, really."

Braxton clenched his fists at his sides. He didn't need this prick to tell him about his family's debt. He could see the bank statements and spreadsheets in his mind…complete with the red text and negative signs.

"I'm here to offer you a boon, of sorts," Veneziano said. "I'm prepared to lend you four million dollars."

Braxton swallowed. He knew people like the Santioris never gave something for nothing. But that amount…. Braxton couldn't stop himself from mentally calculating what that much money could accomplish.

It could keep his family's empire afloat long enough for Braxton to win the tournament and set everything right himself.

"And what will I have to give you in return for your generosity?" Braxton asked, trying think over the drumbeat of his pulse.

"Double my investment in the next six months."

Braxton wished Sofia was here right now. His sister could do all the necessary calculations in half a minute.

But there was no chance in hell Braxton was bringing his sister anywhere near these people.

"That's a lot of interest, but it should be manageable if I win the tournament," Braxton said carefully.

"Getting a little ahead of yourself, aren't you, McKaid?" The corner of Rick's lips lifted. "You'll still have to get past me, don't forget."

Braxton used his superior height to look down on his future rival.

Veneziano interrupted the face-off before Braxton could escalate.

"I expect you will win the tournament," he told Braxton.

Rick let out a strangled sound of protest. "I told you I'm gonna win," he complained. He sounded like a sullen child.

Veneziano held up his hand for the second time, dismissing his son from the conversation.

"Double my investment within six months if you win," he told Braxton again. "But if you lose and can't repay your debt—"

"Which is what's going to happen," Rick interjected.

"—the McKaid empire, or whatever is left of it, will be mine. Your restaurants, your properties, your family. You will work for me in whatever capacity I dictate. In a word, Braxton, your family will belong to me."

Braxton tried to breathe. No matter how confident he was about winning the tournament, this deal was still an insane risk.

"So, let me get this straight," he managed, speaking through his swirling thoughts. "No matter what happens, you come out ahead."

Either Braxton won Hex Kitchen and still had to repay a massive debt, or his entire family would belong to Veneziano Santiori.

"I like to hedge my bets," Veneziano said with a knowing smile.

Braxton couldn't agree to this. He'd be a fool to agree to anything Veneziano Santiori proposed.

And yet….

If Braxton couldn't save their restaurants, then it would be like losing Aidan all over again.

Their father had barely survived the loss of one of his children. He wouldn't survive the death of his dream.

Braxton needed to buy enough time to keep his family's tenuous hold on everything they'd built. And Veneziano Santiori was offering him just that.

He met Veneziano Santiori's dark eyes. Braxton stretched out his bloody and dirt-encrusted hand toward the other man.

"We have a deal, Mr. Santiori."

CHAPTER 4

KENZIE

A harsh buzzing pulled Kenzie out of a troubled sleep. She grabbed her phone to turn off her alarm and froze.

It wasn't her alarm. It was an incoming call.

From Rikers Island jail.

The last thing Kenzie wanted to do right then was talk to her dad. Her mind was still reeling from what had happened at the diner yesterday, when she'd somehow conjured an illusion of a Spanish oasis. And she hadn't even had her coffee yet.

But she'd ignored his last three calls.

Kenzie answered the phone.

A recording informed her that Walter Ashner was calling and that she would be responsible for the cost.

"Accept," Kenzie said in a voice that warbled only a little.

There was a crackle of static, and then—

"Kenzie? Hello, Kenzie?"

"Dad." Kenzie swallowed. "Hi."

Because, really, what were you supposed to say to your incarcerated father, who you'd been ghosting for the last two months?

"How are you?" he asked in a gruff voice, which he hadn't had before jail.

"Um—"

I cooked for the first time in five years, and I did something insane to the food. I'm freaking out and don't know what's happening to me. I'm afraid it'll happen again.

I'm afraid it won't.

"I'm fine," Kenzie said. "How are you?"

Her dad hesitated. "I'm fine, honey."

His response was even less convincing than hers, but neither of them called each other out on their bullshit answers.

"It's been a while," her dad said. "I was starting to think you were avoiding me."

Because you're a murderer! she wanted to shout. *I know you didn't do it on purpose, but your carelessness killed that boy.*

And you left me.

Usually, negligent homicide came with a sentence of two to ten years in prison. Her dad was in for life.

The boy who'd died in her dad's restaurant came from some fancy-ass family with a whole team of lawyers and politicians behind them. Kenzie's dad hadn't stood a chance.

Not that he'd even tried to defend himself. He'd given up so easily.

Kenzie had been the only one to fight his sentence. She'd written letters, appealed to politicians' assistants who barely bothered to take her calls, and hired lawyers with money she definitely didn't have. In the end, none of it had mattered.

She didn't say any of what she was thinking out loud. Instead, she left it at, "Sorry, just been busy."

Avoidance was a skill Kenzie had learned to sharpen and wield like a weapon.

"So, what have you been up to?" her dad asked after an awkward pause. "Are you thinking about applying to culinary school again?"

The question startled Kenzie, even though it shouldn't have. All through high school, that had been her plan. She'd even been accepted into The Culinary Institute of America in New York.

And then, in one night, everything had changed.

"No," she said, when she realized the silence had stretched on. "I think I'm going to stay in Tennessee for a while."

"I thought we discussed you getting an education," her dad said, an edge to his tone.

Kenzie bristled.

"We did," she agreed. "And I decided that I'm going to stay in Tennessee a while longer."

If you think I'm dragging my butt back to New York for more scrutiny and scandal, then you don't know me at all, Dad.

"There's still time," her dad insisted, clearly not taking the hint that this topic was off limits. "You're just so talented, it would be a shame for it to go to waste." He hesitated. "I worked so hard to make Ashner's successful so you could have opportunities I never did. I want this for you."

Back in the day, she would have done anything for her dad. One of his favorite sayings was *Making a sacrifice for a person you love is the greatest gift you can ever give.*

All of that had changed the night her father destroyed everything.

"I'm twenty-two, Dad. The college ship has sailed. Besides, I don't especially care what you want anymore."

Maybe that was a tad harsh. She could pretend like it was her lack of coffee that was making her especially bearish.

The truth was she was angry with her father. Even five years later, her resentment hadn't cooled. He was the one who had broken his promise. He'd abandoned her. And he had the nerve to talk about how she wasn't living up to expectations?

"Have you heard from your mother lately?" her dad asked, since today was clearly *Dredging Up Unpleasant Topics Day.*

"Nope."

The word hung between them as they both floundered for something to say.

"I miss you, Kenzie." The words were gentle and more reminiscent of the father she remembered.

Oh, no. She wasn't going to cry right now.

"I miss you too, Dad," she said, swallowing down the salty burn.

"Send me a picture or two when you get a chance?" He stated it like a question. "I know I can't be there for you, but I…I miss seeing you."

"Yeah. Sure." She blinked rapidly. "Of course."

When Kenzie's alarm notification sounded, she almost wept with relief.

"Dad, I've gotta get ready for work," she said. And then added, "Love you."

Her dad didn't hesitate. "Love you too, honey."

✳ ✳ ✳

Kenzie was so full of her own thoughts that she wasn't paying attention to her surroundings as she pedaled down the road to the diner. She was still replaying her conversation with her dad, so it took her brain a few seconds to register what her eyes were seeing.

Holy—

It was barely seven AM, and *Good Ol' Apple Pie's* gravel lot was full. Like spilling onto the street full. Like people lined up around the building full.

"There she is!"

A camera flashed in Kenzie's face, blinding her. Before she could so much as blink, she heard the *click click click* of more cameras. She flinched as people touched her shoulders and back, begging for an autograph or a demonstration.

Kenzie clutched her bike handles to try to ground herself. And to keep from passing out.

Oh God. Was that her left arm tingling? Was she going to have a heart attack and croak here in the parking lot?

Who would feed Kiwi if she was dead?

The moment Kenzie stepped into the diner, Loretta offered her a genuine, there's-a-first-time-for-everything smile that put her even more on her guard. Loretta slapped a newspaper in Kenzie's hands.

"She was a food critic for *The New York Times!*"

"Er, what?"

Loretta made a throaty sound of impatience.

"The customer you served yesterday. The one you made that egg skillet for…the one you performed *magic* for."

"It wasn't magic," Kenzie began weakly, but Loretta carried on like she hadn't even spoken.

"That lady was a food critic for *The New York Times,* and she wrote a whole article about you." Loretta took back the paper and held it an inch from her face. "Listen to this. 'Ms. Brookerton created a dish that was so delicious it made me doubt my own sanity. The heat of the spice didn't just evoke thoughts of Spain…it made me believe I could *see* Spain. I know it was the elegance and poise of the meal that gave me the vision, but as I ate, I truly felt like I was experiencing magic. I can honestly say it was the best meal of my life.'" Loretta let out a delighted chuckle.

Kenzie tried to formulate some kind of reasonable response, but her boss didn't give her a chance.

"The article just came out this morning, and look at it out there!" Loretta peered out the foggy window at the waiting customers. "We're all going to be famous!"

Kenzie put a hand on her stomach. "I think I'm gonna be sick."

"Oh no, you aren't," Loretta informed her, putting two meaty hands on her shoulders and steering her toward the kitchen. "You're gonna to tell Max what ingredients you need for the day, and then I'm gonna to rewrite the menu. Think of how much money we'll make!"

Kenzie tried to tamp down her queasiness before she hurled up the coffee that was rebelling in her stomach.

"I don't know how you did it," Loretta carried on, "but I know what I saw, and that beach resort thing you did wasn't just in that woman's head. I saw it myself."

"Me too," Max piped up. "Incredible, Kenzie. Seriously."

Kenzie managed a weak smile. How was she supposed to explain what she'd done, when she was as confused as everyone else…maybe even more so?

"You get cooking, now," Loretta ordered Kenzie. "I have to make some calls before we open. Would you believe reporters want to interview me? *Me!*"

Loretta shuffled away at twice her normal speed.

Kenzie stood in the middle of the dining room and tried to get a grip.

Loretta was already on the phone with someone, waffling on about freaking magic, and Max was looking at her like she was some kind of prophet or something.

Who the hell was she?

Kenzie wasn't sure she wanted to know.

CHAPTER 5

BRAXTON

Braxton took in a slow breath.

He'd survived a collapsing building and a beat-down from a Chicago mobster. He could handle five minutes with his father.

So, why did it feel like a boulder had settled in his ribcage?

Braxton eased open his parents' bedroom door and forced himself to step over the threshold.

"G'day, Dad."

His father, who was sitting up in bed, looked like an old man. His chest was sunken. His thick espresso hair had been reduced to a few stray tufts of white. The frown on his father's face was familiar, and one that hadn't lifted in five years.

This frail, morose body was nothing like the man who, in his heyday, had been one of the best culinary magicians in the world. Seeing him now, it was hard to believe Braxton and Aidan had inherited their ability from him. There was nothing left of the passionate man who had put in eighty-hour weeks in the hopes of turning his small magical deli into something more.

"How are you feeling today?" Braxton asked.

Instead of answering, his dad looked past Braxton at the empty doorway. The boulder in Braxton's chest turned into a mountain, because he knew who his dad was looking for.

I miss him too, Dad, Braxton wanted to say. *Every goddamn minute of every goddamn day.*

"Dad, I have some good news." Braxton pushed past the lump in his throat. "I'm going to Hex Kitchen."

His dad blinked once. Twice. And then focused on him for the first time in what felt like ages.

"Aidan won the tournament last decade." His father's voice was rough from disuse. "He'd be twenty-three now."

"Same age as me," Braxton replied, hating the way his voice caught.

His dad squinted at Braxton, searching for something he wouldn't find. Braxton and Aidan were fraternal twins but had looked nothing alike. Aidan had gotten their father's darker complexion, while Braxton and Sofia looked like their mum. Braxton and his sister both had blonde hair and green eyes, and the two of them looked more like twins than he and Aidan had.

"You going to come to the tournament and cheer me on?" Braxton asked before thinking better of it. It was stupid to ask questions he already knew the answer to.

"I can't," his father said in a hoarse whisper. "This world let my son be killed while his murderer survives. I want nothing to do with any of it.

"Most days, I don't see the point of anything."

The blood in Braxton's veins turned to ice.

"Dad," he choked. "You still have me and Sofia and Mum. We need you."

"I wish I saw a reason to carry on," his dad murmured. "I just…don't."

Braxton wanted to tell his father that he was working on a solution…that he was going to give his whole family the justice they craved. But he didn't want to offer his father false hope.

"I'll—uh—come see you later," Braxton stammered, already backing away.

He had to get out of there before he broke down.

Braxton didn't breathe until he was out of the bedroom and in the elevator that led down to their restaurant. He used those twenty seconds of solitude to compose himself. When the doors opened, he stepped into the restaurant's controlled chaos.

Wait staff fluttered around, folding crisp white linens, polishing glasses, and reviewing everything for the evening's tasting menu. Sunlight streamed through the floor-to-ceiling glass windows that overlooked Sydney's Darling Harbour. Diners had a first-row view of the docked ships and glittering financial district skyscrapers. This restaurant was in one of the premier locations in the city.

But people didn't come here for the view. They came for the food.

The main dining room was a normal gourmet restaurant for normal guests—well, if a three-star Michelin restaurant could be considered *normal*. A secret entrance through the coat closet led to the separate dining room that was invitation only. That was where guests went to eat something a little more magical.

The non-magic section of their restaurants served as a front for the more lucrative part of the business. Their hidden magic dining rooms were what had made them famous in the culinary magic world and accounted for over ninety-percent of their profits. More importantly, the magic part of their business was the last connection any of them had to Aidan.

"Hey, Boss," someone said, pulling Braxton out of his depressing thoughts. "Try this."

A wine glass was pressed into Braxton's hand. The sommelier hovered over him as Braxton swirled the glass and inhaled the wine's floral bouquet.

"Jasmine?" Braxton took a sip, letting the flavors roll around on his tongue. "And pear?" *And a hint of lychee, too*, he thought.

"Yessir. And lychee. I think it'll be a good pairing for the Mediterranean flavors for tonight's menu."

Braxton nodded.

A spoon appeared in front of his face. Braxton obediently opened his mouth for Natalie, the restaurant's sous chef, to feed him.

"What do you think?" she asked.

The buttery sea bass melted on his tongue. The fish's sweetness was accentuated by dehydrated cherry tomatoes, and paired well with the salty Taggiasca olives they imported from Italy. He took the spoon from her and dipped it into the smear of puree underneath the fish filet. Earthy, sugary steam curled up from the plate.

"It's good," Braxton said. "Beetroot puree could use more seasoning."

"Ha!" Natalie elbowed one of her colleagues in the ribs. "Told you."

Braxton gave the other man an apologetic shrug.

"I'm thinking of adding a coral tuile garnish," the other chef told Braxton, probably to interrupt Natalie's gloating.

"Try black," he suggested. The crisp wafer would make for a good contrast in color and texture to the sea bass.

"Mr. McKaid?" The maître d' held out a phone receiver. "For you."

"Braxton McKaid," he said, balancing the receiver with his chin so he could sign off on a bill that appeared in his hands.

"Mr. McKaid," a silky female voice said. "Justine with the Coultin Group here. I'm calling because we're having a little trouble with your bank. It seems the funds haven't been transferred."

Braxton loosened his grip on the receiver before he broke the thing.

"I'm sorry about the delay, Justine," he said, trying to sound charming rather than desperate. "I know it's a lot to ask, but could you give us just a couple of days? We'll be able to transfer the money by Friday."

Because I got into bed with an American mobster….

"I'm sure that won't be a problem," Justine said generously. "We heard about your acceptance into the tournament. Congratulations, by the way. We're all rooting for you!"

"I appreciate that," he replied. "And I'll owe you one."

Justine giggled. "You can make it up to me by taking me out for a drink sometime."

Braxton didn't bother explaining that if he had any time or cash to spare…which he definitely didn't…he'd find better uses for both.

"It's a date," he said smoothly.

Braxton handed the phone back to the maître d' and made a beeline for the kitchen. He skirted around the busy chefs and let himself into the private cooking area adjoining the main kitchen. It was stocked almost as well as the restaurant's main kitchen, but he was the only one who ever used it.

As soon as the door closed and he was alone, Braxton hunched over the island and let out a groan.

"What a fucking mess, Aid," he said to the empty room.

Because that was what crazy, desperate people did: they talked to their dead brother like he was standing right there.

Braxton shook his head and rolled his shoulders. Then, he went around to the fridge and gathered ingredients for the dish he'd been practicing for weeks. It was one of Aidan's recipes and was deceptively complicated. Braxton was thinking it would be a good one for his final dish at the tournament…provided he could get it to work a little more consistently.

It started with a delicate merengue, molded into the shapes of birds, that were cooked until their peaks just began to brown. That was the easy part.

Infusing a dish with magic required a balanced interplay between the ingredients and power. The magic worked by bringing intrinsic aspects of a completed dish to life. One of Braxton's mentors had explained that it was like a tapestry, where the interwoven threads worked together to produce a coherent whole. One wrong move, and the entire creation would fall apart.

With this dish, the magic was as fragile and fussy as the merengues.

When the merengue birds were ready, Braxton arranged them on a serving platter.

Time for the hard part.

Braxton closed his eyes and forced his mind to clear.

He inhaled, drawing in the light scents of vanilla and toasted sugar. He imagined the slight crunch, followed by pillowy softness, that came from biting into one of the merengues. He felt the sugary egg whites disintegrate on his tongue like snowflakes.

Strands of pearly white magic appeared in the darkness. The threads were only visible in his own mind, and if he lost concentration for even a second, they would disappear. The magic was delicate as spider silk.

Braxton tried not to be too eager as he reached out with his mind. Sweat beaded on his forehead. His labored breathing filled the otherwise silent room.

Come on.

All at once, the tension he felt within his own mind eased. The pearly strands of magic solidified. Braxton's eyes snapped open.

The meringue birds were hovering a foot off the serving dish.

Hell. Yes.

"Good work," he whispered to the inanimate birds like the psycho chef he was definitely becoming. "Ready to fly?"

Braxton stayed motionless, his fingers gripping the stainless steel until his knuckles turned white. The meringue birds, however, were anything but stationary. They flapped their small wings and parted their beaks, like they were ready to burst into song. The birds floated up to the ceiling and began to fly in a slow circle.

Braxton tugged on the magic until the birds were engaged in a synchronized dance. Braxton held out his arms, and the birds landed on his palms. He was panting like he'd just run a marathon, but he was also smiling like a fool.

Not too bad, huh Aid?

He could almost see his brother's half-smile and hear his voice saying, *Not bad, but I can do better.*

The kitchen door opened, and Braxton jumped. The meringues dropped out of the air and hit the spotless floor. The delicate shells broke, and pieces scattered across the tiles.

"Seriously, Sofia?" Braxton glared at his sister.

Sofia fisted her hands on her hips and glared back. "You're not going to be competing in a vacuum, Brax. If you're going to win, you need to be able to handle the sound of a door opening."

She was right, and that only pissed him off more.

"I assume you have a reason for being here." He glowered at his sister. "Aside from being a pain in my ass?"

"Three deaths from the collapse," she announced in her direct, no-nonsense way. "All things considered, it could have been worse."

Braxton thought about the man he'd been forced to leave behind. He knew he'd never forget the sound of that woman screaming her husband's name.

"I'm dealing with the fallout and repairs," Sofia continued.

"How can I help?" Braxton asked.

He hated that so much of the restaurant grunt work fell on Sofia and their mum, since Braxton was so busy preparing for the tournament and their father was…indisposed.

Sofia waved a hand. "I've got it covered. I actually wanted to show you something, but you better drink some water first. You look like you're about to keel over."

"Sure thing, *Mum*," he said with as much ire as he could muster. He really was beat, and his mouth felt dry as dust.

Meringues crunched under Sofia's four-inch heels as she crossed the room. She grabbed two waters out of the fridge and tossed one to Braxton. She assessed the merengue birds that had managed to land back on the plate, grabbed one, and bit off its head.

Because that was how Sofia rolled.

She strode over to him and set her laptop down on the counter.

"I thought you'd want to see this." She tapped the spacebar, and the video on her screen began to play.

"We're here at the *Good Ol' Apple Pie* diner in Ellingreer, Tennessee," a chipper American reporter said into her microphone.

The video cut to the inside of a dingy restaurant. A chef who looked like she was around his and Sofia's age was standing at the edge of the frame. She was watching a man lift a red velvet cupcake to his lips.

As soon as the man bit into the cupcake, his brown hair turned cherry-red.

The camera zoomed in on the man as he took another bite of his cupcake. White streaks appeared in his hair, just like the ribbon of frosting he'd just eaten.

Either it was a really good trick of the light, or it was magic. Braxton couldn't tell for sure from a video, but he guessed it was the latter.

The chef in the video tried to edge away from the camera. When it followed her, she cringed.

With those big eyes, she looked like a doe facing off against a predator.

"She's hot," Braxton observed. He wasn't usually into girls with tats, but on her, they somehow worked. Her eyes were a smoky gray color, and her long black hair fell over her slender shoulder. *Definitely hot.*

"I don't recognize her," he said.

The fact that he didn't know her was strange, since there was a finite number of culinary magicians worldwide…especially with that kind of ability. All of the most powerful chefs in their community at least knew of each other, and the less powerful ones were recorded in the Gourmands' databases.

Culinary magicians could enhance their innate ability with study and practice, but the ability itself was inherited directly from one's parents. Thus, it wasn't like new ones randomly cropped up.

Braxton figured this girl's mysterious identity was probably why Sofia was sharing this video…rather than just to show him some eye candy.

"The regular news is chalking it up to some kind of optical illusion trick," Sofia said, "but my contacts are all pretty sure it's a rogue culinary magician."

Braxton turned his attention back to the chef in the video. She didn't have the look of someone bold enough to go up against the Gourmands.

"Who is she?" Braxton asked.

Sofia offered him a grim smile. "Kenzie Brookerton."

There was something in his sister's voice he couldn't discern.

"Is that name supposed to mean something to me?"

Sofia shook her head. "She changed her last name when she left New York."

New York. If there was a single city Braxton could permanently wipe off the map, it would be the one where his twin had been stolen from him.

Their whole family had gone to Manhattan to recruit some new talent for their quickly-expanding network of restaurants. Braxton had been thrilled because he'd gotten out of midterms for the trip, and he and Aidan had a bet going about which of them could bed an American woman faster.

And there, at a swanky New York restaurant, Aidan was killed by a fucking non-magical chef. He was eighteen years old.

Negligent homicide, they'd called it.

"Aren't you going to ask what her last name used to be?" Sofia asked, her impatient demand pulling Braxton out of the darkest memory of his life.

"I'll bite," Braxton said. "What was her last name?"

"Ashner."

Braxton froze. The water in his stomach turned to acid.

"It's his daughter," Sofia said, her mouth twisting from the same hatred that had Braxton's insides in knots. She pointed at the screen. "That's Walter Ashner's daughter."

Braxton stared at the laptop screen, which was paused on an image of the girl's—Kenzie Ashner's—face. He couldn't imagine how he'd ever thought she was attractive.

In his statement to the police, Walter Ashner had claimed it was an accident. But people didn't *accidentally* cook food that contained enough poison to burn through someone's entire digestive tract after a single bite.

Whatever that bastard had done to the food Aidan ate, there was no doubt it had been intentional.

Braxton had always wondered if Walter Ashner had some culinary magic. Aidan's toxicology report hadn't been able to come up with any known poisons that could be responsible for the destruction done to his body. Culinary magic seemed like the only reasonable explanation, but there was no evidence of it anywhere in the Ashner family tree.

And it was simply unheard of for a family to avoid the Gourmands' notice.

If Kenzie Ashner had culinary magic, though—and it certainly seemed that way from this video—then that meant she'd inherited it from one of her parents. It was too much of a coincidence that Walter had killed Aidan with a poison no regular medical professionals could identify, and now his daughter was performing magic.

"I knew Walter Ashner was a culinary magician," he told his sister. He forced himself to release the tension in his jaw before he cracked a tooth.

Sofia nodded. "Their family isn't registered with the Gourmands, and there's no evidence of magic in any of their ancestry, but I think you're right."

Braxton's mind was reeling too much for him to be able to appreciate his sister telling him he was right.

Walter Ashner was a culinary magician. However impossible, he'd somehow slipped through the cracks. And he'd used his ability to kill Aidan.

"If there was a way for me to get into that jail," Braxton growled, "I'd strangle that bastard with my bare hands."

"No you wouldn't," Sofia said, tossing her long hair over her shoulder. "Because I'd already have killed him myself."

For several seconds, they both just stared at the image of Kenzie Ashner. Braxton had never met the girl, but he hated her almost as much as he hated her father.

After her father's arrest, Kenzie Ashner had hired lawyers to try and soften the jail sentence. Nothing she'd tried had worked, but all her efforts had forced Braxton's family to interrupt their grieving to deal with her shoddy team of lawyers.

"If it makes you feel any better," Sofia said, "Those two aren't going to be long for this world. Once the Gourmands find out the Ashners somehow slipped past their radar and have been practicing culinary magic without going through the proper channels, they're going to kill both of them." She cocked her head. "Well, maybe they won't do anything to Walter, since he's already in prison. But there's no way they're going to let his daughter keep getting away with this." She pointed at the screen.

Sofia was right.

As Braxton chewed that truth over, a crazy possibility began to take shape in his mind. He turned to his sister.

"If the Ashner girl is going to die anyway, then maybe we could find a way to make her death mean something."

Sofia's brows pulled together. "How?"

Braxton lifted a shoulder as he continued to glare at the screen.

"Walter Ashner killed our brother. Maybe if we took away his daughter—before the Gourmands get to her—it would be like retribution, or something. You know, even the score between our families?" He swallowed. "Maybe that would make Dad believe the world is fair, and he'd feel like life was worth living again."

Maybe it would bring him back to us.

Sofia's eyes were bright, and Braxton knew she was sharing his thoughts. They both missed their father.

If Kenzie Ashner was bound for death anyway, then maybe they could take matters into their own hands to bring about a little good. God knew his family deserved a little justice after what happened to Aidan.

Braxton would remember his dad's screams and his mum's sobs until his dying day.

"What exactly are you thinking?" Sofia asked.

Braxton couldn't believe what was about to come out of his mouth.

He wasn't a murderer. Hell, he rarely even raised his voice.

But this was different. Walter Ashner's daughter was showing off culinary magic and living her life without a care in the world. Meanwhile, Braxton's family was drowning in debt, his father was too depressed to get out of bed, and Aidan's legacy was *literally* crumbling into dust.

"I know someone," Braxton said. "A poisons expert."

Sofia huffed out a laugh. "You can't be serious, Brax."

"This could work," he said, as much to convince himself as Sofia. "I'd have to make some calls, but the person I'm thinking of can make a poison that will never be traced."

"You trust this person?" Sofia asked, a fierce hope lighting her face.

Braxton almost couldn't believe his sister seemed to be going along with this.

He nodded. "I know something about her. If it ever got out, it would ruin her. She won't want to risk me telling anyone."

Sofia *hmmed* in thought. "There really is no telling when the Gourmands will take this girl out. If we get to her first and poisoned her like Aid was, then Walter will know his daughter's death was his fault. It would be a kind of poetic justice for what happened to Aidan."

Maybe, just maybe, this was the first step in allowing his family to move on.

He and Sofia exchanged hesitant smiles as they allowed themselves to imagine a scenario that, a few minutes ago, had felt utterly impossible.

"What do you think?" Braxton asked his sister.

He was usually more thoughtful when it came to big decisions…and this definitely counted as a big fucking decision…but he didn't want to hesitate for even a second. If he let the image of his family healing and moving on together fade, it would be replaced by the unsettling knowledge of what he was planning to do to another human being.

It was better not to think about that part at all.

Sofia stared at her laptop screen for so long Braxton wondered whether she'd gone into some kind of trance.

"Do it," Sofia said, snapping her head up to look at Braxton. "I want that family to suffer. I want Walter Ashner to know that the person he loves most in the entire world is dead. I want him to know exactly what he did to us."

Braxton nodded. "I'll make the call."

CHAPTER 6

KENZIE

It was the butt crack of dawn, and already, the diner's gravel lot was full of cars and people.

So many people.

After yesterday's craziness, Kenzie had thought she was prepared for all the cameras and people and noise.

She'd been wrong. So very wrong.

Her pulse was fluttering like a hummingbird's wings. She couldn't stop herself from flinching when people reached out to touch her, like she was some kind of celebrity.

Kenzie had come halfway across the country to escape the limelight.

Even the best-laid plans....

"She's here!"

"I want to do magic tricks for my school's talent show. Can you teach me how you do it?"

"What are you making for us today?"

The questions swirled through the air from everyone crowded into the parking lot. Their voices built into a cacophony that matched the scream tearing through Kenzie's mind.

Kenzie concentrated on not fainting.

A microphone was shoved in front of her mouth.

"Can you tell us how you're doing it?" a reporter asked Kenzie, using his elbows to keep the fifty other reporters from getting to her. "Are you using special lighting to make your dishes feel magical?"

I have no frickin' clue! she wanted to shout.

"Err," was what she actually said. Because Kenzie was eloquent like that.

"Just give us something, Ms. Brookerton," the reporter wheedled.

She couldn't even if she'd wanted to. And instinct told her not to reveal that, whatever was happening, it wasn't some light trick. It was real.

"I—I'm sorry," she managed, trying to forge a path through the ravenous crowd. "I really can't say any more at this time."

This wasn't Kenzie's first rodeo with the press. If she convinced everyone this was just some silly gimmick, maybe they'd get tired of her. Maybe she'd be a fad…like rainbow bagels and raindrop cakes.

"You're my hero!" a woman screeched from the crowd, knocking the reporter aside and thrusting a diner menu in Kenzie's face. "Will you sign this?!"

Or, maybe not.

"Excuse me, pardon me, folks. Comin' through!" Loretta was attempting to waddle through the throngs. Her progress was stymied by the giant bags she was toting.

Yesterday, they'd run out of plates and produce before lunch, and poor Max had been making trips back and forth to replenish their supplies to keep up with demand.

Kenzie made a mental note to tell Loretta to give that kid a raise, too. *God knew their boss wouldn't come up with that bright idea on her own.*

"G'day, madam," a deep, accented voice said to Loretta. "Can I help you with that?"

Even with all of the people milling around, Kenzie had no trouble identifying the source of that voice. She was actually proud of herself that she managed to keep her tongue from falling out of her mouth like Kiwi's when he was eyeing a particularly juicy roach. Because the most drool-worthy man Kenzie had ever laid eyes on was taking Loretta's bags.

Not that Kenzie was prone to drooling. Especially over a guy. In fact, she hadn't felt more than a vague, passing attraction for anyone since Danny. But no woman in her right mind could be unaffected by this man.

Even without his accent…and *damn* that accent…she would have known in an instant he wasn't a local. His sun-kissed golden skin and wavy, beach blonde hair gave that away easily enough. He looked like he belonged on the cover of a surfer magazine instead of carrying bags full of cookware into the sagging diner.

As Mr. Surfer Model reached the door, he turned and locked gazes with Kenzie. The first thing she noticed was that his eyes were so green she wondered if he was wearing colored contacts. Her second observation was that the easy smile he'd offered Loretta was now nowhere to be seen. He stood perfectly still, unlike everyone else in the parking lot who was jumping up and down and babbling. He wasn't looking at her with the awe that she'd seen from all of the other customers who'd visited the diner over the last two days.

Kenzie didn't think she was imagining the emotion burning in his eyes. It was hatred.

❋ ❋ ❋

Kenzie breathed a sigh of relief when she finally made it into the kitchen's relative safety.

"Phew." Max bustled in, looking even more frazzled than usual. His uniform was skewed, and his hair was sticking up in every direction. He'd apparently given up shaving in the madness of the last couple of days, and his cheeks were covered in patchy bristles. "This is nuts."

"Tell me about it," Kenzie replied, helping to unload all of the ingredients she'd written down for him the night before. "Thanks for getting all this stuff."

Max beamed. "Do you need me to do anything else?" he asked. "You know, like adjust the blinds so the lighting is right, or cause a scene to make people look away while you do—" He flailed his hands and bulged his eyes. "—you know, whatever it is that you do?"

Kenzie gave him a little smile and shook her head. "I've got it covered," she told him.

Liar, she thought. She didn't have a clue about what was going to happen to her food today.

For all she knew, the Moroccan beef stew she was planning to make would turn everyone who ate it into alligators. Or, worse yet, it would just be regular old stew.

Oh, the horror.

Loretta would totally fire Kenzie if her food didn't do anything magical beyond being insanely delicious.

Kenzie had hoped that cooking yesterday would bring her some clarity about what was happening to her food. The only result of a twelve-hour shift of constant cooking was that Kenzie was even more confused than ever. She'd spent most of her life in a kitchen, and nothing remotely strange had ever happened to her food.

Either she'd unwittingly ingested some freaky hallucinogens and was tripping, or something had changed. For the life of her, she couldn't figure out what.

While Max started on the daunting task of getting waters—with double lemon—for a gazillion hungry people, Kenzie tried to lose herself in the familiar rhythms of the kitchen.

While the meat for her stew browned in a pan, she chopped onions, carrots, garlic, and dried apricots. She removed the browned meat from the pan and added the veggies, letting them soften in the fat left over from the beef. She added paprika, cumin, cinnamon, and beef broth. She drained the chickpeas she'd left soaking overnight and measured out golden raisins. Soon, the kitchen was filled with warm scents that made Kenzie think of sand dunes and spice markets.

There was a small Moroccan restaurant around the corner from her nana's house in Queens, and for the year when Kenzie had lived with her grandmother, they'd eaten at the restaurant every Sunday night. The stew she was making now reminded her of dozens of cold Manhattan nights she'd spent with Nana. They'd devoured the thick, savory broth while Nana complained about her arthritis and politics.

Kenzie's paternal grandmother was the only relative she'd had in her life besides her father. Poppie, her grandfather, had died before Kenzie was old enough to really know him. So, after her dad went to prison, Kenzie's only real option for a guardian was Nana.

Nana had taken care of Kenzie. She'd cooked her oatmeal every morning, made her go to school, and protected her from the reporters who hung around for weeks after her dad's arrest. She'd been kind, but not overly affectionate. She and Kenzie had existed in the same house, but their conversations stuck to logistics like who was doing the grocery shopping and what time Kenzie would be home at night. It had always felt like they were two ships passing each other in the night.

And then, barely a year after Kenzie moved in, Nana had a massive stroke.

Kenzie had come home from school to find her grandmother face-down on the kitchen floor. She'd died in the hospital later that night.

As the diner kitchen filled with the aromas of ground cardamom and cumin, Kenzie could almost see her nana's wrinkled face break into a smile as the stew's fragrant steam fogged up her glasses.

An expectant silence filled the restaurant when Kenzie delivered the first tray full of bowls. She held her breath along with everyone else as the customers dipped their spoons into the broth.

It looked like normal stew. It smelled like better-than-average stew. The taste of the rich and salty broth still sat on her tongue, along with the sweetness from the dried apricots and carrots. But if there was anything more to the food, then it had happened without Kenzie's say-so.

The elderly woman who had just swallowed her first mouthful began to cry.

Oh no. Had she done something wrong? Was the stew doing something…bad?

"I haven't heard my mother's voice in twenty years." The woman leaned back against the plastic booth and closed her eyes as tears continued to track down her cheeks. She sniffed. And then, she smiled.

Kenzie jumped when another woman let out a delighted giggle.

"I didn't even know I had this memory," the woman said, clapping her hands in delight. "My first day of grade school, and oh my." She giggled again. "Would you look at those shoes? What *was* my mother thinking?"

The woman reached out to Kenzie. Not knowing what else to do, Kenzie took the woman's bony hand in her own.

"Thank you," the woman said. "Your stew is so delicious, it made me remember moments from my past I didn't even know I'd lost."

"You're welcome," Kenzie managed, trying to keep her freak-out private.

Her stew wasn't *that* delicious. There was definitely something…unnatural…happening to her food.

"Oh!" A man at the next table bounced up and down in his booth, making the plastic squeak.

His smile took up his entire face as he said, "I'm seeing my first communion. It was so long ago, I didn't think I even remembered it." He closed his eyes. "Oh look! There's Aunt May and Uncle Enzo." The man waved, like his family was standing right before him.

"Max, get more bowls," Loretta ordered. As the busboy-turned-waiter scurried into the kitchen, Loretta wrote "Forgotten memory stew" on the chalkboard next to the cash register.

When she passed by Kenzie, Loretta said, "I'm putting out advertisements in the *Ellingreer Tribune*. Soon enough, everyone will know this isn't a trick. My old eyes don't lie, and this is magic!"

"It's not," Kenzie began, but Loretta was already gone.

Over the fifty-or-so people packed into the restaurant, Kenzie's attention was pulled to the far corner, where the surfer model was leaning against the wall. He didn't wear that goofy, impressed expression that everyone else had on. His narrowed gaze was fixed on her.

A whole-body shudder went through her. This time, her physical reaction had nothing to do with his uncommon good looks. He looked dangerous.

CHAPTER 7

BRAXTON

Braxton watched Kenzie Ashner. There was no doubt she knew her way around food. Braxton had no interest in tasting her concoctions, but the smells filling the dining room told him that Walter had taught his daughter well. The peppery heat of Moroccan spices hung in the air. Her plating was far more rustic than anything that would appear in a McKaid restaurant, but this was a diner, after all.

It was also clear to Braxton that, as adept as Kenzie Ashner was at cooking, she was utterly clueless when it came to her magic. He'd been watching her face when she served those first bowls of stew, and Kenzie had been as surprised as any of her patrons that her stew unlocked memories.

What Braxton couldn't figure out was how she was employing such advanced magic techniques in such a haphazard way. Culinary magicians were specialists, and it took years of training to hone the ability they naturally inherited.

In two days, this girl had altered the food with her little illusion. She'd also affected the eaters by changing their hair color and making them recall forgotten memories. That was abnormal, to say the least.

And that was just the magic that others had witnessed. Braxton wondered what else she'd accomplished with her cooking. Although, judging from the dazed expression in her eyes every time she saw one of her dishes perform, her magic was newly-awakened.

She was old to just be finding her magic, but there wasn't a specific age when culinary magicians' power emerged.

The oddness of Kenzie's magic didn't really interest Braxton. All that mattered was that Kenzie Ashner was getting famous, while Braxton's twin was ash on the wind.

Braxton closed his hand around the tiny glass bottle in his pocket. The hardest part about getting the poison had been actually having a conversation with Crazy Esther.

Esther was the culinary magical world's poisons expert and Braxton's future tournament competitor. She also lived somewhere in the Canadian wilderness, and it had taken all of Braxton and Sofia's considerable resources to track her down. Once he'd gotten a hold of her, though, Esther had been more than happy to share a recipe that matched his criteria.

Braxton had been forced to endure an hour of Crazy Esther ranting about how civilization has made people soft and useless. She'd talked about survival of the fittest and weak humans living on hospital generators…and about how her poisons could help equalize out the imbalance that humans had brought on the natural world.

Braxton's synopsis of the rant was that Crazy Esther just really, really liked making poisons.

Her eagerness had waned slightly when Braxton had dropped the news that he knew Crazy Esther's secret…and that he wasn't afraid to use it if she ever mentioned the poison to anyone else.

Braxton knew he was playing with fire, but he didn't regret any of what he was planning. Kenzie Ashner was going to die anyway. If Braxton could use her death to avenge his twin's murder and give his father a reason to get out of bed, it would all be worth it.

Besides, it wasn't like she was an innocent by anyone's standard. She had supported her father and shown no hint of remorse for what happened. Her death would show Walter Ashner exactly what he'd done to Braxton's family.

So, Braxton stood at the back of the crowded diner and waited for an opportunity to get Walter Ashner's daughter alone.

It was close to midnight before the heavyset woman who appeared to be the owner of this establishment finally started locking the place down. Braxton followed the rest of the restaurant's patrons outside. He went around back and let himself in through the narrow doorway that led into the diner's kitchen.

The busboy was loading silverware into a dishwasher that looked like it was from the 1920s…or whenever dishwashers first came into being. Braxton waited until the kid disappeared into an adjoining room—probably the freezer.

Braxton strode up to Kenzie, who had her back turned to him and was pouring sugar into an empty cannister. He rearranged his expression into one that was more flirty than…murderous. He leaned over the counter and cleared his throat.

Kenzie spun around. A dusting of sugar arced through the air, but she didn't seem to notice. Her eyes widened as she spotted him.

"You," she said. Pink blossomed on her pale cheeks. "I just mean, I saw you earlier today."

"I'm flattered you noticed me with all of your other admirers." Braxton forced a smile.

The Ashner girl would have a Snow White thing going on with her black hair, pale skin, and cherry lips…if it wasn't for the tattoo sleeves. The tats were an odd contrast to her naturally innocent, doe-eyed appearance.

As he looked closer, though, he realized there was nothing innocent about her eyes. He'd never met anyone with slate-gray irises. They were a little hypnotic.

Kenzie crossed her arms and squinted at him. "So, are you claiming to be one of my admirers?"

"Do you want me to be?" Braxton swept his gaze up her body, lingering on her lips before he met her smoky eyes again.

Even pretending to flirt with this girl made Braxton want to vomit.

A smile played at the corner of Kenzie's lips. "I can't imagine why else you would have hung out here all day, especially when you didn't even have the decency to taste my food."

Braxton arched an eyebrow. "So, you've been watching me. Little stalkerish, don't you think?"

A pretty blush stained her cheeks. "You're the one lurking around *my* restaurant, buddy."

Braxton smirked. "I didn't know lurking was illegal in your country."

Kenzie peered at him, like she wasn't sure if he was making fun of her or not. She fiddled with the frilly edge of her uniform. "Listen," she began. "If you're after my recipes, then you're wasting your time."

Braxton studied her. "Is that what you think I'm doing here?"

"Isn't it?" she countered.

Braxton closed his hand around the smooth glass container in his pocket. "No," he told her.

Kenzie scoffed. "Right. You flew all the way here from—" She waved a hand in his direction. "Britain? Australia? Wherever…because I seem like a nice girl. Right?"

"Is that so impossible?" he replied.

"Yes." Kenzie frowned. "Either you're after my recipes or my ass."

Braxton released a surprised chuckle. This girl certainly didn't suffer from shyness.

"Why not both?"

Kenzie's eyes widened a fraction, but she recovered quickly. She huffed out an annoyed breath. "Well, first, I'm not in the business of training beginner chefs."

Braxton pursed his lips to hide his amusement.

"And second, with your surfer dude thing going on, I'm sure you get girls with much better asses than mine."

"Hmm," Braxton said. "Maybe food is the way to my heart, in which case…." He leaned farther over the counter and gave her a suggestive smile.

"Are you seriously offering to *let* me to cook for you?" she demanded. "When we haven't even exchanged names?" Her voice radiated irritation, but there was a glimmer of amusement in her gray eyes. "That's a little forward of you, don't you think?"

Oh yeah. He had her right where he needed her.

"Fair point." Braxton pretended to consider their conundrum. "How about this? Let me buy you a drink, and then we can properly commence with the introductions."

Kenzie's entire body tensed up.

Huh.

She hadn't gotten offended when he was talking about her ass, but apparently he'd crossed some kind of line in offering to buy her a drink.

"I don't drink," she said curtly. "Thanks anyway."

Okay. A chef who didn't drink was like a doctor who didn't get vaccinated.

"Do you drink coffee, then?" he asked, keeping his tone casual. He didn't want to scare her off.

"Does a bear shit in the woods?" Kenzie retorted.

Braxton couldn't hold back a laugh.

The tension eased out of Kenzie's shoulders. She tucked a loose strand of hair back into her high ponytail. "I guess one cup wouldn't hurt."

"Why don't you relax, and I'll make it?" Braxton suggested.

Her lips parted in surprise. "I didn't peg you as the kind of guy who makes his own coffee."

Braxton quirked an eyebrow at her. "I can do a lot more than make coffee. You might be surprised."

"Doubtful," Kenzie replied. She settled herself on a rickety metal stool and watched him as he got the coffee going.

He felt Kenzie's eyes on him but didn't turn around.

The stool scraped against the tile floor as Kenzie pushed away from the counter.

"Where are you going?" he asked as the aroma of coffee filled the small kitchen.

"I'm hankering for an almond biscotti," she said absently, reaching up on her toes to grab a cannister of flour off a shelf. "You?"

"Definitely." Braxton's gaze flitted to her bare and toned calves before he yanked his attention back to the coffee.

Kenzie hummed to herself as she whisked flour, baking powder, and salt in a ceramic bowl. A smile played at the corner of her red lips.

Braxton cleared his throat. Kenzie started.

"Oh, I forgot you were here," she said, a sheepish expression crossing her face.

"Now I'm offended." He pulled his eyebrows together and gave her an exaggerated glare.

Kenzie laughed. "Don't be. I forgot how everything else just fades away when I'm cooking." She chewed on her bottom lip. "This…being back in the kitchen…is kind of new for me. I took a break from cooking after some…life stuff. It's good to be back." She turned her attention on the butter and sugar she was in the process of creaming together.

Braxton bit the inside of his cheek hard enough to draw blood. *Life stuff* was one way of qualifying it.

The other was that her dad had fucking killed his brother.

But Kenzie was already back to humming, seeming more concerned with the dough she was rolling out than the *life stuff* she'd so casually mentioned.

Braxton turned to the coffee. Glancing over his shoulder to make sure Kenzie wasn't looking, he grabbed two mugs off a shelf and slipped the vial from his pocket. Crazy Esther had told him he only needed a single drop to kill the girl.

He added three.

He checked to make sure Kenzie's attention was still on her dough before capping the mostly-full bottle and returning it to his pocket.

Braxton poured the coffee, careful to keep track of which mug held the poison. If he accidentally killed himself, Sofia would find a way to pull him out of the afterlife just so she could murder him for his stupidity.

"Thanks." Kenzie smiled as she reached for the mug.

Braxton faltered as an unexpected pang of regret tore through him. *Was he really about to do this?*

Kenzie's slate-gray eyes met his. "Everything okay?" she asked.

Braxton realized Kenzie's hand was stretched out toward the mug, which he was still in possession of. He swallowed and nodded.

"Good. Then quit hogging all the coffee. I'm starting to get the shakes over here."

Aidan, he reminded himself. He was doing this for Aidan.

He wanted to know that Walter Ashner was going to suffer the way Braxton and his family had.

Still, craving revenge was a very different beast from committing murder. Braxton had been so wrapped up in the former than he hadn't given the latter enough thought.

Crazy Esther had assured him the poison wouldn't be detected by any toxicology screenings, so he wasn't worried about getting caught. But could he really do this? Could he kill an innocent woman in cold blood?

She's not innocent, he reminded himself. She fought her father's sentence. She'd gone on with her life like nothing had changed. She probably didn't even know Aidan's name.

Braxton thought of his dad, who had tried to take his own life after Aidan's death. He thought about his mum and Sofia, both of whom were working themselves into the ground to keep the family business afloat. He thought of his twin.

The food Walter Ashner served that night had dissolved Aidan's entire digestive system. He'd died quickly, but not before Braxton saw the pure agony on his brother's face.

"Hello? Earth to surfer dude?" Kenzie tapped her foot in impatience. "Did you fall asleep on your feet or something?"

"Surfer dude?" he repeated in a hoarse voice.

"Well, you never told me your name."

"Braxton," he said, intentionally not offering up his last name. He watched her closely for any sign of recognition.

As he expected, there was none. There hadn't been a trial, since Walter Ashner had pleaded guilty before the case ever made it into a courtroom. And Kenzie clearly hadn't bothered to find out anything about the victim's family.

"Braxton," Kenzie repeated. "Got it. Now, hand over the goods. I don't want to have to get violent."

As Kenzie's fingers closed around the mug's handle, their fingers brushed. Her soft skin sent a jolt straight up his arm. Kenzie's gaze found his.

"Loretta?" the busboy called from the freezer. "I need you."

The heavyset woman burst through the swinging doors a second later, making Braxton and Kenzie jump back. The mug slipped out of Kenzie's grip and hit the floor. Coffee and pottery shards went everywhere.

"Shit!" Kenzie gasped, hopping back before the coffee splashed onto her bare legs.

Loretta took in the two of them and the spilled coffee.

"I don't pay you to stand around flirting," she told Kenzie. Her frown softened a little as she fixed her beady eyes on Braxton. "Honey, I'm gonna have to ask you to wait outside while my employees finish their work."

"Loretta, hurry," the busboy's voice called again.

Loretta snapped her fingers at Kenzie, pointed at the spilled coffee, and stalked off to the freezer. Braxton and Kenzie were left alone.

"Isn't my boss an angel?" Kenzie asked with a little chuckle. She grabbed a towel and started cleaning up the mess.

Braxton's mouth had gone too dry for him to speak. His entire body was shaking.

Kenzie tossed Braxton another towel. "Here, make yourself useful," she told him.

Braxton did as he was told as he tried to get himself under control. He still had a mostly-full bottle of poison. He just needed to stop freaking out long enough to do what he'd come here to do.

They were both on their hands and knees, looking for stray pottery pieces, when they heard footsteps.

Braxton raised his head, expecting to see Loretta or the busboy. Instead, he caught the barest glimpse of a man in a suit, just before he disappeared through the swinging kitchen doors. A few seconds later, the sound of screeching tires came from the parking lot.

Braxton peered out the dusty window at the back of the kitchen. A dark-colored SUV was tearing down the street.

"What the hell?" Kenzie asked, peering through the window alongside him.

"Max?" Kenzie called. "Loretta?"

No answer.

An eerie quiet had descended on the kitchen.

Kenzie tossed her dirty towel in the sink and went into the back room to investigate. A few seconds later, the silence broke.

Kenzie screamed.

CHAPTER 8

KENZIE

The echo of Kenzie's scream still rang in her ears. She clutched the open door to the walk-in freezer and just…stared.

She'd seen Loretta and Max walking and talking not five minutes ago. And now they were…they were….

"Kenzie?"

Surfer guy—Braxton—came to a sliding stop next to her. He looked into the open freezer, and all the color drained from his face. She saw him take in the scene she was still trying to process.

Loretta and Max were sprawled out on the floor, their limbs askew. Max's head was lolling to the side. Kenzie didn't need to be a doctor to know his neck was broken.

Loretta was laid out beside him. Her eyes were open and unseeing, and her mouth was contorted like she'd died in terrible agony. There was a deep gash that cut all the way across her stomach. Blood was still oozing out, and there was something glistening just beneath the skin that looked like hamburger meat.

Kenzie tried to take a step forward, but her legs gave out. She fell to her knees and retched.

"We have to call the police," she gasped, wiping her mouth with the back of a trembling hand.

Braxton seemed to snap out of his horrified trance. "I don't think that's going to help."

"What do you mean?" Kenzie's voice came out about two octaves higher than normal.

Braxton dragged his gaze away from Loretta and Max's…corpses…before fixing his green eyes on her. "Your boss wasn't being quiet about your magic. The wrong people were bound to take notice, sooner or later."

"So, this is my fault?!"

Kenzie felt completely unhinged. What the hell had she gotten messed up in?

"Look, there are rules to what we do, and you haven't been following them," Braxton said.

Kenzie had no idea what he was talking about. All she knew was that she was staring at her boss and coworker's mutilated bodies.

"Police," she said, getting to her feet and stumbling back toward the phone. It took her shaking hands two attempts to get the receiver off its cradle. She had punched in 9-1, when a pounding on the diner's back door made Kenzie scream and drop the phone.

"Kenzie Brookerton?" a muffled female voice called from the other side of the door. "Darling, please open up."

Kenzie searched the kitchen frantically for a weapon. She grabbed a serrated knife she'd used earlier to slice artisan bread.

"Who are you?" she called out, just as Braxton reappeared from the freezer.

"Polly Berrywhite, dearest," the woman called. "I have a very special invitation for you."

Braxton walked over to the door.

"What the hell are you doing?" Kenzie hissed, but it was too late.

Braxton pushed back the lock and opened the door.

Kenzie had been expecting an assassin with a ski mask and gun to come through the door, so it took her brain an extra second to process the image before her.

A plump woman with smile crinkles around her eyes stepped into the kitchen. She looked to be in her sixties or early seventies, and was wearing a fuchsia skirt and tweed jacket. As if the color wasn't a bold enough choice, she'd paired the outfit with a diamond necklace and chandelier earrings. Even the chain around her glasses was studded with diamonds. Her wispy white and blue-streaked hair was piled on her head like a cloud of cotton candy.

"Are you real?" Kenzie asked dazedly.

Maybe she was on one of those prank shows. Kenzie glanced around, searching for hidden cameras. Because that was the only plausible explanation for everything that was happening to her.

"Of course I'm real." The woman chuckled and reached out her hand to Kenzie. "I'm Polly Berrywhite, dearest."

She certainly sounded and felt real.

"And, oh!" She gave a delighted little squeal. "I didn't expect you to be here Braxton. This is lovely. So very lovely." She pulled Braxton's face down to her level and kissed his cheek.

"It's an honor to meet you in person," Braxton told the bejeweled grandma. "I'm a big fan."

Polly giggled and hid her face in her chubby hands. "You are too much, Braxton! If you don't stop, I'm going to get all atwitter."

"Are you here because of the bodies?" Kenzie asked stupidly.

"Bodies?" Polly's smile faded. She looked from Kenzie to Braxton.

"The diner owner and busboy are dead," Braxton explained. He seemed far more in control of his faculties than Kenzie. She was shaking like a leaf. "We—I mean, I—assumed the Gourmands took them out for talking about culinary magic."

Gourmands? Culinary magic? What?!

"Those people didn't kill me," Kenzie pointed out. "And I'm the one actually doing…."

Well, she had no clue what she was actually doing.

Polly gave her a pitying smile. Braxton looked at her in a way that made it clear she was woefully ignorant.

Well, no shit!

"Show me these bodies," Polly said, as calm as if she was asking for a tour of the diner. "And then I think we need to sit down and have a little chat."

* * *

Kenzie was too shocked to grieve. She numbly watched two men carry away Loretta and Max's bodies in black bags. All Kenzie could think was that she'd been one room away, baking biscotti, while they were being murdered.

The men had shown up twenty minutes after Polly made a call on her cell phone. They'd had a whispered conversation in the kitchen. Now, they were loading the bodies into their trunk.

Kenzie could only clutch onto the counter and try not to throw up again.

"I don't want you to think violence is commonplace in our world," Polly said, giving Kenzie's arm a sympathetic squeeze. "It's simply that you didn't know the rules. You can't blame yourself."

Kenzie whirled on Polly. "Are you saying that the reason they're dead is because I—I did—*magic*?"

Polly rubbed soothing circles on Kenzie's back. "You didn't know, dearest. This is all brand new to you."

Kenzie was about to reply, but she was distracted by the two men who had returned, sans body bags. They began to douse the freezer with liquid bleach.

"We need to call the cops," Kenzie said, looking around for where the phone had fallen.

"There's nothing the police can do," Polly said, taking Kenzie's arm in a gentle but firm grip and steering her toward the dining room. "We handle these matters ourselves."

"*What* matters?" Kenzie whirled on Polly. "What the hell is going on?"

"I promise to tell you everything, darling," Polly promised. She looked over her shoulder as she nudged open the swinging doors. "Braxton? Be a dear and bring in those biscotti. I've always found it's easier to have difficult conversations when there's dessert involved." She winked at Kenzie.

Kenzie allowed Polly to lead her to one of the plastic booths, mostly because she didn't have the strength to resist.

Braxton put down a plate of the biscotti Kenzie had made—before her boss and coworker had been *murdered* and stuffed in the freezer. He sat down in the booth across from her. His stone-faced expression revealed nothing about what he was thinking.

Polly patted her cotton candy hair, and then she reached for a biscotti. Kenzie, who didn't think she'd ever have an appetite again after what she'd witnessed tonight, just watched her.

Between bites of biscotti, Polly Berrywhite began to tell Kenzie about an underground world of *culinary magic*.

"So, it's real?" Kenzie asked cautiously, like she was about to be led into a trap…or become the butt of a cruel joke. "You mean, I'm actually doing magic with my food?"

She'd been wracking her brain for some kind of logical explanation, but she hadn't been able to come up with anything. But still, *magic….*

"It's real, dear," Polly said gently.

When Kenzie looked at Braxton, he gave her a short nod.

"Are you one of these magic chefs?" Kenzie asked Polly.

"We call ourselves culinary magicians," Polly gently corrected. "And yes I am, although I'm afraid I'm well past my prime." She patted her round stomach and grinned. "We're a lot like professional athletes in the sense that most of us reach peak performance in our twenties." She chuckled. "And I'll just say I'm a few years past my prime." She winked.

Kenzie tried to smile back. She managed more of a grimace.

"I haven't cooked in years, I'm afraid," Polly continued. "Now I'm more of a figurehead for the culinary magic community." She brightened. "I've diverted most of my energy into funding the largest culinary magic food bank in the world." She rested a hand on her heart. "I also started a program for troubled youth who are culinary magicians."

"Oh, that's really awesome," Kenzie heard herself say. Half her mind was on the conversation with Polly. The other half was too busy freaking out to pay attention to what was coming out of the other woman's mouth.

Loretta and Max are dead. I'm a culinary magician. What the hell is happening?!

"It is, isn't it?" Polly sighed happily. And reached for another biscotti. She blushed at the sight of the empty plate. Aside from the untouched biscotti in front of Kenzie and Braxton, Polly had eaten all of them.

"I take it as a compliment," Kenzie assured the older woman, who visibly relaxed.

"So." Polly rubbed her hands together, making it clear she was finally getting down to business. "Are you certain neither your mother nor your father ever exhibited magical tendencies with their cooking?" Polly wiped crumbs off her fuchsia lapel.

Kenzie shook her head. She sure as hell would have noticed if her dad could do magic.

"How very curious." Polly adjusted her glasses on the bridge of her nose. "Don't you find that curious, Braxton?"

Braxton's eyes snapped up at the mention of his name. Kenzie could tell he hadn't been listening to a word Polly Berrywhite was saying.

"Yes, madam," Braxton said. His gaze flicked to Kenzie.

His flirtiness from earlier in the night seemed like a distant memory. There was a severity to his expression that was closer to what she'd seen the first time they locked gazes across the parking lot. Kenzie wasn't sure if it was hatred now, but there was definitely anger.

She must have offended him somehow, although hell if she knew what she'd done. And at the moment, she didn't particularly care. She had bigger problems.

"Are you one of these…culinary magicians, too?" Kenzie asked Braxton.

Polly's pleasant laughter set the remaining crumbs on her jacket to dancing. "Braxton is one of the premier culinary magicians in the world."

Kenzie looked at Braxton for confirmation.

"Guilty as charged," he said with a small shrug.

Damn. She was in the presence of like…culinary royalty, or something.

Kenzie groaned inwardly. No wonder she'd pissed him off. She'd implied that he didn't know how to brew coffee. The man's ego was probably bruised.

Well, so much for the possibility of breaking her self-inflicted dry streak with the hottest man who would likely ever cross her path.

You win some, you lose some.

She swallowed down a burst of hysterical laughter. How could she possibly be worried about a near-stranger's opinion of her after what had happened tonight?

"Oh, and that reminds me." Polly Berrywhite rifled through her large handbag. She fished out a piece of cardstock with gold script. It looked like one of those personalized menus they used to print at Ashner's for special events.

Kenzie took the cardstock after Polly's cheerful, "Go on, dearest" and began to read.

Ms. Kenzie Brookerton,

You have been selected as the eighth and final competitor in this decade's Hex Kitchen. Should you choose to participate, you will need to make yourself available from April 1-14. Further details to follow.

April 1 was tomorrow…well, given that it was past midnight…today.

"I don't understand," Kenzie said, looking from Polly to Braxton.

Polly smiled at her in understanding. Braxton was busy staring out the dark window. Clearly, he wouldn't be any help.

"I'll happily explain everything to you, but—" Polly glanced around the empty restaurant, her mouth pinching. "I think we might all feel better if we went someplace away from all this unpleasantness. Your residence, perhaps?"

Leaving the building wasn't going to help Kenzie to stop picturing Loretta and Max's mangled bodies. She was pretty sure that was a sight she'd carry to her grave.

She didn't bother saying any of that to Polly. Nor did she mention that her *residence* was a crappy apartment that was barely big enough to hold the three of them. She did have to get back and feed Kiwi, though. May as well make a party out of it.

"I don't have a car," Kenzie said.

"I do." Polly stood and swung her bag over her shoulder. "Come. I promise I'll do my best to answer all of your questions. I'm sure you have a few." She winked at Kenzie and led the way out of the restaurant.

CHAPTER 9

KENZIE

In the four years since Kenzie had moved into this apartment, she'd never had a guest. Now, she had two.

Polly Berrywhite was perusing the embarrassingly-empty cupboards in the tiny kitchen. Kenzie took the opportunity to clean out Kiwi's habitat and adjust the incandescent bulb that regulated its temperature. The normalcy of the task made her feel a little less unbalanced.

Braxton stood in the center of the room, his hands shoved into his pockets, his expression unreadable.

Kenzie had no excuse for why she'd let this sexy surfer into her apartment. All she could do was plead insanity or hypnosis.

When he'd started flirting with her, Kenzie couldn't pretend she wasn't just a little flattered. The guy was burn-girls'-panties-off hot, *and* he knew how to brew a pot of coffee.

It had been the first almost-date she'd been on since high school. Unless she counted her few one-night stands, which didn't really fit the definition since Kenzie had peaced out before they reached the cuddling portion of the evening. The experiences had left her feeling emptier and more alone than she'd been before, and so she'd quit men cold turkey. Ever since, her love life had become a solo event.

It wasn't like she expected to find love again after Danny. Lightning didn't strike twice, and after she lost him....

"You've caused quite a stir in our circle, dearest," Polly Berrywhite said, peeking around the ingredients she'd hobbled together and giving Kenzie a kind smile. "Quite a stir."

Kenzie shook her head. "I still don't understand. Those people who…killed my boss and coworker…."

Polly didn't wait for her to try and untangle her muddled thoughts.

"I know it seems harsh, but we have to keep our special brand of cooking secret from the general public. At all costs." She squeezed back out of the kitchen and joined Braxton over by the ratty couch.

"I don't get why it has to stay secret," Kenzie protested. "And I really don't understand why the secret is worth killing over."

Polly's smile faded. "You've seen how much attention your cooking drew in just a few days," she pointed out. "Think about how everyone would have reacted if they had known you were indeed performing magic, rather than some clever feat of technology."

"But—" Kenzie began, but Polly wasn't finished.

"Your boss and coworker recognized your work for what it is: extraordinary. That made them a threat to our world. And, as harsh as it sounds, threats need to be eliminated."

"That's barbaric," Kenzie said. "Not to mention freaking illegal."

"We do abide by normal laws, most of the time," Polly conceded. "But we also have authorities—we call them the Gourmands—who carry out justice on behalf of all of us. It's the ugly side of what we do, but there's a beautiful side, too."

Kenzie looked at Polly. The older woman had her hand curled around Braxton's biceps and was half-coaxing, half-dragging him into the kitchen.

"Go on," Polly told Braxton, giving him a pleading look over the rim of her glasses. "It won't kill you to show off a little."

Braxton let out an indulgent sigh. Polly gave him a gentle push in the direction of the counter, where she'd lined up a few ingredients.

"Um." Kenzie held up a finger as Braxton went for the first bag. "Those are mealworms…. You know, for my chameleon."

Braxton raised his eyebrows, his expression going from annoyed to amused.

Polly laughed. "Don't you worry, darling. He won't hurt your chameleon." She wandered over to Kiwi's habitat and bent down so she was level with the glass. She started making kissy noises.

Kiwi's skin went from green to brown as he crawled on top of his rock and turned his back to Polly.

"Don't take it personally," Kenzie told Polly, who was looking a little hurt by Kiwi's dismissal. "Reptiles aren't known for being warm and cuddly."

"Shh."

The sharp command came from Braxton, who had made a small salad out of the collard greens, raspberries, and mealworms that Polly had laid outon the counter. He was hovering his hands over the wriggling mealworm salad. His eyes were closed, and his breathing was unsteady.

Kenzie was about to ask what exactly he was doing, when she caught sight of faint shimmers of light hovering over Kiwi's food dish.

As Kenzie watched, the strands of light began to move. It looked almost like a spiderweb, with the silky white threads connecting the mealworms in the salad to Kiwi, who was watching the proceedings with mild boredom.

When Braxton opened his eyes, the pearly threads vanished. Braxton wiped a hand across his forehead, which was dotted with perspiration in spite of the fact that the apartment was freezing.

Kenzie's stupid landlord always refused to turn on the heat until she was at risk of actual frostbite.

"You're just going to love this," Polly assured Kenzie.

Kenzie's breath caught as the mealworms and shredded greens began to wiggle around inside the dish. Then, like they were engaged in some kind of choreographed dance, each ingredient began to wriggle up the sides of the container.

The mealworms, shredded greens, and halved raspberries inched along the counter in a perfectly straight line. They made a beeline for Kiwi's habitat, where they deposited themselves through the small hatch at the top.

"Wow," Kenzie whispered.

Polly chuckled. She watched Kiwi prowl around on his rock, eyeing the mealworm salad as he decided whether it was worth his time. When he closed his eyes and went back to napping, Polly turned back to Kenzie.

"Most of us inherit our ability from one or both of our parents," Polly explained. Her smile faded away as she twirled the diamond-studded chain around her eyeglasses between her fingers. "Dearest, are you absolutely certain neither of your parents have this gift?"

It was the third or fourth time Polly had asked some variation of this question.

Kenzie gave the woman a helpless shrug. "My dad is—was—an amazing chef."

Out of the corner of her eye, she saw Braxton's body go rigid. His cheeks hollowed out like he was clenching his teeth. Ignoring his strange reaction, Kenzie focused on Polly. "And my mom—" She almost choked on the word. "Well, if she had that kind of ability, I'm sure she would have used it."

Kenzie heard the bitterness in her own voice, but there was nothing she could do to mask it.

Polly *hmmed* in thought. Then, she shrugged. "Why don't you give it a whirl, darling? Let's see what you can do."

"Um, you mean I should make the mealworms crawl around the apartment?" Kenzie asked.

Polly waved her hand. "Try whatever feels natural to you."

Movement from the chameleon's habitat caught Kenzie's gaze. Kiwi, who had opened his orb-like eyes, was watching the mealworms with new interest. Quick as lightning, his long tongue darted out to snap up one of the insects.

"Better do something before he eats them all," Braxton said, lifting his chin in a challenge.

Kenzie felt like retorting that she had no idea what the hell she was supposed to do. It was like she was standing in the middle of a stage and expected to perform, but no one had given her a script.

Dance monkey, dance.

She closed her eyes in an attempt to calm herself. That was when she noticed those pearly-white threads of light appear over Kiwi's habitat. She blinked. Now, even though her eyes were open, she could still see the light.

Weird.

"What do I do now?" Kenzie whispered. She kept her attention on those gossamer threads, knowing instinctively that they were the key to whatever was supposed to happen next.

"Anything you want," Polly said in a soft, encouraging voice. "Touch them with your mind. Let your magic do the work."

Uh, okay….

Kenzie looked to her pet for inspiration. Kiwi's bulging eyes were fixed on a raspberry. His tongue darted out and snapped up the fruit.

Thanks for all the help and support, bud.

Kenzie was still trying to figure out what to do when she noticed Kiwi jump off his rock with a dexterity her lazy little pet rarely exhibited. Kiwi stood on his hind legs—something else he'd never done—and started to…dance?

"Are you doing this to him?" Kenzie asked Braxton, a little alarmed.

He shook his head. "You are."

Kenzie was about to call bullshit, but she was too preoccupied by her chameleon's strange behavior. Kiwi's little front claws bobbed up and down as he shimmied his hips. Like he was a freaking hula dancer. No…wait.

Kiwi was doing the Macarena. And, yep…there was the butt wiggle.

Polly applauded.

"I seriously must be tripping," Kenzie muttered.

"Did you mean to make him dance?" Braxton asked. "Or did it just happen?"

Kenzie gave him a little shrug. "I was thinking about performing myself, so maybe my subconscious did this?"

Braxton nodded like it all made sense.

Crazy. Cra-zy.

As Kiwi continued to rotate through the Macarena steps, his skin transformed to an electric blue color Kenzie had never seen on him before. In the blink of an eye, his color shifted to neon yellow. And then hot pink.

"Dear heavens," Polly whispered.

When Kenzie glanced over, she saw that Polly's jaw had slackened. She and Braxton were staring from Kiwi to Kenzie. Braxton seemed dumbstruck. Polly looked a little afraid.

"Um…problem?" Kenzie asked.

As far as she was concerned, Kiwi's new color palette was far less disturbing than the way he was shimmying his butt.

Braxton was the one who finally answered.

"It's impossible for a culinary magician to control more than one power at a time. Even if a dish is complex enough to allow for multiple magical properties—which is incredibly rare—then only one can be initiated at a time."

They all looked back at Kiwi. He was still rotating through insane and unnatural colors as he danced.

To Kenzie's relief, her pet settled down a few seconds later. He changed back to his resting color, climbed onto his favorite branch, and promptly fell asleep.

"What else can we put magic into?" Kenzie asked, feeling as dazed as she sounded.

"I beg your pardon?" Polly quirked a snowy eyebrow at her.

Kenzie shrugged. "Could I, like, make my apartment turn into a castle or something?"

Kenzie did not appreciate the hearty chuckle she got out of the other two, like she was their night's entertainment.

"No, darling," Polly said, wiping away a tear of mirth and adjusting her glasses. "Our magic only works with food. It's just the way it's always been."

"That's why it's called *culinary* magic," Braxton added dryly.

Well, thank you so much, Mr. Helpful. That clears up everything.

"Got it," she said stiffly. "And what's the deal with this tournament?" Kenzie held up the invitation.

Polly sat in one of the two chairs that had come with the apartment. "Braxton, love, will you tell Kenzie all about it? All this excitement has tuckered me out."

Braxton's green eyes fixed on Kenzie. For a second, she could almost see the pure intensity radiating off him. Instinct told her the flirty, easygoing version of him had been fake. This was the real Braxton.

Unease shimmied up her spine.

"The Hex Kitchen tournament is held once a decade," Braxton said. "There are eight participants—"

"The other seven have already been selected, dear," Polly jumped in. "Braxton is favored to win, but so much can happen that anything is possible."

Braxton seemed neither surprised nor flattered by Polly's assessment. Kenzie couldn't decide if that meant he was pompous, or if he was really just that good. Possibly both.

"Most of us are champions from the smaller culinary magic tournaments." He turned to Polly and said, "Not to be rude or anything, but why was she invited?" He pointed at Kenzie. "It's not like she's been around the culinary magic scene long enough to prove herself."

Please. That was totally rude.

Kenzie couldn't really blame him for asking, though. The man had a point.

"Oh baloney," Polly said pleasantly. "In just a few short days, Kenzie has already proven she's special." She winked at Kenzie.

When it was clear Polly wouldn't offer any further explanation, Braxton continued.

"There are three rounds. For the first two, we'll compete in pairs. The challenges for those two rounds stay secret until right before they begin. After each round, one pair is eliminated. For the final round, the four remaining participants compete as individuals and get to prepare any dish we want. The winner gets a wish truffle."

"A wish truffle?" Kenzie repeated, hearing the wariness in her own voice.

Braxton's lip quirked. "Exactly what it sounds like. It's a white chocolate truffle infused with strawberry liqueur and filled with—" He broke off and frowned. "Actually, I have no idea what it's filled with. I do know that the magical ingredient inside it—that's the wish part—grows once a decade on top of the Shishapangma mountain in China. Hence why the tournament is held only once a decade."

"There's just one culinary magician in the world who knows how to harvest the ingredient and prepare the wish truffle," Polly added, looking wistful.

"The winner gets the truffle," Braxton continued. His gaze sharpened. "Eating the truffle will earn you a single wish. Whatever you desire most will come about."

Kenzie had to repeat that sentence twice in her head before the full meaning penetrated.

"No friggin' way." She shook her head.

"Way," Polly replied with another wink.

"Does a genie pop out?"

Polly laughed. Braxton did something with his mouth that could have been amusement or disdain.

"I like your sense of humor," Polly told Kenzie.

Kenzie decided not to say that she'd only been sort-of kidding. A chocolate truffle that could make your greatest desire come true?

If it hadn't been for everything else that had happened over the last couple of days, Kenzie would have been sure she was being pranked.

"You'll be a bit behind the other participants in terms of preparation," Polly told Kenzie. "The other seven competitors' magic emerged at a young age, and they were all classically trained. Not to worry, though." She gave Kenzie a kind smile. "You have a great deal of natural talent. Plus, your partner will help you along. That is, if you wish to participate."

"You mean, I have a choice?" Kenzie asked.

She felt dumb for asking. Although, really, this whole thing was outrageous from beginning to end. Kenzie's brain felt like it had been run through the meat grinder they'd used at Ashner's to make their own sausages.

Magical cooking competition? Truffles that could fulfill wishes?

Kenzie wanted to laugh. Except, was it really that much of a stretch after what she'd seen her own food do over the last few days? Inexplicable hallucinations…stew that brought back old memories…a dancing chameleon….

"So, what do you say, darling?" Polly asked. "Can I report back to the other judges that you've accepted our invitation?"

"Other judges?" Kenzie asked, surprised. "Are you one of them?"

Polly sat a little straighter in her chair and beamed at Kenzie. "I certainly am. I'll also be emceeing the tournament. It'll be my fourth decade, and I have a feeling this one will be the most exciting yet." She grinned broadly. "So, what do you say?"

What did she say?

One look in Braxton's direction, and any illusions she might have had about winning that coveted wish flew right out the window…along with her sanity, apparently.

She was actually considering accepting the invitation.

It would be nice to understand what was happening to her and her food, she reasoned. Besides, it wasn't like there was anything tying her down in Ellingreer, Tennessee. Her quiet little life had been blown to smithereens. Loretta and Max were…gone.

If Kenzie stuck around here, she'd be reminded of their deaths every minute of every day. It would be like New York all over again. If she left and did this tournament, then maybe she'd give herself a fresh start.

Kenzie practiced avoidance the way some people practiced religion. *Devoutly.*

"Where's the tournament?" Kenzie asked.

"Manhattan," Polly said brightly.

Oh, hell no.

"Yeah, that's not going to work for me," Kenzie said. "I…don't like New York."

One glance at Braxton told her that he shared her opinion. There was a veritable storm brewing in his green eyes.

"You won't have to worry about a thing," Polly assured Kenzie, misunderstanding her growing panic. "Your living quarters have already been prepared. Everything is taken care of. All you have to do is arrange travel for any immediate family members who will be watching you compete."

Kenzie hid her snort with a cough. "I don't think I need to worry about that."

"Ah. Alright, then." Polly cleared her throat. "You'll receive a small stipend while you're in the tournament to take care of any necessities. Of course, we'll cover all of your food costs."

Kenzie hesitated. She was pretty sure if she set foot back in the city where her life had fallen apart, she'd either have a panic attack or do something rage-driven and wildly inappropriate. Not to mention, did she really want to get involved with a group that murdered people just for talking about magic?

But when else in her life would she be offered the chance to understand what had been happening to her? To meet others like her?

"We can't let such a talented young culinary magician slip through our fingers," Polly said, as Kenzie continued to deliberate. "Don't you want to learn more about your unique abilities?"

Polly had her there. But would Kenzie really risk exhuming all of the memories she'd tried so hard to leave behind?

Polly's encouraging smile faltered. "It really would be best if you came with us." She twirled her eyeglass chain. "There are strict rules in our community about revealing what we can do to outsiders, as you've seen for yourself. You'd be so much better off under our protection."

Kenzie stared at the older woman. Was Polly threatening her?

If she didn't go along with all of this, would she be carried out of here in a body bag like her coworkers?

"Braxton," Polly wheedled. "Tell Kenzie she positively must come with us. It'll be fun."

When Braxton turned the full force of his gaze on her, Kenzie found she couldn't breathe. There was no denying this man had an effect on her. She just didn't know if it was a good or bad thing.

Okay, that was a total lie. Absolutely nothing good could come from a guy who looked at her like *that.* Like he could chew her up and spit her back out.

"Come with us," Braxton said, repeating Polly's plea with far less enthusiasm than the sweet old woman. When he smiled, it looked a little sinister. "It'll be fun."

Kenzie bristled. Did he think he could scare her off? Intimidate her? *I don't think so, bud.*

"I'll come," Kenzie announced before she could think better of it. "But I'm bringing my chameleon."

CHAPTER 10

BRAXTON

If Braxton was wound any tighter, he'd snap. He hadn't had a second alone with Kenzie since Polly showed up.

He'd been so close. So goddamn close.

Two more seconds, and Kenzie would have taken that mug of coffee and drank the poison. She'd be dead, and Braxton could go home and tell his father that there was justice in the world, after all.

And then you'd be a murderer.

Braxton needed to get his head on straight, otherwise he'd never be able to finish this.

Polly had insisted that Braxton, Kenzie, and Kenzie's pet chameleon accompany her on her private plane (*paid for by the Gourmands, dears. They're very generous to an old woman.*).

The convenience of a free ride had been eclipsed by the company.

He'd been sitting mere feet from Walter Ashner's daughter and couldn't do a damn thing about it.

They had just landed in New York, and already, Braxton felt a heavy weight descend on his shoulders.

Christ, he hated this city.

As they taxied on the runway, Braxton tried to mentally regroup. Tonight was the tournament's opening ceremony, where they would meet the two mystery judges and be assigned their partners.

All during the limo ride that brought them from the private airfield to the tournament arena in Midtown, Manhattan, he and Kenzie were silent. Braxton didn't know what she was thinking, but there was a vacant expression in her gray eyes that probably matched his own.

"Here we are, dears," Polly announced. She popped out of the limo with far more enthusiasm than either he or Kenzie displayed.

The last time Braxton had been inside the Empire State Building—or more accurately, beneath it—he'd been thirteen years old and nothing more than a spectator.

He followed Polly through the underground parking garage to a small elevator bank. Instead of stepping into one of the waiting elevators, Polly led them to a door that said *Emergency Exit Only*.

When she pushed the door open, no alarm sounded.

Polly turned her body to the side to fit through a pitch-black space that no one in their right mind would enter unless they knew what was on the other end.

Kenzie whispered, "This isn't sketchy. Nope, not sketchy at all."

They walked steadily downward for several minutes, using the wall and their cell phone flash lights to guide their path. Polly opened another door that was illuminated by the tiniest sliver of light. There was a single elevator, which they took down to the third level. When the doors opened, they were inside the tournament venue.

A long corridor, wide and high enough to allow for food deliveries and a thousand audience members, stretched out before them. It sloped downward, leading even deeper underground. There were doorways on both sides labeled with plaques that denoted storage areas, pantries, and meeting rooms.

"Shortcut, dears," Polly said cheerfully as she opened a door to a giant walk-in freezer.

A gust of frigid air lifted the hairs on Braxton's arms as they walked past packages of ground beef and enormous bags of French fries. Polly pulled up a hidden lever, and the back wall of the freezer slid away.

Beside him, Kenzie gasped.

They stepped into a circular room with thousands of red-velvet chairs that climbed all the way to the rafters. The room's centerpiece was an enormous glass dome.

The dome, which looked like a giant fishbowl, was made out of hundreds of glass panels that fit together almost seamlessly. The black tile floor shone from the dozens of spotlights hanging from the ceiling. There were four pristine cooktops spaced equidistant around the dome, as well as a raised platform where the three judges would sit.

Giant cameras positioned at every angle were ready to capture the activity inside the dome.

As Braxton stared at the rows of empty audience seats, he couldn't help but be transported ten years back in time. His whole family had been here. He could almost see the starry-eyed expression Sofia had worn, and the way their parents had been bursting with pride. Aidan had been as calm and sure of himself as ever, despite the fact that he was the youngest contestant ever to compete.

"You'll both want to get settled into your suites and get acquainted with your kitchens," Polly said, breaking into his reverie. "I'm off to hair and makeup." She patted her wild hair and shouldered her handbag. "I'll see both of you tonight at the opening ceremony."

Polly gave each of them a hug that smelled like the caramels she'd been eating during the flight. Then, she was hurrying off.

Tournament employees arrived a few moments later to bring them to the competitors' living quarters.

Braxton had once asked his parents how such a large venue could exist beneath the Empire State Building without the general population being aware of its existence. His dad had explained that the building's lead architect was from a culinary magic family.

"This is so intense," Kenzie whispered, speaking for the first time since they'd landed in New York.

"Just wait until tonight," Braxton told her. "All those seats around the dome will be full." Bookies would be taking bets, and tournament employees would be selling all kinds of Hex Kitchen swag.

This tournament was the single biggest money-maker in the world of culinary magic. The tickets for non-family audience members were exorbitant, but that only accounted for a small fraction of the profits. The real money was made in the gambling that went on throughout the competition.

People bet on everything from who the guest judges would be, to which two teams would make it to the finale, to whether anyone would be seriously injured or killed.

Braxton hadn't handed over a penny to the bookies, but he felt like the biggest gambler of them all. All of the investors who had a stake in the McKaid empire had bet millions that he would win the tournament. If he met expectations, then his investors would get a nice payday.

If he lost, well…. It didn't bear thinking about. Because it wouldn't fucking happen.

Kenzie disappeared into her suite first, while Braxton was led to the end of the hall.

"Here you are, Mr. McKaid," the man carrying his suitcase said. "I hope you don't mind." He hesitated, shifting from foot to foot. "I, ah, thought you'd like to have the room your brother occupied when he was a competitor."

A jolt went through Braxton's system.

"This was Aidan's room?"

The man nodded. "If you don't want it—"

"I want it," Braxton said hurriedly. *Christ, he wanted it.*

He took the gold key the man handed him and unlocked the door.

When the man continued to hover behind him, Braxton muttered, "Right, sorry." He pulled out his wallet.

"No. Please." The man held up his gloved hands and took a step back. "I was just wondering if maybe…." He fumbled in his back pocket and pulled out the latest issue of *Magical Cuisine Quarterly*. He opened the magazine to a page that had a giant image of Braxton's face. He gave Braxton a bashful look and held out a pen. "Would you mind?"

"Not at all, mate." Braxton signed the man's magazine, smiled, and gently closed the door between them.

He stood on the threshold of his suite and took it in. There was a modest living room area that contained a white couch and glass coffee table. There were no windows since they were underground, but the white lights and modern-style standing lamps brightened the room. A decent-sized bedroom and bathroom with all the usual fixings were just off the sitting area.

The suite's shining star was the kitchen. It was bigger than the rest of the rooms put together. There were two cooktops with eight burners each, double sinks and dishwashers, three ovens, and a refrigerator that was big enough to live in. All of the appliances were top-of-the-line.

"Not bad, Aid," Braxton said as he wandered into the bedroom. As he sat on the edge of the bed, a strange tingling came over him. It was like déjà vu, except not, since he'd never been here before.

It was stupid to feel closer to Aidan here. It wasn't like the sheets had been preserved for the last decade, for Chrissake. But when Braxton stretched out on the duvet, he felt closer to his twin than he had in years.

Instead of letting himself dwell in the bittersweet sensation, he sat up and pulled out his phone to call Sofia.

She picked up on the first ring. Braxton could hear the hustle and bustle of one of their restaurants in the background, and it sent an odd pang of homesickness through him.

"You in New York?" his sister asked.

Sofia wasn't big on hellos. Or goodbyes. Or anything that didn't have a specific purpose. Given that she was now in charge of keeping the books and dealing with all money-related problems for their failing empire, Sofia didn't have time to be anything but efficient.

"Yeah," Braxton replied. "They gave me Aid's old room."

He heard his sister's small intake of breath.

"Is it weird?" she asked, her voice softer than it had been before. The background kitchen noise went quiet as Sofia closed herself inside somewhere more private.

"No. It's actually…nice."

A few seconds of weighted silence hung between them.

"So, is it done?" Sofia asked.

She didn't have to explain what…or specifically *who*…she was referring to.

Frustration slammed into him. *If only he'd been quicker with the coffee. If only he hadn't hesitated.…*

"Working on it," Braxton replied. "You know the tournament organizers picked her as the eighth contestant?"

"I heard," she said, sounding as displeased by the development as Braxton. "You'll have to be even more careful. You'll also have to do it before she figures out who you are."

He hadn't told Kenzie his last name, but given her complete lack of recognition when he told her his first name, he wasn't sure it would matter. Clearly, Kenzie had put the past behind her.

At least no one in their world seemed to have realized the history between Kenzie and Braxton's families. Kenzie had done a good job of hiding her identity, and there were few people who had both Sofia's network of contacts and determination.

"I'll get it done," Braxton promised, rubbing at his gritty eyes.

"Good." Sofia sighed. "I gotta get back to work."

The call ended.

Braxton flopped back on the bed. "What do you think, bro?" he asked the empty room. "You gonna help me win this thing?"

A knock came at the outer door to his suite, and fuck if Braxton's heart didn't beat a little faster. When he opened the door, he half-expected to see his twin grinning at him from the other side of the threshold.

It wasn't Aidan. Obviously. But that didn't stop Braxton's knees from going weak with disappointment.

Idiot, he told himself.

"Hiya, stud."

The culinary world's poisons expert was standing outside his door. Her long, platinum-blonde hair hung in dozens of messy braids that were looped through with small rings of metal. She wore leather shin guards and a cape that looked like it was made out of grizzly bear fur. Heavy eyeliner made her pale face and eyes look a little feral.

She looked like she'd walked right out of a Viking movie.

"Uh, hey Cr…I mean, Esther."

Braxton didn't know exactly who had given Esther her moniker or when, but there was no question why her title of *Crazy Esther* had stuck. Nevertheless, after everything he'd heard about her, and their brief phone conversation a few days ago, Braxton knew better than to call her *Crazy Esther* to her face. If even half the rumors about her were true, she'd probably stab him with the hunting knife hanging off her belt. Or shoot him with the bow and arrows strapped across her back.

Seriously? Did none of the security guards think to take those away from her?

"You look as tasty as your picture in *Magical Cuisine Quarterly*," Crazy Esther informed him.

She flounced into the room without waiting for an invitation and stretched out on Braxton's couch. She bent her leg in a suggestive way and waggled her eyebrows at him.

"What can I do for you, Esther?" Braxton asked, using the voice he adopted with especially irate patrons at his family's most expensive restaurant.

Esther tossed her head, making her braids flip over her shoulder. "Did you use the recipe I gave you yet?"

Braxton's hand twitched, wanting to feel the outline of the vial in his pocket.

"I made it," he replied.

I just haven't been able to use it.

"It's a good one." Esther nibbled on her bottom lip as her eyes darkened in excitement. "It'll be slow and painful, and it's impossible to reverse once it's ingested."

Braxton took no pleasure in the thought of causing Kenzie excruciating pain. In fact, the entire business was starting to make him feel sick.

All he wanted was to restore the balance between their families so his could move on. He wanted to put Aidan's ghost to rest and bring his father back from this purgatory he'd been in for the last five years.

"I used it on a hunter who killed wolves for the hell of it," Esther said, her voice taking on a dreamy quality. "The fucker didn't need the meat or pelt…just liked shooting big game. So, I put a few drops of the poison into his canteen while he was sleeping." Esther sighed in satisfaction. "It took him two days to finally croak."

Braxton winced, which seemed to delight Esther.

"Just out of curiosity." Crazy Esther peered up at him. "Who are you going to use it on?"

"None of your business," he said shortly. "And don't forget about our agreement. You keep my secret, and I'll keep yours."

Esther's lip curled, making her look like a snarling animal.

Another knock came at the door, and Braxton had never been more grateful for the interruption.

"Come in," he called.

Kenzie ducked her head into Braxton's suite. She'd changed out of her frilly pink uniform and was wearing a pair of dark skinny jeans and a black tank top. The shirt's thin straps bared the tattoos that covered both of her arms.

Her left arm looked like a tattoo garden. There were butterflies, flowers, and vines that wound around her skin. Her right arm didn't seem to have a particular theme. There was a boat, a Turkish evil eye, music notes, and an incredibly detailed dragon that curved around her shoulder and stretched across her collarbone.

Braxton wondered if she had tattoos anywhere else on her body. Disgust at himself followed on the heels of that fleeting thought. He wanted to kill her…not seduce her.

"What's up?" Braxton asked.

"Sorry." Kenzie's gaze darted to Esther, who was still sprawled out on the couch. "Just wanted to tell you we're supposed to go to the dome now."

"Hi, Number Eight," Esther purred. She got off the couch and walked around Kenzie, studying her like she was a slab of meat. "You're a pretty little thing, aren't you?"

"Uh, thanks." Kenzie stepped back to put some space between them. "Nice…cape."

Esther smoothed her hand over the fur. "It's despicable that civilization has turned people into useless automatons who don't know how to live in harmony with nature," Esther said.

"Esther specializes in backwoods cooking and foraging," Braxton explained, seeing the confusion on Kenzie's face. *And poisons.*

"Oh," Kenzie said. "That's cool."

"It's not *cool*," Esther snapped. "It's a way of life. And I'm going to prove that to everyone when I win this tournament." She loomed over Kenzie. Her height and overbearing demeanor only seemed to emphasize how tiny Kenzie was.

"Esther, leave her alone," Braxton ordered. As soon as the words were out of his mouth, he was surprised he'd said anything at all. Kenzie's full, red lips turned down in a frown, making it clear she didn't appreciate him coming to her defense.

What the hell was the matter with him?

"Someone's touchy," Crazy Esther said, tossing her blonde braids and flicking Braxton's chest.

"If you're done with your diatribe," he told Esther irritably, "maybe we can go to the dome?"

When Esther turned to the door, Kenzie caught Braxton's eye and swirled her finger around her ear in the universal crazy sign. Braxton found himself grinning back.

Braxton's moment of levity passed as soon as he remembered why they needed to go to the dome.

It was time for the opening ceremony.

CHAPTER 11

BRAXTON

All eight competitors were brought into their own changing rooms before the opening ceremony. Braxton didn't know what was going on in the other rooms, but in his, a highly caffeinated woman was flitting around him like a hummingbird.

"No thanks," he grated, when the lady came at him with some fruity-smelling hair spray.

"You're gorgeous," the woman told him in a breathy voice. "I'm just going to make you a little more gorgeous. And cover up those under-eye circles."

Braxton had been awake for forty-eight hours straight. Under-eye circles were the least of his worries.

When a security guard poked his head into the room to announce it was time, Braxton could have kissed the man.

Braxton was escorted to the waiting deck outside the dome. He was handed a crisp, white chef coat with his name sewn onto the front. As he put it on, he got a little choked up thinking about Aidan's, which was framed and hanging in their family's penthouse.

The eight competitors were led into the dome one at a time. Braxton, as the favorite, was the last to enter. There was only a small audience for the opening ceremony—usually just the competitors' family and VIPs—but he was still greeted with enthusiastic applause when he joined the rest of his competitors. His gaze immediately went to the section of audience seats that had been cordoned off for his family.

Braxton had known they would be empty, but the sight of those lonely seats still brought a pang of sadness.

Braxton ignored the audience and focused on the dome itself. The judges' table was empty, but the rest of the eight competitors were already milling around the waxed floor.

In the *avoid at all costs camp*, there was Crazy Esther and Rick Santiori.

Braxton hadn't seen Rick since his father's goons had beaten Braxton up in his own garage. It would have been bad enough if Braxton's only concern was needing to compete against this slimy bastard. Now, just the sight of Rick's face served as a reminder that, if Braxton lost the tournament, his own family would belong to Rick's.

Polly had been right when she said anything could happen at Hex Kitchen. All of the competitors were talented, and after Braxton, Rick was most favored to win.

Rick was also the only one of them who had competed in Hex Kitchen before. In fact, as far as Braxton knew, Rick was the only loser to be asked back to compete a second time. Last decade, Rick had lost to Aidan.

And this decade, he'll lose to me. End of story.

"Hiya, loves." Farley, an Irish girl with an Irish temper, gave all of them a handshake that was hard enough to crush bones.

Farley's magic only worked with pressure cooking, and Braxton didn't see her as much of a threat.

Sébastien was a Frenchmen whose family had been at the forefront of magical ceviche for generations. He had dark skin and close-cropped black hair. The best word Braxton could use to describe the man was *tidy*. His glasses made him appear even more studious and serious. Sébastien was so introverted that Braxton didn't think he'd ever heard the man speak.

Philippe, who was also from France, was a more talented and fun version of Sébastien. His wild hair and beard were just an extension of his free-living spirit.

Braxton had spent a weekend with Philippe after a culinary magic institute he'd done in Paris. It was one of the most fun…and drunkest…weekends he'd had in recent memory.

Finally, there was Hiroto. Hiroto's mother was the Japanese ambassador in London, and their family travelled constantly. He liked to joke that his English was better than Braxton's.

Braxton went over to Hiroto and Philippe, exchanging back slaps and handshakes. The three of them had seen each other at various magical culinary competitions over the years and had developed a friendly rivalry.

"You blokes can't get enough of losing to me, can you?" Braxton teased.

Hiroto elbowed Braxton in the ribs. He was wearing an extra-large T-shirt under his unbuttoned chef coat that had a picture of a cake and the tagline *I like big bundts, and I cannot lie.*

Philippe slung an arm over Braxton and Hiroto's shoulders. "Ah, but this time will be different."

Braxton raised an eyebrow.

Philippe checked to make sure the cameras overhead weren't rolling yet, and then leaned in secretively. "I've got motivation this time."

Braxton scoffed. Philippe was a talented chef, but he'd always been more interested in partying than winning.

"And what kind of motivation are we talking about?" Hiroto asked Philippe. "Besides embarrassing yourself in front of the entire culinary magic community?"

"Asshole." Philippe punched Hiroto in the arm.

Braxton snickered.

"But no," Philippe continued. A smile stretched across his face. "Raina's pregnant."

"No shit," Braxton said.

Raina was a sweet girl Philippe had been in love with since the two of them were in diapers.

"You gonna marry her?" Hiroto asked, giving the other man a congratulatory hug.

Philippe's gaze darted around the room to where the other contestants were mostly standing by themselves. Then, with a face-splitting grin, he reached into his pocket and pulled out a jewelry box. He snapped it open to display an engagement ring.

"I'm gonna ask her during the finale," Philippe said, smiling even wider. "I would do it when I win the wish truffle, but—"

"You know Braxton's going to win," Hiroto finished.

Philippe shrugged. "If I can get to the finale, I'll be a happy man."

"And an engaged one," Braxton said, shaking his head in amazement. "Congratulations, mate."

Philippe closed up the ring box and put it back into his pocket.

Braxton couldn't help but notice how Philippe kept his hand curled protectively around the bulge in his pocket, the same way Braxton kept feeling for the bottle of poison in his pocket.

Thankfully, there wasn't time to consider that disturbing parallel further. Polly Berrywhite entered the dome to more applause from the audience. She blew kisses and thanked everyone profusely before going over to the judges' table. Her blue-streaked hair bobbed with her every movement. All the diamonds she wore absorbed the white lights and reflected tiny rainbows everywhere.

"So exciting." She nudged Kenzie, who was standing closest to her.

Kenzie offered a small, nervous smile in return. Her attention kept going to the cameras. It looked like she was hunching her shoulders to make herself seem smaller.

Braxton was glad for the cameras. At least this way, his family would be able to watch him on the closed network that was only accessible to members of the culinary magic community.

Polly gave more or less the same welcome speech she delivered every decade. She thanked the competitors, the Gourmands, and even worked in a plug about where to make donations to her magical food bank.

As Polly waffled on, Braxton tried not to look directly at her, lest he be blinded by her diamonds. He remembered at the last tournament, an eleven-year-old Sofia had loudly asked their parents why Polly didn't sell her diamond necklace if she loved her charities so much.

All eight participants lined up in front of the judges' table as they waited to find out who the other two judges would be. Polly wasn't a secret, since she'd been emceeing and judging the event for just about forever, but the other two changed every year.

Braxton's heart sank to his toes when the second judge entered the dome. Chef Elyannah Levy, an Israeli who was a world-renowned magical food critic, had been the bain of Braxton's existence since the McKaids opened their first restaurant a decade ago. Chef Levy was rumored to have been part of the Mossad before she got into magical cooking. The woman was scary as hell. She'd once written that Aidan's food *lacked soul*, and that Braxton's dishes were a *piss-poor copy of another man's attempt at genius.*

That quote had been published in four of the biggest culinary magic magazines. Their dad had responded by building a huge bonfire in their backyard and tossing every issue of the magazine he could scrounge up into the fire. He'd invited a few hundred guests, including some esteemed food critics and reporters.

After all the guests went home, their family had sat around the bonfire. Their dad had let them taste brandy, even though Sofia was only fourteen at the time, and their mum told ghost stories.

It was one of Braxton's favorite memories.

It was also the only happy memory he had that involved Chef Levy. That woman had made it her personal mission to criticize every dish ever served in a McKaid restaurant.

"I expect you'll all play by the rules," Chef Levy said in lieu of a greeting. "And I implore you not to be boring with your magic. Don't make me regret the long plane ride I took to get here."

In that moment, the snarly chef reminded Braxton a little of Sofia. That helped ease the knot of tension in his stomach…a little.

Braxton perked up when the third and final judge entered the dome. Chef Yamosato Sakai was renowned for his magical kaiseki—a Japanese style of artfully preparing a multi-course meal. Kaiseki was all about presentation and precision, and most closely matched Braxton's own style.

Chef Sakai had taken some heat over the last few years for his radical notion that magical food should be shared with the non-magical world. He'd also written an unpopular editorial about how magical chefs relied too heavily on pomp and circumstance to mask inadequate technique.

Chef Sakai regarded the competitors with a critical gaze. "I want you all to know that just because a muffin levitates or can induce euphoria in the one who eats it, it doesn't make the meal a work of art. Food must entice each of the senses. The most memorable dishes often convey their strength with a whisper rather than a shout." He rubbed a palm over his bald head before tracing the thin trails of his black goatee. "Truly remarkable food tells a story in which all of the senses and the magic work together to create harmony."

"What Chef Sakai is saying," Chef Levy added in a terse voice, "is that we're looking for perfection. Pure and simple." She sneered at all of them. "Since you are allegedly the best culinary magicians in the world, I expect perfection should be well within your reach."

No pressure or anything....

"Tough beans," Hiroto whispered, looking as unhappy about the lineup as Braxton.

"How wonderful," Polly Berrywhite gushed. "Are all of you as excited as we are?"

"Yes, Chef!" seven of them replied.

Kenzie, Braxton noticed, wore a dazed expression as she tried to take everything in. He couldn't blame her. This was a lot for anyone to wrap their heads around, and she didn't have the benefit of a lifetime of being immersed in this world like the rest of them.

Braxton was overcome by an urge to go over there and…stand next to her, or something. Which was insane, considering he was planning to poison her the first chance he got.

"Now, for those of us who are new," Polly said, smiling at Kenzie. "We're going to review the rules."

Rick Santiori let out a scoff that echoed in the lofty dome. He eyed Kenzie the way a dog might stare at a juicy steak. Braxton didn't like it.

"You think you can come out of nowhere and compete against the world's best?" Rick asked Kenzie in a haughty voice. The question was pitched loudly enough for all of the contestants on the floor to hear, but not loud enough for his voice to reach the judges' stage or be picked up by the mikes spaced around the dome.

Kenzie turned to Rick. "Sorry." She blinked at him. "I've heard of everyone else here, but who are you, again?"

Rick's upper lip quivered, like he was some kind of feral animal.

"Atta girl, Kenzie," Philippe called, giving her a thumbs-up.

"Love havin' another lady with some zest around these parts," Farley said in her heavy Irish accent.

"Once the tournament begins," Polly continued, completely oblivious to the tension taking place on the floor, "your participation is binding. No one can leave unless the judges deem your dish unworthy and you're sent home."

None of the contestants reacted.

Polly continued. "There are three rounds. You will compete in pairs for the first two rounds, with one pair being eliminated after each. For those rounds, you are inextricably linked with your partner. You are only as strong as your weakest link."

The thought made anxiety gather at the base of Braxton's spine. He could be sure of himself, but the other participants were less reliable. Braxton made a subtle shift so he was standing closer to Hiroto and Philippe. Maybe the judges would take the hint and pair him with one of his friends.

"For the final round, the remaining four contestants will compete as individuals. There is only one wish truffle." Polly paused to give her words extra emphasis. "If you win the finale, the truffle will be yours. Any questions?"

"Who are the pairs?" Rick demanded, earning some appreciative chuckles and claps from the audience.

"Quite right," Polly said, giving him a broad smile.

The three judges conferred.

"We have chosen the partners," Chef Levy announced. Her pale blue eyes seemed to hold an edge of malice as her gaze snagged on Braxton before moving on to the other competitors. "The first team will be Hiroto and Philippe."

Braxton's hopes sank.

"Sorry, brother," Hiroto told him, before exchanging a handshake with Philippe.

"Team two is Farley and Sébastien."

The two reluctantly made their way toward each other. Their styles of cooking were as opposite as their personalities. If Braxton was a betting man, he'd guess they would be the first team out of the tournament.

Now that those two were paired up, that left three potential partners for Braxton…all of whom were equally unpalatable. Rick was the most talented chef, but Braxton would rather chew glass than work with that asshole. Crazy Esther was, well, crazy. And he couldn't be with Kenzie because—

"Rick and Esther will be team three."

For just a second, the room spun.

No.

No fucking way.

This wasn't happening. This couldn't be happening.

"And the judges have decided to pair our newest and most experienced contestants. Team four will be Kenzie and Braxton."

Newest and most experienced…. What a load of bullshit. It was more likely that the Gourmands had discovered Kenzie's real name and were doing this to mess with Braxton's head.

Kenzie offered him a hesitant smile. She said something, but the words didn't penetrate the roaring of his own mind.

He was partnered with Kenzie Ashner. That meant that, for the first two rounds of the tournament, their fates were intertwined. If he killed Kenzie, he'd get himself kicked out of the tournament. His family would have to pay back loans with money they didn't have, and they would be ruined.

That gave him only one option.

Not only would he need to train a chef who hadn't even known she possessed magic a week ago, but he'd be working side-by-side with his family's enemy.

Bloody fantastic.

CHAPTER 12

KENZIE

Everyone else gathered with their partners and started to talk strategy. Since Braxton had left the dome as if a pack of hellhounds was on his heels, Kenzie went back to her suite alone.

She didn't want to be anyone's dead weight, and she didn't blame Braxton for feeling like he'd gotten the short end of the stick. Every other competitor had been doing this magical cooking thing for years. From what Kenzie had gathered, they'd all proven themselves to be the best at what they did in a myriad of other magical cooking competitions. Kenzie, on the other hand, had spent the last four years of her life working as a waitress at *Good Ol' Apple Pie.*

Kenzie wasn't exactly pleased by her pairing with Braxton, either. She didn't have anything against Braxton, specifically. It was just that Kenzie preferred to work alone. The one lesson her mother had taught her, and which had proven itself to be true time and again, was that the only person she could trust to look out for her was herself.

Why had she come here, again? And, for that matter, She why had she even been invited her to compete?

Sighing, she grabbed her phone off the bedside table. Kenzie felt a small pinch of guilt when she saw a missed call from her dad. She'd talked to him only a few days ago, but it felt like a lifetime's worth of drama had happened since then.

What would a conversation with her dad even sound like right now?

Oh, hey Dad. I'm just in an underground tournament venue for people who can make their food do magic. No biggie. What's new with you?

Swiping the missed call away, she brought up her contact list for another unpleasant conversation she'd been putting off.

Kenzie was sure she hadn't inherited her magical cooking ability from her father. She'd spent every day with him for the first seventeen years of her life, and they'd been closer than close. He never would have kept a secret like that from her.

That left only one other possibility for magical inheritance.

Kenzie glanced at Kiwi, who was slowly crawling up one of his branches. His skin was the same tan color as the branch.

At least he hadn't been put out by his interstate trip and seemed to be settling in just fine. His round eyes swiveled around to regard her before he continued on his journey.

"Just get it over with, huh?" Kenzie asked the little chameleon.

Kiwi didn't respond.

Sighing, Kenzie tapped on her contact for Denise and pressed send.

A chipper voice answered on the second ring. "Manhattan drug and alcohol rehabilitation center. How may I direct your call?"

"I'd like to speak to Denise Werrimeth," Kenzie said, ignoring the way her stomach turned over at just speaking that name.

"I'm sorry," the woman on the other end of the line said after a pause. "Ms. Werrimeth is no longer with us."

Of course, she's not.

"Do you have a number where I might be able to reach her?" Kenzie asked. "It's really important."

"Just a moment," the woman replied.

A few minutes later, Kenzie was dialing a new number.

"Yeah?" a male voice said when the call connected.

"Is Denise there?" Kenzie asked.

She could hear music and voices in the background on the other end of the line.

"Who's askin'?" the man demanded.

"Her daughter." Kenzie managed to say the word without choking…much.

"Huh."

He didn't say anything else.

Kenzie could still hear the music and voices, so she knew the man hadn't hung up on her. A few seconds later, heavy breathing came across the line.

"*Yesh?*"

Kenzie's stomach roiled at the sound of that voice. Her nausea only got worse as she heard the unmistakable clink of ice cubes in a glass.

She'd be willing to bet the wish truffle that the glass wasn't filled with water.

Kenzie could almost see Denise's glazed-over gray eyes. Kenzie avoided face-to-face interactions with her mother like the Plague…not least because it was always a little like looking into a mirror that displayed a fucked-up version of her reflection.

"It's Kenzie," she said. "I need to talk to you."

"Wha'? Speak up," Denise slurred. "'s bad connection."

Holy hell. It was seven o' clock in the evening, and Denise was already sloshed.

"I need to talk to you," Kenzie practically shouted, even though she knew there was nothing wrong with the connection.

"M'kay."

"Listen, can we meet up tomorrow or something?" Kenzie asked. "I'm in New York, and—"

"You're in New York! Oh, tha's nice." Denise burped.

"I'll text you where to go," Kenzie managed, clutching her phone so hard she was surprised it didn't crack. "Security will meet you and bring you to my room."

"Oooh, security, huh? Fancy schmancy."

"Just come by as soon as you can," Kenzie said through gritted teeth.

As soon as you're sober, is what she really meant.

"And don't say anything to anyone about this," she added as an afterthought. Whatever her feelings were about Denise, Kenzie certainly didn't want her ending up like Loretta and Max.

Kenzie hung up before she said something she'd regret. She texted the address and threw her phone onto her nightstand. She fell back onto the mattress and stared up at the speckled white paint on the ceiling.

This was why she hadn't wanted to come back to New York. She could have happily spent the rest of her life hiding out in Tennessee and never encountered a single relic from her past. Instead, she was inviting Denise over to her place. Soon enough, she'd have to walk by Ashner's, and then she'd probably call her dad. And then her dreams would turn into nightmares featuring Danny's smashed car and all those flashing lights.

Kenzie closed her eyes and tried to breathe.

"You know you're not on holiday, right?"

Kenzie let out a little yelp and clutched her racing heart. Braxton loomed in the doorway to her bedroom. His eyes were slitted in irritation.

"Jeez." Kenzie scowled at him. "Ever consider knocking?"

"Your door was open," he pointed out. "Figured it was as good as an invitation."

"Well, you figured wrong."

"Sorry for disturbing you," Braxton said, his voice dripping with derision. "Maybe I should come back after you get your beauty rest?"

"What happened to Mr. Can I Buy You a Drink?" Kenzie asked.

"Gone," Braxton replied shortly. "We have work to do."

Kenzie briefly wondered whether she was dealing with a multiple personalities kind of situation.

Nah, just a douche, she decided.

Kenzie was two seconds away from biting his head off, but she stopped herself before the verbal assault made it out of her mouth. It wasn't Braxton's fault that she was in a crappy mood.

"Look," she began in an attempt at being conciliatory. "I can imagine you're not pleased about being partnered with a total newb."

Hell, the guy had looked like he'd been two seconds away from fainting when the partners were announced.

"But I do know how to cook," she continued. "And I'm going to do my best not to get us kicked out in the first round. So just chill, okay?"

Braxton snorted. "Thank you so much. All my concerns have been alleviated."

"Good," Kenzie chirped. "Now, do you plan on watching me get my beauty rest, or should we cook?"

If he wanted to take the sarcasm route, she'd match him step for step.

"Cook," Braxton replied, looking mildly chastened.

Hah.

✳ ✳ ✳

Steam puffed out of the oven, and Kenzie stifled a moan as the scent of cinnamon, ginger, and cloves tickled her nostrils. She brought the fresh gingerbread over to a rack to cool.

"Smells nice," Braxton conceded, flicking his hair out of his face as he spooned icing into a piping bag.

"I don't believe it," Kenzie said in mock surprise. "Was that an actual compliment that just came out of your mouth?"

"It's been known to happen," Braxton said, his lip twitching. "Just don't get used to it."

"Wouldn't dream of it," she replied.

They moved around each other as they worked, finding an easy rhythm the chefs in her dad's restaurant had called *the dance*. They each did their own part, hardly needing to speak as they brought their dish together.

"Why do you do that?" Braxton asked.

"What?" she replied, pausing as she cut through the cooled gingerbread.

"Hum while you cook."

Did she do that? She hadn't even noticed.

"I guess because…I'm happy." Kenzie shrugged.

"Happy," Braxton repeated, like the emotion was foreign to him.

"Yeah. I mean, when I'm cooking, I go into this peaceful place where everything just flows. It makes me happy."

Braxton made a noncommittal noise.

Silence stretched between them as they continued to work.

"I'm sorry," Braxton said, startling her enough that her knife hand slipped and made a jagged line across the gingerbread. "I know I've been kind of a—" He paused, searching for the right word.

"Dick?" Kenzie supplied.

Braxton gave her a crooked grin. "Yeah. That."

She smiled back. "Now, admitting that wasn't so hard, was it?"

He shook his head. "It was actually quite painful."

"Poor baby," she crooned. "Here. Have something sweet." She held out a small piece of fresh gingerbread.

Braxton took the piece of cookie from her outstretched hand and popped it into his mouth. The sound he made as the sugar and spices dissolved on his tongue went straight to Kenzie's nether regions. The guy was sexy without even trying. It was beyond unfair.

"Okay, ready for the hard part?" Braxton asked.

"Um, what exactly are we going to do?" she asked, eyeing the gingerbread with new trepidation.

"Just watch."

Braxton placed both of his palms on the counter, making the muscles in his shoulders bunch against his shirt. He closed his eyes.

Kenzie was about to tell him that she didn't see anything, when tiny flickers of light began to shimmer above the gingerbread trays. As she watched, the threads thickened and multiplied. They wove an intricate and mesmerizing pattern in the air. All at once, the lights vanished.

"Did you just—" Kenzie stopped talking and just watched as the panels of gingerbread began to move on their own. They stood up on the tray and started to arrange themselves.

Kenzie stared in amazement as the gingerbread house—which was turning into more of a castle, complete with turrets and a drawbridge—assembled itself.

By the time the castle was finished, Braxton was breathing hard and his golden skin was a shade paler.

"That's incredible," Kenzie whispered.

This was so much cooler than changing someone's hair color or bringing back forgotten memories. *He'd built a freaking castle…with his mind.*

Braxton looked exhausted, but his hand was steady as he piped roof tiles and icicles onto the gingerbread castle.

"Now you," Braxton said. "See what magic comes to you."

Feeling a little self-conscious, Kenzie closed her eyes and searched for the threads that had appeared when Braxton was doing his thing. Nothing happened.

"It's not working," she said, stating the obvious.

"You need to find an interplay between the ingredients and the magic," Braxton said. "The end product needs to combine the two in a way that makes sense."

Kenzie gave him a withering look. "Braxton, none of this makes sense."

"How did you do the other magic stuff?" Braxton asked.

Kenzie gave him a helpless shrug, keeping her eyes shut so she wouldn't have to see the frustration and annoyance she heard in his voice. "I felt inspired to make the dish, and then the magic just kind of…happened."

"But the gingerbread house was my idea," Braxton said.

He was quiet for a few seconds. When he spoke again, his voice came right at her ear. She felt his sleeve brush against her bare arm.

"Focus on your senses," Braxton said. The low pitch of his voice sent a tremor straight through her. "Smell the spices. Feel the texture of the pastry. See the molasses. Taste."

Kenzie tried to do as she was told, but she kept getting distracted. She was thinking about the structure of the castle…all those little rooms Braxton had built…and the gingerbread soldiers who would live in them.

The gossamer threads began to appear in Kenzie's mind. A tune popped into her head, and she began to hum.

"Look," Braxton breathed. He was so close to her that his warm breath fanned across her cheek.

Kenzie opened her eyes.

Holy….

Gingerbread men were lifting themselves off a sheet of uncut pastry and marching over to the castle. They formed a perfect line, and each one paused just before reaching the drawbridge to salute her. Then, the little gingerbread people filed into the castle.

"How—" Braxton began, but Kenzie held up a finger.

The pearly threads hovering over her gingerbread men were still there. She gave one of the strings an experimental tug.

All the castle windows lit up at once, as though someone had flipped on a light switch inside the fragrant building.

Cool.

Kenzie tugged a different string, while maintaining her hold over the others in her mind. Tchaikovsky's "Dance of the Sugar Plum Fairy" wafted out of the open windows.

Kenzie felt the strings bearing down on her mind, but she still wasn't finished. One final tug had smoke wisping out of the gingerbread chimney. It smelled like oranges and star anise.

Kenzie held onto the strings of magic…or whatever…for as long as she could. When stars began dancing across her vision, she released all of the threads the same way she might let go of a bunch of balloons.

The lights in the castle winked off, the music stopped playing, and the smoke vanished. Kenzie sagged.

Her flailing hand missed the counter. Her face was about to collide with the unforgiving floor when a pair of strong arms hauled her back up.

"Easy there," Braxton murmured. He kept a steadying arm around her waist as he half-dragged, half-carried her over to the sofa.

Kenzie sagged back against the cushions. She squinted to block out the harsh white ceiling light.

"I feel like I just got hit by a truck," she complained.

"If I'd known you were going to push yourself to your breaking point, I would have warned you to slow down," Braxton said irritably. He went over to the fridge, took out a bottle of water, and brought it back to her.

"Drink," he ordered.

"Yessir."

Kenzie guzzled half the bottle and then pressed the cold plastic against her clammy face.

"This didn't happen to me when I was making magical food in the diner," Kenzie protested.

Braxton nodded but didn't say anything. When Kenzie searched his face, she saw that his brows were furrowed.

"What is it?" she asked, almost not wanting to hear.

"It's just—" Braxton paused. "What you did just now shouldn't be possible. It's kind of a law of culinary magic that it's only possible to control a single magical property at a time.

"I could go as far as moving two different components of a dish at different times, since it's relying on the same inherent magic. Like, I could move one part of the dish in a circle and then make another part fly, but—" He trailed off and shook his head. "You were controlling four distinct types of magic simultaneously. That's…bloody impossible."

She remembered Braxton and Polly saying something to that effect when they'd been in her Tennessee apartment. She hadn't given it much thought at the time.

"So, I'm a freak of magical nature?"

Braxton smiled wryly. "I don't know what you are, Kenzie."

That made two of them. She tried to ignore the flutter of anxiety that filled her stomach.

"Anyway," Braxton said, shaking his head again as though to clear it. "You weren't just using four different types of magic; you were drawing on multiples senses to do it. It's like any kind of physical exertion. If you push yourself too hard too fast, you'll burn out." Braxton crossed his arms and stared down at her. "You overdid it."

"Well, it's not like we have time to build my magic muscles, or whatever," she grumbled.

"No, we don't." Braxton frowned.

"Gimme one of those gingerbread men," Kenzie ordered. The tray was ten steps away, but it might as well have been at the top of Mount Everest. "Those little bastards are going to pay the price for zapping all my energy."

"Ruthless little thing, aren't you?" Braxton arched an eyebrow at her, and in that look, Kenzie thought she saw something a little like respect.

"You have no idea," she replied.

Grinning, Braxton brought her one of the cookies. He chuckled when she bit off the gingerbread man's head without an ounce of pity or regret.

Braxton went over to the fridge and perused its contents. He grabbed another water and a bottle of beer.

"Will it bother you if I drink this?" he asked, holding up the beer.

Kenzie was oddly touched, both that he'd remembered she didn't drink, and that he was considerate enough to think she might be uncomfortable with others drinking in her presence.

"Be my guest," she told him. "I don't mind if other people drink, I just don't do it myself."

Braxton nodded, and again, Kenzie appreciated that he didn't bombard her with questions about why she was anti-alcohol. Most people were stupid when it came to that sort of thing.

Kenzie tucked her feet under her to make room on the couch for Braxton. He handed her the water before settling on the other end.

"You're going to want to sleep that off," Braxton said, giving her a knowing look as she massaged her throbbing head. "Tomorrow, we'll work on figuring out your magical strengths so we can prepare for the first round."

"So, I'm not completely dead weight after all, huh?" Kenzie couldn't help but needle him.

"I didn't say that," Braxton muttered.

"Uh-huh." She slugged back more water. Braxton had been right; it really did help. She was already feeling almost back to full capacity.

"So, where are you from?" Kenzie asked. She tossed her empty water bottle at the trash can on the other side of the room. She scowled when she missed by a solid foot.

"Australia," Braxton replied curtly.

"Well yeah, I figured that with the accent and all." Kenzie rolled her eyes. "Is there a particular city you call home, or have you just claimed the entire continent for yourself?"

He was arrogant enough that the latter was a genuine possibility.

"Sydney."

"I've always wanted to see the opera house," Kenzie said, feeling the need to babble when faced with so much brooding silence.

When Braxton didn't reply to that, she forged on. "So. What's your story? You know, do you have siblings, what do you do when you're not making food fly, etcetera, etcetera?"

Kenzie hadn't meant to be offensive, but it would have been impossible to miss the way Braxton tensed up. His gaze was no longer semi-friendly, and he was strangling the neck of his beer bottle hard enough that his knuckles were white.

"Sorry," she said, putting up her hands like she was dealing with an untamed creature. "I just thought—"

"It's fine," Braxton said gruffly.

It clearly wasn't.

"I get it," she told him, because she did. "I like my privacy, too. We don't have to play get-to-know-you games or anything like that, okay?"

Braxton opened his mouth, but his response was drowned out by a ruckus in the hallway. They exchanged a look and rose from the couch.

Braxton looked back at her and put out a hand, like he was ready to catch her if she collapsed.

"I'm good," she assured him.

She opened the door just in time to see paramedics wheeling a stretcher down the hallway. They stopped outside one of the suite doors.

"Farley's room," Braxton said from behind Kenzie.

He was so tall he didn't even have to crane his neck to see past her. He just looked right over the top of her head.

A few minutes later, the paramedics returned. They carried a stretcher that held Farley, the Irish contestant. Her face was ashen, and her open eyes were glassy.

The guy who'd been paired with her— Sébastien, Kenzie thought his name was—followed them out. His fists were clenched at his sides, and he was grumbling in French.

All the other competitors were poking their heads out of their doors, too. Philippe, the other French guy who'd been talking with Braxton in the dome, let out a low whistle as soon as the small horde of people had disappeared down the hall.

"What happened?" Braxton asked.

"According to Sébastien?" Philippe chuckled. "Farley almost blew the roof off this place with her chicken and dumplings. Sébastien tried to tell her she was going too hard, but she kept telling him moderation is for chumps."

Someone let out a scornful laugh.

The sound came from the other American contestant, an anemic man with dark brown hair and ridiculous sideburns whose name Kenzie couldn't remember.

He said, "That Irish lump is deranged if she thinks her magic pressure cooking will get her past the first round."

It was because of people like this guy that Americans always got a bad rap.

"I know it's difficult for you, Rick," Philippe said, "but try not be such an asshole."

"He can't help it," Braxton said. "It runs in the blood."

Rick and Braxton exchanged a glare. As Kenzie looked between them, she saw something in their expressions that went beyond petty cruelty. There was no doubt that these men had history. And it wasn't a pleasant one.

"Besides," Hiroto, the Japanese man who had actually taken the time to introduce himself to Kenzie earlier, said. "Some of us are sensitive about our weight." He patted his rotund stomach.

Hiroto was wearing a T-shirt with a head of lettuce and the words "Smile and *romaine* calm."

Kenzie wished she'd been paired with him instead of Braxton. She wondered what it would be like to have a partner with a sense of humor….

A screeching, feminine curse came from inside Rick's suite.

"Sounds like you should be a little less worried about Farley and a little more concerned about your own partner," Philippe told Rick.

Rick muttered something under his breath before retreating into his suite and slamming the door.

"Dinner in a bit?" Hiroto asked Braxton.

Braxton nodded. "Lemme shower and I'll be over."

"You're coming, too," Philippe informed Kenzie. "If you spend too much time with Braxton, you'll be in danger of forgetting the meaning of fun."

Kenzie grinned. Braxton rolled his eyes.

"You know, your face could freeze like that one day," Hiroto warned him.

"It's a risk I'm willing to take," Braxton replied dryly, but he gave Hiroto's arm a pat as he walked past him to his own suite. He didn't so much as glance back at Kenzie.

CHAPTER 13

BRAXTON

Braxton must have unwittingly entered some kind of alternate reality. It was the only explanation for why he was sitting on the floor of Kenzie's suite, along with Hiroto and Philippe, and laughing as Kenzie's chameleon climbed all over Hiroto like the guy was a human tree. Eventually, Kiwi perched on top of Hiroto's head. The chameleon turned his green skin black to match the hair he was nested in, and fell asleep.

They were all sitting around a giant bowl of pho, a Vietnamese beef and noodle soup.

The steam curling from the bowl immediately brought Braxton back to the hole-in-the-wall Vietnamese restaurant he, Aidan, and Sofia had frequented every Saturday afternoon during secondary school. They'd get fresh fruit smoothies while they argued about what food to order, since the portions were huge and everything always tasted better when it was shared. In the summer months, they usually settled on lemongrass chicken with chili and fish sauce. In the winter, when the sky was bleak and their fingers were numb from the walk over, they ordered pho. There was something about the umami broth and slippery noodles that made whatever bad tempers they'd come into the restaurant with fade away.

Hiroto and Philippe had made a traditional pho, with thin, rare slices of beef floating on top of the rice noodles and scallion rings. Hiroto dipped his chopsticks into the soup, poking the meat down and covering it with the rice noodles to finish cooking it through.

Philippe passed around small bowls and ladle-like spoons, and they all helped themselves to the soup. Next to the pho, there was a plate piled with cilantro, Thai basil leaves, lime wedges, and bean sprouts. Braxton added some of everything to his bowl, covered all of it with the fragrant broth, and then used his chopsticks to fish out slices of meat and translucent noodles. He dolloped on some sticky-sweet hoisin sauce, added a drizzle of hot chile sauce, and dug in.

The buttery meat melted in his mouth. The fresh lime juice added a burst of freshness that balanced out the heat from the chile sauce.

"Mmm," Kenzie said appreciatively as she slurped up a noodle. "So good." She started to fan her face. "And hot."

Braxton glanced over at her, which was a mistake because she was stripping off her sweatshirt to reveal a red tank top.

Braxton quickly looked away, but not before he noticed a sliver of smooth, creamy skin across her abdomen.

"Your tats are badass," Philippe told her, raising his ceramic cup of rice wine to her in a toast.

"Thanks." Kenzie held out her arms, displaying the ink designs that covered most of her skin.

"What do they mean?" Hiroto asked. He turned his head slowly to keep from disturbing the chameleon sleeping on his head.

Braxton had been wondering about the tattoos, too, but he hadn't asked. He didn't want to know anything about her. She was a means to an end for him, and that was all. He needed her help to get to the tournament finale. And her death would show Walter Ashner the meaning of true pain.

Braxton reached into his pocket for the bottle of poison. He panicked when his seeking hand found nothing except some lint, before he remembered he'd locked the poison in his suite's wall safe.

"Tattoos don't always have to mean something," Philippe said. "Raina has one—" He gave them all a suspicious look. "Actually, never mind."

Braxton and Hiroto chortled at that. Neither of them had any interest in Philippe's soon-to-be-fiancé's tattoo.

Kenzie's, on the other hand….

In a serious voice, Kenzie said, "My tattoos are a secret map to buried treasure."

"Really?" Philippe's eyes widened.

Braxton snorted.

"No." Kenzie grinned. "I just felt like a change, you know?"

"Can't say I do," Philippe replied. He sighed in contentment as he put down his empty bowl. "I've spent my entire life in a tiny town outside Paris, and I never plan on leaving." He grinned. "Raina and I are going to start up our own restaurant once the baby comes."

"Gonna be awkward if she doesn't say yes to your proposal," Braxton observed.

"She'll say yes, jackass." Philippe's confident expression faltered. He turned to Kenzie, the token female of their little group. "Won't she?"

"If she's got half a brain," Kenzie assured him. "And if not, I'll marry you. This pho is amazing."

Philippe laughed in delight and leaned over to kiss her cheek.

Braxton checked his watch. "Time to go," he announced. To Kenzie, he said, "We're up early tomorrow, and I don't need you staggering around from a magic hangover."

Kenzie gave him a snappy salute. "Aye aye, Captain."

Braxton's traitorous friends snickered.

Philippe and Hiroto both hugged Kenzie before letting themselves out. It was an unwritten rule that whoever cooked dinner escaped cleaning. That meant Braxton and Kenzie were left to gather up the dishes and scrub out pots.

"I like your friends," Kenzie said, taking the clean bowl he handed her and drying it.

"They're good blokes. But don't forget this is a tournament and they're our competitors." Braxton frowned. "Speaking of which, you need to start locking your door."

If he could just wander into her room while she was asleep, so could anyone else.

"You think Philippe and Hiroto will murder me in my sleep?"

A muscle ticked in Braxton's jaw.

"No, not them," he said quietly.

He could feel Kenzie's penetrating gaze on him as he studiously washed an already-clean bowl.

"Rick and Esther?" Kenzie guessed.

Braxton nodded, still unable to meet her eyes. She had no idea that the biggest threat to her stood a foot away.

Braxton was saved from having to say anything more when a hard knock came at Kenzie's door.

"Miss Kenzie?" a deep, male voice called from the other side. "There's a woman by the name of Denise Werrimeth here to see you. Says you invited her."

All the color drained from Kenzie's face. She swayed on her feet, and Braxton quickly put a hand on her back to keep her upright.

"Shit," Kenzie whispered. "Shit, shit, shit." She stared at the closed door like a monster was about to break through.

"Who is this person?" Braxton asked, growing alarmed by the expression in Kenzie's gray eyes. She looked almost haunted.

"No one. I just—" Kenzie shook her head. "I have to talk to her." She headed for the door.

"Kenzie—"

"You should go," she told him absently.

Yeah right. With the way she was acting right now, he wasn't leaving her alone with whoever was on the other side of the door. He wouldn't risk her getting hurt before the first round.

Kenzie opened the door. The woman leaning against the doorjamb looked…wrong. It took Braxton a few seconds to work out why. He noticed the track marks on her bare arms, sores around her dry lips, and the fact that he could see her individual ribs through her shirt. But those details barely registered.

This woman had Kenzie's eyes…or the way he imagined Kenzie's eyes would look if she had a few more decades and had lived a life of misery. The woman also had Kenzie's black hair and pale skin. On Kenzie, it was striking. On this woman, it was disturbing. Her skin looked papery and more gray than white. Her hair was thin and ratty. But her eyes….

Braxton didn't scare easily, but those empty, lifeless eyes were the stuff of nightmares.

Braxton hoped for Kenzie's sake this woman was a very, very distant relative.

"Wowww, check it out." The woman snapped her gum as she peered into the suite. "Nice digs."

"Hello, Denise," Kenzie said without enthusiasm.

"Long time, huh?" Denise asked, still craning her neck to see inside the room.

"Yeah, it's been a while," Kenzie said.

There was no mistaking the bitterness in her voice.

If Denise noticed, she didn't give any indication. Her appraising gaze stopped taking in the room and moved to Braxton. The woman hadn't so much as glanced at Kenzie, but she was now eyeing Braxton like he was edible. The woman licked her scaly lips and smoothed a hand down her emaciated hip in a way that had Braxton repressing a shudder.

"You're done good for yourself, girlie," Denise told Kenzie. To Braxton, she said, "Where do I get me one of you?"

"You don't," Kenzie said, saving Braxton from responding. "And I asked you here for a reason, so I need you to focus."

"Sweetums, where are your manners?" Denise whined. "Ask me in and gimme a drink. Then, I'll tell you anything you want."

"From the smell of it, you've already had plenty of drinks tonight," Kenzie said. "And you're not coming inside."

Denise jutted out her lower lip and gave Braxton a pleading look.

Braxton crossed his arms and glared at the woman.

"So, this is how you treat your mother?" Denise complained.

That one word almost knocked Braxton on his ass. *Mother?* Holy shit.

He looked at Kenzie, but she was locked in a staring battle with her—*Christ,* he couldn't even think the word.

And he thought he had a complicated home life.

"You're only my mom when you need something from me," Kenzie said. "I've never asked you for anything. Now, I'm asking. I need you to tell me if—" She glanced at Braxton, seeming to just remember that he was there. Color filled her cheeks, and Braxton saw shame burn in her eyes.

Without consciously making a decision to do so, Braxton rested his hands on Kenzie's shoulders and gave her a light squeeze. He could feel tiny tremors going through her body.

"Ask your question," he told her in a gruff voice. To Denise, he said, "You're going to tell Kenzie what she needs to know, and then you're going to leave."

Braxton didn't like the calculating look that had emerged in those lifeless eyes. And he really didn't like the effect this woman was having on Kenzie.

Kenzie cleared her throat. "Have you ever cooked anything…magical?" she asked her mother.

Denise let out a peal of laughter that was like nails on a chalkboard. When she smiled, Braxton saw that her teeth were yellow and chipped.

"Magic?" Denise repeated. "Like abracadabra, poof, you've been turned into a rabbit?" She laughed some more.

"Not like that." Kenzie's voice was tight, like she was forcing the words out through clenched teeth. "When you cooked, did anything inexplicable ever happen?"

"Sweetums, if I could do magic, I'd be living in a mansion instead of an apartment that belongs to a seventy-year-old lawyer with erectile dysfunction." Her unsteady gaze lifted to Braxton. "Unless you're in the market for some sugar. I bet I've got a trick or two more up my sleeve than my daughter." She giggled.

Braxton's gorge rose. He forced himself to loosen his hold on Kenzie when he realized he was gripping her shoulders hard enough to cut off her circulation.

"Annnnd, we're done here." Kenzie gave Denise a small push, and the other woman almost fell over.

"Now, that's no way to treat your mother." Denise hiccupped. "I need money."

"I can't help you," Kenzie replied.

Denise folded her arms across her emaciated chest. "It was my birthday last week, and you didn't send me a present. I need money. Gimme a hundie and call it my birthday present."

Kenzie crossed her arms. It was disturbing to see the way the two women were standing in mirrored poses. The resemblance between them was undeniable…if one looked past the ruin that Denise had brought on her own body.

"Well, I don't have a half-used bottle of drugstore nail polish or a belly-up goldfish like the last present you gave me," Kenzie said. "So I guess you're out of luck."

Fuck. Had her mum really done that to her?

"I was going through a rough patch," Denise whined. "Not that I'd expect you to understand anything about that." She waved a hand at the room that Braxton was using his body to block. "If you'd had to struggle like me, you wouldn't be so heartless."

Kenzie laughed, but there was no humor in it. "Heartless?! Okay, let's talk heartless. The last time I saw you…my own mother…was when I was sixteen. You went on a rant about everything Dad made for dinner—"

Kenzie was still talking, but Braxton fixated on that one word. *Dad.*

As in Walter Ashner. As in the man who had stolen Aidan's life and plunged Braxton's family into ruin. As in the reason why Braxton needed to kill a woman who was seeming more and more like a genuinely decent person.

"—ate all the baked Alaska," Kenzie was saying. "—my favorite, by the way. After you'd thrown it back up, you told Dad you'd fight for partial custody if he didn't give you a thousand dollars."

"Well, I," Denise began, but Kenzie wasn't finished.

"And, go figure, as soon as Dad was arrested and you found out all his money was locked up in lawyer fees, I never heard from you again."

An unwelcome sense of guilt shot through Braxton. He knew why Kenzie's father had spent all of his family's money on lawyer fees. Until this moment, Braxton would never have felt anything except satisfaction at the thought of Walter Ashner being broke. But his financial troubles had clearly hurt Kenzie, too.

"Fine, be that way." Denise sniffed. "I know when I'm not wanted, and I'm certainly not going to beg my own daughter for a little compassion when she clearly doesn't have any to spare."

Enough was enough, Braxton decided.

"Time for you to leave," he growled, surprised by the fury heating his blood.

"I need bus money," Denise complained.

Sickness washed through Braxton as Kenzie pulled a few crumpled bills out of her pocket and slapped them into Denise's waiting palm.

"Sweetums—"

"Leave," Braxton ordered her. "Or I'll have security drag you out of here."

He'd do it himself, but he got the unpleasant sense Denise might actually enjoy that.

"Fine." Denise took a few stumbling steps before regaining her balance and sauntering down the hall.

When Kenzie turned to him, there were tears in her eyes. Braxton's chest gave a painful squeeze.

"I didn't think I'd gotten my magic from her," Kenzie said in a flat voice. "But I had to be sure."

Braxton nodded in understanding.

"Kenzie," he began. He wanted to offer her some comfort…to explain his certainty that she'd inherited her magic from her father, but he didn't even know where to start.

"I want to be alone now," she told him.

When Braxton opened his mouth to speak, she shook her head.

"Seriously, Braxton. Just let it go."

So, he did.

"Lock your door," he told her as he left.

When Braxton was enclosed in his own suite, that entire conversation with Denise played over in his mind.

No wonder Kenzie avoided alcohol. If he'd been related to someone like Denise, he would have done anything and everything in his power to be the exact opposite of her.

Braxton went into the kitchen and started pulling out the ingredients to practice his merengue birds, but he couldn't concentrate. He kept replaying that conversation between Kenzie and her mom.

Damnit. He didn't need this right now. He needed to be planning for the possible challenges they'd face during the first round. He needed to be thinking about the finale.

Instead, all he could see were the tears glimmering in Kenzie's big eyes.

Tonight hadn't changed anything about the reality of their situation. Braxton still needed Kenzie to get to the finale. He still needed to kill her to set things right for his family.

But nothing about this felt right.

CHAPTER 14

KENZIE

Kenzie dreaded seeing Braxton. She had barely slept last night as she replayed her conversation with Denise over and over again. And Braxton had been there to witness all of it.

If she'd had her head on straighter, Kenzie would have made him leave before he witnessed her humiliation. But Kenzie was never fully in her right mind when dealing with the woman who had birthed her and then given her up.

She groaned when she heard Braxton's knock at her door.

He was going to have questions. Or worse, she'd look into those incredible eyes and see pity. Then, she'd probably have to kill him. And then she'd get kicked out of the tournament before she figured out why her magic didn't work the way it was supposed to.

The suckiness was real.

Kenzie didn't know what to expect when she opened the door for Braxton. What she got was a steaming cup of espresso in her hand and a gruff, "Ready to cook?"

For the next five hours, they made everything from delicate savory souffles to macarons to sushi. Then, once they had a feast laid out around the suite, they started in with the magic.

Kenzie's misguided attempt to magically flambé her custard without touching it ended with a smoking hole in the coffee table. She'd also done something to her souffle—hell if she knew what—that filled the entire suite with a rotten egg smell.

She would have felt worse about her blunders, but Braxton hadn't left their practice session unscathed. He'd blown the top off a pot pie and made filling explode across the entire kitchen because he'd been trying to magically transform the chicken into turkey. He'd also made a piece of tuna sashimi scream…like actually scream.

Poor Kiwi had taken refuge under a leaf in his habitat and refused to come out, even when Kenzie tried to temp him with crickets.

They cooked the entire day through without stopping. Their clothes were stained, singed, and torn. There was a stack of dishes in the sink that reached halfway to the ceiling.

Kenzie couldn't remember the last time she'd had this much fun.

"What do you think of this?" Braxton asked, holding a spoon to her lips.

Kenzie opened her mouth. Their eyes locked for just a second as Braxton slid the ruby currant syrup between her lips.

"Mmm." She closed her eyes to savor the sharp burst of tartness, followed by a fruity sweetness. It would pair perfectly with her fontina and basil crepe.

Kenzie licked her lips to chase the lingering taste.

When she opened her eyes, Braxton was staring at her. A stain of pink had emerged on his defined cheekbones.

"Braxton?"

"Yeah?" His voice had gone deep and husky in a way that made her all warm and tingly.

"Did you forget something?" She smiled sweetly at him.

Braxton's eyebrows drew together, and then he looked down. Cursing, he pulled his saucepan off the flame as ruby syrup boiled over. Kenzie tried to hold back a guffaw and failed. That earned her a glare from across the kitchen, where Braxton was trying to salvage what was left of his syrup while wiping up the spill.

Taking pity on the man, she dipped her spoon into the almond-y amaretto whipped cream she'd just finished. She brought the spoon over to Braxton, who leaned down so she could reach his mouth.

Instead of feeding him the whipped cream, she dolloped it on the tip of his nose.

Braxton's eyes widened. Then, his lips twitched.

"Gotcha," she taunted.

"You're going to pay for that, baby," Braxton growled.

And *whoa*. That Aussie accent. The low timbre of his voice. The word baby….

Kenzie barely resisted the urge to fan herself.

Braxton, smug bastard that he was, gave her an evil smile. He knew exactly the effect he had on her, and he liked it.

"Bring it on, *baby*," she replied, because Kenzie had never been one to back down from a fight. She gave her spoon a little flick, sending a poof of whipped cream onto his forehead.

Bull's eye.

Braxton didn't so much as pause to wipe his face. He leapt toward her.

Kenzie yelped and darted behind the couch. She feinted right and then raced left. Braxton didn't fall for it.

He caught her around her waist and lifted her up like she was weightless. Her butt hit the counter.

Braxton leaned closer, until she could see the flecks of light and dark green in his irises. He still hadn't wiped the whipped cream off his nose. Kenzie was trying to decide whether she was brave enough to lick it off, when Braxton reached behind her.

She expected to feel his arm curl around her back, but it never came. Triumph lit Braxton's eyes. And then a handful of whipped cream was connecting with Kenzie's face.

"What the—" she spluttered.

"Don't fuck with a master," Braxton taunted, easily sliding away from the dish towel she hurled in his direction.

"Come back here, you worm!" she fumed, blindly racing after him as dollops of whipped cream plopped off the ends of her hair.

Laughing, Braxton reached the door and threw it open.

Kenzie, determined to get him back before he made his escape, didn't expect him to come to a screeching halt in the doorway. She ran into his back with an affronted *oof*.

"What the hell, Braxton?" she complained.

When he moved aside and Kenzie saw who was standing in the hall, all of her humor vanished.

"Chef Sakai," Braxton said, lowering his head in deference to their judge. "Uh, I apologize."

The judge looked from Braxton to Kenzie. Instead of cracking a smile like Kenzie had hoped, his expression darkened. He grunted out something in Japanese, which probably translated to *Fuckin' kids*.

"The first round begins in ten minutes," Chef Sakai informed them.

Braxton and Kenzie exchanged a horrified look.

"We have two more days," Braxton choked out.

"Ten minutes," the judge replied. "Don't be late."

With that, he was gone.

"He's joking," Kenzie reasoned.

"Yamosato Sakai never jokes," Braxton said grimly.

"We can't compete right now!" Kenzie was starting to feel a little unhinged. "I need a shower, and a nap, and—"

Kenzie hadn't gotten to the point where she was magically hung over, thank God, but she wasn't exactly firing on all burners. Neither was Braxton. They'd been cooking all day…and now they were supposed to compete?!

They spent the next thirty seconds cursing enough to make a sailor blush. Then, they sprang into action. Braxton raced back to his suite.

Kenzie didn't bother showering. She just dunked her hair in the sink, rinsed out the whipped cream, and threw on cleanish clothes. She stumbled into the hallway five minutes later, where Philippe and Hiroto were looking equally bewildered.

"What's going on?" Farley, the Irish woman, demanded. She had something smeared on her cheek that might have been blueberry compote, and half her hair was scorched black.

"Judges moved up the first round to screw with us," Philippe answered. He tilted his head as he regarded Farley. "You okay, by the way? We saw the paramedics carrying you out of here and didn't know what was up."

"I'm alrigh'," Farley said with a brisk nod. "But my partner's a pain in my arse, ya know?"

Sébastien, his dark skin dusted with what appeared to be powdered sugar, muttered something under his breath in French. Whatever he'd said made Philippe, the other Frenchman, chuckle.

"Well, we're glad to see you're feeling better," Hiroto told Farley. "We were worried about you."

"Oh, I'm fine," Farley replied in her heavy brogue. "Just got a little overdone." She twisted her scorched hair into a bun and stuck a chopstick through it to keep it in place.

Rick and Esther—or Crazy Esther, as Braxton called her—were the last to emerge. Unlike everyone else, they seemed neither flustered nor annoyed.

Rick took in everyone else's ragged appearance and chuckled. He was wearing a crisp button-down and slacks. His brown hair was gelled close to his scalp, which made his sharp cheekbones and dark eyes even more prominent. He smelled annoyingly good…like aftershave and hair product, rather than the mish-mosh of food smells that Kenzie was rocking.

Crazy Esther was wearing a white fur dress and fur boots. Every time she moved, the blue stones she'd braided into her white-blonde hair clicked together. Her long earrings were arrowheads, and she wore a necklace that was some kind of animal's tooth strung onto a leather string. She'd rimmed her cornflower-blue eyes in black liner, which made her look at once terrifying and majestic. She seemed more prepared for a battle than a cooking tournament.

Although, Kenzie supposed this was a battle of sorts, just not the lopping off heads kind…*she hoped.*

This was one woman Kenzie definitely didn't want to piss off.

"You don't seem surprised about this," Philippe accused Esther and Rick.

"What can I say?" Rick flicked an imaginary speck of dust off his sleeve. "When you have money and influence, people tell you things. Secret things. Money is power. Don't you think, Braxton?"

The two men glared at each other. Kenzie could almost feel the testosterone rolling off them.

"What's your name again?" Kenzie asked in a loud voice. "Dick, was it?"

Hiroto snorted.

Rick slowly turned away from Braxton and to her. He studied her the way someone might regard a squished bug on the bottom of their shoe.

"Rick," he said flatly.

"Isn't that what I said?" She batted her eyelashes at him and offered an innocent smile.

"Put your little dog on a leash," Rick muttered to Braxton before stalking off.

When Kenzie caught Braxton's eye, she saw appreciation in his gaze. Maybe even respect.

"We better get moving," Philippe said. "If we're late, the judges'll probably make us cook whole sheeps' heads, or something."

"See, that right there is why civilization is going to destroy itself," Crazy Esther said. "All parts of a carcass have a purpose and should be used. If you lived out in the wild, you wouldn't let a sheep's head…or any other part of the animal…go to waste."

"Just a little advice for ya, love," Farley told Esther in her thick Irish brogue. "Don't say *carcass* in front of the judges. It'll put 'em off their suppers."

"Bite me," Esther hissed back, pairing her threat with a snap of her teeth.

Alrighty, then.

"Is this normal?" Kenzie asked Braxton as they reached the tunnel that led to the dome. "You know, the judges springing surprises on us like this?"

Braxton nodded. "They've never changed the timing of the rounds before, but yeah, the judges sometimes try and throw the competitors off their game."

Kenzie would have said more, but a man wearing a belt with makeup brushes grabbed her chin and dragged her under a light. While he undertook the daunting task of making her presentable, he clucked about how the makeup artists were always the last to know everything.

He perked up a little as he fussed over Kenzie's gray eyes, but his mood soured again when he discovered the dried whipped cream still clumped in her hair.

The others were being similarly assaulted. The nervous butterflies battering around Kenzie's stomach eased somewhat as she listened to Braxton argue with his makeup artist about the shimmery bronzer she wanted to use to accentuate his bone structure.

They were each given their chef coat that had their names stitched onto the front. What felt like seconds later, they were being paraded into the dome.

Kenzie's ears were assailed with loud music, Polly Berrywhite's magnified voice, and the thunderous applause of a full audience.

A full freaking audience.

"Ohmygod," she gasped.

The last time she'd been in the dome, it had been intimidating enough, and that had been when there was only a handful of people in the audience. Now, with cameras flashing every millisecond and the spotlights moving around the dome, she was ready to keel over.

She felt like that belly-up goldfish Denise had gifted her on her sixteenth birthday.

Being in this glass dome, with all the lights shining down on her and thousands of people staring at her, brought her right back to her Dad's arrest. There'd been reporters clustered around Ashner's and cameras flashing in Kenzie's face, just like the spotlight that was following her everywhere she moved.

It had been the same at Danny's funeral. There'd been so many people. She didn't remember anything else about that day except for all of the goddamn people. They all wanted to talk to her…to hug her…when all she wanted was to curl up next to Danny's casket and cry.

"You okay?" Hiroto asked, giving her arm a small pat. "You're looking a little green."

"Fine, thanks."

The response sounded far away and too high-pitched to be hers. She heard Hiroto talking to someone nearby, but none of his words penetrated her frantic mind.

So many people. Kenzie could feel them staring past her tattoos and side-swept bangs and recognizing the girl she'd stopped being when she left New York.

Brookerton, she reminded herself. She was Kenzie Brookerton now.

Kenzie Ashner was dead.

"Kenzie. *Kenzie.*" A sharp tug on her arm had her looking away from the crowd outside the dome and into green eyes.

She glanced back at the horde of people. Either they were coming closer, or the dome was lowering to the ground. Shapeless blobs were turning into actual faces.

Oh God. The dome *was* moving. It was gently descending from the arena's ceiling until they were no longer above the mob but directly in their midst.

Braxton took her chin in his hand and forced her to meet his gaze.

"What's wrong?" he demanded.

Just a minor impending heart attack…no biggie.

"Just…a little stage fright," she managed.

"Better get your partner under control if you don't want to get kicked out in the first round," Rick said, smiling nastily at Braxton as he brushed past to take his place beside Crazy Esther.

A muscle pulsed in Braxton's neck, but he didn't tear his eyes off Kenzie. Instead, he took her hands in both of his.

"Christ, your hands are freezing," he murmured, rubbing his thumb across her knuckles.

His touch infused her with enough warmth that her violent shaking began to ease.

"I'm okay," she told Braxton, letting her hands drop from his grip. "Promise."

Braxton didn't look like he believed her. Hell, she didn't believe herself, but it wasn't like there was any other option. Music was blaring through the speakers that hung from the transparent ceiling, and the three judges were being introduced by a disembodied voice that seemed to come from everywhere at once.

Kenzie forced her knees to unlock so she could take her position next to Braxton at their cook station. The competitors all stood quietly while Polly Berrywhite thanked them for their participation in *the most exciting tournament we've ever held!*

Kenzie felt Braxton's worried gaze straying to her, but she kept her eyes glued to Polly Berrywhite. There was something soothing about the grandmotherly vibes the woman gave off. Kenzie clung to the gentle confidence radiating off the woman.

Polly Berrywhite was resplendent in a gold gown and her trademark diamonds. There were even some studded in her cotton candy hair, which Kenzie was beginning to suspect was a wig…or at least some serious extensions.

When Kenzie broke her own vow to herself and looked back out at the crowd, she realized she was facing a roped-off section of seats that was labeled with each competitor's name.

Kenzie's attention drifted to the section for her. It was empty.

Not that she'd expected anything else. Her dad was in prison, her mom was…well, Denise was who she was. Kenzie didn't have siblings, and Nana was dead. So was Danny.

Kenzie was alone. And for the first time in five years, that didn't feel like a good thing.

As if sensing her bleak thoughts, Braxton shifted his weight so they were close enough for their sleeves to brush. Curious, Kenzie glanced into the section reserved for Braxton's family. It was empty, too.

On a whim, Kenzie shifted so her fingertips touched Braxton's. He didn't take her hand, but he didn't move away. Grounded by that gentle touch, Kenzie turned her attention back to Polly Berrywhite.

The judge and emcee had finished her plug for the charities she ran and was reintroducing each of the competitors.

"And finally," Polly said, her diamond necklace winking in the three spotlights that were trained on her. "We have Kenzie Brookerton and Braxton McKaid."

The audience erupted in hearty applause, but Kenzie wasn't paying attention to the crowd anymore. She realized it was the first time she'd heard Braxton's last name. There was something about it that tickled a memory. She couldn't quite put her finger on it, but there was something—

"Are all of you ready to hear your first challenge?" Polly called, addressing the eight of them at their stations.

"Yes, Chef!" they shouted back.

"Then, welcome to Hex Kitchen. Let the tournament begin!"

CHAPTER 15

BRAXTON

The only reason Braxton wasn't in a complete panic was because he could tell how freaked out Kenzie was. They couldn't afford to have both of them distracted. If they were going to make it to the second round, he needed to be at the top of his game.

And Braxton was making it to the second round.

"You will find an assortment of common ingredients at your stations," Polly Berrywhite was saying.

Braxton looked down at the canister of flour, quart of milk, dozen eggs, and a few other staples that were neatly gathered at the edge of each of their stations.

"There are eight specialty ingredients positioned around the dome," she continued.

Small, colored spotlights appeared over eight previously-dark spots around the dome. Two small crates dangled from metal chains on the ceiling. Three others were glued to the walls. Two were hidden beneath a transparent trap door beneath the judges' table. The last was in a cloth bag that was taped to the glass on the outside of the dome.

"Your first task," Chef Berrywhite explained, "is to use only magic and the ingredients at your station to reach the specialty ingredients positioned throughout the dome. I repeat, you may not leave your stations to access the hidden ingredients."

Chef Berrywhite paused to let all of them absorb that information. Braxton tried not to look too pleased. The two ingredients tied to the dome's ceiling practically had his name written all over them. He could just use food levitation to access those without breaking a sweat.

We've got this, Aid.

"Once each pair has successfully brought your two mystery ingredients back to your station, you will be free to access the pantry." The glass enclosure at the back of the dome lit up. Rows of produce, raw meat, and exotic spices filled the space.

Braxton glanced at his competitors to see how they were absorbing the news of their first challenge. Rick, as expected, didn't seem in the least bit surprised about anything Chef Berrywhite was telling them.

Because the motherfucker had bribed someone to tell him the challenge in advance.

The rest of the contestants seemed excited. Ready.

Kenzie was the only one who looked terrified.

Braxton suppressed a groan. The others would take one look at her and smell blood in the water. He'd seen the same thing happen in past years, when an especially weak team was targeted by all the others to get them out quickly.

Braxton couldn't let that happen.

Polly Berrywhite continued, "If any chef moves more than three feet away from their station in any direction, it will result in that pair's automatic disqualification. Furthermore, each individual is responsible for bringing one, and only one, secret ingredient back to their station."

Damn. That meant Kenzie would have to get their second ingredient.

All of Braxton's anticipation from a few seconds before turned to anxiety. Kenzie hadn't managed to levitate anything yet.

"Obviously," Chef Berrywhite continued cheerfully, "there's an advantage to obtaining your two mystery items quickly. The sooner you have them, the sooner you can begin constructing a dish that features those two ingredients." She paused. "But remember. You cannot begin cooking your final dish until *both* mystery ingredients are at your prep station."

Which meant each pair was limited by their weakest link. *Bloody fantastic.*

"Each pair will present a single dish to the judges. Your mystery ingredients must be the star of the dish. We'll be judging you on presentation, flavor, and magic. You will have two hours for this first challenge."

Polly pointed at the large digital clock that hung from the dome's ceiling.

"Are we ready, competitors?"

"Yes, Chef!" they all chorused.

"Let's cook some magic!"

All around Braxton, the dome devolved into chaos. Inside his own mind, it was quiet. He began measuring out yeast, sugar, and water into a bowl. Once the yeast dissolved and started to froth, he added flour to make a simple dough.

"Do you have a plan?" he asked Kenzie as he worked.

"Umm," Kenzie replied.

Braxton's hands continued their task as he turned his attention on her. He knew she was out of her depth, but he didn't have time to talk her through this.

Damn the judges for teaming the two of them together. If only he'd been paired with Hiroto or Philippe....

Out of the corner of his eye, Braxton saw his two friends laughing as they worked.

"I think the ingredient hanging outside the dome will be easier to get than it looks," Braxton decided. "And I'm guessing it won't be the first the others go for. All you need to do is make something that'll break through the glass and then bring the ingredient back here."

"That's all?" Kenzie asked with more than a bite of sarcasm.

Braxton was about to retort, when he realized Kenzie's hands were visibly shaking.

"Do you think you can manage to make a rope out of dough that can crawl its way over there and grab the ingredient?"

It was easier to make ingredients crawl than fly. Although it would take longer.

"I think so?" She chewed on her bottom lip. "But how do I break the glass?"

"I'll take care of that," Braxton replied.

The judges had said each participant needed to bring one ingredient back to their station. They hadn't said anything that would prevent him from helping Kenzie get to her ingredient in the first place.

Braxton planned to take advantage of that particular loophole. Kenzie clearly would need all the help she could get.

Braxton started preheating his oven, when another time-saving idea occurred to him. He didn't even need to cook the dough…he just needed it to reach one of the mystery ingredients.

He quickly shaped his pastry dough into the shape of a hand and forearm. Then, blocking out all other distractions, he reached for his magic.

Braxton felt the elastic pull of the dough and allowed the smell of yeast to surround him. He saw the hand-shaped pastry begin to move in his mind. He felt the weight of it, mentally calculating the distance it needed to go.

The pearly strands of magic appeared through the darkness. Braxton didn't hesitate before winding them together until they made a rope that wouldn't fray or break. Then, he sent his dough-shaped hand off to gather his ingredient.

Braxton didn't need to open his eyes to know his dough was on the move. The noise from the crowd told him that his technique was as flawless in reality as it was in his mind.

Braxton opened his eyes when he felt his dough reach the top of the dome. He tweaked the ropes of his magic, guiding the dough fingers so they grasped onto the crate's lid.

The audience erupted into applause.

There was a rattling sound as the crate wobbled in its rope cradle. Then, it came loose. The crate was heavier than it looked, and Braxton's hold on his magic-infused dough faltered. He heard the audience let out a collective gasp as the dough-fingers fumbled.

The crate slipped out of Braxton's control and fell to the ground.

A tiny glass vial rolled out of the crate, displaying the mystery ingredient to everyone. *Saffron.* The golden-orange threads looked almost luminescent with the way the spotlights all congregated on the small container.

Braxton felt a rush of triumph. It was a good ingredient. There were about a hundred dishes he could think of off the top of his head that would feature the spice.

But he wasn't alone in his thoughts.

Rick, who had been unsuccessfully attempting to dislodge one of the treasure boxes pinned to the wall, was laser-focused on the saffron. Braxton saw the moment Rick realized it would be far easier to steal an ingredient Braxton had already brought halfway to their stations than to do his own work.

The éclair Rick had made was slithering across the floor like a snake. It was heading straight for the container of saffron.

I don't think so, mate.

Braxton turned and flashed the audience a grin. Then, he tightened his mental grip on his own pastry. The dough hand used its thumb and index finger to walk across the stage to Rick's éclair, which was slowly nudging the saffron closer to his prep station.

Braxton tugged on the magical threads connected to his dough. It reared up on its doughy elbow and wagged its index finger at Rick's éclair. Then, Braxton made his dough fingers flick the éclair away. The audience roared in approval.

He could have achieved the same ends with far less fanfare, but as Kenzie had informed him the day before while they were practicing, cooking was supposed to be fun. And he was definitely having fun.

Braxton's dough lifted up the container of saffron, flew across the dome, and delivered the ingredient into Braxton's waiting palm.

Hell yeah.

He was the first competitor to retrieve his ingredient, and it had taken him only ten minutes.

Not too shabby, huh Aid?

Braxton turned to Rick and took a bow. He knew he was playing with fire, but it wasn't like the two of them were ever going to be mates, anyway. If he hadn't glimpsed Hiroto's little sister sitting in the front row, he would have made a far ruder gesture at Rick.

Feeling his nemesis's glare burning a hole in his back, Braxton refocused. This round wasn't even close to over. Now, he needed to help Kenzie.

CHAPTER 16

KENZIE

You've got this," Braxton told Kenzie for the hundredth time.

No, she really didn't.

Kenzie wanted to scream.

Everyone else had their ingredients. All of the other pairs were well into preparing their dish. There was only half an hour left in the challenge, and Kenzie was still trying to get her goddamn mystery ingredient.

She'd tried to make a hand out of dough like Braxton, but the thing just kept flopping around like a limp noodle. The audience was in stitches at her expense. Braxton looked like he was about to have an aneurism. And Philippe and Hiroto were already starting to plate their final creation.

"Just make something that can crawl up the side," Braxton begged her.

"How do I get through the glass?" she asked, even though the point was moot. She had no idea how she'd get anything to crawl anywhere.

"I can't get your ingredient for you," Braxton said, "but the judges didn't say anything about helping you reach it."

"Okay...."

Braxton grabbed a lump of discarded dough and formed it into a ball. Kenzie waited for him to start magicking it. Instead, he pulled his arm back like he was a pitcher on a baseball field. Kenzie snorted when she realized what he was about to do.

Braxton threw the ball of dough. The pane directly beside the mystery ingredient shattered.

"Whoa!" Polly called from the judges' table. "Nice aim, Braxton!"

"Lazy," Chef Sakai grumbled. "Should have used magic."

The audience was hooting with appreciative laughter.

Kenzie turned her attention on the cloth bag dangling beside the broken glass pane. So close, and yet so far....

"Now all you have to do is get your dough up there," Braxton said.

Easy, right?

Freaking impossible.

"Visualize it in your mind," Braxton said. "Feel the weight of your dough. Smell the raw flour. Use those senses to take control of the magic."

It was the same advice he'd been giving her for the last twenty minutes.

It wasn't working.

"Kenzie." There was desperation in Braxton's voice that was mirrored in his eyes. "Please. I...I need you to do this."

I'm trying! she wanted to shout. She was sweating so much her shirt was plastered to her like a second skin. She probably looked constipated with the way she kept squeezing her eyes shut and trying to make the magic come. No matter what she did, the only thing her dough hand was managing to attract were dust bunnies.

"Kenzie—"

"Give me a second," she snapped, and then immediately felt terrible. She was the weak link in this partnership. Braxton didn't deserve to be kicked out because of her incompetence.

She wished she could have snuck Kiwi into her pocket and brought him into the dome with her. She could use something like her little chameleon's sticky tongue right now. When he saw something he wanted, he didn't sweat and hesitate like she was doing now. He just unfurled his tongue, and—

Ohmygod. That's it.

Those pearly threads of magic—so infuriatingly absent for the last hour-and-a-half—began to swirl around in her brain. She took her dusty lump of dough, quickly reshaped it, and then let the magical spiderweb strengthen as the strands wound around and around her dough.

Everything else slipped away. She blocked out Braxton's voice and the shouts of the audience. It was just her and her food. And the magic.

Kenzie rolled and stretched the dough until it was barely the width of a pencil. She kept going until she estimated the length of dough would be long enough to reach the bag hanging outside of the dome.

She coiled up the dough and gripped one end. Then, she let the magic take hold.

The dough let out a soft hiss that was barely audible over the other sounds in the dome. The coil of dough flicked into the air. It unspooled as it flung itself in a perfect arc at the missing panel in the dome's wall.

Come on. Just a little bit more….

The last little bit of dough unfurled and latched around the cloth bag, exactly the way Kiwi's tongue snatched up tasty mealworms.

The dough version of Kiwi's tongue, and the cloth bag, ricocheted back and landed with a dull thud on Kenzie's station.

She'd done it. Relief hit her with so much force she almost keeled over. Instead, her shaking fingers fumbled for the drawstring on the cloth bag. A wrapped package of beef tenderloin tumbled onto her work station.

"Five minutes to go, chefs!"

Kenzie looked at the giant digital clock.

4:58.

Kenzie stared at Braxton.

4:56.

Braxton let out a low, tortured groan.

"Carpaccio," Kenzie said, snapping her fingers in Braxton's face to get his attention. "Make a dry rub with the saffron."

She began trimming the ends and sinew from the meat with quick, clean strokes of her knife.

Normally, the raw meat needed time to marinate in the rub and firm up in the fridge. At Ashner's, her dad had served a beef carpaccio coated in crushed pink peppercorns and flash-seared in hot olive oil, thyme, and garlic. It was delicious. And way more time consuming than she could afford right now.

2:59.

Braxton shoved a shallow dish at her that had coarse-ground sea salt, pepper, and saffron threads.

Kenzie rolled the meat in the mixture, trying to make an even crust around the edge of the meat.

"There's no magic," Braxton said, his eyes wide with panic. "We need—"

"What we need is to get something on the plate," she said firmly.

They couldn't both be losing their minds at the same time.

Kenzie meticulously sliced the meat into ribbons that Braxton arranged on a clean plate.

0:58.

Hands shaking, Kenzie sprinkled a few saffron threads over the raw meat. She dashed on a few capers from the jar Braxton thrust into her hand, along with a pile of peppery arugula.

"Time, chefs!" Polly Berrywhite called. "Hands in the air!"

Kenzie stepped back and raised her hands. They were shaking.

She surveyed their plate.

It was a disaster. No, that was being too generous. It was a calamity.

She didn't want to look at Braxton and see the betrayal and defeat on his face. When she forced herself to glance at him, her stomach turned over. He had his fist pressed to his mouth like he was trying not to throw up. His eyes were squeezed shut. His lips were just barely moving, and Kenzie thought she heard him whisper *I'm sorry.*

Kenzie didn't know what to say, so she didn't say anything at all. It wasn't like her apologies would prevent them from getting kicked out of the tournament.

As the audience applauded and Polly Berrywhite spoke into her microphone, Kenzie's guilt began to transform to irritation. She hadn't asked to get partnered with Braxton. She didn't even care about winning the stupid wish truffle. She just wanted to learn more about her magic and this underworld she hadn't even known existed.

This was why she was better off alone. When she was by herself, there was no one else to disappoint or let down.

"Okay, competitors," Polly said, offering each of them a broad smile. "Time to decide which teams will be moving on to the second round, and who will be going home."

Kenzie wasn't looking at Braxton, but she could feel his misery rolling off him. She once again tamped down the urge to apologize.

Dramatic music blared through the speakers as all three judges walked down the steps from their elevated stage. Kenzie's ears ached. So did her chest, which was where all her guilt had congealed like heartburn.

The judges went to Philippe and Hiroto's station first.

Everything was broadcasted onto screens around the dome, so spectators in the farthest seats would be able to see every detail of the dish.

"What were your ingredients?" Chef Elyannah Levy barked.

That woman was four-and-a-half-feet of pure terror. Kenzie would take on Rick or anyone else in this competition before she'd want to get in a fight with Chef Levy.

"Asparagus and lavender flowers," Hiroto replied.

"Ooh, tough ones, boys," Polly said into her microphone. "Let's see what you conjured." She winked at the audience.

Kenzie watched as Philippe lifted the cover off their serving dish with a flourish.

"We call this dish springtime in Manhattan," Hiroto said, as the cameras zoomed in on their creation.

Kenzie had no idea what the magic part of their dish was, but the focaccia bread was beautiful. It looked more like a painting than food.

Stalks of asparagus and lavender flowers were cooked into the bread, along with slices and spirals of other vegetables. The colorful veggies baked into the bread were designed to look like a field of trees and flowers. Pitted olives at the bottom of the scape mimicked a line of ants. Spiralized butternut squash was baked into the upper corner of the bread, looking like the sun. Radish slices, dill fronds, and blooms of red onion completed the gorgeous display.

"And here, we have a honey-lavender butter," Hiroto said. He offered Chef Levy a small pot. "If you pour it over the garden, the magic will be initiated."

As soon as the melted butter hit the bread, the dish came alive. The asparagus stalks swayed, like they were trees caught in a breeze. The olive ants began to march across the bottom of the bread. The spiralized butternut squash sun grew brighter, turning from orange to a fiery red, to purple…just like a sunset.

"Oh, how lovely, dears." Polly clapped her hands.

She took the knife and serving spatula Philippe handed her and cut off small wedges for herself and the other two judges.

The audience went silent as the judges bit into the focaccia. From where Kenzie was standing, it looked perfectly cooked—golden on the outside and springy on the inside.

Damn those two and their magical focaccia.

"Hmph," Chef Sakai said. "Too much lavender in the butter."

"I'll have to disagree with you there," Polly said pleasantly. She'd polished off her slice and was cutting into the focaccia for a second piece. "This might be the most delicious creation I've ever sampled. It's fresh and light and reminds me exactly of spring. You have truly elevated these two ingredients. Well done, chefs!"

Philippe and Hiroto's thanks were drowned out by Chef Levy.

"This tastes like cow dung!" she bellowed.

For someone so small, she had quite a pair of lungs.

"No salt." She thrust the rest of her piece back on the plate. "Were you never taught how to season your food, chefs?"

"Sorry, Chef," Philippe mumbled.

Hiroto hung his head.

"Let's move on," Polly said hastily.

Kenzie glanced at her and Braxton's dish. *Holy shit.* If the judges had complained about that focaccia masterpiece, then what were they going to say about this magic-less pile of raw meat?

Take a hike, most likely.

Crazy Esther and Rick were up next. Their ingredients were rhubarb and pig's blood. They'd made a pyramid of decadent treats featuring their ingredients. Every time one of the treats was removed from the pyramid, a new one magically appeared to take its place.

"If that rhubarb galette was the only food left on earth, I'd happily starve to death!" shouted Chef Levy. "The crust is burnt, and is there anything in that filling besides sugar?!"

"Hmph," Chef Sakai grunted.

"Delightful!" cried Polly.

Kenzie held onto the edge of their station to keep herself upright. These dishes were the most incredible culinary creations she'd ever seen, and the judges were ripping them apart.

"Next up, we have Farley and Sébastien," Polly said in a bright tone.

"Looks like they're saving the best for last," Rick said out of the corner of his mouth to Braxton.

When Braxton didn't respond, Rick laughed.

Kenzie considered throwing the plate of carpaccio in his smug face. At least then their poor excuse for a dish wouldn't be a total waste.

"What do you have for us, chefs?" Polly asked Farley and Sébastien.

The pair in question didn't even seem to realize the judges were standing in front of their station. They were in the midst of a heated argument that looked like it was about to come to blows.

"We're not interrupting anything, are we?" Chef Levy barked at the pair.

"No, Chef," they both said, before stepping away from each other and clasping their hands behind their backs.

Chef Levy raised a single eyebrow.

"We've prepared a potato volcano with duck egg yolk lava," Farley told the judges. "Please enjoy."

She started to open the lid of her pressure cooker.

"No." Sébastien put a hand over hers to stop her. "Too much magic was infused. It's…not good."

"It's perfect," Farley hissed. To the judges, she said, "Sébastien's a coward." She glared at her partner. "He's using the rules of magic as an excuse for a bad imagination."

"I'm not a coward," Sébastien mumbled. "There are limitations to the magic."

"Well, forgive me if I don't want to just reinvent the wheel!" Farley retorted. "You might be happy to be boring, but I'm an inventor."

At least, that was what Kenzie thought the other girl was saying. Farley's accent was so heavy it was difficult to keep up.

"Sure, Farley," Philippe said under his breath. "You're basically the Thomas Edison of culinary magic."

Hiroto chuckled. Braxton's stony expression didn't change.

Chef Levy tapped her foot impatiently, while Chef Sakai's brow was furrowed in deep disapproval that seemed to encompass all of them.

"Farley, do you stand by this dish?" Polly asked, her forehead puckered in concern.

"Of course," Farley answered without a moment's hesitation. "This meal is not only perfectly prepared, it's a magical anomaly. These other dishes are variations of magic you've seen before." She waved a dismissive hand at the competition. "My dish will blow you away."

With a flourish, Farley pulled off the top of her pressure cooker.

The audience oohed and ahhed. What appeared to be a miniature, purple volcano was growing out of the pot.

The sides of the volcano were made out of mashed purple potatoes that had been molded together until they held their shape. A heavy dusting of pepper along the outside made it look like the potato volcano was covered in ash. Steam poured out of the volcano's crater, filling the dome with the smell of butter and chives.

The volcano continued to grow until it enveloped the pressure cooker. By the time it stopped expanding, it was as tall as Kenzie.

It looked awesome…although not as appetizing as the other two dishes.

A gurgling sound came from the volcano's depths. The outer layer of potatoes began to ripple and bubble as the pressure within built. Golden flecks of yolk began to spurt out of the top.

Just as it started revving up, the steam and dollops of yolk stopped. The volcano's rumblings went still.

Kenzie wondered whether Farley's great creation might be a dud.

Then, a high-pitched whistling filled the air. Kenzie felt a subtle vibration in the counter beneath her hands and the floor underfoot. She barely had time to register the source of the shaking, when the potato volcano exploded.

Someone screamed. Kenzie watched in horror as boiling yolk surged out of the volcano. It kept coming and coming. Kenzie saw the boiling liquid blast Farley in the face. Pieces of potato shot out in every direction.

What was left of the volcano's outer shell exploded outward. Dollops of steaming mashed potatoes rocketed in every direction.

The heat must have hardened the mashed potato. The chunks blasted right through the dome's walls. All around them, glass panels were shattering.

Someone wrenched Kenzie's arm hard enough for her vision to go white for a second. She didn't have time for so much a squeak of protest.

Kenzie hit the ground, hard, a second before Braxton's crushing weight settled on top of her. One of his hands cupped the part of her face that wasn't pressed into the floor, shielding her from the glass that was raining down on them.

All Kenzie could think was that Braxton was a lot heavier than he looked. She could barely breathe.

Braxton's heart thrummed against her back as he held her in place. Somewhere nearby, an alarm blared.

Kenzie had no idea how much time passed before Braxton rolled off her. Dazed, she sucked air into her starving lungs as she took in the ruined dome. The glass panels were mostly obliterated, and the audience had fled. It was just the contestants and the three judges…all of whom were crouched around something on the floor.

"You okay?" Braxton asked in a husky voice.

"Yeah. Um. Thanks for saving me."

Adrenaline was coursing through Kenzie, making her knees wobble.

"Well, I couldn't bloody let you die on me before we get into the finale," he said gruffly.

Kenzie didn't believe that for a second. While it was true enough that he needed her to get through the next round, there hadn't been time for him to do anything except react. Braxton was a good person, pure and simple.

"You averse to compliments, or something?" she asked him with a shaky laugh.

"Just from you," he muttered.

At that moment, Chef Sakai stood up from where he'd been kneeling on the floor. That was when Kenzie caught sight of the reason why all the judges had congregated around that spot. Farley's unmoving figure was stretched out on the ground.

Kenzie could feel her head moving back and forth as she tried to make sense of what she was seeing. Beside her, she heard Braxton draw in a ragged breath. She grabbed onto his arm to steady herself, because at that moment, her limbs had forgotten how to work.

The Irish woman's freckle-dusted cheeks were covered in blisters and deep gashes. It looked awful. Agonizing.

Why wasn't Farley screaming her head off?

If it had been Kenzie, she'd be writhing and moaning at the very least. But Farley was perfectly still.

Too still.

Kenzie's gaze dropped below the other girl's face, and that was when she understood.

Oh. My. God.

There was a wedge of glass impaled in Farley's throat.

Kenzie couldn't breathe. She couldn't bear to look, but it was impossible to turn away.

Chef Sakai was staring at Farley's unmoving body with an expression of horror in his dark eyes. He was tracing his goatee with a finger over and over again. Polly was holding a dish towel to her face as she sobbed.

Chef Levy, her arms covered in blood and smears of yolk from trying to staunch Farley's wounds, got to her feet. Everyone went quiet as they waited for what she would say. Even the alarm stopped.

Chef Levy's heavy voice filled the silence.

"Farley is dead."

CHAPTER 17

BRAXTON

Farley was dead.

No matter how many times he repeated those words to himself, he couldn't quite bring himself to believe them. A little while ago, he'd seen Sébastien being escorted out by security. Even that hadn't been enough to completely convince Braxton that what he'd seen in the dome was real. It felt more like a nightmare.

The six remaining contestants had gathered in Crazy Esther's suite to decompress after the paramedics dealt with their minor injuries. Braxton had gotten thirteen shards of glass taken out of his arms and back. Sébastien had needed to go to the hospital for second-degree burns. Everyone else had come out mostly unscathed…physically, at least.

It was late, but none of them seemed interested in going back to their own suites. Even Rick was being subdued.

An official announcement had gone out that Farley and Sébastien were eliminated from the tournament by default. That meant Braxton and Kenzie were moving on to the second round.

Christ. The only reason he was still in the tournament was because a woman had died.

As much as it filled him with self-loathing, Braxton couldn't ignore the relief coursing through his system.

"Is this the first time?" Kenzie asked, her soft voice breaking through the tense quiet. "I mean, is this the first time someone's died in the tournament?"

"Someone died three decades ago," Philippe replied. "But it wasn't cooking-related. It was the chef favored to win, actually. He just died in his sleep."

"Aren't you adorable?" Crazy Esther cackled. "He was poisoned."

Yeah, poison was definitely not a topic Braxton wanted to think about at that moment.

"That's just a rumor," Hiroto said, coming to Philippe's defense.

"No, it's a fact," Rick retorted. "They called it an accident because a murder at the tournament would have been bad for viewership. The Gourmands didn't want to scare off the best chefs from participating."

"Who are the Gourmands, exactly?" Kenzie asked.

"No one you'd know," Rick said. "They're powerful members of the culinary magic community and don't deal with amateurs." He gave her a disparaging smile. "You don't need to worry your pretty head about them."

Anger flushed across Kenzie's cheeks, but she must have made the same calculation Braxton had: no good would come from tangling with Rick.

"They're just super rich dudes who keep in the background," Philippe told Kenzie. "They're the authorities who keep culinary magic hidden from the rest of the population."

Kenzie turned to Braxton.

"They're the ones who killed Loretta and Max, aren't they?" she asked in a whisper.

He nodded.

Kenzie curled her hands around her coffee mug and stared into space.

He knew he should say something to her. This whole shitshow of a night was a lot to take in, even for those of them who had been a part of this world for their entire lives. Kenzie was actually handling everything better than Braxton could reasonably expect.

Unfortunately, that wouldn't be good enough to get through the next round. The six people in this room were the most talented culinary magicians in the world. None of them would make the kind of mistake Farley had.

Except maybe Kenzie.

"I think we need to talk about something positive," Hiroto announced, shooting a worried look in Braxton's direction.

Braxton tried to bury his turbulent emotions and rearrange his facial expression.

"Let's talk about what we're going to do when we bite into that wish truffle," Hiroto said, licking his lips. Today, his T-shirt had the quote *Come on, just take a* whisk.

"Hypothetically, of course," Philippe said with a weak grin. "Since we all know I'm going to win."

"Riiiight," Rick drawled.

"I'll go first," Esther said, scooching forward on the couch and tracing the handle of the hunting knife tucked into her belt.

Before they'd gone into the dome, Braxton had heard her arguing with tournament security about bringing it with her. They'd ended up taking the weapon away from her but returning it at the end of the first round.

She also had her bow and quiver of arrows resting on her lap.

You know…just in case a herd of reindeer happened by….

"When I win," Esther said, "I'm going to wish that backwoods cooking becomes the norm for every chef and culinary magician in the world. Everyone will realize modernity is an illusion, and the only way for humanity to survive is by living a minimalist life in nature." She sighed, losing herself in the wretched fantasy.

"And on that note, I need another drink," Rick muttered.

"Oh no you don't," Hiroto said jovially. "Share your wish first."

Braxton thought Rick wouldn't answer, but then their gazes locked, and Rick's eyes lit with malicious intent. "Well, I certainly don't need to wish for money, because my family has so much." He chuckled.

Don't say it, Braxton warned himself, feeling the retort hover on the tip of his tongue. *Don't say it. Don't—*

Braxton said, "All that money, and you can't even buy yourself a decent reputation." He shook his head in mock disappointment. "It must be hard to be back here, you know, after you lost the last time."

Yeah, he said it.

"I can imagine your bitterness," Rick sneered. "Your brother wasted his wish on building your restaurant empire, and now it's failing because he's dead."

Braxton felt his face go hot. The smart course of action would be to say nothing at all, but he'd be damned if he gave Rick the last word.

Braxton leaned forward until he was invading Rick's personal space.

"Must suck that you're still not favored to win, even though you have the advantage of having done all this once before. Not to mention the fact that you've probably bribed your way into finding out the next challenge, too."

Rick stood up so fast the drinks on the coffee table wobbled. Braxton stood, too.

"Whoa, whoa, whoa." Philippe put out his hands like he was a cop directing traffic. "Easy, gentlemen."

Braxton didn't relax even when Rick let out a forced chuckle.

"Odds are nothing," he told Braxton, "if you can't actually close."

Braxton had nothing to say to that, because Rick was right. After what had happened today, no one needed to remind Braxton that his participation in the finale was by no means guaranteed.

"I didn't know chefs could compete in the tournament more than once," Kenzie said.

Braxton couldn't tell if Kenzie was genuinely curious or if she was taking a jab at Rick. Either way, he had a passing urge to reach out and squeeze her hand. When she gave him a quick wink, that urge escalated to a desire to kiss her.

The look that crossed Rick's face was nothing short of priceless.

"The win was stolen from me last time," he grumbled.

Hiroto and Philippe shot worried looks at Braxton, but he just laughed.

"Stolen by the best culinary magician. But I wouldn't call that stealing."

"If I win," Philippe said loudly, "I'm going to wish that grouchy old Monsieur Renouard sells me the restaurant he's been hanging onto for fifty years."

"You need that specific restaurant?" Hiroto asked.

"Hell yes. It's the perfect size, perfect location, and most importantly, my girlfriend loves the building.

"Raina and I want to make good food where locals can just chill."

"That's a really nice wish," Kenzie said, earning her scoffs from Esther and Rick.

"I'm not here for the wish truffle," Hiroto said. "Honestly? I just want my little sister to be proud and know she can do anything she wants if she works hard enough." He turned to Braxton. "How about you, man?"

No way in hell was he talking about his family's woes in front of these people. Even if he'd been alone with Philippe and Hiroto, Braxton wouldn't have said anything. Family business was private.

Luckily, he was spared from having to say anything at all because his phone chose that moment to start buzzing. When he dug it out of his pocket and looked at the screen, he saw he had three missed calls from Sofia.

"Gotta take this," he said, holding up his phone in explanation and retreating toward the door.

He waited to call Sofia back until he was locked in the privacy of his own suite.

"You're one lucky son of a bitch," his sister said in lieu of a greeting.

"Hey to you, too," Braxton replied. "And can we not talk about how I got lucky off of someone dying?"

"It is what it is," Sofia said.

Braxton could picture her shrugging.

"You can't cut it that close in the second round," she told him.

"Don't you think I know that?" Braxton let out a breath, trying to get a hold on his frayed temper.

"If you'd killed the Ashner girl before the tournament, you probably would have been partnered with Hiroto or Philippe," she continued.

"Well, I didn't, and I'm not," he snapped.

Braxton massaged his head, which was starting to pound.

"I'm sorry," Sofia said after a pause. "I can't imagine what it must be like to have to work with Walter Ashner's daughter."

Braxton opened and closed his mouth. No sound came out.

It came as a shock to his system to consider how, aside from their disastrous performance during the first round, working with Kenzie hadn't been even close to terrible. She might be green when it came to magic, but there was no denying she was a talented chef. She was also pleasant to be around.

Pleasant. Right, mate. Because *pleasant* didn't explain why yesterday, when they'd been chasing each other around with the stupid whipped cream, he'd come dangerously close to kissing her.

"I'm handling everything," Braxton promised his sister. "Today was a fluke. It won't happen again."

"I know."

Braxton could hear Sofia's nails tapping away on a hard surface through the phone…a clear sign she was stressed.

Sofia was even more of a control freak than he was. It had to be killing her that their entire family's fortune rested on his shoulders.

"What's wrong?" he asked. "I mean, aside from the obvious?"

Sofia blew out a breath.

"Sofe?" he pressed.

"Okay, fine. Some of our investors weren't exactly impressed with your first-round performance. They think Kenzie is going to get you kicked out in the second round, and they're starting to get scared."

"Tell them to keep their shirts on," Braxton said through gritted teeth. "It was Kenzie's first time competing. The second round will be better, and then she'll be irrelevant."

In the finale, they would all compete individually and make whatever dish they wanted. Braxton would be in charge of his own fate. The tournament would be his to lose.

"I've been getting calls from the Santiori family," Sofia said.

Braxton's head began to throb. He hadn't told anyone in his family about his agreement with Veneziano Santiori. He hadn't wanted them to worry.

Liar. He'd been hoping he would win the tournament, pay back the loan he'd gotten from the Santiori family, and his mum and sister would never be the wiser.

He should have known better.

And now, those assholes were harassing his sister.

"Did Rick call you?" he asked, his voice deceptively calm.

"No, but his dad and uncle have been leaving messages." She tried to sound nonchalant, but her voice wavered at the end, betraying her. "What did you do, Brax?"

Braxton resisted the urge to slam his fist into the wall.

"Listen," he told his sister. "If they call again, don't pick up. Tell Mum not to talk to them either. Okay?"

"Okay."

Braxton thought he heard a tiny sniffle, but that was impossible. The only time Sofia cried was when she was shedding crocodile tears.

"Brax?"

"Yeah?"

"Things are going to be better when you win, won't they?"

Braxton's chest hurt. His family had been shouldering so much for so long, that most of the time it didn't even register. For Sofia's mask to slip now, when she knew how much pressure Braxton was under, meant that things were worse than she was even saying.

"Yeah, things will be better," he assured her.

The words rang false in his ears. Even if he won the tournament and restored his family's restaurant empire, Aidan would still be gone.

Braxton cleared his throat. "In two weeks, we'll have enough money for all of our restaurants and then some. Dad will see his dream coming to life and Aidan's legacy living on, and he'll get better. And then we'll all go on holiday."

Sofia let out a choked laugh. "Deal. But I'm planning the trip. Remember when Mum and Daddy let you plan your sixteenth birthday?"

Braxton felt himself grinning. "Hey, I had a good time."

"That's because you met a Mexican princess our first night and spent the rest of the trip in her mansion. Meanwhile, Aid and I were slumming it back at that awful hostel you booked."

Braxton laughed. "Yeah, that was pretty lousy of me. If it makes you feel any better, she was a terrible kisser."

Sofia thought it over. "I guess I do feel a little better now."

"Later, sis."

As soon as he'd hung up, Braxton's fleeting good mood vanished like smoke. Rick's family was harassing his sister. Their other investors were pulling out. And he was hanging onto this tournament by a thread.

Braxton needed to talk to Kenzie. They had to get their act together and make sure that what happened today didn't happen in the second round.

Going to see Kenzie would have the additional benefit of keeping him from doing what he really wanted to do, which was bust into Rick's suite and beat the shit out of that pompous little prick.

He could almost hear Aidan's voice in his head telling him, *It's not worth it, mate.* And his mum saying, *Never get into a fight with a pig, Son. You'll both get dirty, and the pig'll like it.*

When Braxton opened his door, it was to find tournament security officials escorting two police down the hall. They stopped in front of one of the suites and spoke to each other in low voices. Then, they knocked on the door.

Kenzie's door.

CHAPTER 18

KENZIE

When Kenzie opened the door, her heart lurched into her throat. Cops outside one's door was never a good thing. Her first thought was that something had happened to her dad. She grabbed onto the doorframe for support.

"Yes?"

Her voice came out as more of a squeak.

"Are you Kenzie Ashner?" one of the cops asked.

"Brookerton," she whispered.

At the confused look the cops gave her, she clarified, "I changed my name."

"But are you Denise Werrimeth's daughter?"

Kenzie's whole body jerked, like an electric current was running through her. She opened her mouth, but no sound came out.

She knew why the cops were here. It didn't take a genius to read their grim expressions. This was the knock at her door that she'd been expecting for most of her life.

Kenzie stood there, frozen and mute, as the words *heroin overdose* and *no evidence of foul play* filled her ears.

"Kenzie?"

Braxton's voice somehow cut through the scream that was building in her mind. He pushed his way through the police to her.

Kenzie barely knew Braxton. And yet, that didn't stop her from colliding with the front of his sweatshirt. After a second, his arms came around her. She felt the rumble of his voice through his chest, but she couldn't hear what he was saying. Awful, gut-wrenching sobs were tearing out of her. Her tears were soaking the front of Braxton's shirt, but she couldn't make herself stop.

She hadn't shed a tear over her mother since she was old enough to understand there was nothing she could do to change Denise. Now, all those years of not-crying were coming out at once…like a monsoon after years of drought.

Oh God. Her mom had asked for money, and Kenzie had callously refused because she'd assumed Denise just wanted to use it for more drugs. *What if she'd needed that money for rehab? To escape an abusive boyfriend? To…*whatever.

Kenzie had refused to let her mother so much as set foot inside her suite.

"I'm a monster."

Kenzie didn't even realize she'd spoken out loud until Braxton's hand on her cheek forced her to meet his gaze.

"This isn't on you," he told her. And then he said it again.

The cops began to talk about medical examiners and funeral homes and a hundred other things that didn't make it through the fog of Kenzie's brain. Braxton kept one arm around her so she didn't collapse into a useless puddle on the floor. He took notes on his phone with his free hand.

Even after the cops gave their final condolences and left, Braxton stayed with her.

"I knew this was going to happen," Kenzie said dully, since it felt like she needed to say something. "Even when I was a kid and my dad would be all hopeful because Denise had gotten into this or that rehab program, I knew." Kenzie forced herself to say the words she'd always known but never spoken out loud. "My mom didn't want to get better."

"And that's on her." Braxton let his arm drop from around her shoulders, and Kenzie immediately felt cold emptiness rush in to take its place. "I know that doesn't make any of this easier, though."

No, it didn't. "Thanks for understanding," she whispered.

When she looked at Braxton, she didn't see any hint of pity, only understanding and sympathy. Kenzie appreciated that more than she could ever put into words.

"I guess we better get back to work," she said, realizing that was probably why Braxton had come to her suite. She'd botched the first round so thoroughly she should have been thrown out of the dome…or burned at the stake. She was Braxton's weak link.

Braxton shook his head. "Not tonight."

"But I'm fine," she insisted.

Cooking right now would probably be a disaster, but the thought of being alone in her room was so much worse. She remembered how it had been after Danny died, and—

Nope. Definitely not going there. Just thinking his name made her eyes start to well up again.

"Let's go for a walk," Braxton suggested.

Ignoring her weak protests, he took her hand and tugged her down the hall.

"Where are we going?" she asked, hurrying to keep up with his long strides.

"Anywhere we want." Braxton offered her a little smile. "The city is ours tonight, Kenzie."

She liked the sound of that. Curling her fingers around his, she let him lead the way out of the building and into the bustling New York night.

✳ ✳ ✳

There was a heavy weight on Kenzie's heart, but this walk was exactly what she'd needed. Talking with Braxton was easy. They chatted about all sorts of things while skirting around anything painful. He coaxed laughter out her with his stories about his first attempts at culinary magic.

She told him about how, a week after she'd gotten Kiwi, the mischievous little chameleon jail-broke out of his habitat. He'd somehow made it all the way to her landlord's apartment on the floor below.

Braxton artfully steered the conversation away from any mentions of his family. Kenzie wasn't sure if it was because he was trying not to make her think about Denise, or because he had baggage of his own.

They walked through Bryant Park and lost themselves in the glittering hubbub of Times Square. They held hands the whole time, but it didn't feel like a date. It didn't feel platonic either, though. Maybe it was just that she hadn't done anything like this—just walking and talking with a guy she was attracted to—since Danny.

And there was no denying she was attracted to Braxton. *Although, really, how could she not be?* Kenzie didn't think there was a heterosexual woman alive who could resist those green eyes, tousled blonde hair, and golden-toned body.

"Earth to Kenzie?"

She started. "What? Sorry."

Braxton grinned. "Something the matter with my face?"

Kenzie wrinkled her brow. "Why would there be?"

Braxton lifted a shoulder. "You've been staring at me and haven't heard a word I said."

Don't blush, she ordered herself.

"You're blushing, Kenzie," Braxton teased.

"Oh, don't flatter yourself," she snapped, which only made Braxton's smile widen. He even got a swagger in his step.

Jackass.

Kenzie had never been shy about going after what she wanted, but Braxton wasn't just some random guy she'd met at a coffeehouse. She valued this budding friendship…or whatever it was. Besides, there was no way she'd jeopardize their professional relationship by hitting on him.

"I…was just…." Kenzie stuttered.

Braxton took pity on her and changed the subject.

Kenzie was so focused on their conversation and the solid pressure of his hand in hers, that she didn't even realize where she'd led them until her feet halted of their own accord.

Braxton must have read something from her body language, because he stopped mid-sentence and looked at the building in front of them.

It was still a restaurant, but the name was different. The white-washed front was now more of a sandy-brown color. The other notable difference was that there wasn't a line of people eagerly waiting outside the door.

"This used to be my dad's restaurant," Kenzie said, so Braxton didn't think she was just gawking outside some random building.

She knew it would be better to keep walking, but her feet were cemented to the ground. She'd grown up in this restaurant. She'd learned how to cook here. She and Danny had snuck in when the restaurant was closed and made out behind the bar. She and her dad had stayed late on Saturday nights…really Sunday morning by the time everyone else had gone home…drinking hot chocolate and discussing the new menu.

Kenzie jolted out of her reverie when Braxton's hand slid out of hers. He hadn't said a word the whole time she'd been lost in her memories, and when she turned to him, she realized he looked…distraught.

Tension was etched into the hard line of his jaw and the strained tendons in his neck. His fists were balled at his sides.

"What's wrong?" she asked.

Braxton didn't seem to hear her. All of his attention was on the building that used to be Ashner's.

"Braxton?"

He jumped when she touched his arm. When his eyes met hers, she recoiled. There was a wild look in his eyes that she didn't trust. It was almost violent.

All at once, she was reminded of the way he'd looked at her the first time she saw him at *Good Ol' Apple Pie*. There's been hatred in his eyes then.

And it was there now, too.

"What's going on?" Kenzie asked.

Braxton blinked, and the fury in his eyes receded.

"Kenzie." He cleared his throat. His gaze flicked to the restaurant before coming back to her. "There's something I need to tell you."

CHAPTER 19

BRAXTON

In all of Braxton's machinations, telling Kenzie who his family was and how their paths had crossed before had never been part of the plan.

But everything was different now.

Fighting through the first round with her…practicing with her…. Holding Kenzie after she'd found out her mother was dead from an overdose….

Yeah. That changed things.

Braxton ran a hand through his hair as he stood in front of the building where his family had lost everything.

"Does the name Aidan McKaid mean anything to you?" he asked before he could second-guess himself.

Expressions cycled across Kenzie's face so fast it was almost comical. Confusion…understanding…horror.

Oh yeah. That name meant something to her.

"McKaid," she whispered. "I knew it sounded familiar when Polly said it before, but I couldn't place it. Was he…how was he…I mean…."

"Aidan was my brother," Braxton said. "My twin."

"Oh my God." Kenzie leaned over and clutched her knees. "Oh my God. Braxton. I heard Rick say your brother was dead, but I never thought…." When she straightened, tears were slipping down her pale cheeks.

Braxton had the strangest urge to comfort her, even though he was the one who had lost everything.

Kenzie wrapped her arms around herself as her whole body started to shake.

Braxton pulled off his sweatshirt and offered it to her. Kenzie didn't even notice.

"I should have known right away," Kenzie said, not looking at him. "But the truth is, I couldn't let myself think about your brother. I didn't want to know anything about him because it would make everything more…real." A shuddering sigh escaped her lips. "My dad was everything to me, and after what he did, I started to hate him. I felt so much disgust…so much shame. I couldn't handle it."

She looked at him. The apology and horror he saw written all over her face made the backs of Braxton's eyelids sting.

Oh hell. This was not where he'd planned on this night going.

"I know this probably isn't at all what you want to hear," Kenzie said, "but my dad isn't a bad person. He has a big heart."

Anger rose up, clogging Braxton's throat.

"Big-hearted people don't do what your father did to my brother," he said, somehow managing to keep his voice below the level of a shout. "That much poison doesn't get into someone's food by accident. And if you think that was all it was, then you're delusional."

Kenzie's shoulders hunched. "My dad had this friend…a chef who was always travelling to weird places to forage from ingredients. He would bring berries and mushrooms and stuff back for my dad to use in his dishes." Her expression darkened. "I told my dad not to use anything the guy brought us. I told him it was dangerous to use ingredients when we didn't know exactly where they'd come from, but my dad didn't listen to me."

Braxton realized he was holding his breath and let it out in a rush. This part of the story hadn't made it into any of the legal transcripts. Braxton absorbed every detail like a man who was dying of thirst and had been offered a few drops of water.

Kenzie's words didn't change anything, but that didn't stop him from wanting to hear every word.

"That night…the night your brother died…. My dad was using ingredients that his friend had foraged. There were all sorts of weird flowers and leaves that he claimed were edible, but which I'd never seen before. And I think—" She squeezed her eyes shut before continuing. "Some of those ingredients weren't what the forager thought they were."

Braxton coughed, but it failed to dislodge the lump that had formed in his throat.

Kenzie hurried on. "I'm sure that whatever garnish my dad used on your brother's plate that night was poisonous. It wasn't intentional, but if my dad had been more careful and only used ingredients from reputable distributors, that never would have happened to your brother."

She spoke everything in a single breath, like if she didn't get it out in one shot, she'd never get it out at all.

"Is it possible," he began, choosing his words carefully, "that your dad created magic that killed my brother, rather than that forager delivering rotten ingredients?"

Kenzie's lips moved, like she was repeating his words to herself.

"No!" Her ponytail whipped back and forth as she shook her head. "My dad doesn't have culinary magic. He's just a regular chef."

"But you didn't get it from your mum," Braxton pointed out. "You had to have inherited it from one of your parents."

"Maybe I'm an anomaly," Kenzie said stubbornly. "My magic already acts weird, so maybe the way I got it is weird too, right?"

Braxton didn't say anything. He could see the resistance in Kenzie's mind giving way to the irrefutable truth.

Her father, for whatever reason, had managed to hide the fact that he was a culinary magician from everyone, including his daughter.

"I guess it doesn't really matter," Braxton said heavily. The specifics of the details didn't change what had happened.

He needed this conversation to end. The whole thing was messing with his head.

"I'm sorry," Kenzie said. She tilted her head back to meet his gaze. "I know it can't change anything, but I'm so damn sorry. I'll never stop being sorry for what happened to your family."

"It wasn't your fault," he told her in a hoarse voice.

It wasn't until the words were out of his mouth that he realized he truly believed them. And that he no longer felt a shred of ill will toward Kenzie.

There was what her father had done, and then there was Kenzie. They had started off as a single entity in his mind. That wasn't the case anymore.

Kenzie wasn't her father. She didn't deserve to pay for his mistakes.

"You were a victim too," he said. It had never occurred to him before, but it was true. "Your dad betrayed you too, in a way. And then you lost him."

Because Braxton's family had thrown every dollar and resource in their possession at making the bastard who had killed Aidan pay.

Fuck. That must have been terrible for Kenzie.

During the arrest and everything that came after, Braxton had never once considered what would happen to Walter Ashner's teenage daughter when he was sent to prison for life. If Braxton had given it any thought, he would have assumed Kenzie went to live with her mother. Except, he'd met Kenzie's mother….

"Who did you live with after that?"

"My nana," she replied. "My dad's mom," she clarified. "She was my only other living relative who I'd ever had any relationship with, and since she already lived in the city, it made sense." Kenzie picked at a thread on her shirt. "She had a massive stroke almost exactly a year after I moved in with her. That was when I decided enough was enough and got the hell out of New York."

"I'm sorry," Braxton murmured. It felt like a completely inadequate thing to say, but it was how he felt. He could barely begin to process how much sympathy he was feeling for someone he'd spent most of the last five years hating.

"And it wasn't just thinking about Aidan that I couldn't handle," Kenzie said in a soft voice. "I was so messed up with other stuff from that night that I was barely holding myself together."

"Was your mum giving you problems?" Braxton guessed. His voice came out rough and jagged, like he'd swallowed a handful of sea salt.

Kenzie shook her head.

"That night…the night your brother died…. Something else happened. We were understaffed because the flu was going around and our sous chef and two waitresses were out sick." Kenzie's voice was devoid of emotion, and her gray eyes had gone vacant. "I'd been cooking all night. Danny, my boyfriend, was coming to help, too."

She managed a wobbly smile. "He couldn't cook for shit, but he was good at waiting tables, and it was so busy we needed all the help we could get."

Braxton remembered how the small restaurant had been packed that night. His family had waited almost an hour to get in. They'd passed the time by playing some trivia game Sofia had downloaded on her phone.

"It was around the time when your family would have been in the restaurant," Kenzie continued. "Before…everything that happened with your brother." She squeezed her eyes shut.

Braxton held his breath, worried that any sudden move would make Kenzie stop talking.

"I remember how I was freaking out because my sauce was too thick and I didn't have time to start over. I was crying about it. A goddamn sauce." Kenzie let out a humorless laugh. "That was when I got the call—"

Kenzie pressed her hand to her mouth, but it didn't stop the muffled sob from breaking free.

"You don't have to tell me," Braxton whispered.

After everything this girl had been through, he couldn't begin to imagine what had gone down to make her look so broken.

"Drunk driver," Kenzie said. "Danny was on his way here…and a drunk driver fucking—"

Kenzie wasn't crying, but Braxton wrapped his arms around her and held her. Christ. In one night, she'd lost her father and her boyfriend.

Kenzie stepped back. "I didn't want to believe it. I even went back to my sauce, because as long as I focused on something normal, then maybe the rest of my life would go back to normal, too. You know?" She swiped at the tears gathering on her lashes. "And then, after I got my sauce right, I just lost it. I ran out of the restaurant and called Danny's mom. By the time

I got back after, well, everything, your brother had died. And the police were arresting my dad."

"Shit," he said. Because, really, what else was there to say?

All this time, Braxton had assumed Walter Ashner's daughter had skipped off merrily into the sunset while his life imploded.

Kenzie's small gasp drew his attention back to her face, which was now alight with hope.

"Ohmygod. I didn't even think about it before. This wish truffle—"

Braxton held up a hand to stop her right there. He knew what she was going to say, and he wanted to stop her before her hopes ran away with her.

"Can't bring back the dead," he finished.

As quickly as it had come, the hope faded from her eyes.

"The truffle isn't that powerful," he explained. "It's only strong enough to make changes that are actually possible. So, you can wish for money or fame or anything like that, but—"

"The dead stay dead."

Braxton nodded, hating himself a little for destroying her hope.

"Any other limitations to this whole wish thing that I should be aware of?" Kenzie asked, her tone a little acerbic.

"Yeah, actually." Braxton kept forgetting how little Kenzie knew about their world. "Technically, you can wish for anything that could reasonably happen, like I said, but there have been some…cautionary tales over the years. If you wish for something that draws attention from the non-culinary magic crowd, or if the wish is super greedy, the Gourmands put a stop to it."

Kenzie glared at a spot on the pavement. "Put a stop to it. Like what they did to Loretta and Max."

"Yes." Braxton wanted to reach out and put a comforting hand on her arm, or something. Instead, he explained, "There was a Hex Kitchen winner from Zimbabwe a while back. She wished for infinite wealth. It caused hyperinflation that almost collapsed the entire country."

"And the Gourmands killed her?" Kenzie asked.

"Yep. That's why you need to be cautious about your wish."

Kenzie chewed on her bottom lip as she considered everything he was telling her.

"Aidan won the last Hex Kitchen," Braxton blurted out. He didn't know where the words had come from, but he couldn't make himself shut up. "His wish was to transform our dad's single restaurant into dozens all throughout Australia."

"Your brother sounds like he was ambitious," Kenzie said carefully.

Braxton shook his head. "He did it for our dad." It took him a few seconds to compose himself before he could explain. "Our father opened a restaurant before we were born. It was good, and he had a hidden culinary magic deli attached, but his dream was to expand. He just could never make enough of a profit to buy any more properties." Braxton managed a small laugh. "Our dad always talked about the restaurant empire he wanted to build one day. So, when Aidan won Hex Kitchen, he used his wish to make it happen."

Because that was the kind of person Aidan had been.

"Your brother sounds amazing."

"He was," Braxton said, speaking through the tightness in his chest.

They were both silent for a minute, lost in their own thoughts.

Kenzie sighed. Then, just as she must have done so many times in the past, she lifted her chin and smiled.

"Okay." She linked her arm through his and steered him away from the building that used to be Ashner's. "How about wishing for wings? I've always wanted to fly."

Braxton grinned, relieved their conversation was steering away from such depressing topics.

"If that was really your greatest desire, you could wish for your own plane," he suggested. "But probably not the wings."

"Damn." She snapped her fingers. Then, getting serious, she said, "I just want you to know that I don't care about the wish. I mean, I know I wouldn't be able to beat you, anyway, but even if I could, there's nothing I want to wish for. I just want to understand more about culinary magic and learn from the best of the best. I can do both without having to compete with you for that truffle."

"I am unbeatable," Braxton said, giving her a teasing smirk. He pulled her closer and slung an arm over her shoulders. He felt lighter, somehow, and he didn't want to descend back into their pasts. Right now, he just wanted to be in this moment. With Kenzie.

"Feel like grabbing a nightcap somewhere before we head back?" he suggested. "A non-alcoholic one," he quickly clarified.

Between her mother and what happened to her boyfriend, this girl had more reason for avoiding alcohol than anyone he'd ever met.

"Ooh, yes," Kenzie said, picking up her pace and putting even more distance between them and the building that was the source of their shared hell. "I know a great café nearby. And bonus, there's this dessert place next door that makes a mean baked Alaska."

He remembered her mentioning before that was her favorite food.

"Now you're talking my language, baby."

He leaned down and kissed the top of her head before thinking twice about it. Her hair smelled like apples—a little tart and a little sweet. "You're alright, Kenzie Ashner. You know that?"

"Brookerton," she said firmly.

She tipped her head to the side, her pretty lips pouting as a thought occurred to her.

"Hang on." She pinned him with an accusatory glare. "You knew who I was when you came to Tennessee, didn't you?"

Every muscle in Braxton's body seized up. His guilt must have shown on his face, because Kenzie jabbed a finger in his chest.

"You came to the diner that day to get your revenge, didn't you?"

Braxton swallowed. Nodded.

To his utter shock and amazement, Kenzie didn't start screaming or try to run away.

"Huh," she said, smiling a little. "I was wondering why you were looking at me like you wanted to kill me."

"How are you taking this so calmly?" he demanded.

Kenzie lifted a shoulder. "The drunk who killed Danny died in the accident too, but I've fantasized about what I would have done to him if he'd lived." Her arm tightened around his waist. "I get why you'd want to take your revenge out on me, especially since you couldn't get to my dad."

"I like this violent Kenzie," Braxton told her. "It's hot."

She shot him a look, catching her lower lip between her teeth. And wow…. This girl was Trouble. With a capital T.

Braxton let go of her and put a little distance between them.

"Besides." Kenzie tossed her hair in a casual move that was undermined by the flush across her cheeks. "You wouldn't be the first person to threaten my life recently."

Braxton whirled on her. "What are you talking about?"

"Rick." She rolled her eyes, like it was no big deal. "He came by my suite yesterday for a little chat. Said if I got in the way of him winning, he'd kill me slowly."

Braxton resisted the urge to drive his fist through the nearest wall. Instead, he stopped walking and tugged on Kenzie's arm until she faced him. His jaw was clenched so tightly, he could barely squeeze the words out. "Tell me everything."

CHAPTER 20

BRAXTON

Braxton had always thought *seeing red* was a figure of speech. As he pounded on Rick's door, he realized there was nothing figurative about it. His fist itched to smash the prick's nose.

Braxton could count on one hand the number of times he'd gotten into a fist fight, and all of them had taken place before the age of twelve. But he was ready to throw down now.

"Santiori!" Braxton yelled, pounding on the door again. "Open up, you piece of—"

His fist dropped when Crazy Esther opened Rick's door. She was casually buttoning up her shirt, which was gaping wide enough to show off the fact that she wasn't wearing a bra.

"Hey, stud." Esther licked her lips. "Wanna—"

"Fuck off, Esther," Braxton growled.

He brushed past her and into Rick's suite, relieved to find the other man mostly dressed. At least he was wearing pants.

"I could knife you right now," Esther said, pulling her hunting knife out of her belt and brandishing it at Braxton. "Did you consider that before you barged in here?"

"Yeah, because no one will be able to figure out that you murdered me." Braxton rolled his eyes. "You'll get kicked out of the tournament, among other things, and then everyone will assume all chefs specializing in backwoods magic are as batshit as you."

Braxton was gratified—and more relieved than he'd ever admit out loud—when Esther put her knife away.

"Leave us," Rick told Esther, like he was the boss on some TV mob show. Braxton half-expected him to pull out a cigar and one of those gangster fedoras.

"Fine." Esther flounced past Braxton. "Don't kill my partner before we make it to the finale," she said, reaching up to pat Braxton's cheek. "Once we make it through the next round, though, go wild."

With that gracious offer, she left the room. The suite door clicked shut behind her.

Rick pointedly turned his back on Braxton and bent to pick up some discarded clothes on the floor. "I'm afraid my family can't offer you any more on credit after your embarrassing first round performance. So, if that's why you're here, I'm sorry to say you're wasting your time."

Braxton ignored the jab. "I'm here to tell you to stay the fuck away from my partner." It was an effort to keep his breathing under control.

He wanted to wrap his hands around Rick's skinny throat and squeeze the life out of him.

"And tell your father to stop harassing my family," Braxton added. "If he has something to say, he can say it to me. Leave my mum and sister out of this."

Rick took the time to fold his wrinkled shirt before he replied. "You know," he said, "if you can't pull out a win and pay up, the McKaid family will belong to me."

Braxton stiffened. "Well, then I guess it's a good thing I'm going to win."

Rick snickered. "I can't lie, man. The thought of lovely Sofia on her hands and knees, scrubbing the floors of one of my kitchens, is getting me all kinds of hot." He tapped a finger on his chin. "I think I might need to get a special uniform, just for her. Or maybe have her wear nothing at all."

"Sofia would rip off your balls and feed them to you," Braxton growled.

Rick laughed.

It was a kick to Braxton's gut that, in spite of his bravado, Rick was the one with all the power in this situation. Unless Braxton made good on his promise to win, he was condemning his family to hell.

"Guess I'll never know what it's like to be beholden to the corrupt and slimy Santiori family," Braxton said. "Because we both know which of us is the better culinary magician."

"That remains to be seen," Rick retorted. "This tournament isn't over yet."

They exchanged a glare full of silent menace.

"Stay away from Kenzie," Braxton said. He spun on his heel and was about to stalk out of the room, when he ran into someone.

Not just someone....

Veneziano Santiori, Rick's father, was standing in the doorway. He was wearing a bespoke pinstriped suit with a purple tie and pocket square. He was as thin and pasty as his son, but it didn't make him appear any less imposing.

Two of his muscled and heavily-armed goons stood behind him.

"Papà," Rick said sullenly. "I didn't know you were dropping by for a visit."

"Believe me, Ricardo, this is not a social call," Veneziano told his son. "But I'll get to that in a minute."

Ricardo. Braxton almost snickered at that, but then Veneziano turned away from his son and faced Braxton.

"Mr. McKaid," Veneziano said smoothly. "Wouldn't your time be better spent preparing for the second challenge rather than threatening my son?" He crossed his arms and leaned against the doorjamb. "After your partner's embarrassing display during the first round, I would think you would be off trying to get her into competing shape."

Braxton bristled. "Don't worry," he told Veneziano. "You'll get your money."

Veneziano lifted a shoulder. "It makes no difference to me. Either I get double my investment, or I get control of your family. Either way, I win."

Braxton forced his clenched fists to go loose at his sides. He tried to speak, but fury had made his throat close up. Besides, Braxton knew a losing battle when he saw one. Veneziano's thugs were moving further into the suite. One of them shut the door. The other stood next to his employer with his hand resting on the gun tucked into his waistband.

Not good.

"I'm going to win the tournament, Papà," Rick said in a loud voice, as though to remind his father that he was in the room. "I've made sure of it."

Braxton could have sworn he heard Veneziano sigh as he turned his attention on his son.

"Yes, Ricardo, I'm well aware of your pathetic little power grabs, and the way you've been tossing money around to cheat your way to the truffle." He sneered at his son.

"But—" Rick stuttered. "I thought you'd be proud. I was being proactive."

"Proud!" Veneziano's laugh was high and cold. "I don't think I've been proud of you a single day in your life, Ricardo."

Rick flinched.

If Rick was less of an asshole, Braxton might have felt sorry for him.

Braxton thought it was the right time to make his escape. He started inching toward the door, but Veneziano's goons had other ideas.

"Watch," one of them said to Braxton in a deep, heavily-accented voice. "See what happens when you displease Mr. Santiori."

Braxton had no desire to stick around and see what happened next. From the way the two goons were rolling up their sleeves, he had a pretty good idea of where this conversation was heading.

So did Rick, apparently.

"Papà, don't," Rick said, backing away from the thugs who were converging on him. "I was helping us!"

"No. You were helping yourself," Veneziano corrected. "You are also drawing attention from the Gourmands with your cheating. We do not want to bring that kind of scrutiny onto our family."

"I'm sorry. I won't—"

The breath wheezed out of Rick as one of the goons hit him in the stomach. Before Rick could recover, the other kicked the back of his legs so he fell onto his knees.

Braxton stood frozen in the middle of the room. He hated Rick, but was he really going to stand here and watch him get beaten into a pulp?

As it turned out, the decision wasn't Braxton's to make.

"You may go, Mr. McKaid," Veneziano informed Braxton as Rick let out another squeal of pain. "But just remember. If I can do this to my own son for disobeying me, then consider what will happen to you if you attempt to double-cross me."

CHAPTER 21

KENZIE

So, I think I owe you an apology," Braxton said. He offered Kenzie a half-smile that made her a little weak at the knees.

If he ever called her on it, though, she'd claim she was just faint from hunger and overwork. Seriously. This man was a slave driver.

They'd been cooking for twelve hours straight. Kenzie's eyes were burning, because Braxton had gotten the bright idea to practice magicking raw onions.

Brilliant, that one.

"What are you apologizing for?" Kenzie asked. "Aside from working me half to death." She pressed the back of her hand to her forehead.

"If you faint, I'm not catching you," he warned her.

"Liar." She pffed. "You're gallant. Admit it."

"I admit nothing." He folded his arms across his broad chest.

"You're not off to a very good start with this apology, you know."

"You're right." Braxton sobered. "I think what happened in the first round was mostly my fault."

Kenzie wrinkled her nose. "Can we never talk about that again?"

"I thought you wanted your apology."

Kenzie heaved out a sigh. "Fine. Proceed."

Braxton shook his head. "Every culinary magician I know was trained the same way…using senses and the food's properties to control the magic.

That's what I kept trying to get you to do in the first round, but it's obvious your magic doesn't work the same way."

Kenzie was trying not to think about her strange magic, and Braxton's conviction that she had inherited it from her dad. She couldn't comprehend why he would have lied to her about anything, let alone something so huge.

He wouldn't do that to her. Would he?

"You can just call a spade a spade," Kenzie replied. "I'm a freak of nature."

"Your words, not mine."

"Well, I accept your apology." She kept her tone light, but she was genuinely touched he wanted to take partial responsibility for her failure.

"I'm sorry too," she said in the spirit of fairness. "I saw all those people in the audience and froze. I promise it won't happen again."

"Deal."

Kenzie returned her attention to the red onion on the counter in front of her. Braxton had been trying to get her to make it spontaneously peel and slice itself. Instead, she'd decided to get a little retribution for her burning eyes. She'd cut little holes into the onion skin in the shape of eyes, nose, and a pouty mouth. Breathing deeply, she waited for the strands of magic to shimmer into existence.

It was getting easier to see those elusive threads of magic. She no longer felt like she burst blood vessels every time she tried. It was also becoming easier for her to create dishes with the final magic in mind. Before, she'd made it up as she went along. Now, she was starting to sense which ingredients would pair well with different kinds of magic.

It wasn't easy, but it was all starting to make sense. It felt natural.

Like right now, with this onion.

The onion scrunched up its face and made a pathetic blubbering sound. Juicy tears slid down its purple cheeks.

Hah.

"Cute," Braxton said, watching the onion sob its guts out with a bemused expression on his face. "Really mature."

"I think so, too." Kenzie adjusted her hold on the magic so it looked like snot was coming out of the onion's nose.

Braxton snorted.

"So, what next?" she asked.

The two of them surveyed the kitchen. There were beautifully-plated dishes covering every available space. The only evidence of a dish-gone-haywire were some red splotches along the wall from when Kenzie's tomato sauce had gotten a little over-excited.

"You hungry?" Braxton asked, looking around at all the food. "I just realized we skipped lunch and dinner."

Kenzie groaned. "If I never have to be around food again, it'll be too soon."

A loud knock at the door stopped Braxton from replying.

"Yo, Braxton, Kenzie. You in there?"

When Kenzie opened the door, it was to find the other four competitors waiting in the hall. The smell of expensive cologne teased her nose. The guys were all wearing button-downs, except for Hiroto. Tonight, his T-shirt had a music note and the words *Thyme to Turnip the Beet*. Crazy Esther was wearing a dress that looked like it was made from leather she'd pieced together herself. It also showed enough cleavage that she could have done away with the top part of the dress for all the good it did. At least Esther had left her arrows and hunting knife in her room.

Rick stood a little behind Esther. When the light caught on his face, Kenzie saw that one of his eyes was swollen shut. He was also moving carefully, like he had other injuries beneath his clothes.

Kenzie whirled on Braxton.

"Did you do that to him?"

She'd meant to whisper, but she was so angry that her voice carried to everyone, including Rick.

Rick scoffed. "If you think McKaid could lay a finger on me and live to talk about it, you're dumber than you look."

Kenzie ignored him. All of her attention was fixed on Braxton.

"I didn't do that," he said quietly, holding her stare.

He seemed like he was telling the truth, but then who—

"We doing this or not?" Rick demanded, his voice cutting through the tense silence.

"What exactly is *this*?" Braxton asked.

"We're going out," Philippe informed them.

It felt to Kenzie like they all released a breath at once. The tension seemed to evaporate.

"Come on, you two," Philippe said to Kenzie and Braxton. "Go put on something—"

"Suitable," Hiroto supplied.

Kenzie looked down at her baggy T-shirt and jeans. Both were covered in all manner of stains and crumbs. She was pretty sure she reeked of the onion she'd just been torturing.

She looked at Braxton. His blonde hair was sticking up in every direction, and his clothes were in even worse shape than hers.

"The second round is tomorrow," Braxton said with a frown. "We've got more work to do. Then, we're going to bed."

"Together?" Philippe asked, quirking a dark, bushy eyebrow.

"Separately," Braxton said through gritted teeth.

Philippe and Hiroto snickered.

"He's so easy to mess with," Hiroto confided to Kenzie in a low voice.

She grinned back at him. "You're telling me."

"Don't be a pansy," Esther told Braxton. "We won't be out late. Go put on your big boy pants."

"It'll be fun," Philippe coaxed. To Kenzie, he asked, "Have you ever been to a magic bar?"

She shook her head. "Didn't even know such a thing existed."

"That settles it." Philippe clapped his hands. "Braxton, you've been overruled. Besides, Raina's meeting us at the bar, and Kenzie hasn't met her yet."

"I'd love to meet your girlfriend," Kenzie told him. If Raina was anything like Philippe, she was sure to be a good time.

"Come on, Braxton," Hiroto wheedled. "Stop being a spoilsport."

Braxton looked at Kenzie, a question in his eyes.

"Maybe it would be good to get out for a little bit," Kenzie said.

The others whooped, except for Rick, who wore a sour expression on his bruised face.

Kenzie still wanted to know what had happened to him, but it was clear no one was going to tell her.

"Fine." Braxton sighed. "Give us ten minutes to get ready."

A short while later, Kenzie was rejoining the group. She had put on the one going out-worthy outfit she'd brought with her. It was a light gray tank that made her eyes pop and black miniskirt. She'd put on her customary two coats of mascara and boldened the look with red lipstick. Her outfit was modest compared to Esther's, but Kenzie couldn't stop the little thrill that went through her when Braxton's green eyes rested on her cleavage for a beat longer than strictly necessary.

"Cab or walking?" he asked brusquely, turning away from Kenzie to address the rest of the group.

Braxton studiously avoided looking at her, which gave Kenzie the opportunity to take him in at her leisure. He looked criminally good in a black button-down that hugged his wide shoulders and narrow waist. His jeans looked like they'd been made for him, giving her a view from the back that was as good as the front.

Philippe elbowed Kenzie in the ribs and waggled his brows. She glared at him in return.

"Let's cab," Rick said. "My treat."

He watched Braxton through his good eye as he took out his wallet. He smirked as he thumbed out a few hundred-dollar bills. Braxton's spine stiffened.

There was some serious beef between those two. Kenzie wasn't sure exactly what their deal was, but there was obviously more than just competitive rivalry.

They had to split into two groups on the way to the bar, and with Esther and Rick in the other cab, Braxton relaxed. He even cracked a few smiles as Hiroto and Philippe reminisced about some of the culinary competitions the three of them had been in as kids.

When the cab dropped them off, there was no sign of a hopping bar with people crowded outside. They were in an alley of the Meatpacking District outside a mini mart.

It was colder in New York than it had been in Tennessee, and Kenzie hopped in place to keep warm.

"Where's the bar?" she asked, looking around. Aside from the mini mart, all the other nearby businesses were closed.

A light flickered over the mini mart. Aside from a siren in the distance, it was disconcertingly quiet. Kenzie almost wished Esther had brought along her hunting knife.

"This is gonna be so fun," Philippe said, looping his arm through Kenzie's and tugging her toward the mini mart. "We're popping your magical bar cherry!"

Kenzie allowed herself to be led into the mini mart. The bored-looking teen at the register didn't even glance up as their group headed for the back. They went through a pair of swinging doors into a dingy storage area. There were some empty crates and a soda machine with an *Out of Order* sign taped to the front.

Kenzie was beginning to wonder if they'd brought her here to murder her.

Rick pressed the button next to the picture of bottled water. There were a few metallic clicks, and then the soda machine slid into the wall. A hallway appeared on the other side.

"No way," Kenzie muttered.

"I can already tell this is going to be a good night," Hiroto said, grinning at the awe that was probably written all over her face.

As soon as the six of them were through, the soda machine slid back into place.

At the end of the hallway, there was another door. A skinny man with a taser tucked into his waistband checked their IDs—since apparently the rules about underage drinking applied even in this upside-down world of culinary magic.

Braxton was the last one to pull out his ID. The bouncer, who hadn't spoken to the rest of them, looked from Braxton's license to the man himself. The bouncer's eyes widened.

"I've got two-thousand bucks on you winning," he said in a heavy New York accent. "Can I get an autograph?"

"Uh, sure," Braxton muttered, quickly signing a magazine the man produced from inside his jacket.

"How about the rest of you's?" the bouncer asked, waving his pen at their group.

Rick and Esther brushed past him and disappeared into the bar. Philippe and Hiroto signed the man's magazine like it was no big deal before following the others into the bar.

Kenzie tried not to let her surprise show when the bouncer handed his pen to her. She looked at the magazine, which was titled *Magical Cuisine Quarterly*. It was the special Hex Kitchen edition. Her face was right there along with the rest of the eight competitors pictured on the front cover.

Kenzie signed the magazine, adding a little flourish to the *K*. Grinning, she handed it back to the bouncer.

"Thanks!" he said enthusiastically as he examined her signature like it had made his day.

"Any time," she replied.

She felt a little light-headed, but it wasn't the bad I'm-under-the-spotlight-and-gonna-faint kind. It was just…different. New. Like everything else about her life these days.

The fact that this whole world of culinary magic had existed under her nose, and without her knowledge, made Kenzie's head spin.

"Don't forget to win," the bouncer told Braxton as they said their goodbyes and stepped into the bar.

CHAPTER 22

KENZIE

Holy people everywhere.

A man with a Yankees cap and bushy moustache took one look at their little group and squealed like a girl.

"It's the Hex Kitchen competitors!"

The news spread like wildfire. Within seconds, they were surrounded.

"Congratulations!"

"Ohmygosh!"

"This is amazing!"

"Will you sign my bra?"

The last one was from a model-type in a sequined romper and was addressed to Braxton. He graciously declined, which saved Kenzie from needing to brawl it out with the chick. Not that she really had any right to stake a claim, but Braxton was her partner. People needed to learn boundaries.

The others were busy signing autographs and talking to their fans. A few people—mostly skeevy guys—tried to chat up Kenzie. She had a feeling their interest had more to do with the fact that she had boobs than her participation in the tournament.

"You've been a fabulous audience," Hiroto announced, like he was a circus showman. "But it's time for my friends and I to get thoroughly wasted. No photo evidence, please!"

That earned them a round of applause and a corner table that was quickly vacated.

Kenzie let herself be ushered over to the table. The nervous fluttering of her pulse that came any time she was the center of attention was still there, but she wasn't in full-on panic territory like she'd been in during the first round.

"You look like a deer in the headlights," Philippe said, giving Kenzie a thump on the back.

"I just didn't realize people would recognize us outside of the dome," she replied, having to shout over the music that was loud enough to make the floor vibrate.

"Right now, we're the biggest names in the world of culinary magic," he replied. "No matter how all of this shakes out, you'll still be famous."

Kenzie waited for the familiar squeeze of discomfort that was sure to come on the heels of that statement.

Nothing happened. No ragged breathing or spotty vision or an intense need to puke. She was surprisingly chill.

Kenzie didn't have any love for Rick or Esther, and she barely knew Philippe and Hiroto, but the others made a natural barrier that shielded her from the rest of the bar. She didn't know if they were doing intentionally or not, but she was grateful regardless.

"Raina!" Philippe called out, waving his hands in the air. A petite brunette came hurtling through the packed bar like a torpedo and threw herself at Philippe. The two of them staggered back against the wall. Their mouths met in a sloppy kiss that involved way more tongue than Kenzie needed to see from either of them. But they were also adorable.

Philippe's *very* pregnant girlfriend extricated herself to peck Hiroto and Braxton on both cheeks. She offered Rick and Esther a little wave but didn't approach them.

"Come meet Kenzie," Philippe shouted to Raina over the pumping music.

Raina gave Kenzie a wide smile. She was so tiny everywhere except her stomach. It looked a little like she'd swallowed a watermelon.

"Aren't you gorgeous!" Raina kissed Kenzie on both cheeks and then gave her a hug that squeezed the life out of her. For such a little thing, Raina was strong as an ox.

"I need a drink," Hiroto yelled over the din. "Preferably two. You know, for balance." He held his arms out to the side to demonstrate.

He and Braxton made a path through the throngs to the bar. Braxton leaned over to talk to the bartender, and Kenzie was annoyed to see that his ass had attracted the notice of half the bar. At least, that was how it seemed to her.

When Braxton and Hiroto returned, they each carried a tray of the most interesting drinks Kenzie had ever seen.

Five of the drinks were blood-red and came in tall wine glasses. The liquid was smoking. The last two drinks came in champagne flutes. They were bright purple with yellow ice cubes.

Braxton handed one of the purple drinks to Raina and the other to Kenzie. He leaned down and spoke into Kenzie's ear so she'd be able to hear over the music. "Mocktail. Chew the ice cubes."

She didn't know if he did it on purpose, but his lips grazed her ear as he straightened back up. The small touch zinged through her like an electric shock.

She took a sip of her drink, hoping it would cool her down and make her stop lusting over her tournament partner.

The drink was fizzy and carried the flavors of citrusy lemongrass and sharp mint. Kenzie chased one of the ice cubes with her tongue, finally managing to get it into her mouth. When she bit down, she didn't get the crunch of ice she'd expected. It was more like gelatin and gave easily between her teeth.

She gasped as tart clementine juice hit her tongue. The flavor was too intense, so she spit the other half of her "ice" cube back into her drink. As soon as it touched the purple liquid, it dissolved. The entire drink turned bright orange. When she looked at Raina's drink, hers was turquoise. Raina stuck out her tongue, which had turned the same color as her drink. Kenzie stuck out her own tongue, squinting down to check out its new orange hue.

Cool.

"This isn't permanent, is it?" Kenzie asked Raina.

In answer, Raina took another sip of her drink and opened her mouth to reveal that her tongue had become pitch black.

"Eww," Kenzie gasped, which prompted Raina to try to lick her.

"Your tongue's natural color will come back after the ice cubes fully dissolve," Philippe said, seeing Kenzie's stricken expression and taking pity on her.

The rest of their group had normal-colored tongues as far as Kenzie could tell, but as soon as they sipped from their drinks, they began to breath out smoke rings.

Rick's were the best. He blew out one that shaped itself into a handlebar moustache and settled itself on his upper lip. His next smoke ring took on a distinctly phallic shape and rose to hover directly over Braxton's head.

Kenzie hooted along with everyone else…until Braxton looked directly at her. The intensity in those green eyes shut her up.

"What's going on with you two?" Raina asked, nudging Kenzie.

"Nothing," Kenzie replied. And then guzzled more of her drink.

The other girl laughed. "Yes, I said the same thing when my friends first asked me about Philippe." She rubbed a hand over her belly.

Kenzie's horror must have shown, because Raina dissolved into a fit of giggles.

The music in the bar changed to a song Kenzie had never heard before, but everyone else in the bar started to whoop and cheer. When Kenzie looked at the others for an explanation, she almost choked on air. They were…stripping.

Or, more accurately, taking their shirts off. Crazy Esther was parading around in a bra that was see-through and so skimpy it couldn't have any practical function.

Raina and Philippe were the only ones keeping their shirts on.

"They don't have a non-alcoholic version," Raina told Kenzie with a wistful look at the trays of blue and orange shot glasses that waitresses were bringing to everyone in the bar. "Not to mention, I'd totally kill the mood if I took off my shirt." Raina patted her stomach.

"Nonsense," Philippe said, pulling Raina into his arms. "You're the sexiest woman in this place. In fact, I think it's time we get outta here."

The two of them exchanged a heated glance before making a quick exit.

"Has everyone gone nuts?" Kenzie asked a shirtless Hiroto, since she'd recently lost her culinary magic translators.

"Fire and ice shots," he explained, just as a tray was deposited onto their table. There were fourteen glasses—seven blue shots, and seven orange.

"But why do you have to be naked?" she demanded, doing everything in her power not to look in Braxton's direction.

Like sharks drawn to blood in the water, shirtless women were circling around their table. One leggy redhead, who could definitely benefit from incorporating a hamburger or two into her diet, held an orange shot in one hand and a blue one in the other. She offered Braxton the blue shot glass and stood on tiptoes to say something to him.

Kenzie had no idea what the hell was going on, but she did know she didn't like the way the redhead was accidentally-on-purpose brushing her frilly bra against Braxton's chest.

Have some self-respect, honey. Sheesh.

Braxton looked around the redhead to Kenzie and raised an eyebrow. There was a question in his expression…one she didn't know how to answer.

"I got you," Hiroto told Kenzie, giving her shoulder a squeeze before sidling up to the redhead and taking the blue shot she was still trying to force into Braxton's hand.

The redhead hid her disappointment like a champ and threw back her orange shot. To Kenzie's shock and horror, a line of flames burst through her skin. The flames danced all the way from her collarbone, down between the cups of her bra, to the top line of her booty shorts.

"Holy shit," Kenzie began, looking around for a pitcher of water…or a fire extinguisher.

No one else seemed to be panicking, though. There were some whoops as Hiroto downed his blue shot and knelt in front of the redhead. Kenzie's muted scream was lost in everyone else's cheers as Hiroto licked the flames off the redhead's skin.

And didn't burn himself.

As soon as his tongue touched the flames, the fire disappeared. Neither he nor the redhead seemed to be in agony of any kind. In fact, they seemed to be enjoying themselves. As soon as he was done licking up all the flames, Hiroto got to his feet and the two started making out. A puff of stream erupted from their joined lips.

All around Kenzie, people were downing their orange shots. Fire erupted across their chests. But no one was crying out or calling 9-1-1. Instead, people were coupling up and licking flames off each other's body.

Just a regular evening at a magic bar. No biggie.

Kenzie was watching the insanity unfold around her in mild shock when someone thrust an orange shot into her hand.

"Drink the fire!" the stranger shouted.

"Fi-re! Fi-re! Fi-re!" everyone around Kenzie chanted.

She didn't know what to do. This wasn't exactly the venue for explaining to a hundred strangers why she didn't drink. Before she had to make a decision, the glass was plucked out of her hand. Braxton held her gaze as he threw back the shot.

A second later, his tanned, golden chest broke out in flames.

"You want it?" Crazy Esther dangled a blue shot in front of Kenzie's face.

Unable to take her eyes off Braxton, Kenzie shook her head.

Esther shrugged. "Guess it's your lucky day, stud," Esther called to Braxton. She lifted the shot to her lips.

Screw. That.

The thought of Crazy Esther's tongue going anywhere near Braxton was unacceptable.

Kenzie didn't even process what she was doing. All she knew was that one second the shot glass was in Esther's hand. The next, Kenzie had grabbed it and downed the shot herself.

The flavors that hit her tongue were so strong she got an instant brain freeze. Notes of pine, mint, and lime sorbet flooded her senses. Her mouth felt cold. *Really* cold.

When she blew out a breath, it fogged like she'd just stepped outside during winter. But while her mouth might be freezing, the alcohol was burning up her veins. She felt a little lightheaded as she met Braxton's stare.

"Are you just going to stand there?" he taunted. "Or are you gonna do something about this fire? It tickles something awful."

The alcohol must have been making Kenzie bold. There was no other explanation for why she hooked her fingers through his belt loops and lowered her head to lick at the flames on his stomach.

At the first touch of her tongue to his skin, Braxton's hips shot forward. His hands tangled in her hair in a way that was just shy of rough.

Kenzie glanced up at Braxton, surprised at the effect she'd had on him.

"Sorry." He dropped his hands by his sides and gave her a sheepish grin.

At least the attraction between them wasn't one-sided.

"Behave," she told him with a teasing smile as she bent to lick the rest of the flames away.

As the fire touched her tongue, there was a burst of heat. Then, the ice shot she'd drunk kicked in. The flavors of lime, mint, and pine extinguished the flames before they could burn. The shot's magic clearly protected the rest of her from getting scorched too, because the tip of her nose grazed the flames without being singed.

Kenzie took her time as she worked her way up Braxton's body.

She felt a groan vibrate through his chest as she licked the flames on his pecs. As intimate and arousing as the whole experience was, the flames that danced just below Braxton's neck were the ones that made her heart try to pound its way out of her body. She was getting dangerously close to kissing territory.

When she worked up the courage to look up, she saw Braxton's eyes were heavy-lidded and a darker green than usual. His cheeks were as flushed as she felt.

Kenzie was still holding his unblinking stare, wondering if he was going to lean down enough for her to kiss him, when someone tapped her on her shoulder. Esther handed Kenzie an orange shot.

"You don't have to," Braxton told her, raising his voice to be heard over the music and voices all around them.

Oh, what the hell? She was already in this far.

Kenzie raised the shot to Braxton in a toast and then brought it to her lips. Braxton stopped her with a hand on her arm. She watched his pulse thud at the base of his throat as he reached down and slid his fingers under the hem of her shirt.

Kenzie's breath caught.

"Is this okay?" he asked.

His voice was pitched so low she read the words on his lips rather than heard them. Nodding, she handed her shot back to Esther and raised her arms so Braxton could pull off her shirt.

Once she was standing in only her lace bra—in the middle of a crowded room—she downed the fire shot.

Ginger, white pepper, and chile flooded her senses. Kenzie's eyes watered as the sharp spices burned all the way through her. After a few seconds, the discomfort wore off, and Kenzie just felt warm.

She looked down and gasped. Her chest was on fire.

Braxton had been right—it did tickle. Especially the flames that danced around her belly button.

She forgot all about the ticklishness when Braxton sank down onto his knees in front of her.

Holy hell. That had to be the hottest thing she'd ever seen. When his tongue swiped a line from one hip bone to the other, she had to grab his shoulders to keep from falling over. He pressed his face against her stomach. She thought he was having as much trouble holding himself together as she was, but then his breathing evened out. He quickly licked up the flames, even missing some in his haste, and got to his feet.

He didn't even look at her before grabbing his shirt off the floor and shrugging it on.

Kenzie was left standing there, wondering if the sizzling attraction between them had been in her head all along.

CHAPTER 23

BRAXTON

K enzie, I don't think—" Braxton began, but he didn't get a chance to finish his sentence.

Kenzie took the drink Hiroto handed her and downed it in two seconds. She was overcome by a fit of giggles as her arm tattoos began to move. Her sailboat tattoo crashed against an ink tree, and both burst apart into spidery lines of black ink before they reformed.

"So freaking cool!" Kenzie exclaimed.

"I'll get you another," Hiroto said, heading back toward the bar.

Braxton clamped a hand on his arm. "Lay off, mate," he warned.

"Relax," Hiroto replied. "She's having fun."

That was undeniable, but she'd already taken two shots, and magically-enhanced alcohol was more potent than regular alcohol.

Braxton wasn't usually the type to monitor someone else's drinking, but it was his fault Kenzie had started with that first shot. If he hadn't taken the fire shot himself, she would have stuck to her mocktails.

Guilt sliced through Braxton. He knew how powerful Kenzie's reasons were for avoiding alcohol, and he hadn't wanted her to feel any pressure to drink tonight.

"Wooo!" Kenzie yelled, pumping her fist in the air.

Uh-oh. Kenzie was woo-ing. In Braxton's experience, that meant she was one drink away from dancing on a table. Or passing out. While the former would be undeniably hot, the latter would give her a hangover in the morning that their training schedule couldn't afford.

"Whoopsie!" Kenzie's arms flailed as she tripped on absolutely nothing.

"Easy," he warned, wrapping an arm around her waist until she regained her footing.

"Wanna be my ice?" a man with flames erupting from his chest asked Kenzie. He held out a blue shot in invitation.

"Sure." Kenzie reached for the glass.

Braxton tugged Kenzie behind him.

"Get lost, mate," Braxton told the idiot who was leering at her.

"Why'd you do that?" Kenzie pouted. Then, she perked up. "Eh, it's ok. I wanted another fire shot, anyway."

"Oh, I'll totally do your ice," another bloke in hearing distance offered.

Braxton had no idea where Kenzie's shirt had gone, so he pulled his off and put it on Kenzie.

Almost every other woman in the bar was shirtless, and yet it seemed to Braxton like all the male attention in the room was glued to Kenzie's chest.

He didn't fucking like it.

"S'fun," Kenzie said, slurring a little. "Love magic."

"You know what else is fun?" Braxton asked. "Going back to your suite and sleeping."

Kenzie's face scrunched up as she tried to work through the logic of that suggestion.

"Come on." Braxton offered her his hand. "Let's go home."

"I have a better idea," Kenzie countered, like this was some kind of negotiation. "Let's do more fire and ice shots. Or dance. Oooh, yeah. Let's dance!"

She tried to pull him toward the crowded dance floor. She took a few wobbling steps and would have gone down if Braxton hadn't been there to steady her.

"That's enough," he muttered.

Kenzie's sound of protest was lost in the deafening music as he lifted her into his arms.

"Where are you taking me?" Kenzie demanded.

"Home," he replied shortly.

"But I was having fun," she argued.

"*Was* being the operative word. Now we're going home."

Braxton expected Kenzie to argue or demand to be put down. Instead, she said something that sounded like *Oh poo* and relaxed against him.

Grateful she was a docile drunk, he made short work of getting her out of the bar. He ignored tournament fans who tried to talk to him. He brushed past women trying to shove ice shots into his hands. Not that he could have taken one even if he'd wanted to, since his arms were curled around Kenzie's tiny frame. He tried not to think about why he had absolutely no interest in the beautiful women who were practically throwing themselves at him.

It certainly had nothing to do with the smell of apples, which somehow filled his senses even with all the perfume, body odor, and alcohol smells in the air. And it definitely wasn't related to the waterfall of black hair that was cascading down his bare chest.

Yeah right.

When Braxton finally got himself and Kenzie out of the mini mart that served as a front for the hidden bar, the street was completely deserted. Since he was going to have a hell of a time hailing down a cab when he was shirtless and had a humming Kenzie in his arms, he put her down and pulled out his phone. He called the one security guard at the tournament who he knew personally. The man had gotten into a tight spot while he'd been backpacking through Australia, and Braxton's mum had given him a job at one of their restaurants.

Ten minutes later, the security guard was pulling up to the curb in a beat-up minivan.

"Fire and ice shots?" the man guessed, grinning.

"You know it."

Braxton helped Kenzie into the car, even though she insisted his assistance was *totally unnecessary*, before bumping the driver's fist.

The trip back to the Empire State Building was a blur of small talk and Kenzie bossily controlling the radio.

By the time they got back to Kenzie's suite, it was two in the morning. Braxton unlocked her door, since fitting the key in the lock was eluding her, and guided her inside.

"I don't need your help," Kenzie informed him, batting his hand away as he tried to steer her toward the bedroom.

He let go of her, and she made it two steps before whacking her hip against the side of the table.

"Oh, sugar!" Kenzie yelled, slapping the table in retribution. She shook out her palm and muttered, "Son of a hot dog bun."

Braxton couldn't help but laugh. Kenzie was the only person he'd ever met who cursed less when she was drunk than when she was sober.

"I'm not tired," Kenzie informed him as he lifted her up and carried her into the bedroom to avoid any further injuries.

"You will be," he promised her.

Braxton laid her down on the bed and took off her shoes. Once he was confident she'd stay put, he went back out to the kitchen and started pulling ingredients out of the fridge.

"What're you doing?" Kenzie called.

"Making sure you don't have a hangover tomorrow," he replied.

He put pineapple chunks into a blender, along with fresh orange juice, chia seeds, grated ginger, and a handful of baby spinach. While the mixture was blending, he closed his eyes and focused on the stimulating properties of the fresh ingredients. When the threads of magic appeared in his mind's eye, he wove them together in the hangover remedy a culinary magician had taught him at the start of his teenage years.

He owed the man so much.

"Are you singing?" Kenzie asked.

Braxton froze with his hand on the blender. *Was he?*

"Holy crap, you totally were!" Kenzie gloated. "I'm rubbing off on you!"

In more ways than one.

He brought the smoothie back to Kenzie, who was reclined against her pillows like a princess. Her black hair fanned out over the white pillowcases, and her cherry lips curved into a smile as she held out her hand for the glass.

"This isn't poison, is it?" Kenzie asked. She took a sip of the smoothie before Braxton's hurried "No!"

She downed half the smoothie and then put the glass on her bedside table.

"Kenzie, I'd never—" Braxton stopped right there. He thought about the bottle of poison locked in the safe in his room.

"I'm not going to hurt you," he told her gruffly.

"Because you need me?" She blinked at him, her gray eyes wide and disconcertingly lucid. Given the direction of this conversation, he hoped she was hammered enough that she wouldn't remember any of it in the morning.

"No. I just…wouldn't," he said. "Regardless of the second round."

"Oh. Okay." She yawned and settled back against her pillows.

He was just about to ask if she needed anything else before he left, when she groaned and sat up.

"I'm hot," she grumbled.

Kenzie yanked off Braxton's shirt and tossed it across the room.

Oh Christ. In the dim lighting of the bar, he'd been able to convince himself that he couldn't really see much. Now, with the white bulbs shining down on her, there was no hiding the tantalizing picture she made. Her bra was black lace and showed hints of her creamy skin beneath the fabric.

He had to get out of here.

"I'm still on fire," Kenzie complained.

It wasn't a figure of speech. Tiny flames licked up the sides of her ribcage.

She glared at him. "You did a bad job with your ice shot."

Yeah, because if he'd spent one more second with his lips on her skin, he would have ripped off her clothes and bent her over the bar right then.

"Stay here," Braxton said before going to the bathroom and running a washcloth under the tap.

By the time he got back to the bedroom, Kenzie was in the process of shimmying out of her skirt.

Don't look. Don't look. Don't—

Shit. Her panties were like a force of nature, drawing his attention without his consent. And were those…penguins?

"You look like you're in pain," Kenzie observed.

You have no idea.

"I just never thought I'd be turned on by penguins," he muttered.

Kenzie's brow furrowed in confusion, and then she giggled. "I love penguins. Don't you?"

"Fuck yeah. I think they're my new favorite animal."

That earned him another giggle.

They were quiet for a minute. Braxton hovered beside her, knowing he had to leave now before he lost whatever shreds of his willpower remained.

"Okay, well, goodnight," he said. It caused him actual pain to turn away from her.

"You're leaving?" she asked.

Braxton continued on toward the door, figuring that was answer enough.

"Everyone always leaves me."

The confession was so quiet Braxton almost didn't hear it. He stopped mid-step and spun around.

"What?"

Kenzie lifted a delicate shoulder. "My dad, Denise, Nana, Danny…." Her eyes darted away from him. "I'm tired of being alone."

"Do you—" Braxton swallowed. "Do you want me to stay with you tonight?"

She nodded. "But only if you want to," she amended quickly. "I'm not going to hold you hostage or anything."

Braxton chuckled. "You're too small to make anyone do anything."

"*Wiry*," she corrected. "And I'm stronger than I look. There was this one time in kindergarten when Samuel—he was our class bully—stole my lunch box." She smirked. "Let's just say Samuel thought twice about stealing lunches after that."

"You're a barbaric little thing, aren't you?" Braxton asked, bemused.

"Oh, you have no idea, buddy."

He wanted to, though. He really fucking wanted to. And therein lay the problem.

Braxton went around to the other side of the bed and sat down. He took off his belt but left his jeans on as he eased onto the far side of the mattress. He didn't even get under the covers.

"I don't bite, you know," Kenzie told him.

"How do you know I don't?" he replied.

"Maybe I want you to," she retorted.

"Kenzie," he warned.

"Hmm?" She scooted closer.

If he retreated any farther, he'd fall off the bed.

"Do you have a girlfriend?" she asked.

"No," he replied, before thinking it might have been smarter to lie. He didn't like where this conversation was headed.

Liar. He liked it far too much.

"Lover?" she asked.

Just hearing that word from her mouth sent heat coursing through him. "No."

"Are you attracted to me?"

She'd scooted close enough that her apple-scented hair filled his nostrils. The drinks he had at the bar had barely affected him, but he could get drunk off just her smell.

Braxton looked away from her. "No."

"Hah." Kenzie stared pointedly at the noticeable bulge in his pants. "You, Braxton McKaid, are a terrible liar."

He glared at her. "Fine. Yes, I'm attracted to you. Is that what you want to hear? I want you so damn bad I can hardly think straight. But I'm not going to do anything about it, and neither are you."

Kenzie looked at him, like she couldn't decide whether to laugh or yell at him.

"I fail to see the problem." Kenzie crossed her arms, which drew Braxton's attention right back to the breasts he'd been so studiously avoiding. "We're going to be enemies after tomorrow, anyway. May as well stop fighting our attraction for tonight, right?"

"Wrong," he said through clenched teeth. "First, we're not going to be enemies after tomorrow. And second, you're drunk."

"But—"

"Help me out, Kenz," Braxton begged. "I don't want you to do something tonight you'll regret tomorrow. So, please. Turn your sexy self around and go to sleep."

Kenzie's lips parted, and a tiny crease formed between her eyebrows.

"This conversation isn't finished," she told him before turning over and letting out a soft sigh. "'Night."

Even with Kenzie breathing peacefully next to him, it took Braxton a long time to fall asleep.

CHAPTER 24

KENZIE

Kenzie woke to a pounding on her door. She tried to sit up, but a warm weight was holding her in place. One tanned, sinewy male arm was stretched across her stomach. She glanced to the side.

A wave of tenderness swept through her at the sight of Braxton's tousled blonde hair. He was on his stomach with his face turned toward her.

Contrary to what Braxton had thought, her tipsiness from the fire and ice shots wore off after her first sip of that magic smoothie. Her memory of the previous night was perfectly clear. And as frustrated as she'd been that he wouldn't make a move, she appreciated that he'd played the part of a perfect gentleman.

The banging at the door came again.

Kenzie leaned forward a few inches and kissed Braxton's stubbled cheek.

Green eyes flew open.

"Morning," she said innocently. "Mind if I get the door?"

Braxton blinked at her, like he was trying to put the pieces of his reality back together. And then, he leapt out of bed so fast one would think his ass was on fire.

"I'm awake," he announced.

Kenzie gave him a thumbs-up. Any unnecessary talking before coffee was against her religion.

The pounding came again.

"Jeez Louise, I'm coming!" Kenzie yelled. "Keep your shirt on."

Speaking of shirts…. She needed one.

She grabbed Braxton's off the floor, since the banging was now continuous and his shirt was long enough that it saved her from needing to put on pants.

"Who is it?" Kenzie called as she stumbled out into the main area of her suite.

She really wasn't interested in dealing with Rick or Crazy Esther at the butt crack of dawn.

"Chef Levy," came the terse reply from the other side of the door. "And if you don't open this door in the next second, I'm leaving. The two of you can look like fools for the second time in this tournament."

Kenzie threw open the door just as a very shirtless Braxton emerged from the bedroom.

Chef Levy looked from Kenzie to Braxton. She crossed her arms and did that one eyebrow raise that somehow managed to be both terrifying and offensive.

"Uhhh," Braxton said.

"This isn't what it looks like," Kenzie said, adding to their collective stupidness.

"Please." Chef Levy rolled her eyes. "Do you honestly think that a) I have the slightest interest in your sex life, or b) that you're the first competitors to use your time for something other than winning?" She glared at Kenzie. "Although, after your first-round performance, I would have thought you'd be more interested in *not* embarrassing yourself again."

"I am," Kenzie assured the judge, who was quite possibly the most intimidating person she'd ever encountered.

Last night, Philippe had told her that Chef Levy was in the Israeli Mossad before she became a culinary magician. Kenzie decided right then that she'd happily take a cyanide pill rather than be interrogated by this woman.

Chef Levy hmphed. "Well, anyway, I'm here to tell you that the second round begins at eight o'clock tonight. You have until then to plan a recipe that centers around a theme."

"A theme?" Kenzie repeated.

Chef Levy looked at Kenzie like she was a carton of milk that had been left in the back of the fridge and discovered months later.

"A theme. Such as hope. Or technology. Illusion versus reality…." The judge threw up her hands. "Would you like me to choose one for you? Maybe I can even design and cook your dish? That way, it won't be a pile of shit on a plate like your last performance!"

"Thank you, Chef," Braxton said, recovering first. "We'll get working straight away."

"Just be ready for your makeup people by seven-thirty," Chef Levy snapped. "You won't be allowed to bring anything into the dome with you. All cooking and magic must be completed during your two hours in the dome."

"Yes, Chef," the two of them replied in unison.

Chef Levy was already marching back down the hallway. When Kenzie peeked out her doorway, she could hear Polly Berrywhite explaining the challenge—using far gentler language than Chef Levy had—to Philippe and Hiroto.

Kenzie shut her door and turned to Braxton.

"Okayyy," she began.

"Time," Braxton said, turning and heading for the kitchen.

"It's noon," Kenzie said, reading the digital clock over the stove.

"No. That's our theme for this challenge. Time.

"Aidan did something like this for one of our restaurants, and people were obsessed with it. Come on. It's going to take us all afternoon to get it right."

✳ ✳ ✳

"Are you sure about this?" Kenzie asked uncertainly.

196

Braxton was folded over the counter, his cheeks flushed and his breathing labored.

"Aidan could do this in his sleep," Braxton huffed as he stared at the clock hands that were made out of rolled seaweed. "I'll get it."

Kenzie watched the seaweed clock hands. They quivered. A little.

Sweat darkened Braxton's hairline as the nori hour hand crawled to two o'clock. The sushi made out of egg, scallion, and gold leaf in the two o'clock position began to rise into the air.

The sushi floated at a snail's pace over to the sticky note on the wall that had *Chef Sakai* written on it. Ten seconds later, the sushi completed its laborious journey across the room.

Kenzie stifled a yawn.

"I think it's time we reevaluate our strategy," Kenzie announced, getting a bottle of water out of the fridge and handing it to Braxton, who looked like he was about to pass out.

"I said I'd get it," Braxton replied, his voice thin.

"And I'm saying maybe we're going about this the wrong way."

At the look he gave her, Kenzie put her hands up defensively. "Look, I just think—"

"What?" Braxton snapped.

Kenzie planted her hands on her hips. "I think this flying sushi thing might have been Aidan's specialty, but it clearly isn't yours."

"Thanks for the vote of confidence." He slammed the water bottle down on the table and began to stalk away.

Kenzie didn't miss the way he wavered on his feet before catching himself.

"I'm not saying you aren't a talented culinary magician," she said, resting a hand on his forearm to keep him from running off. "I'm saying you're trying to be your brother, and you're not him. What's your culinary specialty?"

"Are you seriously trying to psychoanalyze me right now?!" Braxton fumed, shrugging out of her grasp.

"Quit being an ass." She grabbed his elbow and hauled him back. This boy was slipperier than the eel she'd fileted earlier during their sushi clock journey.

"Stop being a brat," he shot back.

They glared at each other. And then, they both broke into a grin.

When Kenzie reached up to brush a damp strand of hair from his forehead, Braxton leaned into her touch.

"What is your culinary specialty?" she asked again, softly enough that he had to bend his head even closer to hear her.

"I…don't have one," he admitted.

Kenzie tried not to let her surprise show. All the other competitors had a specialty. She'd assumed Braxton would have one too, seeing as he was the most talented culinary magician in the entire world. This seemed like the type of thing he would have explored in Magical Cooking 101.

"Okay," she said. "What kinds of magical cooking do you enjoy, then?"

"Enjoy?" He stared at her like she'd lost her marbles. "What the hell does that have to do with this challenge?"

Kenzie gave him a *duh* look. "We should play to our strengths out there, rather than trying to replicate someone else's masterpiece. So, what dishes do you like making the most?"

"Idon'tlikecooking."

Braxton spoke so quickly that it took Kenzie a few seconds to untangle what he'd just said.

"What?!"

Braxton lifted a shoulder. "It's always been my life. It wasn't something I liked or didn't like…it just was. And then, after Aid died, it became everything."

There was such intensity in Braxton's gaze that it was difficult to hold his stare.

"My family is depending on me, Kenzie. If I don't win this—" His voice broke.

"Hey." Kenzie reached up and cupped his cheek. "We're going to get through the second round, and then you're going to win this tournament. Okay?"

Braxton gave her a sharp look. "You do remember we're going to be competing against each other if we make it to the finale, right?"

Kenzie scoffed. "Braxton, I'm not an idiot. I know I don't stand a chance against you or the others."

When he opened his mouth to protest, Kenzie held up a hand.

"I'm seriously cool with it," she assured him. "I came here because I wanted to know if this magic stuff was actually real or just some figment of my imagination." *And because Polly made it pretty clear that if I didn't agree, those Gourmand people would hunt me down the same way they did to Loretta and Max....*

She cleared her throat. "And, once I believed it was all real, I wanted to learn more about how it all works. You helped me with that, even though I'm sure it was the last thing you wanted to spend your time doing. So thank you."

Kenzie still didn't know why her magic seemed to work differently from everyone else's and where exactly it had come from. She didn't want to believe her dad had been lying to her for her entire life.

"The truth is," she continued, "even if I was good enough to win the tournament, I don't have some kind of a great, unfulfilled desire." She shrugged. "I don't know what I'd wish for even if by some miracle I got the truffle. So, even once we're in the finale—" *And they would make it to the finale…* "—I'm going to do everything I can to help you win."

Braxton nodded. Cleared his throat. Nodded again.

"Kenzie," he began, and then stopped. He rubbed the back of his neck. He looked…odd. Uncomfortable. *No, vulnerable.*

"My family's in trouble," he said, his attention fixed on the wall behind Kenzie. "I need this wish to fix things for them."

When he finally brought his gaze to hers, the openness in his expression cracked her chest wide open.

Braxton was always so cool and collected. She felt honored that he'd let her see beyond the image he projected to everyone else.

"Well, then." She swept her palm out to indicate the kitchen. "Let's figure out how we're going to blow all the other participants out of the water. Because I refuse to go down to Crazy Esther and Rick."

Braxton smiled. "I like the way you think, baby."

CHAPTER 25

BRAXTON

After what felt like minutes, but was actually hours, the two of them stood in the center of the kitchen and surveyed their creations.

"We might actually pull this off," Braxton said, shaking his head in amazement.

"Don't sound so surprised," Kenzie teased.

She had her hair up in a high ponytail and was wearing only a tank top and denim shorts. Braxton had no idea how he'd managed to accomplish any cooking with the way she paraded around the kitchen in that little outfit. Every time she turned around and he glimpsed the way those shorts hugged her curves, he had to swallow a groan.

Kenzie tossed him a water and then pulled herself up onto the counter. She swung her legs as she twisted the cap off her own bottle.

"You know," she said, "I think I'm getting the hang of this magical cooking thing." She stretched her arms over her head and flexed her fingers.

"You're getting better," he acknowledged.

Kenzie scoffed. "I'm getting *fantastic*, I think you mean."

Braxton shook his head, although he couldn't disagree. Over the last few hours, he'd witnessed a change come over her. She was more sure of her food and her magic. More than once, he'd found himself just stopping to watch her. There was a quiet confidence about her as she moved around the kitchen.

Kenzie's dishes were imaginative and complex. She didn't abide by any of the rules he'd been trained to follow, and her skills had seemed to grow before his eyes.

Braxton went to join Kenzie, leaning against the cool granite counter.

"Thank you," he murmured.

"For what?" Kenzie quirked an eyebrow.

"All of this." He gestured to the magical dishes they'd created together. "I…had fun."

The observation was a shock to his system. Braxton had lost his love of magical cooking—if he'd ever had it in the first place—the day Aidan died and their family's future fell on his shoulders.

It was more than his enjoyment of cooking that Kenzie had awakened, though. Braxton's magic was more powerful because he'd given in to his instincts rather than leaning so heavily on Aidan's past successes.

"You were right," he admitted.

Kenzie perked up at that. "Of course I was."

"And so modest," Braxton grumbled.

Kenzie laughed, and the sound filled places inside him he hadn't even known were empty. Kenzie plucked a chocolate-covered strawberry off the tray of fruit they'd magically enhanced to start yelling at whoever ate them.

"Murderer!" the strawberry cried. "Cutthroat! Savage!"

The accusations became more muted and garbled as Kenzie chewed and swallowed.

Braxton watched her as she licked melted chocolate off her fingers.

Did she have any idea what she did to him?

Their gazes locked. There was no mistaking the way Kenzie's gray eyes sparked with…something. She cocked her head at him. It looked like an invitation.

Braxton pushed off the counter and faced her. Kenzie's legs parted, making a space for him that he didn't hesitate to move into. With her sitting on the counter, they were the same height.

He leaned in, stopping when his lips were a hair's breadth from hers. Kenzie closed the gap. Their lips fused together in a kiss that instantly stole the breath from his lungs.

She tasted like chocolate strawberries and something uniquely Kenzie. With his first taste, he was addicted. He'd never get enough of her.

Braxton thrust his hands into Kenzie's hair, guiding her face to the angle he wanted. Kenzie moaned into his mouth, and all thoughts of going slowly vanished.

His kiss was rough to the point of bruising, but he couldn't make himself ease up. Judging from the way she locked her legs around his waist, she didn't want him to.

Braxton pulled back to look at her. Their ragged breathing filled the kitchen.

"Why'd you stop?" she whispered.

He waited a second for his thundering pulse to quiet. "Do you want this?" he asked.

What he really meant was, *Do you want* me?

Kenzie's legs tightened around his waist in answer.

Braxton cracked a smile at that. "You've got a possessive streak, don't you?"

He leaned forward until their foreheads rested against each other.

"Just in case you still have any doubts about my feelings," Kenzie murmured, "try this on for size. When I close my eyes, there's only one man's face I see." She reached up to cup Braxton's cheek. "Yours."

Her words untangled the tension knotted in his stomach.

"Yeah?" He brushed his lips over hers. Even that gentle contact sent his pulse skyrocketing.

"Mhm."

Braxton was about to lose himself in another kiss, when Kenzie's door opened. Hiroto stood in the doorway with his chef coat on. His focus zeroed in on Braxton and Kenzie, and he let out a hearty guffaw.

"Oh, hell yeah!" Hiroto pumped his fist.

Braxton reluctantly backed away from Kenzie and raised an eyebrow at his friend.

"Philippe and I had a bet going," Hiroto explained, still grinning like a fool. "He didn't think you two would get it on until the tournament was over. But I had more faith."

"Uhhh," Kenzie said.

"How much did you win?" Braxton asked, curious.

Hiroto's face fell. "One USD."

Braxton snorted.

Hiroto wandered into the kitchen, eyeing the chocolate-covered fruit platter on the counter.

"Do your friends often make bets on your love life?" Kenzie asked Braxton.

Hiroto scoffed. "What love life?"

Kenzie's lip twitched, but she gave no other indication about what she was thinking.

Braxton glared at his friend. Hiroto shot him a panicked look and mouthed *Oops.*

It was true Braxton didn't usually hesitate around someone he wanted to sleep with. But Kenzie wasn't just some itch he needed to scratch.

After he won the tournament, some of the weight of his family's empire would be lifted off his shoulders. Maybe he could convince Kenzie to come back to Sydney with him instead of returning to dreary middle-of-nowhere Tennessee.

Let's not get ahead of ourselves, mate.

They still needed to get through this tournament. And that meant eliminating another team from this round…ideally Crazy Esther and Rick. And if the clock hanging on the wall was any indication—

"Holy shit," Braxton exclaimed. "We need to get to the dome."

"Never thought I'd see the day," Hiroto said, shaking his head. "The unflappable Braxton McKaid has been thoroughly flapped." He gave Kenzie a thumbs-up. And then he popped a chocolate-covered cherry in his mouth.

A muffled "Fuck you, bitch!" came from the cherry in Hiroto's mouth.

* * *

By the time they reached the private hallway that led from their living quarters to the dome's entrance, the rest of the competitors were already there. Rick, whose bruises had almost completely healed, was exchanging smirks and secret looks with Crazy Esther. Philippe's face was white as a sheet, and he was standing a little apart from the rest of them. Their makeup artists buzzed around them.

Braxton felt serene as he buttoned his chef coat. He was confident in the dish they'd conceptualized together, and more than that, he was confident in his partnership with Kenzie. They'd gotten their kitchen dance into such a honed rhythm that they didn't even need to talk. They both knew what had to be done, and they did it.

In two hours, they'd be in the finale.

"Good luck, mate," Braxton told Hiroto, holding out a hand as the applause on the other side of the door grew louder.

He offered his hand to Philippe, who hesitated before shaking it.

"You okay?" Braxton asked, noticing the sweat beaded on Philippe's brow.

His friend offered a wobbly smile. "Just nerves. Never done anything this big before."

"We'll try not to embarrass you all too badly," Kenzie piped up, giving Philippe a warm hug.

Braxton heard Rick's derisive snort, but he didn't so much as look in the asshole's direction. Soon, Braxton would be done with Rick and free from the Santiori family's hold over his own.

Soon, his family would be free.

The six of them entered the dome to the roar of the crowd. Braxton watched Kenzie to see if her stage fright would emerge, but she looked as calm and ready as he felt.

Braxton noticed that the dome's glass panes had all been repaired since the disastrous first round.

As they all lined up in front of the judges, Braxton glanced out at the audience. His seats were still empty, but the sight of Hiroto's sister waving frantically at her brother raised his spirits. The chubby little girl was holding up a sign in each hand, one in English and one in Japanese. The one in English was written in clumsy block lettering and said, *My brother is the best chef EVER!!!*

"You've really got your sister fooled, mate," Braxton joked to Hiroto as Polly Berrywhite explained their second-round theme challenge to the audience.

"Don't I know it," Hiroto replied, giving his sister a small wave.

Philippe still seemed to be suffering from a bad case of nerves. Braxton hoped for all of their sakes that he pulled himself together. He really didn't want him and Kenzie to have deal with Esther and Rick in the finale. At least if he was competing against his friends, he knew no one was going to play dirty.

And yeah, Rick and Esther were definitely planning something dirty. While Polly droned on, Braxton caught the pair exchange more than one knowing look.

Instead of simply focusing on his dish, Braxton would need to be on the watch for those psychos trying to knife him and Kenzie in the back.

Bloody fantastic.

The mood turned somber when Polly asked everyone to observe a minute of silence for Farley. As soon as the minute was up, Polly's smile returned.

"Best of luck to all of you," she boomed, her voice filling every corner of the dome. "Not that any of you will be needing luck, of course. Just your skills, determination, and a little bit of magic." She winked at them.

"Any questions?"

"No, Chef!" they chorused.

"Let's cook some magic!"

After that, Braxton's world narrowed to Kenzie, their food, and his magic. Nothing else existed.

Thanks to Kenzie's reworking of his original plan, they were making a trio of cakes, stacked one on top of the other. Each cake contained a different flavor and magic based around their time theme. Three cakes for three elements of time: past, present, and future. A clock face made out of fondant numbers would hover over the entire concoction.

Braxton knew the idea would be a winning one, since it was a rule of magic that culinary magicians could only control one kind of magic at a time. They'd be doing several…because the rules of magic didn't apply to Kenzie.

As Braxton watched her move around the kitchen in a blur of controlled motion, he couldn't help but be awed by her. At the start of all of this, he'd thought he was getting the short end of the stick by being assigned to be her partner.

He couldn't have been more wrong.

Braxton might be the one with all the magical experience, but she'd taught him just as much.

"So, chefs, what have we got here?"

Braxton looked up from his work and into Polly Berrywhite's smiling face. She'd added another choker of diamonds, and with the spotlights directly over their work station, her jewelry was blinding. The other two judges stood on either side of Polly with their arms crossed and wearing matching frowns.

"Our theme is time," Kenzie answered. She held up a sprig of thyme and grinned. "Get it?"

Polly clapped her hands and cooed. "Wonderful, dears. Just wonderful!"

"I certainly hope you've got more than a homophone if you're expecting to get to the finale," Chef Levy groused, making Polly's friendly smile fade.

"We do," Kenzie assured the sour-faced judge as she used a pair of tweezers to position white thyme flowers on top of her of cake.

Braxton focused on shaping the fondant minute hand he'd just rolled out. They wouldn't be relying on Aidan's magic for the main part of their dish, but their performance would still be a tribute to his twin's magic.

Braxton held up a ruler to the fondant number 2. He used a paring knife to straighten the edges.

He put down the fondant number and turned to his saucepan. He swirled the sugar, which would be the basis for his bacon brittle…part of the *past* cake.

"And what's the magic?" Chef Sakai asked. He dipped his finger in a bowl of in-progress batter, tasted it, and grimaced.

Just wait, you cantankerous ass.

"Past, present, and future," Braxton answered. "Three kinds of cake, magically infused with memories, clarity, and future predictions that will be tailor-made for each of you.

All three judges' eyebrows rose in tandem.

"That…isn't possible," Polly said slowly.

"It is for us," Kenzie said brightly.

Polly looked troubled. The other two judges just seemed like their perpetually-annoyed selves.

"Hope you idiots haven't bitten off more than you can chew," Chef Levy grumbled.

"Hmph," said Chef Sakai.

"I simply can't wait to taste your creation!" Polly gushed. She looked at the digital clock hanging over their heads. "And look at that. It's almost *time*."

With that witty observation, she ambled off after the other two judges.

Braxton turned to Kenzie, who was holding a spoon out to him.

"Taste," she commanded.

He did, closing his eyes when the salty and sweet caramel ganache hit his tongue.

"More sugar?" Kenzie asked, her voice barely audible over the other sounds in the dome.

Braxton nodded and then leaned in so his lips were at the level of her ear. "I'm going to need a lot more sugar from you later." He gave her a look that made her cheeks turn a pretty pink. "But the ganache is fine."

Kenzie let out a bark of laughter as she turned back to her cake. With their station hiding their lower bodies from view, and the judges' attention elsewhere, Braxton gave Kenzie's butt a little smack.

He'd never had so much fun cooking in his entire life. And it was all because of her.

"Ohh, you're going to pay for that one, mister," Kenzie warned. "Just you wait."

Braxton raised an eyebrow and grinned at her. "Bring it, baby."

CHAPTER 26

KENZIE

Kenzie was having a blast. She wasn't worried about the thousand people who were staring at her like she was a specimen in a tank. She barely even noticed the audience.

The other participants were running around the dome like headless chickens. Crazy Esther and Rick seemed to be in the midst of a heated argument about something, but Kenzie didn't care enough to try and listen in.

She was too busy putting the final touches on their masterpiece.

The cakes looked beautiful. Every component was delicious. And their magic was flawless. It was the trifecta of a finale-worthy dish. She couldn't wait to see the crow-eating expressions on Chef Levy and Sakai's faces.

Since Kenzie and Braxton hadn't even gotten to present their dish during the first round—not that she was complaining—they were first up this time. Braxton carried their trio of cakes to the judges' table. He was using his magic to levitate a clock made out of fondant high enough over the dish that everyone could clearly see it.

Kenzie followed behind, trying not to draw attention to the awkward angle of her hands. She didn't want to make anyone suspicious about the final part of their dish.

While everyone's attention was on Braxton, she quickly slid her invisible load onto the corner of the judges' table.

"The theme we chose is time," Braxton said, flourishing his hand at their clock-shaped tower of cakes. "Obviously." He turned to the audience and offered them a grin and a little shrug.

Appreciative laughter resounded from the crowd.

As Kenzie listened to Braxton describe their dish, she almost didn't recognize him as the same person she'd cooked with during the first round. He was relaxed, and amusement was sparking in his green eyes.

It was probably egotistical of her, but Kenzie couldn't help but think she was the catalyst behind Braxton's newfound joy in the kitchen.

"Three cakes," Braxton was explaining to the judges, "each to represent the past, present, and future. We'd like to invite you into the past with a flavor that is both salty and sweet."

He's killing it, Kenzie thought, trying not to let her delight be too apparent on her face. Even the impossible-to-impresses Chefs Levy and Sakai were on the edge of their seats.

You've got this, Kenzie thought as Braxton closed his eyes.

He didn't disappoint.

The audience oohed and aahed as the fondant clock hands hovering above the cakes began to move. Braxton made them spin backward, as though time were reversing itself.

The clock hands moved faster and faster until they were a blur of motion. After a few seconds, the clock hands stopped.

"Let's see if you're anything more than a clever storyteller," Chef Levy grumbled. She squinted at the caramel frosting that was studded with sea salt and shards of maple bacon brittle.

Braxton took the knife and spatula off the judges table and gave them a winning smile. "Allow me," he offered.

This next part was all up to Kenzie.

While Braxton slowly and methodically cut the salted caramel cake, Kenzie focused on her magic. She knew she could do it; she'd done something similar back at *Good Ol' Apple Pie*, back before she'd had any clue what she was doing.

The magical spider web appeared in her mind without much effort, since she'd already known exactly what she was looking for. She wove the threads together so they connected the slices of cake to each of the judges. She plucked on the invisible threads of magic like they were musical instruments that existed only in her mind.

As soon as the judges took their first bites, the shimmering threads of magic became stronger. Kenzie began to get glimpses into the judges' minds. The point was to impress them, not piss them off, so she made sure the memories the chefs were about to see were happy ones.

When Kenzie was finished, she gave Braxton a subtle nod.

Chef Sakai and Levy examined their slices of cake. Chef Sakai took a measuring tape out of his pocket, held it up to the frosting, and frowned. Chef Levy had her nose almost buried in the cake.

Sweet, old Polly Berrywhite didn't bother with looking for flaws— which, by the way, didn't exist—and shoved an enormous bite into her mouth.

"Mmmm!" she exclaimed as she chewed.

Now or never, Kenzie told herself.

She tugged on the loose strands of magic that connected Polly to her slice of cake. She concentrated on the flavors…salty and sweet—the tastes of the past. She looked into Polly's gentle, wrinkled face and let the magic take hold.

Polly's fork was poised over her slice of cake when she froze. Her eyes widened comically.

Kenzie got a glimpse of the woman's memory seconds before a stream of mist rose and congealed above Polly Berrywhite's head for everyone to see. Unlike her forgotten memory stew that she'd made at the diner, these conjured memories weren't just inside the eater's head. It was like watching a grainy movie on a pixilated screen: the images were blurry but legible.

A young girl skipped through a park, singing to herself and dragging a doll through the long grass.

"My heavens, that's me!" Polly gasped.

The little girl in the memory let out a squeal of delight as a tall man came into the image and scooped her up. He spun her around in a circle, making the little girl's dress fan out as she giggled and hung onto his neck.

"I love you, Daddy!" Little Polly said as she kissed the man's cheek.

The mist dissipated, and quiet descended on the dome.

The silence was interrupted when Polly loudly blew her nose into a napkin.

"That is one of my most joyful memories," she said in a wobbly voice. "My father's been dead for thirty years." She gave Kenzie and Braxton a wobbly smile. "Thank you, my dears."

The other two went similarly. Chef Sakai's memory was of him making mochi beside his grandmother. When the memory ended, Kenzie got her first glimpse of a smile on the chef's face. Chef Levy's memory was of her, floating in the Dead Sea. She was hand-in-hand with boy who had tanned skin and a devastating smile.

Chef Levy's expression didn't change, but Kenzie thought she saw a shininess to the judge's eyes that hadn't been there before. And when Chef Levy criticized their dish, her insults didn't hold their usual rancor.

Braxton made the hands of the clock spin again. This time, they moved forward in time. Braxton stopped them at 8:05; the exact time that was reflected on the dome's digital clock.

"Time for the present," Braxton announced.

The olive oil and thyme sponge covered with cream cheese frosting had an intentionally gentler taste compared to the other flavors.

While the judges ate, Kenzie began to tug on the strings of magic that she'd woven into the fondant numbers earlier. Shifting closer to Braxton, she slipped her hand into his.

This was the most complicated part of their performance, since both of their magic needed to work together. Kenzie made the fondant numbers unwind from their original shapes and transform into letters.

Braxton made the letters rise even higher into the air, where everyone could see them as they arranged themselves into words.

The quote, *Live in the now* hovered in the air where everyone could see it.

Kenzie waited until the audience's applause died down before magically untwisting the letters and forming them into a new message.

Today is a gift.

Kenzie wasn't normally big on inspirational quotes, but it had been surprisingly difficult to think of twelve-letter messages that revolved around time and the present moment. Besides, with the way the audience was cheering, Kenzie didn't really think anyone cared what words the letters spelled. They were just excited by the magic.

So was she.

After Kenzie returned the fondant to their numerical shapes and Braxton had settled them back into the shape of a clock, she turned to look at him. They were both breathing hard, but energy coursed between them. She gave his hand a quick squeeze, which he returned.

Last up was the future cake.

Braxton made the hands of the clock spin forward. Kenzie sliced the orange blossom and honeysuckle sponge cake with lemon poppyseed buttercream. The flavors were light and tasted like new beginnings.

As soon as the judges' attention was on the cake, Braxton released his magical hold on the fondant numbers. He caught them as they fell out of the air and put them on the side of the judges' table, so he'd be ready for their final display of magic.

"Too much orange zest," Chef Sakai grumbled.

"If there's lemon in here, I can't taste it," Chef Levy griped.

"I could eat this for days!" Polly said, polishing off her entire slice and gesturing for Braxton to cut her another.

"Where's the magic?" barked Chef Levy.

Holding back a grin, Kenzie released the last bunch of magical threads she'd been controlling. The invisible plate she'd put onto the judges' table earlier shimmered into existence.

It was a small cake that was an exact replica—albeit larger—of the wish truffle that the tournament winner would receive. She'd made the filling and Braxton had decorated it, since he was the only one of the two of them who had ever seen a wish truffle before.

The cake's rounded top was covered in a glossy strawberry ganache that was pale pink in color. Beneath the ganache was a white truffle shell. They'd had to make an educated guess about the interior's flavors, since apparently only the truffle's maker knew the actual ingredients that went into it. They'd made a champagne mousse infused with elderflower. Elegant and delicious.

Using magic he'd learned from his brother, Braxton floated the truffle cake off its tray until it hovered directly between him and Kenzie.

The audience roared in approval.

"I think this cake is trying to tell you something about the future, Chefs," Braxton said, somehow managing to keep a straight face.

Polly stood up from her chair and applauded them.

"I don't know how you managed all that magic for a single dish," she said, giving Kenzie a strange look that was a mix of appreciation and puzzlement. "But I think we can all agree that what you've accomplished is *impressive.*"

Chef Levy and Sakai stayed seated, but Kenzie didn't think she was imagining the amusement on their faces.

She glanced at the audience outside the glass-paneled dome. Every single person was on their feet, cheering and shouting their names.

Kenzie turned to Braxton. She raised her hand for a high-five. Instead of slapping her palm, he lifted her off her feet and spun her around. The cheers from the audience grew deafening.

When Braxton put her down, Kenzie caught sight of Rick and Esther. The two of them wore matching expressions on their faces. It wasn't friendly.

Mental reminder: lock suite doors until the finale....

Kenzie barely managed to keep from skipping as she and Braxton went back to their stations. After what they'd just accomplished, there was nothing the other competitors could do to outshine them. There was no way Kenzie and Braxton wouldn't make it into the finale.

All eyes turned on Philippe and Hiroto as they brought their creation to the judges' table. The two of them were carrying what looked like an edible chess board. It was wobbling a little because Philippe was shaking. His face was shiny from sweat, and his lips were pressed so tightly they'd gone bloodless.

For someone who always seemed so easy-going about everything, Philippe looked ready to keel over.

Kenzie tried to give him an encouraging look, but all of his attention was on his edible chess board. They all breathed a sigh of relief when the pair managed to get the chess board down on the table without Philippe's nerves ruining their creation.

It really was beautiful. Their theme was light and dark, and every time the judges ate a chess piece, there was a corresponding burst of white or black sparks that hovered above the judges' table for a few seconds. They started with the pawns. When the judges got to the bishops and knights, the white and black sparks shot higher.

Chefs Sakai and Levy complained about the flavor of each chess piece. The white pieces had been made with light ingredients, like coconut and ricotta. The pair had used dark-colored ingredients, like coffee and black sesame, for the black pieces. When Chef Sakai and Chef Levy ate the white and black rooks at the same time, a simultaneous burst of white and black sparks flew into the air. The colors intermingled, illuminating the entire dome in shimmery black and white. The queens had an even bigger reaction. Black and white sparks showered down from the dome's ceiling like fireworks.

Everyone held their breath as they waited for the climax, when Polly picked up the black king and Chef Levy raised the white king to her lips.

"Wait," Chef Levy commanded.

Polly's expectant gaze fell. She closed her mouth and looked longingly at the edible king in her palm.

Chef Levy sniffed the white king. "Who made this?" she barked.

"I did, Chef," Hiroto said, stepping forward.

"What's in it?" she snapped.

"It's vanilla bean cheesecake, Chef," Hiroto replied, turning to give Philippe a puzzled shrug. "There's sour cream, vanilla extract, eggs—"

"It smells bitter." Chef Levy loudly sniffed the chess piece. She thrust it at Hiroto. "I wouldn't feed this garbage to my dog. If you're so confident in your cooking, you eat it."

"Yes, Chef."

Hiroto took the king piece and, without an ounce of hesitation, bit the top off.

Kenzie realized she was holding her breath, even though she didn't know what she should be nervous about. Vanilla cheesecake wasn't exactly rocket science.

When Hiroto didn't immediately keel over, she relaxed.

The audience began to applaud as a shower of white sparks bounced off the ceiling and fell back down. Kenzie joined in the applause as Polly stuffed the black king in her mouth and black fireworks joined the white.

"Wow," Kenzie said to Braxton, needing to shout over the deafening applause and crackling sparks that continued to fall. "This is amazing."

Not as good as their time cakes, but a close second.

Braxton didn't respond. He was looking up at the fireworks, his brow creased. He looked mad, or worried….

The black sparks had faded away, but the white were still going strong. In fact, they were getting brighter.

No…not brighter. They were transforming into balls of fire.

What the—

Braxton grabbed Kenzie and shoved her toward the exit, just as the flaming particles began to multiply. One of the fireballs struck Hiroto and Philippe's stove. There must have been some oil on the surface, because the fireball transformed into a wall of flame.

Heat blasted Kenzie's cheek as white fire erupted from the stove. An acrid smell filled the air.

Everyone was running and shouting. The dome had turned into complete chaos.

Kenzie had almost reached the exit when she saw Hiroto go down. At first, she figured someone had tripped him. Then, she saw his body start to convulse. Thick, white foam bubbled out of his mouth.

Kenzie screamed and started toward him.

"Go!" Braxton shouted, giving her push toward the exit before doubling back for Hiroto.

Yeah right.

Kenzie followed, almost getting trampled by Esther, Rick, and Polly who were racing in the opposite direction. Philippe was on his knees beside

Hiroto. He was tugging on his partner's arm, trying to get him away from the spreading flames.

"Come on," Philippe begged Hiroto as he struggled to haul the other man to his feet. But Philippe was about as wide as a twig, and Hiroto was easily double his weight.

Braxton bent down and lifted Hiroto's torso. Kenzie grasped one of his legs while Philippe took the other. The three of them shuffled Hiroto's dead weight out of the dome as the white fireballs continued to fall around them.

Kenzie cried out when one burned through her sleeve and scorched her skin, but she didn't let go of Hiroto.

They didn't stop until they'd gotten out of the dome. Then, they all just collapsed.

Philippe, his leg dripping blood, crawled over to his partner. "Hiroto. Hiroto!" He shook his friend, who was still convulsing and coughing up white foam.

Hiroto's eyes were wide with terror. He was trying to speak, but all that came out of his mouth were more choking sounds.

"Help!" Kenzie yelled. "Someone help!"

Seconds or minutes later, paramedics were there, loading Hiroto onto a stretcher and taking him away.

More paramedics swarmed Kenzie, Braxton, and Philippe. The judges hovered nearby, their heads bent close together as they spoke in quiet voices.

…pushed his magic past its limits.

…ingredients that shouldn't have been combined.

…terrible accident.

Kenzie's first and only thought was *No freaking way.* Hiroto was too talented to not understand his limits or mix toxic ingredients. This had been done to him. And she had a damn good idea about whose fault it was.

Swatting away the paramedic who were trying to bandage her forearm, she marched down the hall, ignoring Braxton as he called after her.

Kenzie headed straight for Rick's suite.

CHAPTER 27

KENZIE

Kenzie slammed the door to her suite hard enough to make the whole wall rattle.

She was furious. Like punch someone in the face furious. She wasn't normally a violent person, but there was only so much she could take.

"Guilty until proven innocent," she mimicked, repeating what those worthless judges had told her. She continued to mock their useless platitudes as she banged around the kitchen in her suite.

When she confronted Rick and Esther after the disaster in the dome, they'd been quick to point out that they weren't anywhere near Hiroto and Philippe's station during the entire two hours. That fact had been corroborated by tournament security people reviewing all the video feeds.

But Kenzie wasn't an idiot. She knew someone had tampered with that game piece, and it didn't take a genius to know it was those two. She just couldn't prove anything.

Braxton had gone into Philippe's suite to be with him while they waited for news about Hiroto. Kenzie, with nothing else to do but fume, had decided to cook dinner. It was either that, or go back into Esther's room and kill the crazy bitch.

Kenzie could hear music coming from Esther's room, where she and Rick had been toasting their default entrance in the finale for the past hour.

And judging from the loud moans and wall thumps coming from that direction, they were doing a whole lot more than drinking.

Kenzie cursed and just barely resisted the urge to throw something.

Chef Sakai had come by their rooms earlier to deliver the curt decision he and the other judges had made. Simply that, even if Hiroto got better and was able to compete, the *mistaken* mixture of ingredients in his chess piece warranted elimination from the finale…even without them tasting Rick and Esther's dish. That meant Braxton, Kenzie, Esther, and Rick would be competing in the finale for the wish truffle.

Philippe had been informed that he needed to pack and vacate the premises by midnight.

"Just a mistake," Kenzie mimicked, repeating the words Yamosato Sakai had told her. "Terrible things can happen when magic is misused. *Meh meh meh meh meh.*"

She worked the dough for her homemade linguini until it was the right consistency. Then, she cut the dough and fed pieces through the pasta extruder. When they were the right thickness, she dusted the strands with flour and set them on a sheet to dry.

What Kenzie really wanted was a punching bag, but since she didn't have one, she was attempting to cook off her frustration. After the day they'd had, she figured she, Braxton, and Philippe at least deserved a good dinner. So, she was making Ashner's signature dish—linguini with squid ink sauce.

She'd already cleaned and cut the squid and prepared the ingredients for her sauce. All that was left was to combine them and cook her pasta.

Kenzie added her tomato, garlic, onion, and parsley puree to a pan of hot olive oil. There was a harsh sizzle as the ingredients hit the pan before everything settled to a pleasant simmer. Kenzie's face was bathed with garlicy-herb steam.

Once the flavors were combined, she added the squid ink, along with a bay leaf and fresh ground pepper.

She hadn't made this dish in five years, but it was so familiar she barely needed to think about what she was doing. As her hands put the ingredients together, her mind was free to recall all the times she'd made this dish while standing side-by-side with her father.

He would make the linguini while she focused on the sauce. They'd both be belting out the lyrics of whatever band Kenzie was obsessed with at the moment. Sometimes, Danny was there, too. He'd be chopping onions, and her dad would make fun of him for crying because he was so happy to be with them.

Kenzie stared into the black squid ink sauce. She'd been making this very dish when she found out her boyfriend was dead.

Fucking hell. Why hadn't she decided to make pizza for dinner?

She glanced over at her phone resting on the edge of the counter. With everything that had happened in the last week, she hadn't called her dad back. As she prepared her father's signature dish, she was overcome with an urge to talk to him.

Kenzie even wiped her hands on a dish towel and went over to her phone. She picked it up, debating whether she was ready to talk to her dad. She brought the phone back over to her sauce. She stirred while contemplating whether to make the call.

Kenzie was just about to dial the number when movement in her open doorway made her forget all about her phone.

Braxton stood there, staring not so much at her as through her. His hair was wild and his eyes bloodshot.

Kenzie didn't say anything. As long as the silence continued, there was hope…some possibility that whatever Braxton was about to tell her wouldn't be horrible.

"He—" Braxton began. "Hiroto—"

Braxton sagged against the doorframe.

"He didn't make it."

Kenzie stood there, her hand still mechanically stirring her sauce, as her brain tried to make sense of Braxton's words.

He didn't make it.

"I'm gonna go help Philippe pack," Braxton mumbled. "He's…fuck, Kenzie. He's wrecked."

Even though Kenzie's body had gone numb, she started toward him, stopping when Braxton put up a hand and shook his head. "I can't," he said. "I'll come see you once Philippe's gone." He turned and disappeared back down the hall before Kenzie could get a word out.

She was debating whether to go after him, when the door across the hall opened. Esther, her leather dress askew, poked her head out.

"Something smells…interesting." She swiped her tongue over her lips and pranced into Kenzie's suite without waiting for an invitation.

Not that she would have gotten one.

She knew Esther and Rick were responsible for what happened to Hiroto. She knew it in her bones. She just couldn't prove it.

"Get lost," Kenzie snarled at the other girl.

Esther ignored the command. She came into the kitchen and put her face over Kenzie's squid ink sauce. She inhaled.

Crazy Esther let out a high-pitched squeal of delight.

"Was that going to be for me or Rick?" she asked, bouncing on her bare feet in excitement.

"Neither of you," Kenzie snapped.

Esther's smile broadened. "You're going to kill Braxton?! Oh!" She clapped her hands. "I didn't think you had it in you, Number Eight."

Kenzie was torn between kicking this psycho out of her room and demanding to know what the hell she was talking about. She went with the latter.

"What the hell are you talking about?" Kenzie demanded.

Esther flashed Kenzie a smile that was all teeth.

"Le poison," she said in a fake French accent. She pointed at Kenzie's sauce.

"It's squid ink, genius," Kenzie told her.

"It's *magically-poisoned* squid ink," Esther said. She hovered her face over the saucepan and inhaled again. "Smells strong. Probably dissolve your entire digestive system."

Kenzie's muscles locked up. Her blood turned to ice.

"You're lying," Kenzie whispered.

"Want me to feed a drop to your chameleon so you can see what it does?" Esther asked hopefully.

"Don't—" Kenzie choked. "Don't you dare."

"Lucky little reptile," Esther cooed in a baby voice, bending down until she was eye-level with Kiwi's habitat. To Kenzie, she said, "I know my poisons. And that?" She twirled her finger at the sauce. "Is one powerful poison."

"Get out," Kenzie whispered.

"Wanna sell me the recipe? I'll pay you—"

"Get out!" Kenzie shrieked.

Esther gave her a pouty look before flouncing out of the suite and slamming the door behind her.

Kenzie had no idea how long she just stood there. Her sauce boiled down to the dregs, until all the liquid evaporated. A charred, acrid smell rose from the ruined pot and finally compelled Kenzie to dump everything in the sink.

Probably dissolve your entire digestive system.

Kenzie remembered her dad's lawyer talking about how the meal he'd fed Aidan McKaid had burned up the boy's whole digestive tract. The medical examiner had been stumped, since Aidan's toxicology report hadn't shown anything that should have caused that kind of reaction.

Somehow, Kenzie had just recreated the poison her dad had used to kill Aidan McKaid.

God, she was an idiot. And naïve. So goddamn naïve.

Kenzie had assumed that, since she'd never seen her dad perform culinary magic, she hadn't inherited her ability from him.

Of course she'd gotten it from him.

Braxton had tried to tell her, but she'd refused to listen. Kenzie hadn't wanted to believe she'd lived with someone who had lied to her for seventeen years. Her dad was the one adult in her life who she'd always trusted without question. He'd taken care of her…loved her. He never would have lied to her, especially about something so important.

And yet, the irrefutable truth was there before her eyes. Her father was a culinary magician. He'd passed the ability to Kenzie. And he'd never told her the truth about what she was.

The only question that remained was whether Walter Ashner had poisoned Aidan deliberately or by accident.

She grabbed her phone off the counter, but she didn't pull up the number for Rikers. Her dad had been lying to her for seventeen years. What made her think he's start being honest with her now?

Kenzie knew that if she had any hope of getting answers from her dad, she'd have to confront him in person.

It was already long past the prison visiting hours for the day.

Tomorrow. Tomorrow, she was going to Rikers Island. She was going to talk to her dad. And he was going to tell her everything.

CHAPTER 28

BRAXTON

Philippe had been shut in his bedroom with Raina for the last hour. Braxton could hear Raina's soft voice and the muffled sound of Philippe's sobs through the closed door.

Hiroto was dead.

Braxton stopped pacing when the bedroom door opened. Raina came out with a small duffle slung over her shoulder. She gave Braxton a wobbly smile. Philippe followed her, rolling two suitcases behind him.

Raina put her arms around Braxton and reached up to kiss both his cheeks. Emotion weighed on him, nearly dragging him to his knees.

"Good luck in the finale," she whispered. "We'll be cheering for you."

Braxton swallowed repeatedly until he could speak without breaking down.

"Thanks, Raina. Do you mind if I talk to Philippe alone for a minute?"

She nodded. "Take your time." She left the suite, closing the door softly behind her.

For a few seconds, the two of them just stared at each other.

"So, uh, look me up the next time you're in France," Philippe said. He started to wheel his suitcases to the door, but Braxton moved into his path.

"Why'd you do it, mate?"

Braxton had meant the question to be an accusation. Instead, he just sounded tired. Defeated.

"Do what?" Philippe shifted from foot to foot.

"Are you really going to play that game with me?" Braxton demanded, his blood heating. "I know you did something to that game piece. I thought you were just nervous before we went in, but it was more than that, wasn't it? You knew something was going to happen."

Philippe mumbled something indiscernible that sounded like *magical mistake*.

In two strides, Braxton had Philippe by his collar.

"Hiroto didn't make magical mistakes," Braxton growled. "So, I'll ask you again. Why. The fuck. Did you do it?"

Philippe stopped his pointless struggle. His entire body seemed to deflate.

"They said no one would end up eating it," Philippe choked, wiping at the tears running down his face. "They said it would make the piece smell rotten enough that the judges wouldn't want to eat it, and then we'd get kicked out. I didn't know. Braxton, I swear, I didn't know—"

He sagged in Braxton's grip, sobbing uncontrollably.

Braxton gave Philippe a hard shake to get his attention. "Who?" he demanded. "Esther and Rick?"

"Just Rick," Philippe managed in a hoarse whisper. "He…he came to my suite. Gave me an ingredient and offered me ten grand to put it into Hiroto's batter. I refused."

Philippe's heavy breathing filled the otherwise-silent room. "Then, Rick said he wanted to show me something. He had a fucking video on his phone." Philippe squeezed his eyes shut for several seconds. "Two thugs had Raina in a room I'd never seen before. She was crying. They had a—" His Adam's apple bobbed as he swallowed several times. "They had a gun to her head, Braxton."

Braxton froze. "Are you serious?"

Philippe nodded. "Told me if I didn't do what Rick said, or if I tried going to the judges or police, they'd kill her."

Braxton shook his head, beyond words.

"I knew I was dicking Hiroto over," Philippe said in a scratchy voice, his eyes wide and tortured. "But what was I supposed to do? It was that or let them kill my pregnant girlfriend."

Philippe exhaled unsteadily. "This tournament isn't worth it. I just want to take my girl home and try and find a way to…live with all of this."

"You have to go to the Gourmands, mate," Braxton said, his voice coming out far calmer than he was feeling. "You have to tell them. Rick can't get away with this."

"Yes, they can, and they will," Philippe spat. "I'm not going to put my girlfriend's life…my *child's* life…at risk again. I'm going to go to my grave regretting what happened to Hiroto, but all I can do now is protect my family." Philippe hands were shaking as he reached up to smooth his messy hair. "If you have any sense of self-preservation, you'll walk away, too. You know Rick would sooner kill you than let you win."

"I'm not a coward," Braxton said without conviction. He didn't have a pregnant girlfriend. He did have a family, though, and he knew there was nothing he wouldn't do to keep them safe.

A hint of accusation hardened Philippe's features. "Rick said he wanted to take you down in the finale. That's why Hiroto and I had to be the ones to go out this round."

"So, you're saying what happened to Hiroto is my fault?!" Braxton demanded, incredulous.

Philippe shook his head. "I'm saying that you have no right to judge me until you've been put in the same impossible situation."

Sickness lurched into Braxton's throat. He couldn't be here anymore. He couldn't look at Philippe.

Braxton spun around and headed for the door.

"No." Philippe grabbed his arm and hauled him back. "You can't go after him."

"Let go of me," Braxton snarled. "If you won't tell the judges the truth, then I will."

Rick needed to be put down like the rabid beast he was.

"Don't you think I'd tell them if I could?" Philippe made a sound of disgust. "It's not that simple."

"We can't just let him get away with this," Braxton said, feeling his anger give way to helpless desperation.

"We have no choice!" Philippe poked a finger into Braxton's chest. "Because if Rick finds out we did anything that might get him eliminated, he'll send his people after our families. *Both* our families. And with all of Rick's connections, a little thing like jail wouldn't be enough to stop him."

That stopped Braxton dead in his tracks. Philippe was right.

Braxton's arms fell limp at his sides as he tried to steady his breathing.

"I really am sorry," Philippe said in a soft voice.

"I'm not the one you need to say that to." Braxton faced Philippe. "Hiroto's parents and seven-year-old sister are probably still at the hospital, though. Maybe they'll want to hear your apologies."

Braxton didn't wait to see Philippe's broken expression. He stalked out of the room and past a startled Raina. He didn't look back.

Once he was back in his own room, Braxton did sit-ups and push-ups until the roaring of his mind quieted enough for him to think. Then, he showered using the hottest water he could stand. He stayed under the scalding spray until he regained some sense of composure.

Braxton had just finished getting dressed when a knock came at his door. His pulse leapt.

Kenzie?

What he wouldn't give to lose himself in her for the rest of the night.

He practically sprinted to the door and threw it open.

He was so prepared for it to be Kenzie on the other side, that it took him several seconds for his brain to catch up to what his eyes were telling him.

Sofia was standing in his doorway, her arms crossed and one high-heeled shoe tapping impatiently on the carpet.

Braxton gaped at his sister. "What the hell are you doing here?"

"Hello to you too, big brother." She rolled her eyes at him.

"What's happened?" he asked, his shock giving way to concern. "Are you okay? Are Mum and Dad—"

"Relax. Nothing's happened." Sofia cocked her head, and Braxton recognized that flicker in her eyes.

She was lying.

"Sofia," he growled.

"Nothing urgent," she clarified as Braxton gave her the infamous McKaid stare-down. "I could have called, but I hated that you were here without anyone sitting in your family section. I wanted to be here for the finale. So, I figured two birds, one stone. You know?"

Sofia let out a squeak of protest as Braxton hugged the hell out of her.

He'd never been an especially affectionate person—and Sofia was as cuddly as a cactus—but Braxton didn't have the words to express his gratitude.

"Don't cry," Sofia warned, her face muffled against his shirt. "You know I hate it when people cry. Gives me hives."

Laughing, Braxton let go of her. He pushed a pile of clean-but-unfolded laundry off the couch and motioned for her to sit.

"It's good to see you," he told his sister.

He hadn't realized until he saw her standing at his door how much he missed his family.

"It's just me," Sofia said quickly, noticing when Braxton's gaze flicked toward the door.

"Yeah," he said, unable to hide the bitterness in his voice. "I guess it would be too much to ask for Dad to come out here and support me."

He understood their mum's absence. She was in charge of all of their restaurants, and with Braxton and Sofia in the States, there was no one to help share the load.

Their father hadn't helped with the business in five years. Hell, he'd barely left his bedroom.

"Brax." The gentleness in Sofia's voice immediately put him on his guard. "Dad's…not doing so well." She let out a shuddering breath. "I'm sure he'll be fine once you win, but he's been all agitated because you haven't been coming to see him."

Braxton started at that. He'd gone to sit with his dad twice a day, every day, for as long as he could remember. It had been months…no, years…since his dad had really acknowledged his presence.

"Mum and I keep telling him you're here," Sofia hurried on, "but he doesn't seem to get it. I think he thinks you died."

Guilt slammed into Braxton. "Christ," he muttered, reaching for his phone.

Sofia put out a hand to stop him. "It won't help, okay? He's not all there." Her tough exterior crumbled. She raised her knees to her chest and wrapped her arms around them, looking more like a kid than the tough-as-nails woman she'd become. "The last couple of weeks have been tough on him. He's getting worse."

Worse? Braxton hadn't known it could get worse.

"He's going to get better once you win and come home," Sofia insisted. "He just needs to hang in there a little more."

From the looks of it, she was trying to convince both of them.

"Okay," Braxton conceded, since there didn't seem to be anything else to say on the topic. He cleared his throat. "How's everything going with the restaurants?"

"Not the best," Sofia admitted. Her long hair fell over her shoulder, hiding her expression. "More investors pulled out."

"But we nailed that last round," Braxton protested.

"I know." Sofia tossed her hair back and looked at him. "But they think what happened with Hiroto was foul play—"

A mixture of grief and anger swept through Braxton at the mention of his friend.

"—and everyone knows you won't cheat. Our investors think you're going to lose."

"Because I'm not a cheating scumbag?!" Braxton jolted to his feet and began to pace.

"Just calm down," Sofia ordered him. "These are short-term problems. After you win, everyone will be throwing money at us, and the rest will just be water under the bridge. Mum and I can keep us afloat until you lock this tournament down."

Braxton nodded. He could do that.

He had to.

"And Mum's staying home and dealing with everything herself?" Braxton asked, unable to keep the worry out of his voice. Their mother was already overburdened, and without him and Sofia to help….

"I can do a lot of stuff virtually," Sofia said. "Don't worry about it."

In spite of her flippant words, Braxton could see shadows under his sister's eyes.

"Sofe—"

"Let's talk about something more pleasant," Sofia announced.

Braxton knew better than to push her.

"You hungry?" he asked, starting for the kitchen. Sofia had a bad habit of forgetting to eat when she was stressed or overworked. He was headed for the fridge when Sofia's next words stopped him in his tracks.

"Now that you're in the finale, when are you going to kill Walter Ashner' daughter?"

Kenzie.

Braxton's attention flitted to the wall safe, where he'd put that poison bottle and forgotten all about it. Kenzie had stopped being Walter Ashner's daughter to him the night her mother died and they'd walked the city together.

"Well?" Sofia followed Braxton's gaze to the safe and raised her eyebrows at him. "I would have thought she'd already be dead since you don't need her anymore."

Braxton thrust a hand through his hair as he tried to figure out how he was going to explain this one to Sofia. Hell, he hadn't even had time to work through his own feelings.

"I noticed you were looking a little cozy with her during the last round," Sofia added.

There was no mistaking the accusation in her voice.

"Yeah, well, things have changed," he hedged.

"Oh bull," Sofia snapped. "Want to know what's changed? Our finances and Daddy's health are more precarious than ever."

"Sofe," he began, but she cut him off.

"I want to be able to call our parents and tell them the man who killed Aidan is suffering as much as we are," she said. "Ergo, Walter Ashner's daughter needs to die. Preferably painfully."

Braxton clenched his fists at his sides. The thought of Kenzie suffering made him want to vomit.

"And it's not just about Daddy," Sofia said, her voice softening. "We lost our childhoods, Brax. I don't resent it, because those restaurants were the last piece of Aidan we had. But I refuse to let all of that work…all our sacrifices…amount to nothing."

Braxton's throat felt like it was full of gravel. He understood everything Sofia was saying, which only confused his own thoughts all the more.

Sofia got up and smoothed her skirt. "Do it before the finale," she advised, heading for the door.

"Where are you going?" he managed. Because he was too tied up in knots—and too cowardly—to tell his sister the one truth that had become apparent amid all the noise.

He couldn't…*wouldn't*…kill Kenzie.

"It's business hours in Sydney," Sofia reminded him. "I have some work to do, and then I'm meeting up with a few investors about our new restaurant."

"How can I help?" Braxton asked, determined to shoulder as much of his sister's impossible load as he could.

"Win the tournament, big brother," she told him. She stopped before she reached the door, backtracked, and gave him a fierce hug.

Braxton held onto her, clinging to the sense of home and familiarity she'd brought with her.

"Where's all your stuff?" he asked when they separated, realizing she didn't have a suitcase or overnight bag.

"I'm staying with friends from boarding school who live a few blocks from here." She gave him a haughty grin. "You think I'd want to hang out in this dump any longer than I have to?"

"Brat." Braxton grinned back. He grabbed a sweatshirt off the floor and pulled it over his head. "Come on, I'll walk you back."

Sofia snorted. "I got myself all the way here from Sydney. I think I can manage walking a few blocks alone." She reached up and tugged on a strand of Braxton's wet hair. Then, raising her voice so she sounded exactly like their mum, she parroted, "You'll catch a cold, love."

They both laughed.

"Fine," Braxton conceded. "But text me when you get to their apartment."

Sofia pinched his cheek.

"Love you," she said as she opened his door.

"Love you too, Sofe."

"Oh, and Brax?" She turned and smiled. "Call me before you kill the Ashner girl. I want to be there when she dies."

CHAPTER 29

KENZIE

Kenzie busied herself around her suite while she worked up the nerve to check on Braxton. She fed Kiwi and made sure the temperature of his habitat was comfortably humid. She changed into clean clothes and brushed her teeth. All the while, she tried to ignore the rapid thudding of her heart. After everything with Hiroto, she knew all of their earlier teasing and flirting wouldn't come to anything tonight.

And that was a good thing, she reminded herself.

After the tournament, they'd go their separate ways. Braxton would return to Sydney and Kenzie would…well, she had no idea what she'd do. Her quiet life in Tennessee no longer held any appeal. The thought of staying in New York was downright repulsive. The idea of starting over somewhere new was exhausting.

The music coming from Esther's room had died down, and a heavy silence permeated the rest of the hall. It was an unwelcome reminder of all the competitors who were no longer with them.

Don't think about it, she ordered herself.

Before she could talk herself out of it, she padded barefoot down the empty hallway to Braxton's door. She knocked before she could talk herself out of it.

Two beats passed before she heard his footsteps. The door opened.

"Thank God," he mumbled, pulling her into the room and kicking the door shut behind her.

His lips were fused to hers a second later.

Kenzie clung to his broad shoulders as her entire world narrowed to Braxton. The taste of mint on his breath and his soapy, masculine smell filled her senses until she was lightheaded. Braxton groaned when her lips parted against his. Her heart pounded against his chest…or maybe it was his heart thudding against hers. She couldn't tell. All she knew was that she never wanted this kiss to end.

Braxton lifted her up without breaking their kiss. The door was at her back and his hands gripped her thighs. Kenzie wrapped her legs around his waist, locking their bodies together. He thrust his tongue into her mouth as he ground his lower body against hers. Kenzie moaned.

All she could think was *more*. She couldn't get enough of this man.

Kenzie reached down for the hem of his shirt, which was trapped between their bodies. Braxton made an impatient noise and lowered Kenzie to her feet so he could drag the fabric over his head. He attacked Kenzie's shirt with enough fervor that she heard fabric ripping. She would have teased him about it, but she was just as impatient.

Braxton broke their kiss and stepped back. They were both gasping.

Braxton's green eyes were smoldering as he ate her up with his gaze. Kenzie's attention dropped to his bare chest. He might be a culinary magician, but he was built like an athlete. He was all sculpted muscle and golden skin.

Uncertainty tempered her desire. She glanced at the floor, where their discarded shirts lay in a heap.

The last time she'd slept with someone who was more than just a warm body…someone she had actual feelings for…it had been with Danny. They'd been kids, learning and exploring together.

Now, seeing Braxton's muscled chest and the feral glint in his green eyes, she was all too aware that there wasn't a shred of boyish innocence in him. Braxton was all man.

Kenzie reached up and rested her palm over Braxton's heart. It was pounding in the same fierce, staccato rhythm as hers.

Was he as nervous as she was?

"Any objections to getting naked and seeing where the night takes us?" Braxton asked in a low, husky voice.

Kenzie managed a breathless laugh. His bluntness was oddly comforting.

She shook her head. "None whatsoever."

Braxton made a sound of approval as he crushed his mouth back against hers.

"Bed. Now." His passion-roughened voice sent shivers through her aching body.

Braxton scooped her up like she was weightless and carried her into the bedroom. Kenzie laughed when he tossed her onto the bed. But when the mattress dipped and he loomed over her, the expression in his eyes was anything but playful.

And *holy shit.* Braxton was naked.

He didn't give her a second to process that fact before he reached under her and unclasped her bra one-handed. He hummed in approval as he pressed a soft kiss between her breasts before moving lower.

He slid his hands under the waistband of her leggings, pulling them down along with her panties in a single motion.

Braxton sat back and took her in. His swollen lips parted.

"You're so beautiful," he rasped.

Kenzie released a breathy laugh. "I'm already planning to sleep with you. You don't need to flatter me."

Braxton frowned. "Have you ever known me to sugarcoat the truth?"

"True," she conceded. "You are kind of an ass."

Braxton grinned before his focus dropped to her body again. All his humor vanished.

"You're gorgeous, Kenz."

Her heart fluttered at that. She loved the nickname, and the way it sounded in his Aussie accent.

Kenzie let her own gaze drift down from those piercing eyes. Her breath caught as she took in all of him.

Whoa. He was a fantasy come to life. Toned and golden and…perfect.

"You're not bad to look at yourself."

Braxton chuckled. "Baby, you really know how to inflate a man's ego."

Kenzie locked her ankles around his waist and gave him a sharp tug, bringing their bodies together. Braxton's whole frame shuddered as he stole her breath in another bone-melting kiss.

"You still good with all of this?" he asked as he teased the tail of her dragon tattoo with the tip of his tongue.

Kenzie nodded and then bit her lip. "It's just—" She hesitated.

Braxton stopped kissing her. "What is it?" His forehead puckered in concern.

She reached up to smooth the wrinkle with her thumb. "It's been kind of a while for me," she admitted.

Instead of tossing a bunch of questions at her or making light of the situation, Braxton leaned down and brushed his lips over hers. The caress was feather-light, and yet, it still made her skin tingle.

"We'll take it slow," Braxton promised.

"Not too slow," she warned.

Heat sparked in Braxton's gaze. Balancing his weight on his left arm, Braxton reached up and traced the contours of her face with a finger. He was trembling, and it eased Kenzie's nerves to know he was as affected as she was.

"Kenzie, I think—" He shook his head. "You know what? Screw it. I don't think, I know. I'm falling for you."

Kenzie sucked in a startled breath.

"You don't have to say—" Braxton began, but she cut him off.

"I'm falling for you, too."

As soon as the words were out of her mouth, she knew they weren't quite true. She wasn't falling. She'd already fallen.

She didn't have a chance to correct herself. Braxton was touching her, and she couldn't have managed a coherent sentence if her life depended on it. After that, there was no more talking. There was only the language of shared breath and two heartbeats that raced ahead until they became one.

CHAPTER 30

BRAXTON

Braxton could have closed his eyes and been asleep in two seconds flat. For once, the constant worries that made him a near-insomniac had been relegated to the recesses of his mind. But Braxton didn't want this night to end. He wanted to lay here and breathe in Kenzie's apple-scented hair and hear her soft sighs as she nestled deeper into the crook of his shoulder.

Braxton kept his arms locked around her, enjoying the warmth and softness of her bare skin against his own.

He couldn't believe how bloody incredible tonight had been. It had also been intimate in a way none of his previous hook-ups had ever been.

In between rounds of the most mind-blowing sex of his life, they'd talked. Braxton had told Kenzie about his dad's suicide attempt and his family's financial problems—topics he'd never voluntarily discussed with anyone besides his mother and sister. And Kenzie had told him about running away to Tennessee to try and forget about everything she'd lost in New York.

She was so easy to talk to. So easy to...*love.*

Braxton was no stranger to lust. But this warmth that started in his chest and drew him to Kenzie like one of his threads of magic was something entirely different. He'd told her he was falling for her, but the truth was that he was head over heels for this woman.

In the morning, he was going to tell her. He was also going to tell her that after the tournament, he wanted her to come back to Sydney with him.

Braxton nuzzled Kenzie's hair, which elicited a sleepy grumble. He chuckled as he pressed a soft kiss to her cheek. He was still smiling when he slipped into the first untroubled sleep he'd had in years.

* * *

Braxton woke to the sound of shrieking. For a second, he thought the smoke detector was going off. But the scream was human rather than mechanical. It was also familiar.

He tried to sit up, but there was a Kenzie-sized lump holding him down.

"Baby, wake up." *Christ, this girl slept like a log.*

"Hm?" Kenzie raised her head, and the cloud of black hair fell away from Braxton's face.

That was when he realized they weren't alone.

Kenzie gasped and clawed at the blanket, drawing it up to her chin.

"What the hell, Sofia?" Braxton glared at his sister, who was standing at the foot of his bed. "What are you doing here?!"

"Me?!" she yelled back. "What the hell are *you* doing?"

"I assume that's rhetorical." Braxton rubbed the sleep from his eyes.

"Are you really so desperate to get laid that you'd sleep with *her?!*" Sofia shouted.

"Shut it, Sofe," Braxton growled. He turned to Kenzie, who still had the blanket drawn up to her chin. She was looking between Braxton and Sofia like they were a puzzle she was trying to solve.

"Kenzie, meet my sister Sofia," Braxton said dryly. "Sofia, mind your fucking manners."

"Oh, *sister.*" Kenzie relaxed a little, even though she kept a tight hold on the blanket. She giggled. "For a second there, I thought maybe you had a psycho ex who was going to kill us."

"Nope. Just a psycho sister." Braxton looked at Sofia's face and added, "Who might still kill us."

"You think this is funny?" Sofia demanded, her voice rising into screeching territory again.

"Actually, I do," he replied. "And if you plan to keep yelling at me, I'm going to need some coffee."

Sofia didn't fire back with a biting retort. That was when Braxton knew something was wrong.

He really looked at his sister for the first time since she'd woken him. She was still wearing the same outfit she'd had on the night before. There were red splotches on her cheeks and neck. Sofia turned away from his scrutiny, but not before he saw the telltale gleam of moisture at the corner of her eye.

Alarm bells rang in his head.

"Sofe," he said, more gently this time. "What's going on?"

Braxton glanced down at the floor, trying to locate his boxers or pants.

"I called you like twenty times," Sofia said, her voice catching.

He looked over at his phone on the dresser, which he'd put on silent the night before.

"Mum tried calling you, too." Sofia bit her lip and turned away from him.

Braxton used the momentary distraction to dive out of bed and yank on his pants.

"Sofia, what happened?" he asked, growing more worried by the second.

She spun around to face him. "Daddy died last night."

CHAPTER 31

KENZIE

Last night, Braxton had confided in Kenzie that his father never recovered from his son's death. His health had been declining, right along with their family's finances, and it was all because of Kenzie's dad.

And now, Braxton and Sofia's father was dead.

Kenzie could hear Sofia crying through the closed door that separated the bedroom from the rest of the suite. Kenzie dressed quickly and silently, and then she sat in the center of Braxton's rumpled bed with her knees drawn up to her chest.

Kenzie startled when the door opened. Braxton, looking gorgeous and broken, stood in the doorway.

She wanted to go to him, but she held herself back. She didn't know if he would want her comfort…not when her father was the reason why Braxton had been deprived of his.

"Sofia went back to her friends' place," he said, gesturing to the empty room behind him.

"Okay. Was it…I mean…what happened?" Kenzie wasn't sure if she was even allowed to ask.

"It wasn't suicide," Braxton said, keeping his gaze fixed on the wall behind her. "His heart just…gave up."

"Oh, Braxton." Kenzie's throat was too tight for her to manage another word.

"Our mum's going to try and arrange the funeral for after the tournament, so I can be there—" Braxton's voice cracked.

Kenzie sprang off the bed. Before thinking twice about what she was doing, she crossed the room and wrapped her arms around him.

Braxton stood rigid for a few seconds, and then he sagged against her.

"I'm so sorry," she whispered as she rubbed his back. "I'm so, so sorry."

She tightened her grip as Braxton's body began to shake. When she felt wetness seeping through her sleeve, Kenzie's heart broke.

What can I do to make this better? she wanted to beg. But she knew from experience there was nothing she could say to ease this kind of pain.

Kenzie thought about how she would feel if their roles were reversed, and what she would want. The answer was simple. *Revenge.* She'd want to kill the person responsible for taking away someone she loved.

"Braxton," she began hesitantly. She had no idea if what she was about to suggest was the worst idea she'd ever come up with. All she knew was that she couldn't stand to see him like this, and that she'd do anything to ease his suffering.

She swallowed and forced out the words in a breathless rush.

"I'm going to Rikers Island today to talk to my dad. I'm pretty sure you were right about me inheriting my magic from him, but I won't know for sure until I ask him to his face." She stroked her fingers through his soft hair while using her other hand to keep rubbing his back. "Do you want to come with me and talk to him?"

When Braxton didn't answer, she babbled on. "I just thought it might give you some sense of closure. But if you don't want to, you don't have to. Obviously."

Braxton extricated himself and looked down at her. His eyes were bloodshot but dry. In fact, there was an emptiness to his expression that scared her more than grief.

Kenzie was about to apologize for the stupid suggestion, when Braxton spoke.

"Yeah." The empty hopelessness in his eyes began to transform into something darker. "I think that's exactly what I need."

Uneasiness began to spread through Kenzie, but it was too late to rescind the offer.

"Maybe we should wait a little while," she hedged.

"No." Braxton started for the door. "I want to talk to him. Now."

As she followed Braxton out, Kenzie uttered a silent prayer.

Please don't let him do something that'll land him in the cell next to my father.

✳ ✳ ✳

By the time they reached the Island, Kenzie was a barrel of nerves. She'd come to visit her father exactly once since he was incarcerated. She had come with Nana a few months after his arrest.

Her father had already aged a decade just during that short time. Kenzie still had nightmares about the metal tables bolted to the floor, security guards standing in every corner, and inmates in their bright orange jumpsuits.

She had no idea what to expect when she saw her father now…five years later.

As they went through the whole process of emptying their pockets, being searched, and signing their lives away, Kenzie found herself leaning on Braxton for support rather than the other way around.

As they followed a security guard through a narrow hallway, Kenzie began to shiver uncontrollably. Braxton pulled off his sweatshirt and draped it around her shoulders.

The two of them sat at one of the bolted-down tables in the large room where other inmates and their families talked quietly. Kenzie waited impatiently for her father to be brought in.

Braxton put a hand on her knee to still the incessant bouncing of her leg. The table stopped vibrating.

"Kenzie."

The hoarse voice came from an old man with a shaved head and deep frown creases around his chapped lips. He wore thick glasses that sat crookedly on his nose.

"Kenzie, it's me, honey."

A horrible, choked sound came out of her. She tried to speak. Failed.

Kenzie jumped to her feet and threw her arms around her father.

She'd barely collided with him before she was being torn back by two security guards. Braxton stood, too. The security guards' hands went to their weapons.

"It's alright," her dad said, holding up his hands and backing away from Kenzie. "My daughter just forgot. It won't happen again."

"Eh, only 'cause it's you, Walt," one of the security guards said in a thick New York accent. The man glared at Kenzie. "Keep your hands to yerself, or you're outta here, kid."

"Understood," her dad said before sitting at the table and motioning for Kenzie and Braxton to do the same. He put his hands on top of the table, his wrist shackles clanking against the metal surface.

"Dad," Kenzie whispered.

"I've missed you, honey." Her dad's fingers twitched, like he was as desperate to reach for her as she was to touch him.

Kenzie looked at the man sitting across from her.

The kind, careless, talented chef was gone. In his place was someone who had been battling life…and losing.

"I missed you too," she managed.

Her throat felt like it had been scraped raw.

Why the hell had it taken her so long to come visit him? Why had she ignored so many of his calls?

Kenzie wiped her nose with her sleeve, before remembering she was wearing Braxton's sweatshirt. That thought shocked awareness into her. From the moment her dad walked into the room, she'd forgotten anyone else existed.

"Um," Kenzie began. Her gaze flicked to Braxton, whose mouth was pressed in a tight line.

Kenzie's dad seemed reluctant to tear his focus away from her, but as soon as he turned to Braxton, his eyes widened. His expression crumpled into unmistakable regret.

"You know who I am?" Braxton asked, his voice cold and flat.

Kenzie's dad dipped his head in acknowledgement. "McKaid," he said softly. "You were sitting next to…him…that night."

"You mean the night you murdered my brother?"

Braxton's harsh question attracted the attention of other inmates sitting nearby as well as the guards, who hovered around their table like circling vultures.

This time, it was Kenzie's turn to press a calming hand on his leg. Braxton released a shuddering breath. Kenzie's dad looked between the two of them, a clear question in his eyes.

"Braxton and I met at a tournament for people like us," Kenzie said, watching her dad carefully for his reaction. "You know, culinary magicians."

"Culinary magicians?" Her father's face scrunched in confusion. He absently began to pick at a scab on his knuckles.

Kenzie's stomach clenched. She wondered what he'd done to cut his hands.

In the last five years, she'd told herself that she stayed away because she couldn't forgive her dad for what he'd done. Now, sitting across from him, she remembered the real reason she avoided him. It was because it was so much easier to be angry with him than to worry about and miss him.

"Are you seriously going to look me in the eye and pretend like you don't know?" Kenzie pressed.

"I don't know anything about…magic," her dad said after a pause, still looking down at his knuckles.

"But you do know something."

Disappointment crashed over Kenzie. Some part of her had still been hoping there was another explanation than the very obvious fact that her father had lied to her for her entire life.

After another minute, her dad nodded.

"I just have one question," Braxton said, his voice coming out as a low growl. "Why Aidan?"

Kenzie's dad met Braxton's fierce stare.

"It was an accident," he told Braxton. "I never meant to hurt your brother, or anyone else. I am so truly sorry."

Braxton made a sound of disgust.

"Dad, you have to give us more than that," Kenzie pleaded, blinking rapidly to clear her vision. "What happened that night?"

Her dad opened and closed his mouth, his attention shifting back and forth between her and Braxton.

"Tell us," she ordered. All of her patience and sympathy were deserting her. "Braxton deserves to hear the truth."

And so do I.

"I can't," her father said, his voice coming out as a defeated groan.

Kenzie looked at her dad…the man who had raised her, protected her, loved her. In that moment, she felt like she'd never known him at all.

"Then, I guess we're done here," she said coldly and stood up.

"Honey, please."

In spite of herself, Kenzie turned back. "The truth, Dad. I want the truth."

Her dad swallowed. "How much do you trust him?"

The chains clanked against the table as her father pointed at Braxton.

Kenzie crossed her arms and sat back down. "I trust Braxton with my life."

Her dad sighed and leaned forward. Kenzie and Braxton did the same, until they made a little enclave between the three of them. As Kenzie waited for her dad to speak, it seemed to her that he aged another decade. The burden of this secret had clearly been dragging on him. At the same time, it seemed to be causing him physical pain to share it.

"I inherited this ability from you, didn't I?" Kenzie asked, trying to give her dad an opening into the conversation.

Her dad shook his head. "Like I said, I have no idea what *magic* you're talking about." He said that word like he was humoring her more than actually believing her.

Kenzie's brow furrowed. "But then—"

"Denise couldn't cook, let alone do anything…magical," he said, reading her thoughts. "We're your biological parents, but trust me when I tell you neither one of us ever had any special abilities."

"Is it possible you're not her father?" Braxton asked from beside Kenzie.

She turned to give him a dirty look, but all of his attention was on her father.

Her dad didn't seem to take offense. He turned to Kenzie when he said, "When I went to court to fight for full custody, genetic testing was part of that. I wouldn't have cared either way, but my lawyers said it would help our case." He held Kenzie's eye. "The test proved I'm your biological father."

"Then you're lying about not knowing about our magic," Kenzie said, feeling tears of frustration prick at her eyes. "I know you killed Aidan with a poison you magically created."

Her father's pasty face turned gray. "Kenzie—"

"Want to know how I know?" she forged on. "Because I recreated the poison myself yesterday."

She ignored Braxton's sharp inhale beside her.

"Kenzie, that's enough," her father hissed, looking around like he was terrified someone might hear.

She ignored him. "Are you still going to look me in the eye and tell me it's a coincidence that I replicated a poison you made five years ago?"

"It's not a coincidence," her dad said, his voice so quiet Kenzie had to lean even closer to hear him. His distrustful gaze flitted to Braxton before holding hers. "Ask your friend what dish his brother ordered the night he died."

"I—" Kenzie began. *What the hell did that have to do with anything?*

"Ashner's signature dish," Braxton said through clenched teeth. "Linguini with a squid ink sauce."

Kenzie looked at her father, who nodded. All the air was torn from her lungs at once.

"After the boy…Aidan…began to choke, I ran back into the kitchen to figure out what had happened with the food," her dad said. "I saw the saucepan. Whatever remnants had been in the pan had burned right through the bottom. There was a hole in the cooktop from the squid ink sauce."

Kenzie tried to breath. Couldn't.

"What am I missing?" Braxton demanded.

"Kenzie," her father said in warning.

Kenzie pressed a hand to her mouth to stifle the wheezing sound that was coming through her parted lips.

"Ohmygod," she gasped.

"Kenzie, *what?*" Braxton demanded.

"It was me," Kenzie whispered. She sank deeper into Braxton's sweatshirt as her shock began to transform to bone-jarring shudders.

"What was you?" Braxton asked, his eyebrows furrowing in confusion.

"Kenzie, don't say any more," her father begged.

She ignored him. All of her attention was on Braxton. "I did it," she said, her voice cracking. "I was making the squid ink sauce that night."

And that could only mean one thing.

Kenzie's father hadn't killed Aidan McKaid. She had.

CHAPTER 32

KENZIE

Braxton stumbled to his feet and ran out of the room like he was going to be sick. Kenzie didn't follow. She didn't think she could have moved even if she wanted to. She was numb.

"What is he going to do?"

Her father's sharp question succeeded in snapping her out of her stupor.

"Honey, is he going to cause trouble for us? If so, we need to get our story straight. He'll never be able to prove anything, but we just need to make sure we're on the same page—"

Kenzie held up her hand to stop him. Her voice trembled when she said, "So, you were telling the truth, then? About you not being a culinary magician?"

Her dad gave her a fleeting smile. "It's the truth, honey. I've never done anything magical in the kitchen…or anywhere else, for that matter."

So, Kenzie hadn't inherited her magic from either of her parents. Which was impossible.

At the moment, though, it didn't matter where her magic had come from.

"And—" Kenzie swallowed. "And you knew I was the one who made the poison from the beginning?"

Her father nodded. "After I saw what your sauce had done, I knew that was what killed him."

"So, you took the blame."

Kenzie was surprised by how calm she sounded, when inside, she was a riot of emotions.

Her dad gave her a helpless shrug. "You were my daughter. What else was I supposed to do?"

Kenzie's temporary hold on her calm began to crumble.

"You gave up your life for me."

Her dad reached across the table and brushed his fingers over hers.

Tears slid down her cheeks and beaded up on the table's lacquered surface.

All this time, Kenzie had thought her dad's carelessness had gotten Aidan killed. She'd been angry with him…resented him for abandoning her…when all along he'd been protecting her.

"Oh my God," she whispered.

"Hey, stop that," her dad said gently.

"I didn't call you," she gasped, finding it impossible to get any air into her lungs. "I didn't come visit you."

"It was for the best." He gave her hand a quick squeeze before pulling his shackled wrists back across the table. "I knew that, whatever you'd done, you didn't mean to harm that boy. It was an accident, and I didn't want you to lose your future."

Kenzie was crying. Ugly crying. The whole table rattled from the full-body shudders going through her. Of all the horrible truths assailing her, one fact kept rising to the surface.

"I abandoned you."

Kenzie had avoided her father. She'd been ashamed of him. And all along, she was the one to blame. She was the one who should be rotting in prison right now.

Kenzie stumbled to her feet.

"Hon, what are you doing?" her dad asked warily.

"I have to tell the truth."

It was so obvious. Her dad had been paying for her mistake for five long years, but he didn't have to live out the rest of his sentence. She would answer for her mistakes. Her dad would go free.

"That's not going to happen," her dad said. His voice was so uncharacteristically sharp that it stopped the wheels churning in her brain.

"I made my decision five years ago, and I've never looked back," he said with quiet certainty. "My testimony has been logged. If you try to tell the cops something different now, they'll just think you're lying to get me out." He looked at her over the rim of his glasses. "I'm sticking to the story I gave from the beginning. Spare us both the aggravation and leave this alone." He gave her a wry smile. "Trust me, honey. You didn't inherit your stubbornness from Denise."

Kenzie shook her head, dizzy and sick with everything she'd learned. She still had so many questions.

Her dad offered her a sad smile. "My only regret is that I couldn't be there as you grew into the beautiful, talented woman sitting before me."

Kenzie let out a choked sob.

"I owe you an apology," her dad said.

"*You* owe *me* one?!" Kenzie let out a shuddering laugh.

Her dad, solemn-faced, nodded. "I was afraid that if you discovered the truth about what happened that night, you would become lost in your guilt. I was afraid you'd become like—"

Denise.

Kenzie's mother hung between them. In that moment, Kenzie realized her dad probably didn't even know Denise was dead.

"Dad, I—" she began, but he wasn't finished.

"I can see now that you're so much stronger than I gave you credit for." He met her watery gaze with his steady one. "You won't crumble under the weight of the past."

Kenzie couldn't speak.

"Time's up, Walt," one of the security guards said, marching over and tapping his watch.

Kenzie's dad nodded before turning back to her. "Making a sacrifice for a person you love is the greatest gift you can ever give."

She was shaking her head. Her dad had said those words to her so many times in her life, but she'd never thought…never once suspected….

Her dad offered her a little smile. "Believe me when I tell you I'm at peace with all of this."

"No, wait," Kenzie began as her dad got to his feet.

"I love you, honey." The chains on his wrists and ankles rattled as he leaned closer. He whispered, "Be happy, and be the best version of yourself. That's all I'll ever ask of you."

And then his feet were shuffling along the brown tiles as he was escorted through a barred door and out of her sight.

CHAPTER 33

BRAXTON

Braxton paced back and forth in front of the prison visit center. His mind was blank…utterly and completely blank. The horror was just too much, and his brain had chosen to shut down rather than implode.

All of that self-preserving numbness evaporated when Kenzie stepped through the doors. As she came closer, Braxton could see the salty tear trails down her cheeks.

He could barely stand to look at her, and yet, he stayed where he was and let her come to him.

How was it possible to love and hate someone at the same time?

"Braxton," Kenzie began.

With that one word, he…broke.

He doubled over as agonizing pain shot through his chest. It felt like he'd been impaled on an iron spike.

"Braxton, please." Kenzie reached a hand toward him, and then quickly retracted it at the look he gave her.

"Tell me how to make this right," she pleaded.

"Make this right?!" He laughed, and the sound was as empty and cold as he felt. "There's no making this right, Kenzie. You'll never be able to make this right."

"I know, I just—"

"I fucked my brother's murderer!"

Kenzie flinched, but he made no attempt to soften the harsh words. The silent tears gathering on her eyelashes made no impression.

Christ. He hadn't just screwed his twin's murderer. He'd done that…with her…on a bed Aidan had slept in.

Braxton felt dirty. Monstrous. Sick.

"You have every reason to hate me," Kenzie said, her shoulders hunching in defeat. "And trust me, no matter how much you despise me, it can't be half as much as I despise myself."

"Doubtful," he shot back.

As soon as the word had left his mouth, part of him rebelled. His heart—that stupid, worthless organ—beat faster at her nearness. It reached for her like some kind of deranged magnet. It told him to gather her into his arms and never let her go.

"Just leave," he told her as a wave of exhaustion swept over him. "I can't spend another second with you."

Kenzie bit her lip hard enough to draw blood. She didn't move.

"Why are you still here?" he growled.

"I told my dad I wanted to turn myself in. I need to make this right—"

"There is no making this right!" He thrust his hands through his hair. "You killed my brother…indirectly killed my father…."

"What can I do?"

She sounded so helpless and pained that Braxton's throat constricted.

"You can leave," he choked out. "Just get away from me."

Kenzie gave him a shaky nod. Then, she walked away.

Braxton waited long enough for two buses to depart the Island before he got on one.

Once he was back in the city, he stood outside the Empire State Building as he debated whether or not he could bring himself to go back inside the tournament venue.

He was desperate to shower away the smell of Kenzie that clung to his skin. He needed to practice his dish for the finale. But the thought of going back to the room that was now more full of Kenzie than Aidan made him want to throw up.

So, he just started walking. He didn't have a destination and wasn't even paying attention to where he was going. He just walked.

He thought about Aidan and everything his brother would have accomplished if he was still alive. Braxton thought about his mum, home alone and arranging her husband's funeral. He thought about the bottle of poison locked up in his safe.

Did he have the balls to use it?

The question kept him moving even after the sky grew dark and the city that never sleeps settled down.

Kenzie Ashner deserved to die for what she'd done to his family.

He thought about the trusting expression that would fill Kenzie's gray eyes when he handed her a glass and told her to drink.

He thought about how Kenzie had slept in his arms.

Kenzie had destroyed Braxton's family, but it hadn't been intentional. Most kids didn't realize they'd inherited culinary magic until some emotional trigger brought it to the surface. For Braxton, it had been a surge of jealousy that was sparked by the emergence of Aidan's magic. Braxton's envy had been potent enough to awaken his own magical gift that same day.

Kenzie's ability had been awoken by her overwhelming grief when she found out her boyfriend was dead. And there had been no one around to recognize what she'd done or help her control the surge of power.

Kenzie had mentioned that she stopped cooking after that. So, there'd been no opportunity for her magic to make an appearance over the last five years. She truly hadn't known what she was capable of.

There was also the anomaly of Kenzie's culinary magic not being inherited. Braxton had been watching Walter's face for any sign of recognition when Kenzie started talking about her magic. He truly hadn't known anything beyond the fact that Kenzie was the one responsible for Aidan's death.

Braxton had also seen the look on Kenzie's face when her father told her about the sauce. She hadn't been lying. She'd spent the last five years believing her father had killed Aidan.

Maybe if she'd been lying to him or set out to deceive him, it would make all of this easier. But she hadn't. If anything, it had been the other way around. He had inserted himself into her life so he could poison her.

Braxton dug his fingers into his skull, which was pounding.

What the hell was he supposed to do?

All at once, he was hit with a fierce, childlike urge to talk to his family. He already knew what Sofia would say to him. She'd tell him to man up and poison Kenzie. He couldn't talk to his father or his brother. With an unsteady hand, he pulled out his phone and called his mum.

She answered after the first ring.

"Braxton."

His mum started to cry. And Braxton broke down.

CHAPTER 34

KENZIE

Kenzie's curse echoed in the empty hallway as she reached yet another dead end. She slammed her fist against the door of a walk-in freezer, swearing some more as pain throbbed through her knuckles.

With her vision blurring from tears she refused to let fall, she turned around and backtracked.

Find the judges. Leave the tournament. Get the fuck out of New York.

It was the same refrain that had kept her going as she got herself more and more lost in the tournament's venue's underbelly. She'd had no idea this place was so big.

It shouldn't be this complicated to quit.

Hours earlier, she'd packed up her suitcase and Kiwi's habitat. She'd tried to sneak out of the venue with her tail between her legs, but two security guards had stopped her. They'd said something about participants not being allowed to leave the tournament unless they were eliminated by the judges. So, she'd gone to look for said judges.

And now she was lost.

Kenzie forged on. As long as she clung to her single-minded purpose of getting out of here, she wouldn't be able to think about her dad rotting in prison for a crime she'd committed. She wouldn't have to face the truth that she'd murdered Aidan McKaid.

Kenzie slapped her hand over her mouth, too late to stifle the sob that echoed down the corridor.

She'd spent the last five years on her own, and everything had been fine. Then, she'd met Braxton and Polly Berrywhite and descended into the world of culinary magic. She'd glimpsed happiness and grasped onto it with both hands. Like she deserved it.

What she deserved was the inside of a jail cell.

The sound of voices floated down the hallway, saving Kenzie from herself.

Thank. Freaking. God.

She made a beeline for the voices, which she recognized as Chef Sakai and Chef Levy. She would have preferred to talk to sweet Polly Berrywhite, but it didn't really matter. All she needed was permission to get the hell out.

She raised her hand to knock on the partially-open door, when the judges' raised voices stopped her.

"We've got to get rid of her," Chef Levy said in a quiet snarl. "She's poison. Kenzie—"

She jerked at the sound of her name. The judge's voice went too low for her to hear anything more.

As the judges continued to whisper about her, Kenzie's mind spun.

Get rid of her? Poison?

Did Braxton already tell them she was the one who had killed his brother?

It couldn't be. If Braxton was going to tell anyone, he'd go to the police. The judges didn't have any authority outside of this competition.

But if they didn't know about what she'd done, then why was Chef Levy so eager to get rid of her? And what exactly did *getting rid of her* entail…?

"I'm a chef, Elyannah, not a politician," Chef Sakai said. "I have no interest in the source of Kenzie Brookerton's magic."

"Maybe you don't, but *they* will," Chef Levy snapped. "You want them in possession of that kind of information?"

"I want no part of this," Chef Sakai said, sounding more nervous than angry. "I'm here to identify the best culinary magician in this tournament. Once I've done that, I'm going home. I suggest you do the same."

Footsteps receded as Chef Sakai disappeared through a doorway on the other side of the room.

Chef Levy shouted something in another language and kicked the wall. Kenzie's pulse skyrocketed as the chef gave the wall another hard kick and then started walking in Kenzie's direction.

Kenzie ducked into a shadowed doorway, which turned out to be a narrow pantry. She retreated farther into the darkness. She couldn't see, but familiar scents told her she was in the presence of herbal cardamom and peppery cloves.

Chef Levy stalked past Kenzie's hiding place without even glancing her way. As much as Kenzie wanted permission to leave the tournament, self-preservation kicked in and told her to stay put. Maybe if she kept wandering around, she'd get lucky enough to happen on a judge who wouldn't bite her head off.

It occurred to Kenzie that Chef Levy might be going back to her room. If that was the case, she might lead Kenzie to the other judges' suites. Then, Kenzie could plead her case to someone who might actually show a little compassion.

In other words, Polly Berrywhite.

Keeping a healthy distance from Chef Levy…who wasn't exactly hiding her presence, with the way she was stomping and cursing to herself…Kenzie followed her.

We've got to get rid of her…. She's poison….

Chef Levy's words played in Kenzie's mind on loop.

Kenzie was getting damn tired of being the last one to know about herself. She wanted answers.

Chef Levy stopped outside a door and rapped sharply. Kenzie hung back, using a bend in the hallway to conceal her presence. A few seconds passed, and then the door opened. Polly Berrywhite poked her head out into the hall.

Jackpot.

Now, all Kenzie had to do was wait for Chef Levy to leave.

Polly was wearing flannel pajamas, along with her signature diamond necklace and earrings. Her cotton candy hair was askew, and her glasses were dangling around their diamond chain.

"Oh, Elyannah." Polly offered the other judge a hesitant smile. "How are you, my dear?"

Kenzie was overcome with a desperate urge to give the woman a hug. She could use some grandmotherly kindness right about now.

"Don't you *my dear* me," Chef Levy spat. "You might have fooled everyone else, but I see you."

"And I see you, Elyannah," Polly said calmly. "I see that you're involved in something that's far beyond you. My advice? Stick to the food, and leave the rest to those who know what they're doing."

Polly Berrywhite let out a little squawk as Chef Levy hauled her out of the room and pushed her against the wall. Chef Levy might be shorter and skinnier than Polly, but Kenzie could see how strong she was. Polly let out a strangled cough as the other judge's sinewy forearm pressed against her throat.

"You may be a big honcho around here," Chef Levy said, "but you don't want to make an enemy of me."

"Are you threatening me?" Polly wheezed, her chin wobbling as she tried to break free.

"Damn right, I am," Chef Levy replied, tightening her hold on the other judge.

Enough is enough, Kenzie decided.

"Excuse me, judges," she called, stepping into the middle of the hallway so they could both see her. "I hope I'm not interrupting anything."

Chef Levy let go of Polly. She glared at Kenzie with enough heat to fry her on the spot.

"What are you doing here?" Chef Levy demanded.

"I wanted to talk to Chef Berrywhite," Kenzie said.

Chef Levy didn't budge. Her suspicious glare moved between Kenzie and Polly, like the two of them were conspiring against her.

"We'll be just fine," Polly said. "Thank you, Elyannah."

The two judges stared at each other for another moment—Polly smiling pleasantly and Chef Levy glaring daggers. Kenzie did a mental fist pump when Chef Levy skulked off.

Polly let out a long sigh. "Come in, my dear," she said, ushering Kenzie into a suite that made her own look like a hovel. "I think we could both use some hot chocolate, and I have some snowball cookies that'll be just the thing to put us to rights." She winked at Kenzie and shut the door behind her. When she reached up to slide in the lock, Kenzie saw that her hand was shaking.

"Are you okay?" Kenzie asked.

"You're too kind, but don't you worry about me." Polly offered Kenzie a wide smile that didn't reach her owl eyes. She patted absently at her wispy hair as she bustled around the kitchen.

Kenzie perched on the edge of a beige leather chair. She looked around, taking in the heavy cream drapes that framed beautiful oil paintings of food. Chandeliers with burning candles instead of lightbulbs made Kenzie feel a little like she'd traveled back in time to a duke's mansion, or something. The light fixtures also screamed *fire hazard*, but Kenzie supposed there wouldn't be fire inspections for a place the normal authorities didn't know existed.

Polly returned with a silver tray that held two steaming mugs of hot chocolate and a plate of powdered white cookies.

"Why was Chef Levy talking to you like that?" Kenzie asked, taking the mug of hot chocolate Polly handed her.

"Oh, it was simply a matter of differing opinions about you, dearest." Polly waved a dismissive hand, like it was perfectly reasonable for the judges to be arguing about her.

Polly studied Kenzie over the rim of her hot chocolate mug. "There are many people in our community who are curious about your talents. You've attracted a great deal of attention due to the…unconventional nature of your ability."

"I want to know why my magic's different, too," Kenzie said, feeling a weird need to explain herself. She might be a deviant, but it wasn't like she'd chosen to be different.

She hadn't chosen any of this.

Polly held out the plate of cookies to Kenzie. Even though she had no appetite, Kenzie took one and nibbled the corner.

Yikes. Polly should stick to judging. There had to be a pound of butter in this one cookie. And talk about confectioners' sugar overload….

"Are you certain neither of your parents are culinary magicians, dear?" Polly asked, devouring her cookie in a single bite.

"I'm sure," Kenzie replied. The heavy weight of that truth settled in her gut.

"Hmmm." Polly dipped another cookie into her hot chocolate. "Well, for now, I just want you just focus on winning the tournament." She winked. "Everything else will work itself out."

"Actually," Kenzie said, putting down her cookie. "That's what I came here to talk to you about."

Polly listened without interruption as Kenzie delivered the story she'd rehearsed while she had been busy getting lost. She spun a yarn about needing to go back to Tennessee, where her dear old (nonexistent) aunt was ailing and desperate for Kenzie's help.

"Poor thing," Polly clucked in sympathy when Kenzie had finished.

Polly frowned into her empty mug. "I wish I could tell you otherwise, but it's in the rules that competitors can't leave the tournament until they're eliminated from a round." She reached out and patted Kenzie's knee. "It's just a few more days, though. I'm sure your aunt will understand."

Kenzie shook her head, trying to keep her panic semi-in check. "I'm sorry. I just…can't stay."

Polly's features hardened. "I'm afraid it isn't up to you," she said. "The Gourmands make the rules, and believe me when I tell you, you do not want to attract their attention…more."

Kenzie bristled. Her brain filled with images of Loretta and Max's corpses.

"Are you telling me I'm a prisoner?" she demanded.

Polly's features softened. "It's not like that, dearest. It's just that this is the biggest even in the culinary magic community. It's important that all participants abide the rules."

So, that was a *yes* to the prisoner question. Super.

"Come now," Polly urged, reaching over to give Kenzie's hand a squeeze. "Being here isn't so bad. Besides, don't you want to show off how much progress you've made in this short time?"

Kenzie shook her head, feeling an embarrassing sting at the back of her eyelids. "I just want to be done with this tournament," she whispered.

Polly pulled a handkerchief out of her pajama pocket and passed it to Kenzie. "I'm so sorry, dearest, but I can't make exceptions for just one of the competitors. I hope you understand."

Kenzie was about to start begging, when Polly's expression lit up.

"Think about it this way," she said, leaning forward like she was letting Kenzie in on a delicious secret. "You've got a one-in-four chance at earning the wish truffle. Wouldn't it be something to be able to wish for whatever you want?" Something like longing sparked in her gaze.

"I don't want—" Kenzie began, before cutting herself off.

She'd come to the tournament to learn more about her magic. She'd known she didn't have a chance at the wish truffle and didn't have anything to wish for, besides.

But that wasn't the case anymore.

Kenzie's pulse hammered at the base of her throat. *How had she not thought of it before?*

If she won the truffle, she could wish for her father's freedom.

Kenzie wouldn't need to convince any lawyers or cops about what had really happened, and since she wouldn't be taking her father's place in prison, he'd have no reason to fight her.

"Can this wish truffle really do anything?" Kenzie asked, her voice cracking.

"Anything that could conceivably happen in the real world," Polly replied. "Think of it as a stroke of good fortune nudging fate in the right direction."

Her father could conceivably be let out of prison. And that meant, if she won the truffle, she could wish for her father to be released.

"Now, don't you feel better?" Polly polished off the last snowball cookie and got to her feet.

Polly continued to chatter, but Kenzie's mind was going a thousand miles an hour. She was going to win the wish truffle to free her dad.

But in order to get the truffle, she'd have to get through three other contestants first.

Braxton.

The thought of him brought all of her machinations to a screeching halt. Kenzie had told him she wasn't competing for the wish truffle.

Braxton needed the truffle to save his family from financial ruin and to keep his brother's legacy alive. How could she take that away from him?

It would be another betrayal on top of everything she'd already done to hurt him.

Her dad or Braxton?

Kenzie wanted to scream.

She said a hurried thanks to Polly and backtracked in the direction she'd come. She took a few wrong turns, but she eventually found her way.

By the time she got back to her suite, she had a plan. She also knew that she owed Braxton the courtesy of telling him why she'd decided to compete for the truffle.

If he'd listen to her.

It took Kenzie an entire hour to work up the courage to go over and knock on Braxton's door. Her pulse thundered in her ears as she waited. Ten seconds passed. Twenty.

She forced herself to knock again.

When she heard no sign of movement on the other side of the door, she skedaddled back to her room. She fought an overwhelming urge to curl up under the covers, the same way Kiwi took refuge behind his favorite leaf.

Coward, she accused herself.

She had just changed into a comfy tank top and yoga pants when a knock came at her door.

Kenzie's pulse stuttered.

"Come in," she called, hating the quaver in her voice.

When had she turned into such a wuss?

When you found out you murdered your almost-boyfriend's twin and then decided to stab him in the back by competing against him. Duh.

The person who strode into her room had McKaid blonde hair and green eyes…but it wasn't Braxton.

"Um, hi Sofia," Kenzie said.

She was instantly aware of how grubby her outfit was compared to Sofia's. The other girl was as model-gorgeous as her brother. Every move she made was graceful. And seriously…who actually had legs that long?

The two of them finished sizing each other up. Sofia offered a smile that was a little too wide. She held up a bottle of wine and marched over to the kitchen like she owned the place. She got wine glasses and a corkscrew, and brought everything over to the table.

Kenzie could do nothing but watch as Sofia opened the bottle and put two glasses full of a sparkling rosé down on coasters.

Sofia took the seat at the head of the table. She gestured for Kenzie to sit in front of the other wine glass. Feeling like a guest in her own suite, or maybe a prospective employee at a job interview, Kenzie obeyed the silent command.

Sofia smoothed a hand over her sleek French braid, which didn't have a hair out of place.

In contrast, Kenzie's hair was a wild mess. She'd spent her day traipsing to Rikers Island and then hauling ass all through the tournament venue. She hadn't touched a comb since her night with Braxton….

And she really shouldn't be thinking about last night when she was sitting across from Braxton's sister.

Kenzie glanced down at Sofia's black patent leather pumps, and quickly tucked her fuzzy socked-feet under her chair.

"Listen, Sofia," Kenzie began. "I'm really sorry about this morning."

Dear God. Had it really been just this morning that she was cuddled up with Braxton?

So much had happened since. It felt like weeks had passed.

Sofia put up a hand. "No offense, honey, but I'd rather *not* be reminded of my brother having sex." She puckered her lips in disgust.

Kenzie managed a chuckle. "Fair enough."

If she knew what was good for her, Kenzie would forget all about last night, too. The realization that none of what they'd shared would ever happen again was so crushing that, for a few seconds, she couldn't catch her breath.

"You look like you could use this," Sofia said, nudging the wine glass closer. "It's my favorite wine. I brought a bottle all the way from Sydney." She smiled. "Let's call it a peace offering."

Guilt hammered into Kenzie. Sofia was here to make peace because she still thought Kenzie's dad had killed her brother. Sofia had no idea she was sitting across from her brother's actual murderer.

And Kenzie was too much of a coward to tell her.

Sofia lifted her own wine glass in a toast.

The last thing Kenzie wanted to do was hurt Braxton's family even more than she already had. So, she held back her usual *Thanks anyway, but I don't drink* speech and raised her glass.

Feeling Sofia's eyes boring into her, Kenzie took a small sip.

The bubbles danced pleasantly along her tongue. The fruity grapes and sweetness of peaches were quickly overshadowed by a sharp, metallic taste Kenzie hadn't been expecting. She wondered if the wine had gone rancid.

"What do you think?" Sofia asked. She hadn't drunk from her own glass yet, so Kenzie didn't know if the other girl would pick up on the bad taste.

"It's delish," Kenzie lied, forcing down another sip.

Sofia cocked her head as she continued to stare at Kenzie, like she was waiting for something.

A strange tingling started at the back of Kenzie's throat. She would have gone to go get a glass of water, but she didn't want to seem ungrateful for the wine. She coughed, but it didn't help. The tickling sensation transformed into more of an ache.

"I know you're the one who murdered my brother," Sofia said abruptly.

Kenzie started. "Sofia, I—" she began, not knowing what to say. *What could she say?*

Sofia held up a hand. "If you're going to give me some pathetic *I didn't know about my magic* excuse, then save your breath."

Kenzie forced herself to release her grip on the wine glass before she broke it.

"So, I guess Braxton told you everything," Kenzie said, hating the pang that went through her at the mere mention of his name.

"No, he didn't." Sofia ran her index finger along the rim of her glass. "Our mother did."

"Oh," Kenzie replied dumbly.

Her vision wavered. *Jeez, she seriously was a lightweight.* Two sips, and she didn't think she could walk in a straight line.

"Did you know that Aidan died in my arms?" Sofia asked, as casually as if they were just two friends chatting.

"I—"

"It wasn't a quick death, either," Sofia continued.

Why the hell was Sofia smiling right now?

Kenzie's stomach was roiling.

"I was only sixteen, and there I was, trying to give my brother CPR." Sofia spun her wine glass on the table, watching the bubbles rise to the surface. "I've never felt so helpless in my entire life."

Kenzie was trying to pay attention to the other girl's words, but Sofia's voice had gone fuzzy. Her face was blurry, too.

Oh shit. Was she going to throw up Sofia's expensive wine right in front of her?

"Sofia, I—I'm sorry." Kenzie staggered to her feet.

And then she collapsed.

CHAPTER 35

BRAXTON

Braxton must have walked ten miles, but he still felt edgy. He considered going for a jog, but that seemed redundant with how he'd spent the last several hours. What he really needed was to forget about everything else and focus on his dish for the finale. He'd been so busy training Kenzie and preparing for the first two challenges that he hadn't practiced the magic he would need to make his dish perfect.

Culinary magic was like a muscle. If he didn't keep building up his skills, he'd lose all the progress he'd made over the past months. Especially since the dish he'd chosen for the finale didn't exactly come naturally to him.

When Braxton let himself into his suite, he found Sofia sitting at his table. She had her laptop open as she jotted notes on a spreadsheet printout. Through the Bluetooth headset she was wearing, Braxton could hear a deep, agitated voice.

Braxton raised an eyebrow at his sister, silently asking if she wanted him to deal with it. She gave him a slight shake of her head.

"I understand your concerns," Sofia told the man, using the same crisply efficient voice she used to manage everyone outside the family. Braxton went over to the fridge and grabbed a bottle of water. He paced around the living room while he waited for Sofia to finish her call.

As he prowled around like a caged animal, his gaze caught on the safe tucked into the wall. He thought about that little bottle of poison inside.

While he'd been walking the city, a single question had filled his mind.

Now that he knew the truth, could he bring himself to poison Kenzie?

Staring at the safe, he knew he'd been kidding himself. He might be able to convince himself that his love had been an overwhelming case of lust. He might be able to tell himself he hated Kenzie with every fiber of his being.

But he knew one fact with utter certainty. He could never hurt her.

In that moment, everything became clear. Braxton would win the tournament. He'd wish for his family's business to be restored and for their money troubles to end. Then, he was going to go back to Sydney and pick up the scattered pieces of his family.

He and Kenzie would disappear from each other's lives forever.

Braxton strode over to the safe. Once he dumped out the poison, he could let go of all these Kenzie-related thoughts swirling around his head. He'd be free of her.

Then, he would be able to devote the rest of his time before the finale to perfecting his pinnacle dish. He'd come here to win the tournament, and that was precisely what he was going to do. Nothing else mattered now.

Braxton punched in the code and waited impatiently for the safe to unlock.

"Let me call you back," Braxton heard Sofia tell the investor she'd been talking to. She closed her laptop and pulled off her headset just as the safe door swung open.

Braxton reached inside for the bottle of poison. His fingers brushed only the felt mat covering the bottom of the safe.

He searched the entire space again. He thrust his head into the opening. He even pulled out his phone and shined the light over every centimeter.

The safe was empty.

"Please tell me your bank passwords are harder to crack than your safe," Sofia said, sidling up to him. "If you keep using Aid's birthday for everything, you're going to be the most hackable person on the planet."

Braxton tore his gaze off the empty safe and rounded on his sister. "Where is it?"

Sofia reached into her pocket and held out the little bottle.

Relief shot through Braxton. He snatched it out of her hand and squinted through the translucent glass.

"Sofia—"

Black dots shimmered across his vision.

The bottle was empty.

"What did you do?!"

"What I've been doing for the past five years…picking up slack and getting shit done." Sofia lifted her chin in defiance. "I did what you couldn't…or wouldn't."

Braxton didn't waste his breath asking for details. He shoved past his sister and raced down the hall to Kenzie's room. He tried the handle to her door, and when it gave, he practically fell into her suite.

His gaze swept the room, landing on the huddled figure on the floor.

"Kenzie!" His voice sounded like a smoker's. He crossed the room in three strides and fell to his knees beside her.

Kenzie was curled around herself, her hand pressed to her stomach and her eyes squeezed shut.

Her face was white as a sheet.

"Baby," he murmured, reaching up to brush her hair back from her sweaty forehead.

Kenzie's eyes fluttered open.

"It's…okay," she whispered. "I understand."

No. No no no.

"I didn't want this," he choked.

Kenzie's lips wobbled into a fleeting smile before she grimaced. "I know I deserve it."

"Never." He was shaking his head as he gathered her onto his lap.

She was light as a feather and cold. So cold. Her gray eyes fixed on his as a shudder wracked her body.

"It hurts," she whispered.

Braxton couldn't breathe. His chest had turned into a bed of live coals. She was in pain. No, she was dying.

Kenzie let out a small cry as he lifted her off the floor and carried her to the bedroom.

"I'm going to fix this," he promised her.

He settled her under the covers and pulled the blanket all the way up to her chin. He pressed a gentle kiss to her icy cheek.

Kenzie huddled under the blanket. She looked so fragile.

"I'm going to be back in a little bit," he promised her. "As soon as I figure out how to undo this. Okay?"

Kenzie didn't answer. She was shivering so hard Braxton could hear her teeth clattering together.

"I'll be back soon," he told her again as he closed the door softly behind him.

His first stop was Crazy Esther's room.

"Hiya, stud," Esther said when she came to the door. "To what do I owe the honor?"

Despite the late hour, Esther was dressed like she was about to go hunting. She had a quiver strapped to her back, her hunting knife at her belt, and she was wearing her grizzly fur cloak.

"Antidote," Braxton managed to choke out. His panic was consuming him the same way the poison was ravaging Kenzie's body. "I need an antidote to that poison you gave me."

Crazy Esther giggled. "I told you before. There is no antidote." She licked her lips. "Slow, painful death with no possibility of survival. That's what you asked for, and that's what I delivered."

Braxton clenched his jaw hard enough to make it ache.

"Is there some way to purge it?" he asked not caring how desperate he sounded. "It's possible it hasn't been fully ingested yet."

"God, you're dumb." Esther rolled her eyes. "Do you really think it would be a good poison if someone could just puke it up after they'd swallowed it?"

"There has to be something," he begged.

The more frantic he grew, the more delighted Esther became.

"There's a tonic that could slow the poison by a day or two and mask the pain for a short while, but it'll just prolong the victim's suffering in the end." Crazy Esther's expression brightened. "Is that what you want, to make the pain last longer?" She pawed at his arm and smiled, like the thought of someone else's prolonged agony was making her euphoric.

"Yes, that's what I want," Braxton managed.

The tonic would buy Kenzie time he desperately needed so he could hunt down every culinary magician who'd ever studied poisons. Crazy Esther might be the world expert, but that didn't mean there wasn't someone somewhere who could help him.

"Hmm." Esther tapped her chin as she considered him. "I don't think I believe you. Judging from the way you came running out of Number Eight's suite like a bat outta hell, I'm going to take a stab in the dark and guess she's the one who drank your poison." She tapped his arm. "You don't want her to suffer. You're downright desperate to save."

Braxton didn't deny it. "Please, Esther," he begged her. "I need to buy her more time until I can figure something else out."

"You're boring me." Esther yawned. "Gimme a potion. Gimme a tonic. *Gimme, gimme, gimme!*" She made a face at him. "You're on your own, stud."

Braxton didn't think about what he was doing. He didn't have room in his brain for rational thought or consequences. All he knew was that Kenzie was suffering. He didn't have time to fuck around.

Before Esther could blink, Braxton grabbed the handle of her knife, pulled it free from its scabbard, and held it to her throat.

"I need that tonic," he said. "Now."

His hand was steady as he held the blade against Esther's neck.

"Mmm," she purred. "I do like it rough, and your attitude is turning me on."

Braxton dug the knife into her neck deep enough to make her gasp. Ruby droplets of blood sprang up along the knife's blade.

"Want to test me some more?" Braxton growled.

He followed her to the kitchen. And then he held the knife to Esther's throat for the entire three hours it took for the tonic to brew.

"Drink some," Braxton ordered her as soon as she'd poured the yellowish liquid into a jar.

"Awww, you don't trust me?"

Esther hissed when Braxton drew more blood to the surface of her skin. She lifted the jar to her lips and grimaced as the scalding liquid touched her tongue.

Braxton watched to make sure she actually swallowed. Then, he waited another ten minutes to make sure she didn't start convulsing. When he was satisfied, he took the jar and carefully closed the lid.

"Thanks," he muttered. "And, uh, sorry about this."

Esther swiped a finger along the cut on her neck and licked off the blood.

"Better hurry along now," she taunted. "You don't want Number Eight to croak before you can get this to her."

Braxton ran straight back to Kenzie's suite, cradling the tonic like it was an infant.

"Kenz?" he called hesitantly as he stepped into her suite, not wanting to startle her.

When she didn't reply, his heart stopped beating. He barged into her bedroom.

Kenzie was holding her stomach and shivering. Her skin was so white it matched the sheets beneath her. But she was still alive.

"Can you sit up and drink this for me?" he asked, sitting on the edge of the bed beside her.

She was shaking too violently to do either. Braxton carefully lifted her up, murmuring apologies as she moaned in pain. He steadied her against his chest and tipped the liquid into her mouth.

He made her drink all of it, even though she was choking and spluttering by the end. As soon as the jar was empty, Kenzie slumped against him. Her body went limp in unconsciousness.

Braxton wanted to force her to wake up, just to prove that she was still with him, but he made himself leave her alone. Unconsciousness would be a respite from all the pain she was in.

Pain he'd caused her.

He settled her back against her pillows. Braxton didn't know if it was wishful thinking, but her shaking seemed to be easing off. There was even a hint of color in her cheeks.

"I'll be back in a little while," he promised her, even though she was still out cold. "I'm going to figure out how to make this right."

As soon as he was out of her room, he pulled out his phone and started scrolling through his contacts. There had to be someone in the culinary magic world who could help him.

He wouldn't rest until he found a way to save her.

* * *

There was no one who could help him.

Five excruciating hours—and about five-hundred desperate phone calls—later, Braxton was forced to accept the truth. There was no antidote to the poison.

That left only one option.

Either he or Kenzie needed to win the wish truffle, and they needed to wish for her recovery.

The finale was in two days. She just needed to hang on until then.

She didn't just *need to hang on...she had to win.*

When he got back to Kenzie, Braxton almost collapsed in relief at the sight of her. She was sitting up in bed and offered him a hesitant smile.

"How are you feeling?" he asked roughly.

She lifted a shoulder. "Like I have the flu and the worst period cramps of my life all rolled into one big ball of fun."

"Kenzie—"

"I actually feel way better than I did earlier," she said, wincing a little when she rested a hand on her stomach. "That stuff you gave me took the edge off, even though I can feel that the poison is still there."

A tormented sound was pulled from him before he could stop it.

"It's okay," she insisted.

This whole situation was so far from okay, Braxton didn't even know where to start. He had no idea why she was being so cool about all of this.

"I've tried everything," he began, going over to sit on the edge of her bed. "There's no antidote, and that means that the only way for you to…."

He cleared his throat. "Get through this, is for one of us to win the truffle and wish for your health."

Kenzie shook her head. "I actually need to talk to you about that." She winced a little as she straightened herself against the headboard. "I know I said I wasn't going to compete with you for the wish, but after everything with my dad, I have to go back on what I promised you." She looked so upset that Braxton almost reached out for her hand. He stopped himself, remembering he was the reason why every movement caused her pain.

"I can't let my dad suffer any more now that I know the truth," Kenzie continued. "At least, I have to try and make things right. I know I don't have much of a chance at winning, especially against you and in my present condition." A little smile flitted across her lips. "But I'm going to try. I have to."

"No." This time, Braxton didn't stop himself from enclosing one of her hands in both of his. Her fingers were ice cold. "You need that wish for yourself. You have to. Otherwise—"

"I'll die," she said softly. "Trust me, I've been through all the options…or lack thereof. My dad doesn't deserve what he's gotten, and I…."

"You don't deserve to die!"

Why had it taken him so goddamn long to realize that? If he had, he could have spared them all of this.

"You're not going to change my mind," she told him. "We both just need to do our best in the finale. May the best culinary magician win, right?"

"Goddamnit, Kenzie," he whispered.

The only reason he wasn't losing his mind at the moment was because of one obvious truth. Even before Kenzie was poisoned, Braxton was the stronger competitor. He was still the contestant with the best chance of winning the truffle.

Except, if he won the truffle and used it to save her, then he wouldn't be able to wish for the return of security and prosperity for his family. He would let all of them down.

He wouldn't be able to repay Veneziano Santiori.

Invisible hands were squeezing Braxton's skull. His brain felt like it was going to explode.

What the hell was he going to do?

Braxton stayed with Kenzie until she fell into a fitful sleep. When he went back into his own suite and saw Sofia, all the conclusions he thought he'd come to began to seem less certain.

Sofia had her laptop open and was talking to their mum, whose tear-stained face took up the whole computer screen.

Braxton sat down next to his sister. He wanted to be angry with her for what she'd done, but everything that had happened was his fault. He'd been the one to get the poison in the first place. It had been his idea to kill Walter Ashner's daughter.

And he'd been the one to betray his family by falling in love with Aidan's murderer.

"I filled Mum in," Sofia said curtly.

When Braxton looked at his sister, he saw accusation glinting in her eyes.

"Son, what on earth is going on?" his mother asked. "Sofia says the two of you…poisoned Walter Ashner's daughter? And now you're going to give up your wish to save her?!"

Braxton turned to Sofia. He hadn't yet discussed his plans with her, but his sister knew him well enough to figure out what he would do before he knew himself.

"I'm sorry, Mum," he said.

Because what the hell else was there to say?

His mum rubbed at her puffy eyes. "I can't believe you…either of you…would think to take another person's life." She shook her head. "I just can't believe you would do such a thing, no matter your reason."

Shame descended on Braxton. His mum was right. Aidan would never have turned to violence, no matter what had happened to him. He wouldn't have wanted anyone else to get hurt for his sake.

Aidan had always been the best of them.

Braxton was about to offer another useless apology, but Sofia spoke first.

"We thought it would bring Daddy back to us." She twisted a lock of hair around her finger in a nervous gesture. "You know how he was always saying that there was no integrity in a world that took away his son and allowed his murderer to live out the rest of his days in jail?"

They were all silent for a minute.

"I understand you wanting to give your father the justice he craved," their mum said. Her shoulders rolled forward, like she couldn't bear the weight of so much disappointment. "But this is no longer just about Walter Ashner's daughter and our family." Her voice hitched. "It's not just the three of us who are affected by your actions."

The three of us. It used to be five. Then four. Now, they were the only ones left.

His mum continued, "We're drowning here, Braxton. We have more than two-hundred employees who are depending on us for their livelihoods. Son, I know the pressure on you is enormous, but you're the only one who can save them."

It felt like a block of ice had settled in Braxton's chest.

"Mum," he whispered. "Kenzie is going to die unless I use the wish to save her."

Sofia, who had been silently fuming, boiled over. "Real quick, let me see if I understand." She turned so fast that Braxton got whiplash from her hair as it thwacked his face. "If Kenzie Ashner was some fat bloke with a neck beard who you hadn't slept with, you think you'd still be all gung ho about using your wish to save him?"

Braxton faltered.

"You slept with her?!" their mum demanded.

"Thanks for that," he muttered to Sofia.

"Any time," his sister retorted. "And for the record? I'm so glad I've been busting my ass to keep our restaurants and Aidan's memory alive while you've been dating his murderer."

"That's not fair, and you know it," Braxton shot back.

"Really?" Sofia was on her feet. "I know that Mum and I are barely managing to keep our family afloat, and all you can think about is Kenzie Ashner!"

"You're not the only one who's made sacrifices!" he roared.

"You're right," Sofia said bitterly. "And I refuse to let you throw all of our sacrifices away, especially for someone who deserves worse than death."

"That's enough," their mother said. "Both of you stop this. Now."

"But—" Braxton began.

"Not another word," his mum warned him. "And Sofia, sit down."

Braxton shut up. Sofia sat.

"Listen to me," their mum said. "We're a family. It's just the three of us, and I'm…I'm not sure…." She broke off on a muffled sob. She turned away to wipe her eyes before returning to her computer. "I'm not sure I can take any more loss."

Braxton's stomach turned over.

"Braxton will win the tournament, because he's the best culinary magician," their mum continued.

Her confidence in his skill helped eased the cloud of tension hovering over him. But the temporary reprieve disappeared with his mum's next words.

"You'll win, and at the end of the day, it will be up to you to decide how to use your wish, Braxton. You'll have to choose what matters more to you. The future of this family and all the people who depend on us to survive, or Kenzie Ashner's life."

CHAPTER 36

KENZIE

Kenzie spent the next day in a fog. She dozed off and on, feeling too restless to fall into a deep sleep but too weak to get out of bed and do anything useful.

Braxton left her suite only twice. Both times, he returned with a bowl of chicken soup. The rich, golden broth was shot through with dill fronds, shredded white meat chicken, and tiny bow tie pastas. The first time Braxton brought her the soup, her stomach had rebelled at the mere suggestion of food.

Braxton had coaxed and cajoled, and finally spoon-fed her like she was an invalid. Which, she supposed, wasn't far from the truth.

Once it warmed its way down to her stomach, she'd realized the soup was more than delicious. The bow ties numbed her throat so she could swallow without pain. The chicken made her throbbing headache abate. And the broth encased her entire body in a warm haze that eased the pain in her stomach…at least for a little while.

Braxton took care of Kiwi and sat outside the bathroom door while Kenzie showered, just in case she needed help. But in spite of the fact that she woke up from her naps more often than not to find him sitting in a chair next to her bed, he barely spoke to her. For that matter, he barely even looked at her.

She kept trying to tell him she didn't blame him. Hell, if she'd been in his and Sofia's position, she probably would have done the exact same thing.

Kenzie had even convinced herself that she wasn't afraid of dying. The sentiment was growing easier to accept as the pain in her stomach became just shy of unbearable.

Braxton looked almost as bad as she felt. There were heavy shadows beneath his eyes, his clothes were rumpled, and his hair was standing on end from all the times he'd run his hand through it.

"You need to sleep," Kenzie informed him, breaking the long silence between them.

He shook his head. "I don't want to leave you."

Kenzie got the strong sense that Braxton was afraid to leave her room because of what he might find when he returned. Every time he came back after making her soup, he rushed into her room with a wild look in his eyes that didn't ease until she moved or spoke.

"Then, sleep here." Kenzie patted the bed next to her.

When Braxton hesitated, she managed a weak eye roll, even though it made the room spin.

"I'm not going to molest you," she told him. "Scout's honor."

Braxton snorted but still didn't leave his chair.

Kenzie's eyes closed and she began to drift off. The rustle of clothes brought her back to consciousness. The mattress dipped, and then Braxton was lying next to her.

It took a pathetic amount of effort for her to turn over so she was facing him. Braxton was lying on his side and looking at her with unmistakable guilt and regret twisting his features.

"Kenzie?" He swallowed.

"Yes, Braxton?" She batted her eyelashes at him.

Clearly, the poison hadn't wrecked her to the point where she could no longer mess with him. She was also getting tired of him tiptoeing around her like she was on her freaking death bed.

Oh wait….

"Can I—" Braxton swallowed again. "Can I hold you?"

Kenzie's heart softened. In answer, she moved closer and lifted her head so he could wind his arm beneath her. He made a small, tortured sound when she pressed her lips to shoulder.

Feeling at ease for the first time since she drank the poison, she laid her head on Braxton's chest and fell asleep.

What felt like seconds later, she was being rudely awakened.

"Baby." A soft kiss to her forehead. "Kenz, you gotta wake up."

"Bastard," she mumbled.

Braxton chuckled. "Not going to argue with that. But we need to be in the dome in half an hour or we're going to miss the finale."

That got her moving.

Kenzie ignored the fiery ache in her stomach and the way her surroundings seemed to tilt as she got out of bed. Braxton tried to help her, but she waved him off.

If she was going to spend hours on her feet cooking the dish of her life, then she'd better muster up the energy to put her own damn clothes on.

Her world upended when she bent down to retrieve her jeans, earning her a curse from Braxton and the taste of bile in her throat.

"Just sit," Braxton ordered, giving her a tiny push that sent her sprawling back onto the bed.

With infinite tenderness, and keeping his gaze averted through the entire process, Braxton helped her get dressed.

"Have you changed your mind about what you'll wish for if you win?" he asked, bending down to tie her shoes.

"Nope," she replied.

Her heart stuttered at the realization that her wish might not work fast enough for her to see her dad before she died. She would have liked the chance to explain things to him.

She knew her dad wouldn't thank her for freeing him when it came at the cost of her own life. She also knew that she couldn't live with herself knowing she had chosen her own life over her father's.

Maybe she could write her dad a note....

In spite of his obvious displeasure at her response, Braxton wrapped an arm around her shoulders and helped her stand. He bore most of her weight as they walked into the hallway to join Rick and Esther.

Braxton stood a little behind her, letting Kenzie lean against him without making it obvious to the others how feeble she was. She didn't need him to tell her what a bad idea it would be to show weakness to Esther and Rick. Those two were like sharks scenting the water for injured prey.

"Looking a little sallow, Number Eight," Crazy Esther said to Kenzie as they lined up outside the dome.

"Never felt better," Kenzie replied in as chipper a voice as she could manage.

"Hey, Braxton," Rick said, "Check it out." He held out his phone, displaying a photo on the screen. There was a blonde model wearing a French maid costume that was comprised of a frilly bra, barely-there panties, and garters.

"Go fuck yourself," Braxton told Rick.

"Won't have to," Rick said smugly. "I'll have the beautiful Sofia at my beck and call."

Kenzie staggered against the wall as Braxton's solid weight was suddenly no longer propping her up.

Braxton's fist sliced through the air. A second later, a wet thud resounded in the corridor. Blood poured from Rick's nose and mouth.

Rick swung back. Braxton didn't even try to get out of the way; he was too busy pummeling Rick.

"Braxton, stop," Kenzie said weakly.

He ignored her. Braxton probably had fifty pounds and a foot of height on Rick, and he used every bit of his advantage to send the other man sprawling. Braxton straddled Rick and continued to rain blows down on his face and chest.

Esther let out an ecstatic whoop and leapt onto Braxton's back. She dug the point of her hunting knife into his neck.

Kenzie shouted out a warning and staggered forward, catching her balance on Esther's long hair. She gave the girl's braids a sharp yank that earned her a face full of spittle and a screech that made her temporarily deaf.

"What in the world is going on out here?"

The four of them went still as Polly Berrywhite, framed in the open doorway to the dome, stared down at them. The other two judges appeared on either side of her.

Even with Kenzie's untrustworthy vision, the judges' fury came across loud and clear.

"Have you lost your collective minds?" Chef Levy hissed. She snapped at someone waiting in the wings. "Get a medic. Now!"

Chef Sakai was trying—unsuccessfully—to part Braxton and Rick.

Chef Levy stalked down the steps. With a karate chop-like move that was as effective as it was badass, she had both guys stumbling away from each other. Crazy Esther's knife skittered out of her hand as she landed on her back. Chef Levy caught the loose knife underneath her sneaker.

When Braxton made a move toward Rick, Chef Levy pinned him with a glare that was scarier than Esther's knife.

"Try anything, and I'll break both your wrists," Chef Levy warned him. "You'll have to forfeit the finale."

Braxton stilled. Esther got to her feet. Rick moaned as a woman in a forest-green jumpsuit tended to his split lip. Their makeup artists circled around them, wielding brushes and powders like weapons.

Kenzie didn't envy the impossible task of making them look presentable. The four of them were a sorry sight.

"I've got to get back in there," Polly said, eyeing the open doorway through which loud cheers were coming. "They'll know something's wrong."

"Go," Chef Levy said tersely. "We'll get these idiots ready by the time you've finished your little speech."

With a wounded look at the bossy judge, Polly did as she was told. Chef Sakai stood over all of them, radiating disapproval. Chef Levy barked orders to a flurry of new arrivals who produced fresh, non-bloody chef coats for Braxton and Rick. Two makeup artists worked to conceal Rick's swollen nose and bloodied lip before coming to Kenzie. They layered blush on her cheeks, all the while informing her that she looked like death warmed over.

Hah.

Kenzie had always been good at avoidance. She'd done it for most of her life to keep from being crushed when her own mother refused to acknowledge her. She'd relied on it after she lost Danny and her father went to jail. She had wrapped avoidance around her like a snug blanket after Nana died and she decided to make a clean break from her life in New York.

Now, that gently-simmered and aged skill helped her to avoid thinking about her imminent death. In her experience, the best way to deal with something unpleasant was simply not to deal with it at all.

"Please join me in welcoming our four finalists!" Polly Berrywhite's voice boomed from inside the dome.

Kenzie regarded the short flight of steps that led up to the dome, which might as well have been a mountain. She prayed she didn't keel over before she even made it into the dome. A second later, she felt Braxton's familiar warmth behind her and a steadying hand against her lower back.

"Smile," one of their makeup people chirped as they filed past.

Kenzie stepped inside the dome. She was instantly assailed by all the lights and the noise. She could barely stay standing as it was, and all the sensations were making her head spin. Sweat rolled down her face, even though she had to lock her jaw to keep from shivering.

She was doomed.

Braxton stayed with her as long as he could, but as soon as their names were called, they each had to move to their own cook stations. It took every ounce of Kenzie's strength to walk the ten steps to her own station without crumpling to the ground.

As she leaned heavily against her counter, Kenzie wondered if anyone would think it strange if she asked to borrow one of the judge's chairs.

"You'll have three hours to complete your final dish," Polly boomed. "Use your time well, chefs."

Kenzie wanted to laugh. She wasn't sure she could stay conscious for three hours, let alone cook for that much time.

Yes, you can, an annoying voice insisted in her head. *You have to.*

Kenzie let out a breath, trying to somehow exhale the sizzling pain in her stomach.

It didn't work.

"Are we ready, finalists?" Polly asked.

"Yes, Chef!" the four of them replied.

"Let's cook some magic!"

Kenzie felt like she was standing in the eye of a tornado, while everything else spun around her. The others raced to get their ingredients. Kenzie walked…slowly.

"Look at that, our dark horse is oozing confidence!" Polly commentated from the judges' table, her voice magnified by the microphone clipped to her lapel.

The other contestants were leaving the supply pantry by the time Kenzie reached it. Braxton met her gaze, a silent question in his eyes.

All good, she replied with a nod.

"Braxton McKaid, the crowd favorite, off to a good start," Polly said a few moments later. "And, whoa, Mr. McKaid! Didn't anyone tell you you're not working in pairs anymore?"

The audience laughed. Some people cheered, while others booed. Kenzie looked back. Braxton was at his station, but Kenzie saw a basket of ingredients left on her counter that hadn't been there before. It was all the heavy things that she had preemptively decided to do away with, since she could barely handle her own weight.

"Only two hours and fifty-two minutes remaining," Polly called. "Ms. Brookerton, let's get a move on!"

Somehow, Kenzie made it to and from the pantry without passing out. She dumped her ingredients on the counter along with the necessities Braxton had already carried over for her. Then, shoving away her pain and fear and insecurities, she started to cook.

CHAPTER 37

BRAXTON

It wasn't easy to concentrate on his dish while he was keeping one eye on Kenzie. Braxton cursed the fact that their stations were as far from each other as they could be. And yet, even at this distance, he could see Kenzie's clumsy slowness.

He was also trying to keep tabs on Rick and Esther. Braxton was under no illusion that those two would leave the fate of this competition up to chance…or pure talent. They might leave Kenzie alone since it was clear she wasn't a threat, but he was a different story. Braxton had no idea what cheap tricks those two had planned for this round, but he did know one fact with utter certainty.

Rick wasn't going to let a McKaid steal his victory a second time.

Okay Aid, Braxton thought as he got on with the mise en place and arranged his ingredients. *Now or never. Help me out?*

Braxton's hands knew what they were supposed to do, even if he was more distracted than he'd ever been. He spiralized his butternut squash and spread the strands out on a baking sheet. Then, he whipped egg whites and began shaping his second batch of merengues…just in case he needed extras.

"What's your dish, McKaid?"

Braxton tore his eyes off Kenzie to look into Chef Levy's frowning face.

"Merengue birds flying out of a butternut squash nest," Braxton said. He forced a friendly grin on his face. "And they'll be bringing themselves right to your mouths for your convenience, of course."

"Sounds charming!" Polly clapped her hands together.

"Hmph," Chef Sakai said. He tapped the first tray of birds that had just come out of the oven. The sound had a hollow ring to it, telling all of them that the merengue was crisp on the outside and soft within. Perfect.

"Why does that dish sound so familiar?" Chef Levy asked, arching an eyebrow as she turned Braxton inside out with just a look.

"It was a dish my brother made," he said.

"I see." Chef Levy scowled at him. "The only problem is, you aren't your brother. Do you have any of your own ideas in that big head of yours?"

Braxton's retort was on the tip of his tongue. But as he met Chef Levy's steely gaze, words Kenzie had said to him more than a week ago filled his mind.

You're trying to be your brother, and you're not him.

That was also the day he'd admitted to Kenzie that he didn't have his own culinary specialty and that he didn't enjoy cooking.

"Actually," Braxton said, his gaze already assessing the ingredients compiled on his counter. "I think I'm going to keep my final dish a surprise for the moment."

"Oh, I do love surprises," Polly said.

"Sloppy," Chef Sakai muttered.

Chef Levy didn't say anything, but Braxton thought he caught something in her expression that might have been approval.

Forgive me, Aid? Braxton thought as he pulled the pan of merengues out of the oven and dumped them in the garbage beside his station. He pointedly didn't look at the first row of seats just outside the dome, where Sofia was undoubtedly glaring daggers at him at this very moment.

The question of what could possibly replace the dish he'd been practicing for months…hell, years…was a harder problem to solve.

Maybe he should have waited to throw out those merengues until he had a plan.…

Braxton wasn't a fly-by-the-seat-of-his-pants kind of person. During the first two rounds of the tournament, he'd done the planning while Kenzie had improvised.

He looked across the dome. Kenzie stopped what she was doing, as though she could feel his attention. She smiled at him.

In that moment, all of his uncertainty disappeared. He didn't have to choose between Aidan's style, Kenzie's, or his own.

Ideas began to cohere into something usable.

Past and present…memory and hope… Genius and passion….

Braxton had spent the last five years living in the past, but in the moments he'd spent alone with Kenzie, he'd been firmly in the present. He wanted his dish to represent a merging of both. A little of Aidan's influence, a little of Kenzie's…until he had something wholly, uniquely his own.

Braxton was already reaching for ingredients before the image in his head was fully formed. Sugar, water, corn syrup, cream of tartar, and food coloring. Saucepan. Candy thermometer. Baking sheet.

Sugar glass was easy enough to make. But for what Braxton had in mind, he'd need every second of his remaining time to assemble and infuse his creation with magic.

He'd never practiced this dish before, and yet, he knew he could do it. He had his brother's voice in one ear, Kenzie's in the other, and his own vision of what he wanted to create.

Let's do this thing.

CHAPTER 38

KENZIE

Half an hour into the challenge, Kenzie knew the ambitious three-course magical dinner she'd planned just wasn't going to happen. She'd scalded her hand when her balance failed and she grabbed the burner to keep from whacking her head on the counter and knocking herself out. Because priorities.

She'd spilled her first attempt at a béchamel sauce all over herself when her muscles seized. And she couldn't taste any of her own food to make sure it was right, because her insides were being devoured by a raging inferno.

It was time to improvise.

Kenzie glanced around at the other competitors. Crazy Esther's work table was covered in the scattered remains of the rattlesnake she was butchering.

Yep, rattlesnake.

Kenzie wasn't prone to queasiness—she was a chef, after all—but that rattler's head staring at her from the edge of Esther's table was unsettling to say the least. Kenzie thanked the culinary magician gods that she didn't need to taste Esther's dish.

Rick was baking. Kenzie couldn't see his creation, but there was no denying the smells wafting from his station were enticing.

Kenzie had no idea what the hell Braxton was up to. He had stopped staring at her with a worried expression on his face every two seconds and seemed utterly engrossed in his dish.

And Kenzie had three partially-finished dishes to show for herself. The only aspect of her meal that wasn't a complete disaster was her passion fruit ice cream, which she'd made for a dessert that she had no hope of finishing. It was hardening nicely in the blast chiller and had a beautiful golden hue.

Here you go, Judges, she imagined herself saying. *A nice bowl of ice cream. Now, can I get that wish truffle, please?*

Damnit. She needed to get her act together…fast.

What could she make in—she glanced at the clock—an hour and ten minutes?

If her dad could see her right now, he'd shake his head in dismay. Her station was a mess. She was a mess.

Think, Kenzie.

If only her head wasn't full of cobwebs and her insides weren't disintegrating. She couldn't remember a thing she'd learned about magic. For some reason, the only semi-relevant memory that was sticking in her head at the moment was of the night she'd done fire and ice shots with Braxton.

Maybe she could get the judges really, really *drunk….*

Shaking her head to clear it, Kenzie tried to find the sense of tranquility that usually enveloped her while she was cooking. She needed to come up with the perfect dish to save her father.

What the hell kind of food was powerful enough to save a life?

Her dad always liked to say the ingredients should drive the dish. He'd look at whatever was fresh and in season, and then he'd design the menu around those ingredients.

In Kenzie's case, she had a vat of passion fruit ice cream.

There were a million dishes she could make that fused tropical flavors, but nothing was jumping out at her as tournament-winning-good.

What would Walter Ashner do with a container of passion fruit ice cream?

The answer was so glaringly obvious Kenzie almost laughed. He'd make her favorite dish in the entire world. Baked Alaska.

The dessert was sponge cake, topped with a layer of ice cream, and then enclosed in a rounded merengue shell. Her dad had made it for every one of Kenzie's birthdays for as long as she could remember. He'd experimented with different flavors, but he never messed with the basics of the dish.

The figurative cherry on top was always when her dad flambéed the dessert. Seeing the liquor-soaked shell erupt in flames never lost its charm.

That was it.

Baked Alaska…with a magical twist.

Kenzie knew it was the right choice, because the sizzling ache in her stomach and blurry vision improved a little. She had an hour left. Just enough time to make the most magical dish of her life.

CHAPTER 39

BRAXTON

Ten minutes remaining, chefs!" Polly called out.

Braxton levitated another piece of red sugar glass, adjusting it in mid-air so it settled itself at the end of his phoenix's outstretched wing.

The towering structure was a foot taller than Braxton, and almost as wide as it was tall. He could feel every pair of eyes in the audience glued to his creation.

Traditionally, the magical part of a dish only happened when the food was being eaten by the judges. But Aidan had always believed part of a dish's magic lived in its formation.

Since this dish was partly for Aidan, it seemed appropriate to build the dish the way his twin would have. With levitation.

Braxton was using a combination of red, orange, and yellow sugar glass in his phoenix. He'd used all kinds of fruit flavorings for the different shards that matched the colors, like pomegranate, apricots, and star fruit.

He would lose points because there was no variety in texture, but he would make up for that shortcoming with his uniqueness and ingenuity.

The entire structure had more than two-hundred individual shards of sugar glass. With the overhead spotlights shining down on the translucent sugar, it looked like the phoenix was on fire. Just like he'd hoped.

Not too shabby, eh Aid?

Braxton could almost picture his brother sweeping off an imaginary hat and bowing in deference to the culinary feat before him.

As their mum had so often pointed out when they were growing up, Aidan had inherited enough modesty to make up for the fact that Braxton and Sofia had none.

"One minute, chefs!"

Braxton's phoenix was finished…at least until it was his turn to go before the judges. Then, he'd bring his magical creation even more to life than it already was. He'd never been more confident of securing the win than he was in that moment.

Now, all he had to do was keep his concentration and maintain his magical hold over every shard of glass in the phoenix.

Braxton was holding two-hundred gossamer threads of magic, each of which connected his mind to one of the phoenix shards. If his concentration broke, the entire phoenix would fall apart.

Fortunately, Braxton had never been lacking in the concentration or will power department.

"Time! Hands in the air, chefs!"

They all stepped away from their creations. Thunderous applause filled the stadium as the audience whooped and whistled. Braxton even caught a few chants of his name.

The four competitors lined up in front of the judges so the audience could scrutinize their final dishes.

Braxton snuck a peek at Kenzie. She looked exhausted, but she was on her feet. Her dish was hidden beneath a silver dome, so he couldn't see how it had come out.

"Esther, will you bring your dish forward, please?" Polly called.

Crazy Esther carried a huge platter covered with fried rattlesnake filets up to the judges' table. The displaced head sat sentry on one side of the plate, while the rattle was on the other.

In terms of presentation, she wasn't off to a good start. Even Polly Berrywhite seemed mildly repulsed, and that was saying something.

"I've deep-fried the meat in panko, flavored with cayenne and lime zest," Esther said. "The crunchy exterior will pair nicely with the mild flavor of the rattlesnake meat."

"Oh," Polly said, sighing a little. "Well, that does sound quite scrumptious."

"This is my life on a plate," Esther told the judges as she set the platter down. "Where I come from, no part of an animal goes to waste. As you will see from my dish, backwoods cooking holds the answer not just to the future of culinary magic, but to a sustainable future."

Braxton returned his full attention to his phoenix while Esther droned on about her lifestyle and backwoods cooking. He shored up his magical threads and made sure there were no weaknesses. When he made his phoenix fly, he didn't want any pieces to get left behind.

He spared another glance at the judges' table as the pieces of fried rattlesnake began to vibrate. Esther's face turned tomato-red as she worked her magic.

Slowly, the slices of rattlesnake coalesced until they joined up with the head and tail. Even though some realism was lost by the breadcrumb coating on the rattlesnake, it looked more or less like the real, live thing.

Everyone in the audience gasped as the rattler raised its head and stuck out its forked tongue.

It was more than likely that at least one audience member had fainted.

The snake's rattle shook. Then, the creature slithered off its platter and onto the judges' table.

"Health standards, anyone?" Rick muttered under his breath.

For once, Braxton didn't disagree.

Esther snapped her fingers, and then the whole rattlesnake returned back to filets that launched themselves directly onto each judge's plate. Another snap of Esther's fingers, and the fine-boned skeleton separated itself from the meat.

"Oh, well done," Polly said, clapping her hands and eyeing the snake cautiously.

Esther spooned a citrus vinaigrette onto each plate and stepped back. From the look on her face, one would think she'd already won the tournament.

Braxton caught Kenzie's gaze. She was standing a little behind Esther, so when she pretended to gag, Braxton was the only one who could see.

His laughter quickly died when Chef Sakai glared at him before taking a bite of his rattlesnake.

"Needs more citrus," Chef Sakai grumbled. "But the breading is well seasoned, and the magic was appropriate. I appreciate your use of the whole animal."

That was the most effusive compliment Braxton had ever heard out of the cantankerous judge's mouth.

"I never thought I'd say this," Polly Berrywhite said, talking around a mouthful of rattlesnake, "but this might be the most delicious protein I've ever tasted." She chewed and swallowed. "These spices really bolden up the mild flavor. I need the recipe so I can make it for my next dinner party!"

"Thank you, Chef," Esther said with a self-satisfied smirk.

Chef Levy stood up from her chair slowly and deliberately. She picked up her plate and walked down the steps until she was standing directly in front of Esther.

Braxton could feel the way the entire audience, along with everyone in the dome, held their breath. The judge's face was inscrutable.

"Chef, can you tell me what this is?" She picked something up from her plate and held it in front of Esther's face.

From where Braxton was standing, he couldn't see what the judge was grasping between her thumb and index finger. Whatever it was, it was no bigger than a needle.

Esther muttered something unintelligible.

"I'm sorry, what was that?" Chef Levy cupped her hand around her ear and leaned closer to Esther.

"It's a bone, Chef," Esther repeated.

Well, that sucks.

This was the finale in the most cutthroat magical culinary competition in the world. A bone left in the food was grounds for immediate disqualification.

While none of the judges directly told her to get the hell out, their faces said it all. Esther was done.

The bright look of victory faded from Esther's eyes, leaving her expression vacant and dull. Her posture drooped. She let her braids fall in front of her face to obscure her hand as she wiped her eyes. Then, she straightened and strode purposefully to the edge of the dome.

The audience clapped politely.

In that moment, Esther didn't look crazy. She just looked sad…defeated. If Braxton didn't have a mountain of his own problems to deal with, he would have felt sorry for her.

"Rick, you're next," Chef Levy snapped.

As Rick left their lineup to retrieve his covered tray, he shoulder-bumped Kenzie. Her legs gave out and she hit the ground.

The audience booed.

Braxton's vision darkened as fury overwhelmed him. He started forward, stopping when he felt a strange tug on his mind. That was when he remembered the two-hundred strings of magic he was holding onto. He quickly focused before he lost control and his phoenix collapsed into a shapeless pile of sugar glass.

When he looked back, Kenzie was staggering to her feet.

"Oops, sorry about that," Rick said.

He collected his tray and headed for the judges' table, detouring past Braxton's station. Rick slowed his steps and spoke out of the corner of his mouth.

"So, you and Number Eight were more than just partners, huh?"

At whatever murderous expression crossed Braxton's face, Rick smirked.

"I didn't know you were into the bad girl look, but I can't blame you for tapping that." Rick's smile broadened. "You know what I just realized? If I did her and Sofia at the same time, it'd be like an angel-devil thing. Hot, don't you think?"

Braxton held tightly to his magic…and his sanity…as his anger simmered.

"Everything alright, Rick?" Polly asked politely.

"Coming, judges." Rick offered them a bright smile before continuing on his way.

Braxton gave his magic an experimental tug. He knew it was a bad idea to engage, but this prick had threatened his sister. He'd touched Kenzie.

So, Braxton threw caution to the wind and emptied his mind of everything except his magic and the shards of sugar glass that made up his phoenix. He focused on the smell of candied fruit. He saw the glossy reds, oranges, and yellows in his mind's eye. He tasted the sharp sweetness on his tongue.

Then, when the phoenix was as present in his mind as it was physically before him, Braxton lifted up the threads of his magic. Imagining a draft sweeping under his creation, he sent his phoenix into the air.

He heard gasps and oohs, but all of his attention was on his phoenix.

Braxton stretched the creature's wings out to their full span. Slowly, so he wouldn't disrupt any of the individual shards, he made the phoenix flap its wings and soar gracefully all the way around the dome.

Polly Berrywhite's applause joined the rest of the audience. "Magnificent!" she cried.

"Don't reveal your hand just yet," Chef Levy said with a dissatisfied frown.

"Oh, I've barely gotten started, Chef," Braxton replied. "Just wanted to give you something to think about while you're waiting for Rick to bring you his dish." He looked right at Rick and bared his teeth. It wasn't quite the one-finger salute he would have preferred, but the message was the same. And no less effective in eliciting the intended response.

The audience hooted. Rick's cheeks turned as red as the glass in Braxton's phoenix.

"What delicious morsels do you have for us, dear?" Polly, ever the peacekeeper, asked Rick.

Shaking off Braxton's insult, Rick concentrated on his dish. "I come from a family of musicians," Rick told the judges in a tight voice. "So, this dish is me."

He lifted the covering to show off a chocolate grand piano. The top of the piano was raised, which offered a view of the assortment of pastries within. Each pastry was molded into the shape of a different instrument.

It wasn't as good as Braxton's phoenix, but it was impressive.

"How delightful!" Polly crooned. She plucked a violin-shaped pastry from inside the piano and put it in her mouth.

"Mmm," she said appreciatively.

As soon as she began to chew, a haunting violin melody filled the dome.

"Might I suggest you sample the cello cannoli next?" Rick said.

Chef Sakai carefully removed the cello-shaped pastry from the piano. The golden shell was shaped to look like a miniature version of the instrument, while curls of ricotta filling bordered the edges. Rows of tiny chocolate chips looked like the instrument's strings.

Chef Sakai finished his inspection of the pastry and took a bite. A few seconds later, a new strain of music joined the first.

With every bite the chefs took, more instruments were added to the music. It began to sound like an entire symphony had taken over the dome.

"Lovely," Polly murmured as the music died away. "Just lovely."

"I would have liked some savory," Chef Levy said.

Chef Sakai nodded in agreement. "Scones were oversweet."

Ouch. Given that the Santiori family owned several of the best Italian bakeries in the US, Braxton couldn't imagine Rick was pleased with that feedback. Still, it was undeniably high praise from two judges who could find fault with even the most flawless dish.

As Rick passed him, Braxton couldn't help a snide, "You think you can be runner-up two decades in a row?"

Braxton knew he'd pushed the other man too far. He tensed for their second brawl of the day, but Rick didn't move. He closed his eyes.

"All good, Santiori?" Braxton whispered.

Rick didn't respond. A few seconds passed, and still, nothing happened.

Braxton exhaled noisily when he felt a sharp yank on the strings of magic he was controlling.

Son of a bitch. Rick was trying to steal control of Braxton's dish.

It was a breach of tournament rules to interfere with another competitor's dish. But by the time the judges figured out what Rick was doing, it would be too late. If Rick ruined the phoenix and Braxton had nothing to serve to the judges, he'd be disqualified.

Braxton gritted his teeth as he fought for control of the threads of magic connecting each shard of sugar glass. He could feel the strands stretching and fraying. Sweat trickled down his brow, but he didn't spare an ounce of his mental energy to deal with the discomfort.

"Thank you, Rick," Polly Berrywhite said pointedly, when Rick didn't return to his station.

Rick ignored her. Redness bloomed in his pale cheeks as he tried to wrest control of the phoenix from Braxton.

Not happening, mate.

Rick continued to stand in the center of the dome, halfway between the judges' table and his own station, as he muttered to himself. He was also looking a little constipated.

"I thought my brother already taught you this lesson," Braxton told Rick, loud enough for the microphones to pick up his voice. "You're never going to win against a McKaid."

Rick released his hold on the shards so suddenly that Braxton had to scramble to rebalance his own magical grasp. He didn't want to crush the delicate sugar under the weight of his control.

No sooner had he reached a sense of equilibrium in his magic, Braxton sensed that something was off. The evil smile Rick offered was all the confirmation he needed.

The bastard was up to something.

At the exact moment Braxton discovered one of the magical threads was no longer in his control, a long shard of yellow glass began to separate from the phoenix's beak.

Braxton was holding two-hundred sugar glass shards together…minus one. Rick hadn't been able to pry all of them away, but controlling one to Braxton's one-ninety-nine was child's play.

Braxton mentally grasped for the shard, but it was far easier for Rick to control a single piece than for him to retrieve it without losing hold of all the others he was maintaining.

If Rick didn't stop this, the judges would eventually figure out he was manipulating Braxton's dish, which was grounds for automatic elimination from the tournament. But even though it was becoming increasingly clear that Braxton would eventually win this battle over the magic, Rick didn't let up.

"Give up, Santiori," Braxton huffed, breathing through a headache that warned him he was pushing the limits of his magic.

Rick appeared just as worn out as Braxton. His hair clung to his damp forehead.

"I can do whatever I want on this stage, to whoever I want—" Rick paused to catch his breath. "—and I'll get away with it."

Braxton's retort died on his tongue as the truth behind Rick's words became clear. Rick didn't care about winning…so long as Braxton lost.

Son of a bitch.

"Quit showing off, Braxton," Chef Levy barked, thinking he was responsible for the shard of glass that was hovering a few feet away from where it was supposed to be embedded in the phoenix's beak.

Braxton couldn't risk taking his concentration away from his phoenix long enough to tell the judges he wasn't controlling the rogue shard.

The yellow piece of sugar glass was moving farther away from the rest of the phoenix. Braxton made another futile grab for the piece, but he couldn't latch onto it without letting go of all the others.

The triangle shard that was now fully in Rick's control was about a foot in length and honed to a wicked point. Its edges were sharp as a knife's blade.

Rick let out a harsh laugh. Then, the shard of glass shot forward…straight toward Kenzie.

"Braxton, stop this right now," Polly ordered, her voice pitched high.

"It's. Not. Me." Braxton was straining to maintain his hold over the rest of his creation.

Too far. The shard was out of his reach. If he moved closer, he'd lose control over the pieces in the rest of his phoenix.

Braxton's choices were to hold his winning dish together and forego that single shard, or he could take back control of that one piece at the expense of all the others.

It would have been an easy decision…except the shard under Rick's command was on track to slice through the back of Kenzie's neck.

"Kenz, move!" Braxton shouted.

She turned her head. Her eyes widened. She took a small step to the side and wavered. The shard adjusted its course and raced toward her.

She was too weak. Too slow. And Rick wasn't backing down.

Kenzie screamed.

Braxton didn't hesitate.

He heard a sound behind him like shattering glass, but he didn't spare his phoenix a thought. He threw himself at Rick.

CHAPTER 40

KENZIE

The knife-sharp piece of sugar glass pricked the skin of Kenzie's throat, right at her pulse point.

She tried to stop it, wrapping her hands around the razor-sharp sides as an unnatural force drove the shard forward. It was going to skewer her.

Blood slid down her forearms. Her whole body shook as she fought the shard.

The little that remained of Kenzie's strength was waning. She felt blood dripping down her neck as the shard's tip broke through her skin.

Then, without warning, the piece of sugar glass stopped driving forward. All the resistance disappeared, and Kenzie was able to wrench the point out of her neck. The shard fell harmlessly onto the ground and shattered.

Gasping and clutching her bleeding neck, Kenzie turned to see Braxton pinning Rick to the ground. When she looked for Braxton's phoenix, her heart stopped.

The gorgeous bird was gone. Broken pieces of colored glass were scattered all over the floor.

"What is going on?!" Polly Berrywhite shouted.

The judges were running down from their stage. The audience had erupted in a flurry of outraged cries.

Kenzie wiped her fingers across her throat, ignoring the metallic smell of blood that filled her nose.

She heard Braxton's low voice as he told the judges that Rick had taken control of the piece of sugar glass that would have killed Kenzie…if Braxton hadn't stopped Rick.

But in order to save her, Braxton had been forced to abandon his dish.

His beautiful, show-stopping, one-of-a-kind creation was destroyed.

Kenzie had known from her first glance at the phoenix that Braxton was going to win. She had no doubt everyone else in the dome and outside it had made the same observation.

"Shameful," Chef Sakai told Rick, shaking his head in disgust.

"Poor sportsmanship, to say the least," Polly agreed. "If your father wasn't on the board of my charity—"

"Disqualified!" Chef Levy grasped Rick's shirt and hauled him to his feet, giving him a hearty shove in the direction of the dome's exit.

Kenzie expected to see humiliation and fury on Rick's face. Instead, as he stalked past Braxton, his expression held only triumph. He spoke quietly, but Kenzie was close enough to hear him tell Braxton, "Hope the bitch was worth it to you. 'Cause your family is mine, now."

Braxton didn't respond. He got to his feet slowly and looked at the sugar glass crystals scattered across the floor.

Kenzie's heart gave a painful squeeze.

A security guard appeared to escort Rick out of the dome. The audience's heckles and boos had no impact the smug little shit. Rick seemed content in his knowledge that he had ruined Braxton's chances of winning.

"In all my years, I've never been at such a loss for words," Polly told the audience. Her face was pinched in apology as she turned to Braxton. "I am so sorry about your dish, dearest. But I'm afraid that without anything to taste, we have to disqualify you from the round."

Braxton nodded, seeming unsurprised by the verdict.

Kenzie gaped at the judges. "That's so unfair!" she raged. "You saw his dish. It was incredible."

Polly nodded sympathetically.

"Rules are rules," Chef Levy said.

If Kenzie was at her normal strength, she would have smacked that judge upside her spiky-haired head.

What the hell was wrong with these people?

"Leave it," Braxton told her in a quiet voice. "It's fine."

It most certainly wasn't fine. Fury and righteous indignation clogged Kenzie's throat.

"Kenzie, dear, is your neck alright?" Polly asked. "Do you need a paramedic?"

Kenzie almost laughed at that. If only the judges knew that the blood trickling down her neck was the least of her problems. Her insides were dissolving.

"I'm okay," Kenzie heard herself say.

Her voice sounded thin. Her mouth was dry as a desert.

"Are you certain you're well enough to present your dish, Ms. Brookerton?" Chef Sakai asked.

"Ashner," Kenzie said quietly, even though it wasn't loud enough for anyone to hear her.

Kenzie's legs chose that particular moment to give out. Instead of hitting the floor, she found herself encircled in the familiar warmth of Braxton's arms.

"I've got you," he said in a rough voice as he supported her.

"Why the hell did you do that?" Kenzie demanded, her eyes pricking with tears as the full weight of Braxton's actions caught up to her.

"Um, because you would have fallen and given yourself a concussion…?" Braxton gave her a quizzical look.

Kenzie managed a weak punch that bounced right off his biceps. "I mean, why would you give up your chance of winning?" Kenzie gestured at the pile of glass that crackled and ground into dust under the judges' shoes.

Braxton brushed her cheek with his knuckles. "I think it's fairly obvious."

"But you would have won," she protested.

Braxton would have gotten his wish and saved his family. Instead, he'd come to her rescue and ruined everything for himself.

Braxton nodded. "I made a choice."

There was a desperate kind of intensity in his gaze as he leaned closer.

"It's up to you, now. You have to win and get the wish truffle. It's the only way for you to live."

As if on cue, the inferno in her stomach spiked. Kenzie doubled over, curling around the pain as she tried to breathe.

She knew Braxton's arms were the only thing keeping her upright. She heard his voice in her ears, but she couldn't make out the individual words. Her insides felt like they were being devoured.

"Kenzie, come on," Braxton urged.

His insistent voice brought her out of the haze of pain that was eating her alive. She had to do this. If she died before she got to present her dish, she'd be squandering the precious gift Braxton had given her. He'd sacrificed everything to give her a chance to win.

"Help me?" she murmured.

"It's against the rules for me to touch your dish," Braxton said.

Kenzie felt her world tilt as Braxton lifted her into his arms. He bent down until she was level with her covered dish.

"Oh, that won't be necessary," Polly said quickly, gesturing to the other judges. "I think, given your injury, we can come to you."

Kenzie almost wept with relief. The simple act of lifting her dish, even without having to concern herself with the weight of her own body, was more than she thought she could manage.

Braxton put her down, but he stayed at her back, giving her a solid wall of muscle to lean against.

"So, what have you got for us?" Polly asked in a falsely cheery voice.

The three judges stood on the opposite side of Kenzie's counter and eyed her.

"The inspiration for my dish comes from a combination of my experiences and the people who have helped me get to where I am in this moment," Kenzie said, forcing her throat to work. She pulled off the cover to reveal her beautifully caramelized and golden merengue. Instead of the traditional rounded shell, Kenzie had shaped the merengue into two interlocking hands.

"Baked Alaska was what my father made every year for my birthday for as long as I can remember," Kenzie told the judges. "There's a dark chocolate sponge layer, followed by a layer of passion fruit ice cream on top. I drizzled mango coulis around the edge of the plate."

"I like that you've taken a traditional idea and elevated it," Polly Berrywhite said approvingly. "But why the hands? Is that symbolic of your relationship with your father?"

"Partially," Kenzie replied. "My father inspired this dish, but there have been many others who helped get me to where I am right now. The hands represent all of those people." She took a second to let a wave of dizziness pass. "I call this dish fire and ice."

She turned and snuck a glance at Braxton's face, wondering if he would get the reference to their night at the bar. From the amusement peeking through his serious expression, she thought he did.

"Sounds like a good balance of flavors and textures," Chef Sakai said, sounding more grudging than complimentary. "And the magic?"

Kenzie managed a little smirk. "I thought you'd never ask."

She reached over to her cooktop for the small pot of brandy she'd been warming over low heat. She gently poured the liquor over the two merengue hands.

Normally, a match or fire starter was needed to flambé the alcohol, but Kenzie had magic. She thought about all the passion she felt for Braxton. The emotion allowed her magic to grasp hold of the alcohol and set the brandy alight. Without so much as touching her dish, the brandy erupted into orange and blue flames.

The fire danced along the interlocking merengue hands without burning through the egg white shell. A sweet, nutty scent rose from the merengue, which was caramelizing without overheating. Kenzie gave her magic a little nudge, raising the flames so they stretched far above the interlocking hands.

"We have the fire," Kenzie said, forgetting about her ravaged body as she lost herself in the magic of her creation. "Now, it's time for the ice."

As soon as she sliced into the baked Alaska, the flames extinguished. Kenzie was relieved to see the ice cream beneath the merengue was still completely frozen and unaffected by the fire.

Kenzie handed out slices to each of the judges. As they scrutinized the layer of dark chocolate sponge and golden passion fruit ice cream, Kenzie thought about her father. She remembered all the times he'd made this dessert, just so he could see her smile. She remembered the determined look in his eyes when she'd seen him in the jail and he told her the truth about Aidan's death.

Kenzie's father had been willing to give up everything for her sake. So had Braxton.

Thinking about their sacrifices touched off another bout of magic. Except this time, there was no fiery burst. The magic began in the ice cream layer and spooled outward. It wound around her, gentle and cool and comforting.

She held onto that feeling as thick, picture-perfect snowflakes began to drift down from the ceiling.

They were already in a glass dome, so it didn't take a stretch to imagine they were inside a snow globe. She heard the audience's awed murmurs and applause, but all of her attention was on what was happening inside the dome. The judges were taking their first bites of her dish.

Braxton gave her shoulders a light squeeze. She held her breath while she waited for the judges' pronouncement.

"Tropical flavors are unusual for a baked Alaska," Chef Levy said, dipping the prongs of her fork into the mango coulis. "It's…refreshing."

The judge seemed as surprised by her positive feedback as Kenzie.

"Good balance of flavors and magic," Chef Sakai said. "A winning dish."

"You cooked from the heart, and it shows," Polly Berrywhite said. To the other judges, she asked, "Do we need to confer, or is our decision unanimous?"

Kenzie's vision wavered. She had to remind herself to breathe before she passed out.

The judges only took a moment to whisper to each other.

"Congratulations, Kenzie Brookerton," Polly announced, giving her a warm smile. "You are this decade's Hex Kitchen champion!"

"Ashner," Kenzie said. This time, she spoke loudly enough for everyone to hear her. "My name is Kenzie Ashner."

CHAPTER 41

KENZIE

Everyone was talking at once. Kenzie's shoulder was almost wrenched out of its socket as Chef Levy shook her hand. Kenzie's ears rang from the audience's thunderous applause. Confetti replaced the snowflakes from her dish, catching in her hair and swirling around her feet.

Braxton was no longer standing behind her. They'd been separated by a horde of well-wishers who were crowding into the dome to talk to her.

An enormous bottle of champagne appeared from somewhere. An unfamiliar man wearing a black suit smiled at her before popping the cork.

Where was Braxton?

All of the sounds and people surrounding her were too much. Bile was flooding her mouth. Her insides felt like lava. If it weren't for all the people crushing in on her, she would have collapsed.

The noise around her reached a fever pitch. A procession of suited men entered the dome, surrounded by security guards. The rest of the crowd made way for them to come straight to Kenzie.

A burly security guard presented a key to one of the suit guys. He was carrying a metal case that was honest-to-God handcuffed to his wrist. He positioned the case on top of Kenzie's counter and opened it.

There was a small glass box inside the case's velvet interior. The man reverently freed the glass box from its cushion and held it up for everyone to see the wish truffle inside.

Kenzie's first thought was, *Really, this is it…?*

The milky-pink truffle was the size of a gumdrop. Honestly, the cake-sized replica she and Braxton had cooked during the second round was a lot more impressive than this dinky little thing.

"The wish truffle, ladies and gentlemen!" Polly Berrywhite called.

Kenzie blinked, and then the glass box was in her hands, along with a tiny gold key that would unlock the lid.

"Don't eat it yet," Polly ordered her. The urgency in the judge's voice drew Kenzie's attention away from the crowd clambering to get a closer look at the truffle. "We need to take some pictures with you holding it, first. Come with me."

Polly's grip was surprisingly firm as she pulled Kenzie toward the exit.

"Ah, running off are we, Polly?" Chef Levy swooped in and took Polly's elbow.

"I beg your pardon—" Polly began, and then let out a yelp as the other judge practically dragged her away.

Kenzie made a feeble attempt to rescue Polly from Chef Levy, but the two of them were already gone, swallowed up by the crowd.

"Kenz."

Somehow, even amid the craziness surrounding her, Kenzie picked out Braxton's voice. He waded through the crowd until he was beside her. He used his body as a shield between her and everyone shouting questions and congratulations.

"What are you waiting for?" he demanded. "Eat it. Now."

When Kenzie just stared at the truffle in its locked box, Braxton made an irritated sound. He took the key from her and unlocked the box.

"Come on," he urged, thrusting the open box at her. "Do it now before you get too weak. Make sure to think your wish clearly, and don't let yourself get distracted by anything else. Just like when we're doing magic—"

He must have read the uncertainty in her gaze, because anger sparked in his green eyes.

"What the fuck, Kenzie?" he growled.

"I told you I wanted to free my dad," she said carefully. She'd been so sure about what she needed to do coming into this finale, but Braxton's sacrifice had made her less certain. He'd given up his own chance of winning to save her

And he expected her to use her wish to save her life…not her father's.

Emotions played across Braxton's face in quick succession. Anger. Betrayal. Fear.

"No." Braxton shook his head. "Please." His voice broke.

"I'm so sorry," she said, having to raise her voice to be heard over the ambient noise surrounding them. "I have to set things right for him."

Braxton thrust his hands through his hair. "Think about this for one goddamned second." He cupped her face in his hands and leaned down until they were at the same level. In spite of the desperation he was so clearly feeling, his touch was gentle.

"I watched my brother die and there was nothing I could do to save him." Braxton squeezed his eyes shut. When he spoke again, his voice was hoarse. "Don't make me watch you die, too. I…I couldn't bear it."

Tears sprang to Kenzie's eyes. She reached up to touch Braxton's face. His cheeks were hot. Or maybe it was just that her fingers were like icicles. She gasped as a world-stopping burst of pain shot through her. She tried to ignore it.

"I don't want to die," she said. "But I can't live knowing my dad is in prison for a crime I committed."

"Your dad wouldn't want you to do this," Braxton argued. "What do you think he'll say when he gets out of prison and finds out you're dead?"

That made Kenzie pause. Braxton was right. She could almost picture her dad's disbelief, which would transform to despair.

Her dad would move on, though. He'd get his life back together. He'd be okay.

Wouldn't he?

Her father's favorite saying came back to her now.

Making a sacrifice for a person you love is the greatest gift you can ever give.

"That's it," she whispered.

All of her uncertainty vanished. She knew exactly what she had to do.

Kenzie reached into the box for the truffle. When she glanced up, she saw Polly Berrywhite making a beeline for her…or at least as much of a beeline as she could with all the people stuffed into the dome.

"Kenzie," Braxton said, his voice a warning and a plea all rolled into one.

Kenzie tucked the empty box under her arm and shoved the truffle into her mouth.

CHAPTER 42

BRAXTON

Braxton was no stranger to helplessness. He'd felt it every single day since he'd lost Aidan and watched his world crumble before his eyes. But as he stood in front of Kenzie, with no power to force her to be reasonable, he realized he was just beginning to truly understand the meaning of the word.

"There you are!" Polly huffed, some of her usual good cheer buried beneath irritation. "Come with me, dear. Hurry up, now." She started tugging on Kenzie's arm. "We need you and that truffle."

Kenzie slid out of Polly's grip and turned back to Braxton. He started to voice one more plea that she use the truffle to save her own life instead of dying for her father's sake, but he never got the chance. Kenzie wrapped her arms around his neck and pulled him down with surprising force. Their lips crashed together.

In spite of the madness surrounding them, everything else faded away. Braxton hooked an arm around her waist to pull her body all the way against his. Kenzie's lips parted for him. Braxton started to deepen the kiss, but instead of the silken glide of her tongue, she thrust something into his mouth.

Something solid.

Something covered in a hard outer shell that held the cloying sweetness of candied strawberries.

Holy shit.

The wish truffle was in his mouth.

Kenzie pressed a finger to his lips, keeping him from either speaking or spitting the truffle out. He stood there, too shocked to do anything, as Kenzie hurriedly spoke into his ear.

"You were right about my dad not wanting me to use the wish for him. He sacrificed his freedom…his life…for me because he loves me." She reached up and brushed a lock of his hair from his forehead.

Braxton leaned into her touch as thoughts and emotions ran rampant inside him.

"I know I can never make up for what I did to your family," Kenzie continued. "But I want to fix some of what I broke." She gave him a crooked little smile. "I would have just made the wish myself, but I wasn't sure exactly what your family needs and I didn't want to mess anything up."

Polly was tugging on Kenzie's arm.

"One second," Kenzie snapped. She was trying to free her arm from Polly, but she seemed on the verge passing out. Her face was shiny with sweat. She was breathing hard and blinking like she was trying to keep her vision steady.

"My dad taught me that making a sacrifice for someone you love isn't really a sacrifice. It's more like…a gift to both of you." "Kenzie looked at him like he was some kind of treasure she'd never expected to uncover. "And I love you, Braxton."

Braxton didn't speak for fear of accidentally biting down on the truffle. He wasn't sure he'd be able to find the right words even if he had the ability to talk.

"This wish is for your family. Rebuild the empire your dad dreamed about. Keep Aidan's memory alive. Give your mom and Sofia the future they've been working so hard for." She gave him a sad smile. "And be happy. That's all I want for you."

"*Kenzie.*" Polly Berrywhite's face was splotchy and her hair was all askew. She gave Kenzie another hard tug, managing to pull her away from Braxton. He heard Polly babbling about pictures and interviews, and then the two of them were melting back into the sea of unfamiliar faces.

Braxton was left alone. The truffle's outer shell slowly disintegrated in his mouth as Kenzie's words rang in his ears.

Kenzie's life. His family's future.

The woman he loved was dying an agonizing death.

But if he didn't save his family's empire, his family would be destitute and beholden to all their unpaid investors. Rick Santiori would be able to do…whatever the fuck he wanted to Sofia. His father's dream would disintegrate into ashes and unpaid mortgages.

Aidan's legacy would be lost and forgotten.

How was he supposed to make this decision?

Braxton knew what Sofia would tell him. It was more or less what Kenzie had said…minus all the parts about love and sacrifice. Sofia would say this was justice…necessary….

His mum would probably say the same. So would his father, if he was still alive to give Braxton advice.

And Aidan?

What do I do, Aid?

Hell, his brother would say that he didn't need a goddamn restaurant empire to be remembered. Unlike Braxton, Aidan had cooked because he loved it…not because he had to. Braxton had never heard his twin say anything about wanting to be famous or memorialized.

In all the years he'd been working toward this future, Braxton had never really thought about whether Aidan would have appreciated all their efforts. Braxton had never discussed it with his parents or sister. Thinking about it now, though, he knew exactly what his twin would say about everything his family was trying to do in his honor.

Aidan would say *thanks, but no thanks.*

Still, Braxton hesitated.

Aidan might not care about legacy, but the threat to their family was real. Rick hadn't been talking out of his ass when he threatened Sofia. The thought of that piece of shit having an iota of control over his sister made Braxton see red.

He stood there like a total fool as seconds turned into minutes. People were trying to talk to him, but he ignored them all.

The truffle was quickly melting in his mouth. He needed to make his decision before he lost his chance.

Forgive me, he thought.

He bit down on the truffle. Sweetness coated his tongue, but he paid no attention to the burst of flavor. He closed his eyes to block everything out.

Braxton made his wish.

CHAPTER 43

KENZIE

It was a relief to be surrounded by quiet after the dome's chaos. For several seconds, Kenzie just breathed. All of the reporters who were supposed to be interviewing her would probably arrive any second, but for the moment, she was grateful for this small gift of peace.

"Where is it?"

Polly Berrywhite's shrill voice made Kenzie jump.

"Where's what?" she asked in confusion.

"The truffle, you fool. Give me the truffle!"

Kenzie stared at the sweet old woman…who wasn't seeming so sweet at the moment.

"Give it to me!" Polly reached for the box that Kenzie still had tucked under her arm.

Something told Kenzie not to reveal the fact that the truffle was long gone. There was a frantic expression in Polly's owl eyes that had never been there before. Kenzie didn't trust it.

Then again, maybe the pain clawing at her insides was messing with her judgment. Kenzie could feel the foul-tasting tonic Braxton had given her the day before wearing off. It was taking almost all of her concentration to stay upright. She was afraid if she gave into her urge to collapse, she'd never get back up.

"What's going on?" Kenzie asked Polly, her words tripping over themselves and slurring together. Even talking was using up energy she didn't have. "Why did you bring me here?"

Polly's laugh wasn't that hearty chuckle Kenzie had heard so many times over the last two weeks. It was high-pitched and maniacal.

Polly made another grab for the empty box in Kenzie's arms.

Kenzie twisted out of reach, using her sleeves to hide the fact that the box was empty.

"I thought we were taking pictures, or something," Kenzie told Polly. She pointedly looked around the empty, windowless room.

"Don't be stupid," Polly snapped. "And give me the fucking truffle!"

Whoa. That escalated quickly.

"No," Kenzie replied. "Not until you tell me what this is all about. Did Chef Levy do something to you? Did she threaten you again?"

Polly let out another nails-on-chalkboard laugh. The woman was unhinged.

"Elyannah Levy is probably combing these halls looking for you as we speak. But by the time she finds you, it'll be too late."

"And why would she be looking for me?" Kenzie asked.

"To protect you from me, you imbecile!"

Kenzie blinked at Polly. The fact that Kenzie could feel death creeping up on her must be why Kenzie didn't feel any fear. She was honestly just confused.

"But—but I thought—" Kenzie broke off and shook her head. A wave of dizziness swept through her.

The other day, when she'd overheard Elyannah and Polly arguing, Kenzie had assumed it had been the other way around…that Elyannah was the one who was up to no good.

"Why would I need protection from you?" Kenzie asked warily.

Polly adjusted the diamond chain on her glasses. "I work for some very powerful people. People who would very much like to know why your magic is different." Polly scrutinized Kenzie, like the answers might be written across her forehead.

"Okay…" Kenzie began. "And who are these people, exactly?"

"The Gourmands?" Polly chuckled darkly. "You'll find out soon enough, *dear*."

The pet name no longer sounded affectionate.

Kenzie swallowed against an unpleasant, coppery taste in her mouth. When she surreptitiously wiped her sleeve across her lips, it came away stained red.

"I don't understand," Kenzie began.

Polly waved an impatient hand. "There will be time enough for all sorts of tedious questions and answers later…once you're in the wolves' den."

Maybe, under different circumstances, those words would have made Kenzie afraid. But Kenzie knew the poison racing through her body would end her faster than these "wolves" Polly was talking about.

"So, this whole sweet old lady thing is an act?" Kenzie asked. If she was going to be locked in this room with Polly, she might as well get some answers out of the deal.

"It is what it is," Polly replied, lifting her chin in the air. "And my employers tasked me with bringing both you and the truffle to them." She held out her palm. "Hand it over, Kenzie. *Now*."

Kenzie didn't move.

Polly's focus zeroed in on the box tucked under Kenzie's arm.

"Trust me, dearest," Polly sneered. "There's no wish that will get you out of what's coming for you."

Kenzie held up the box, getting a rush of perverse pleasure at Polly's horrified gasp.

"Where is it?" Polly cried, throwing herself at Kenzie and grabbing the empty box. "What did you do with it?!"

"It's gone," Kenzie said. "And if you think you're going to hand me over to your employers and be some kind of hero, I'm going to have to burst that bubble, too."

"What are you talking about?" Polly snarled.

"I'm dying," Kenzie said. The words slid out of her mouth without so much as raising her pulse.

Aside from the roiling pain in her stomach, all Kenzie felt was…peace. She'd given Braxton the gift he needed to save what was left of his family. She'd done something selfless for the man she loved.

She knew her dad would be proud of the decision she'd made, and that eased some of her guilt about abandoning him in prison.

"You're…dying?" Polly asked, like she was trying to grasp the meaning of the word.

"'Fraid so," Kenzie replied. "Poison."

And if the pain inside her was any indication, she didn't have much time left. Irritation flared through her at the reminder that she was spending her last minutes with this buffoon instead of with Braxton. The only bright side was that now, at least, Braxton wouldn't have to watch her die.

"N-no," Polly stuttered. True terror filled her eyes. "No. You can't." Her gaze bounced around the room, like she was looking for an escape.

As if on cue, a different door than the one Kenzie and Polly had entered through opened up. Two men in suits strode into the room. Kenzie recognized one of them as the man who had popped the giant bottle of champagne when her win was announced.

"What's this we hear about you being poisoned?" the champagne man asked, his voice eerily toneless.

"Do you need me to spell it out for you?" Kenzie shot back, annoyed now. "I said—"

Kenzie stopped talking. All at once, it was no longer a struggle to breathe. Her limbs stopped quivering. Her stomach didn't feel like it was full of lava.

All of her pain vanished.

She felt great. Better than great, actually.

Kenzie sucked air into her lungs…lungs that no longer felt like they'd been filled with pure acid. She wanted to weep from relief at the absence of that gut-wrenching ache that had become her reality since she first tasted the poison.

How was this happening? She was supposed to be—

No. *No.*

Kenzie bit back a scream.

Braxton, what did you do?!

"A miraculous recovery, it would seem," the man said, watching her with narrowed eyes. "You look healthy as a horse."

He didn't give her time to formulate an excuse.

The two men approached her from either side. Kenzie tensed, although she didn't know what she was preparing for.

"I brought her to you," Polly babbled in a panic-laced voice. "She's here because of me. I want you to remember that. I would have gotten you the wish truffle, too, but it was already gone. I swear, I didn't take it!"

The men ignored Polly as they came close enough for Kenzie to smell their nauseating cologne.

"You were invited to this tournament for a reason," one of the men told her. "Didn't you wonder what you were doing here as an untested novice, when you were competing against seven of the world's best-*trained* culinary magicians who have already proven their skill?"

Kenzie gaped at him. She had questioned her invitation at the beginning, but she hadn't wondered at her presence in the tournament since the first round. She belonged here.

Didn't she?

"Not to worry," the man said with a grim little smile. "We'll have plenty of time to talk. We have a lot of questions for you."

Something occurred to Kenzie at that moment.

"Were you the ones who killed Loretta and Max?"

The men just stared blankly at her.

"At *Good Ol' Apple Pie*," she clarified through clenched teeth. "The older woman and the busboy. Did you kill them?"

"Yes," one of the men replied simply. Like it was no big deal.

"Why?" The word whispered out of her. Her mind was full of Max's broken neck and Loretta's frozen expression of horror.

"They knew you were performing magic," the same man replied. "We take threats to our community seriously."

"They weren't a threat!" Kenzie tightened her fist. Before it could connect, the man grabbed her arm and yanked her back against his chest.

She kicked at his knees, but he absorbed the blow and looped a muscular arm around her neck.

Kenzie managed a hoarse shout as the other man loomed in front of her. He searched her face, like she was a mystery he was trying to solve.

"Let me go!" she shouted, writhing in the other man's grip.

The one standing in front of her offered a cold smile.

"You're coming with us."

"Like hell, I am!"

The man gave her another one of those bone-chilling smiles. Then, his fist connected with the side of Kenzie's head.

Darkness fell, and she knew nothing more.

CHAPTER 44

BRAXTON

Braxton needed to move.

He waded through the sea of people, all of whom seemed to be wearing sinister expressions. Were they here to congratulate or kill him?

Sofia. He needed to find Sofia.

All of their creditors would have seen the finale and would be on their way to collect. Veneziano's thugs would be coming after his family.

He needed to get Sofia and his mum somewhere safe before that happened.

Braxton knew what he'd done to his family. He knew he'd abandoned all the people who had worked for his family for years and left them out to dry. And yet, he couldn't be sorry for his decision. He'd saved Kenzie's life.

At least, he thought he had. Kenzie had disappeared with Polly Berrywhite for some photo op more than twenty minutes ago and hadn't come back.

Braxton would have liked a chance to say goodbye, but there wasn't time. He'd done what he could for Kenzie. Now, he had to worry about his family.

Braxton fought his way out of the dome and smacked right into Sofia. His sister didn't give him a chance to bask in a moment of relief.

"What did you do?!" she yelled.

What I had to.

"Mum is texting me that our accounts have been emptied, and creditors are blowing up my email, and—"

"Come on." He took her hand and pulled her with him through the crush of people. "Text Mum," he shouted at her as he marked out the quickest path to an exit. "Tell her—"

He and Sofia were wrenched apart.

"Hello, beautiful."

Rick. And he was with another, slightly older man who had the Santiori smugness plastered all over his face.

Braxton didn't wait for the older man to reach for the gun that was clearly peeking out of his waistband. Braxton gave him a hard shove, knocking him into a wall of people who shouted and swarmed around him. Then, Braxton turned to Rick.

He was partly disappointed, but mostly proud as hell, at the sight that greeted him. His little sister was beating the shit out of Rick.

"And Daddy said those self-defense classes were a waste of time," she huffed. She gave Rick a final knee to the groin that sent him sprawling.

Braxton would have loved to stop everything and have a party right there over Rick's writhing body, but there wasn't time. More beefy men with dark sunglasses and wires behind their ears were converging on them.

Braxton and Sofia clasped hands so they wouldn't be separated and hurried on.

Braxton didn't look to see if the men were gaining on them. He pushed Sofia ahead of him toward the exit.

Somehow, they made it through the bottleneck. They sprinted down a mostly-empty hallway that led to the arena's underbelly, where all the ingredients for the tournament were stocked in giant pantries and fridges. It was also the way to the underground garage that might just be their ticket out of here.

"We need to get out of here," Braxton said as they ran. "Find somewhere quiet enough for us to call Mum."

"Do you realize how many enemies you made today?" Sofia demanded. "I mean, you didn't just lose. You basically sabotaged your own final dish.

And you managed to not only piss off every one of our investors, but also make an enemy out of all the people who gambled on you winning."

"How is it my fault that other people gambled their money away?" Braxton asked.

As long as he and Sofia were engaged in their usual bickering routine, he could stave off his *What the fuck do we do now?* panic attack he could feel cresting the horizon.

He tried to organize his thoughts into a list of priorities. "First we need to talk to Mum. Tell her she needs to go—"

Where?

"Where is she going to go, Brax?" Sofia asked, echoing his thoughts. "The people we owe money to are probably watching the penthouse right now."

Not to mention, with how much money they controlled, the creditors probably had local cops in their back pockets, too.

"We'll figure it out," Braxton said. "We just need to tell Mum to go to a friend's or something for now. And then we need to go to the airport. We'll go get Mum, and then—"

Sofia's harsh laughter cut him off.

"Thanks to what you pulled tonight, we don't have money or any hope of gaining it in the future. That means we have no way to get to Mum."

Shit. She was right. Why the hell hadn't he thought this whole thing through?

"Okay." He rubbed a hand over his face. "Just give me a second to figure this out."

A door slammed from somewhere nearby.

"There they are!"

Braxton recognized Rick Santiori's haughty voice before the bruised and bedraggled chef appeared at the other end of the hall. He was flanked by four men with guns.

"Oh God," Sofia breathed.

"God can't help you now, sweetheart," Rick chuckled.

Braxton grabbed Sofia and barreled through the first door they reached. It was a long but narrow pantry. Braxton shut the thick metal door and wedged a step ladder under the handle, just as a deafening pounding came from the other side.

"What do we do?!" Sofia whisper-shouted.

The pounding stopped.

"You gonna make us shoot our way in, McKaid?" Rick's muffled voice called from the hallway.

Braxton jerked as bullets struck the metal door's exterior. They didn't penetrate…but *Christ*. They were running out of time.

Braxton flipped on the light switch by the door. He scanned the shelves, assessing his options.

"You can't hide in there forever!" Rick shouted. His fist pounded against the metal. "Open up this door, McKaids."

"Or what?" Sofia shouted back. "You'll blow it down?"

Hmmm. That gave Braxton an idea.

He started pulling ingredients off shelves. A bottle of white vinegar, baking soda, popcorn kernels, some sad-looking russet potatoes, a box of raisins….

"What are you doing? Sofia hissed.

"Relax," Braxton replied. "Aid and I used to do stuff like this all the time."

Well, at least a couple of times….

"Wait." Sofia turned to him with a bemused expression on her face. "You're not about to tell me that *you* started that explosion in your cooking school, are you?"

"Guilty." In spite of their situation, Braxton couldn't help but grin. "I forgot to study for the poultry final, and Aid wanted to get an early start to the weekend."

"You could have been arrested!" Sofia squeaked.

"Nah." Braxton started opening packages. "And lucky for you, I remember the recipe. Now shut up and let me concentrate."

As Braxton started combining ingredients, he realized a certain amount of improvisation would be required. First off, he didn't have any mixing or measuring tools. Second off, he didn't have access to the fresh ingredients he and Aidan had used last time.

As the banging and shooting continued outside the door, Braxton decided to hell with the recipe. He started throwing together anything and everything that could be combined into a batter that he could convince to magically detonate.

He broke up a carrot and tossed it into his growing amalgamation of ingredients. Carrots hadn't been used in Aidan's original recipe, but Braxton remembered when, as a kid, Sofia had tried to prove she knew how to cook by throwing a whole carrot in the microwave. The mineral-rich root had exploded, and it took Sofia hours to clean up all the carrot bits.

It was easier to make the magic work when the recipe's individual ingredients were predisposed to doing what he wanted.

"What can I do to help?" Sofia whispered.

Braxton looked at his pile of food.

"Hot peppers," he decided. "And flour and sugar. Also soft drinks. Oh, and if you can find any matches or a lighter, that would be helpful."

"Dried or jarred ghost peppers?" Sofia called from deeper in the pantry.

"Both," Braxton said, stomping on some raw potatoes to turn them into a gluey mess that he could use to combine his 'dough'.

"You're out of luck with the soft drinks and lighters," Sofia announced from the pantry's recesses.

Braxton didn't bother responding as he finished putting his ingredients together. He did his best to block out everything except the food and his magic. It was easier said than done. He was exhausted from all the effort he'd expended during the tournament.

The sound of a drill coming from the other side of the door didn't ease his sense of urgency.

Braxton piled his concoction right in front of the pantry door. After herding Sofia as far back in the pantry as they could go, he closed his eyes and forced his breathing to slow.

Braxton felt the residue of powdery flour and sugar granules on his hands. He remembered the sound that carrot had made when it exploded in the microwave. He pictured what happened to sugar when it melted and turned to smoke. He held back a cough as he tasted ghost peppers on his tongue. He remembered one of his culinary magician tutors telling him about capsaicin, which was the chemical inside peppers that set a person's palate on fire.

He thought about the night at the bar when he'd licked fire off Kenzie's bare skin. He felt the flames dance on his tongue. He smelled Kenzie's apple-scented hair. He remembered the way his blood burned the first time he kissed her.

He opened his eyes to see that his pile of ingredients was engulfed in flames.

"Wow," Sofia said in amazement. "Aidan could do tiny flames, but I never saw either of you do something like that. How'd you get it to burn so fast?"

Braxton couldn't help a smile at that. "Trust me, sis. You don't want to know."

The pantry door flew open. Two guns were aimed directly at Braxton's chest. Before he could blink, there was a deafening explosion.

Flaming pieces of potato blew up into the goon's face. The man screamed and doubled back, knocking down the other man who'd been standing behind him.

Puffs of flour and burnt sugar smoke clouded the air. For a moment, everything was chaos.

"Come on," Braxton choked, fumbling for Sofia's hand and wrenching her out of the pantry and into the hallway.

They slid past flour-covered people who were blindly stumbling around. More gunshots filled the air.

They ran.

Braxton kept waiting for a bullet to tear into his back. Somehow, they managed to reach the elevator that led up to the garage without dying.

Braxton didn't breathe until they were inside the elevator and the doors closed.

"Okay?" Braxton asked, gasping for air.

Sofia nodded. "You?"

"Still in one piece."

"What now?"

Braxton gave his sister a helpless shrug. "Steal a car?"

Sofia guffawed. "Who are you and what have you done with my brother?"

"I'm adapting."

When the elevator door slid open to reveal the garage, Braxton tensed. When they weren't immediately assailed by gunfire, he let out a breath. He didn't see an army of mobsters waiting to mow them down. Yet.

His fleeting sense of relief was quickly followed by panic. They had to get out of here before Santiori's people caught up with them.

He didn't know how to steal a car. He didn't have money to get a plane ticket. He didn't even have a fucking passport.

"Oh, there you are," a bored voice drawled.

Braxton clenched his fists and moved in front of Sofia as Crazy Esther stepped into view. She had an arrow nocked in her bow.

"Relax, stud." Esther lowered her weapon. "I come in peace."

"You do?" Braxton made no attempt to hide his suspicion.

"*Yes.*" She rolled her eyes. "I like rooting for an underdog." She swept her gaze over Braxton and Sofia's bedraggled appearances. "And you two are definitely underdogs."

"We don't have time for this," Braxton said. "Unless you can get us out of here and back to Sydney without Rick's thugs killing us first, then piss off."

"Oh, what the hell." Esther shrugged. "I'll help you."

Braxton had to pick his jaw off the floor before he could force out a stuttered, "What?"

"I can get you out of here," she said, like it was no big deal. "I know somewhere your family can hide where Rick will never find you."

"Assuming you're not bullshitting me," Braxton said. *And that was a mighty big* If. "Why would you help us?"

Esther picked at a splinter on the curve of her bow. "I'm bored. Besides, I'm sure you'll be able to find some way to repay me."

Braxton didn't like the sound of that. He really didn't like that twisted gleam in her eyes.

"Can we trust her?" Sofia murmured.

"Absolutely not," he replied without hesitation.

"No," Esther said at almost the same instant.

Braxton looked at Crazy Esther. She was in full hunting regalia, with her grizzly bear cloak, weapons, and arrowhead jewelry. She certainly had the look of someone who'd be useful in a fight.

"You're boring me," Crazy Esther pouted. "See ya, losers."

"Wait," Braxton and Sofia said at the same time.

Esther grinned, but there was nothing friendly about it.

"Okay," he said, hating that his only choice was to put his faith…and his family's lives…into Esther's hands. "Get us out of here."

Esther's menacing smile widened. She tapped a finger on Braxton's chest. "Just don't forget, stud. You're going to owe me for this one."

"Agreed," he said through gritted teeth. Thoughts about making deals with the devil swam through his mind, but it wasn't like he had any other option at the moment.

"My truck's over this way. Come on."

Knowing it was probably the worst idea of his life, Braxton followed Esther.

"Honestly, I'm a little surprised you're leaving," Esther told him. "I would have thought you'd be tearing this place apart with your bare hands to rescue your girlfriend."

Braxton stopped walking. "What are you talking about?"

"Braxton, come on," Sofia urged.

He didn't move.

Crazy Esther quirked an eyebrow at him. "You mean, you don't know?"

"Don't know *what?*" he ground out.

Esther shrugged. "Guys in suits took her. They put her in a black car and drove off." Esther tilted her head. "I'm pretty sure she was unconscious."

Braxton's entire body went numb.

No. Esther had to be lying. Kenzie was surrounded by reporters and well-wishers right now. She was fine….

"I actually tried to stop them," Esther said. "I have this thing against men who put unconscious women into cars and drive off, ya know? But they got away before I could get to her."

"When?" Braxton demanded. His throat felt like it was closing off.

"Twenty minutes ago, maybe more."

Braxton's mind spun. *Who were these men? Where had they taken her? What the fuck were they planning to do to her?*

"We don't have time for this," Sofia said. She dug her nails into his arm and gave him a shake. "Mum—"

"You said unconscious?" Braxton asked. It wasn't easy to force out the words when he couldn't breathe.

"Looked that way to me," Esther said cheerfully. "I shot one of them in the leg." She brought the curve of her bow to her lips and kissed it. "But he got into the car with the others before I could get to him."

Unconscious. Men in suits. Black car.

"Rick's people?" he asked, his mind whirling. Was this about him? Had Rick taken her when he couldn't get to Braxton and Sofia?

"Negative," Esther said. "They smelled like Gourmands."

"What do Gourmands smell like?" Sofia asked.

"I was starting to like Number Eight," Esther said, ignoring the question. "She's got a brutal streak, and if she's going to go down, I want it to be against me rather than to some prissy man in a suit." She giggled. "Also, that poison of hers is the deadliest one I've ever encountered. Do you think she'll sell me the recipe…you know, if those guys don't kill her?"

Braxton felt like the ground had been ripped out from beneath him.

"That poison killed our brother," Sofia said darkly. "She deserves whatever those men do to her."

Braxton whirled on her.

"What?" she asked defensively. "It's the truth. If you were thinking with your brain rather than your dick, you'd be saying the same thing."

"I have to find her," he choked out.

"They're long gone, stud," Esther told him, wrapping her hands around one of his arms. Sofia took the other. "Let's get you out of here first, and then we can track down Number Eight."

As much as Braxton hated to admit it, Esther was right. He wouldn't be any use to Kenzie if he was dead, and he still had his mum and Sofia to worry about.

Braxton caught sight of a mud-spattered pickup truck that didn't belong with all the other luxury sedans down here. They'd almost reached the truck when the garage elevator dinged.

"Oh goody," Esther squealed.

Braxton dragged Sofia behind the truck as gunfire exploded in the garage.

Esther stood out in the open, totally unconcerned about the possibility of being shot, as she released one arrow after another.

"Get her, morons!" Rick snarled.

Somehow, the bullets missed Esther altogether, while two of the goons fell with arrows sticking out of their chests. They didn't get back up. A third was whimpering and dragging his bloody, arrow-pierced leg as he tried to reach the elevator.

Sirens echoed down the cement garage.

"Oh fuck," one of the goons swore. "Rick, we gotta get outta here. If we get arrested, your father'll murder us."

They beat a hasty retreat to the elevator.

"We're not done here, McKaid," Rick called. "There's nowhere you can go where I won't find you."

Braxton was too overcome with relief for this reprieve…no matter how temporary…to reply.

"You picked the wrong side, Esther," Rick told her from behind his human shield of thugs.

"No, you did when you went behind my back and started threatening pregnant women during the second round," she replied as the elevator doors closed between them. "And besides. Wrong is my middle name."

"I like her," Sofia whispered.

"Come on," Braxton said, climbing into the truck and finding the keys already in the ignition. He didn't want to be here when the cops showed up, either.

He started the truck, mentally reminded himself that Americans drove on the wrong side of the road, and revved the engine. Tires squealed as he drove around to Esther.

For some reason, Braxton's gaze caught on a tiny flicker of movement as he waited for Esther to scramble in. A cricket hopped off a nearby garbage can and disappeared from view.

Shit. Shit shit shit.

"Drive!" Esther and Sofia shrieked.

Braxton put the truck into park and unbuckled his seatbelt.

"Braxton, what the hell?" Sofia demanded.

"Kiwi," he said. He gestured for Esther to take his place in the driver's seat. Sofia was good at a lot of things. Driving wasn't one of them.

"As in the fruit?" His sister squinted at him.

"No, the chameleon." Braxton cursed again. "Kenzie's chameleon."

"Ohhh no." Sofia put up her hands. She shook her head, like she couldn't even fathom what he was saying.

Frankly, neither could he.

"It'll die," Braxton said.

Christ. He sounded like a bloody moron.

"Then let it die!"

"I can't," Braxton said.

That was it. He'd officially lost his sanity.

"This is the least funny joke I've ever heard." Sofia gaped at him. "Because you are joking. Right?"

Braxton held up his phone as he got out of the truck. "Park somewhere nearby and text me. I'll meet you."

"I'm going to kill you," Sofia shouted at him. "Like, you have absolutely nothing to worry about from the Santioris. Because there is nothing they could do to you that'll be worse than what I have planned!"

"Noted." He threw her a quick grin, hopped over a man with an arrow embedded in his neck, and ran for the staircase.

First, he'd rescue Kiwi. Then, he would get Sofia and his mum somewhere safe. And then he was going after Kenzie.

Just hold on, he thought, desperate for his silent plea to reach Kenzie…wherever she was. *I'm coming for you.*

As for the rest? Well, they'd figure it out. Together.

THE END

* * *

Because reviews are so important for a book to be successful, please consider leaving a brief review on your favorite retailer if you enjoyed *Hex Kitchen*. Many thanks!

* * *

Sign up for Stephanie Fazio's e-Newsletter to learn about upcoming books at:
https://StephanieFazio.com/subscribe/

Acknowledgements

I loved writing this book from start to finish, even if it did make me hungry almost the entire time! Thank you to all of the amazing people on my team who helped bring this story together.

To my editor, Ellen Schaeffer. Thank you for your attention to detail and wonderful suggestions!

To Keith Tarrier, for making such incredibly beautiful covers. Thank you also to Bob Brodsky, Rhoda Schneider, and the rest of my ARC team. Your advice, support, and encouragement are invaluable.

To Mom and Dad, for your endless support and advice. Thanks for always believing in me.

To my incredible readers. Thanks for making what I do matter!

And to Andrew for being the most amazing person ever.

About the Author:

Stephanie Fazio is a fantasy author. She grew up in Syracuse, New York, and prior to writing full time, she worked in the fields of journalism, secondary education, and higher education. She has an undergraduate degree in English from Colgate University and a Master's degree in Reading, Writing, and Literacy from the University of Pennsylvania. Stephanie lives in Austin with her husband and crazy rescue dog. When she isn't writing, she's getting lost in parks, hosting taco nights, or ironically and miserably losing at word games, but having fun while she does it.

Connect with Stephanie Fazio:

Visit her Website: https://www.StephanieFazio.com
Sign up for her newsletter: https://StephanieFazio.com/subscribe/

Discover other books by Stephanie Fazio

The Fount Series

The Prince's Chosen

The Forsaken's Choice

The Chosen Union

Opal Contagion Series

Opal Smoke

Opal Slayer

Opal Storm

Bisecter Series

Bisecter

Halve Human

Dusker Dark

Captain Harkibel

Mags & Nats

The Nat Makes 7

Mag Subject 6

Steel for 5

www.ingramcontent.com/pod-product-compliance
Lightning Source LLC
Chambersburg PA
CBHW051213190726
48288CB00006B/1937